DISSIDENT GARDENS

Jonathan Lethem is the *New York Times* best-selling author of nine novels, including *Chronic City*, *The Fortress of Solitude*, *Motherless Brooklyn*, and the non-fiction collection *The Ecstasy of Influence*, a National Book Critics Circle finalist. A recipient of the MacArthur Fellowship and winner of the National Book Critics Circle Award for Fiction, Lethem's work has appeared in the *New Yorker*, *Harper's*, *Rolling Stone*, *Esquire*, and the *New York Times* among other publications.

JONATHAN LETHEM

Dissident Gardens

A Novel

VINTAGE BOOKS

London

Published by Vintage 2014

2 4 6 8 10 9 7 5 3 1

Copyright © Jonathan Lethem 2014

Jonathan Lethem has asserted his right under the Copyright, Designs
and Patents Act 1988 to be identified as the author of this work

First published in the United States in 2013 by
Doubleday, New York

First published in Great Britain in 2014 by
Jonathan Cape

Vintage
Random House, 20 Vauxhall Bridge Road,
London SW1V 2SA

www.vintage-books.co.uk

Addresses for companies within The Random House Group Limited
can be found at: www.randomhouse.co.uk/offices.htm

The Random House Group Limited Reg. No. 954009

A CIP catalogue record for this book
is available from the British Library

ISBN 9780099563426

The Random House Group Limited supports the Forest Stewardship
Council® (FSC®), the leading international forest-certification
organisation. Our books carrying the FSC label are printed on FSC®-
certified paper. FSC is the only forest-certification scheme supported
by the leading environmental organisations, including Greenpeace.
Our paper procurement policy can be found at:
www.randomhouse.co.uk/environment

Printed and bound by CPI Group (UK) Ltd, Croydon, CR0 4YY

For my father at eighty

Dissident Gardens

Part I   Boroughphobia

Quit fucking black cops or get booted from the Communist Party.
There stood the ultimatum, the absurd sum total of the message conveyed to Rose Zimmer by the cabal gathered in her Sunnyside Gardens kitchen that evening. Late fall, 1955.

Sol Eaglin, Important Communist, had rung her telephone. A
"committee" wished to see her; no, they'd be happy, delighted, to come
to her home, this evening, after their own conference just across the
Gardens—was ten too late? This a command, not a question. Yes, Sol
knew how hard Rose labored, what her sleep was worth. He promised they wouldn't stay long.

How did it happen? Easy. Routine, in fact. These things happened
every day. You could get exiled from the cause for blowing your nose
or blinking at suspicious intervals. Now, after so long, Rose's turn.
She'd cracked the kitchen window to hear their approach. Brewed
some coffee. Sounds of the Gardens filtered in, smokers, lovers, teenagers sulking in the communal lanes. Though winter's dark had
clamped itself over the neighborhood hours ago, this early November night was uncannily balmy and inviting, last pulse of the earth's
recollection of summer. Other kitchen windows were spilled to the
lanes, voices mingled: Rose's plentiful enemies, fewer friends, others,
so many others, simply tolerated. Yet comrades all. According Rose

their respect even through their dislike. Respect to be robbed from her by the committee now entering her kitchen.

There were five, including Eaglin. They'd overdressed, overcompensated with vests and jackets, now arraying themselves on her chairs like some Soviet oil painting, postured as if on some *intellectual* assignment. In pursuit of that chimera, the Dialectical Whosis, when really there was to be no dialectic here. Only dictatorship. And the taking of dictation. Still, Rose sought to be forgiving. These men were too young, apart from Eaglin, to have survived like she had the intellectual somersaults of the thirties, the onset of European Fascism and of the Popular Front; they'd been children during the war. They were drones, men costumed in independent thought who'd become slaves of party groupspeak. None mattered in this room except the sole independent or thoughtful among them, a true and famous *organizer*, after all, a man of the factory floors, Sol Eaglin. And Rose Zimmer's former lover. Eaglin in his bow tie, hairline now gone behind his high cranium's arc like the winter's sun setting. Eaglin the only among them man enough *not* to meet her eye, the only to grasp anything of the shame of it.

Here was Communist habit, Communist ritual: the living-room trial, the respectable lynch mob that availed themselves of your hospitality while dropping some grenade of party policy on your commitment, lifting a butter knife to slather a piece of toast and using it in passing to sever you from that to which you'd given your life. Yet that it was Communist habit and ritual didn't mean these boys were good at it, or comfortable: Rose was the veteran. She'd suffered one such trial eight years ago. They sweated; she felt only exhaustion at their hemming and throat-clearing.

The oil painting made small talk. One leaned over and noodled with Rose's Abraham Lincoln shrine, the small three-legged table bearing her original six-volume Carl Sandburg, a photograph of herself and her daughter at the memorial's statue in D.C., propped in a little frame, and a commemorative fake cent-piece the circumference of a slice of liverwurst. The young man was fair, like Rose's first husband—her only husband, yet Rose's brain persistently offered this slippage, as though some next life lay before her, waiting to be enumerated. The man hefted the medallion and tilted his head idiotically, as if being impressed with the weight of the thing constituted a promising avenue of discourse.

"Honest Abe, then?" he said.

"Put it down."

He produced an injured look. "We're aware you're a civil rights enthusiast, Mrs. Zimmer."

It was typical of such an evening that every remark found itself getting to the point, whether it wished to or not. Here was the crime the party had invented for Rose, then: excess zeal in the cause of Negro equality. In the thirties she'd been what would later be called, by Redbaiters, a *premature anti-Fascist*. Now? A too-sensuous egalitarian.

"I had a few slaves," said Rose, "but I freed them." At best, a poke at Sol Eaglin. Certainly lost on the young man.

Eaglin stepped in, as he'd been destined to all along, to "handle" her. "Where's Miriam tonight?" he asked, acting as though his knowledge of her daughter's name mitigated his incongruous presence in Rose's life: neither friend nor foe, despite that they'd a hundred times groped at each other's forms in the darkness. Eaglin was a mere bland operative, an automaton of party policy. Tonight was definite proof, like she'd needed proof. You could harbor a man in your bed or your body, play on his nervous system like Paderewski at the keyboard, and not shift his brain one inch out of the concrete of dogma.

Or, for that matter, the concrete of police work.

Nor, incidentally, had she dislodged either man from his wife.

Rose shrugged in reply. "At the age she's reached I shouldn't ever know her location, apparently." Miriam, the prodigy, was fifteen. Having skipped one grade already she was a high-school sophomore, and a virtual runaway. Miriam lived in other families' homes and in the dining hall at Queens College, flirting with Jewish and non-Jewish intellectual phonies, boys who'd a year or two before been scratching their nuts and slapping one another with rolled-up comic books on spinning stools in soda fountains or on the elevated trains, the kind of boys who fell silent, who even quaked, when they shared sidewalks with Rose Zimmer.

"Playing footsie with Cousin Lenny?"

"Sol, the one thing I can say with assurance is she's anywhere but with Cousin Lenny." It was Rose's second cousin Lenin Angrush who'd in fact gifted Rose with the bogus giant penny. A numismatist, he called himself. Lenny, getting the time of day from fifteen-year-old Miriam? He could dream.

"Let's not waste any more time," suggested the young man who'd been at her Lincoln stuff. Rose shouldn't underestimate the brutal authority of youth: He had some. Eaglin wasn't the sole power in the room just for being the sole power Rose chose to acknowledge. This young fellow was eager to distinguish himself, likely in the context of some jousting with others present, for status as Eaglin's protégé. That itself, only a prelude to stabbing Eaglin in the back. Surely that was it.

Poor Sol, really. Still neck-deep in the paranoid muck.

Rose poured them coffee, this brave cohort who'd come to declare she'd picked the wrong Negro. They were talking; she really ought to listen to the verdict. Short of severing the affiliation, Rose would no longer be welcome to the privilege of acting as recording secretary at meetings with union officials, including the union at her own work-place, Real's Radish & Pickle. Her last duty in the party, stripped. There at Real's, Rose enjoyed the honor of serving in horrified silence as her ham-fisted comrades bullied workers whose daily facts, whose solidarities, forged side-by-side plunging elbow-deep in barrels of chill salt brine, put to shame the abstractions of the posturing organizers, those arrayed in their dapper suspenders and unwrinkled plaid, not knowing enough to be unashamed of these Halloween-hayride prole-tarian costumes.

These men in her apartment, they could needless to say go to hell.

Yet Rose's usual fury was inadequate to the occasion. This kitchen-ful of moral bandits, even Eaglin, appeared to her sealed in distance, voices dim. The room's events unspooled before her as if scripted, something happening not to her but to another. A one-act play, wor-thy of Sunnyside's Socialist theater troupe, set in Rose's kitchen and starring her body—her body's behaviors being the matter under disputation—but no further portion. Heart, if bosom contained one anymore, not in attendance. *Rose no longer here.* This excommuni-cation something that had already long ago been concluded. She warmed and refilled coffee, gracing the lynch mob with use of her mother-in-law's Meissen china, even while they alluded, in terms just oblique enough to salve their own shame but not hers, to Rose's sex life. Presumed to tell her who to fuck. Who *not* to fuck, exactly. Or, not to fuck at all. Not to make her own bedroom solidarities with men who, unlike themselves, had the stature and self-possession to want her, to be undeferential to Rose.

For these occupiers of her kitchen, even in their executioner's errand, were pathetically deferential: to Rose's force, to her history, to her chest twice the circumference of theirs. She who'd marched in protest of Hitler's New York birthday party on Fifth Avenue, while American brownshirts pelted her with rotten vegetables. She who'd marched for blacks practically before they marched for themselves. Bringing revolution to Negroes, fine. To have one particular black cop in her sheets, not so fine. Oh hypocrites! Their incessant, mealy-mouthed usage, again and again droning out of the fog of their talk, was "associations." They were troubled by her associations. They meant, of course, the *association* of her rapidly aging Jew Communist vagina with the black lieutenant's sturdy and affectionate penis.

Yet Rose took orders like a mad lobotomized waitress: A little milk, or cream? With sugar? Oh, you like it black, perhaps? *So do I.* Her tongue stayed stopped, wit unexpressed. A recording secretary, she recorded. Shorthanded her own tribunal as she would that of another, onto some distant mind's tablet. Shorthand, even mental shorthand, an act of fingers scratching at some page barely registered by the mind itself. Here's Rose Zimmer, née Angrush, the scourge of Sunnyside, she who ought to be punching like a boxer against the elastic shadows that filled her kitchen, these ghastly shades of doctrine, and she couldn't care. This second trial was, really, only a lousy parody of the first. That first one, *that* had been something. Then, Rose was important in American Communism. Then, she'd been importantly Communistically married, about to be importantly Communistically divorced. Then, she'd been young. She wasn't anymore.

Now mental pen quit scraping mental tablet. Rose receded even further from the events before her, a present life under assault of disarrangement. "Eaglin?" she said, interrupting some droning insinuation.

"Yes, Rose?"

"Come outside."

The nervous glances that ensued, Eaglin quelled, using his brow like an orchestra conductor would a wand, to cease his players' tuning. And then he and Rose stepped outside, into the air of the Gardens.

The ashtray was a pure fetish: obloid, smooth-polished black granite, weighing enough to use as a stop against a pressure-hinged door or indent a man's skull. Finding it full yet again of Pall Mall stubs, you'd lug it to the kitchen with both hands to overturn it in Alma Zimmer's trash. Then rinse it in the sink, for Alma, Rose's unwilling mother-in-law, had made it plain she liked to see it come back gleaming again—never mind that three or four smokers, Albert's comrades, might be waiting to stub by the time you returned. Imagine making room for that ashtray in your bags as you fled Lübeck! Alma had done so. Who knew who'd hoisted that baggage, whose wrists the ashtray and the load of paper-wrapped Meissen had strained? Surely not Alma's. Porters, Rose supposed, and when no porter was available, Alma's brother, Lukas, or Alma's son, Albert. Albert Zimmer. Rose's future husband, a rich Jew deluded he was German even as the Nazis marched.

And who could say what other treasure had been left behind, in favor of these things? The ashtray, souvenir of Alma's deceased husband's bank desk, was a chunk of German reality, imported against absurd obstacles, to prove the unreality of Alma's present circumstance. That being: Broadway and Ninety-Second, the Knickerbocker Apartments. A one-bedroom on this island of Manhattan, furnished conspicuously with what could be saved apart from the ashtray, the half set of china, a crucial framed photograph or two (showing Alma among cousins, on Alpine vacations, they might as easily have been Nazi memorabilia to Rose's eye), Viennese-lace curtains. An apartment less a home than a memorial to the life abandoned. Two windows staring onto Broadway traffic to replace a house placed high enough in Lübeck's posh district to give panoramas of both river and mountains, next door to none other than the family home of Lübeck's great scion Thomas Mann, the *Buddenbrooks* house. Alma and her banker had more than once conversed with the visiting author, across the distance of two back porches. Another life. Before exile. Alma, formerly an opera singer on Lübeck's greatest stages. Alma, flower of Lübeck. (Rose got her fill of this word, this holy name, *Lübeck*.) More German than German, barely Jew at all until the degraded sons of Bavaria had wrenched the nation to pieces. All this is what that ashtray knew, up to and likely including the exact sums Alma had used to buy herself and her brother, Lukas, and her son, Albert, escape to New York, at that last minute when, after the approaching nightmare had induced the banker's heart attack, Alma's and Albert's denial had been torn from them: *Jew, not German*. Alma had had to sell it all, maybe was lucky even to keep the ashtray.

Here at the Knickerbocker was the "parlor," the sole public room, really, where, sitting over cups of tea, Rose abased herself to Alma's contempt in order to win grudging approval to marry. Albert was that much a mother's boy. Here, the same room, Rose had then learned to open her voice at serious Communist meetings, to smoke and argue with the men, while Alma, sealed in her aristocratic German, unwilling or unable to learn English, had, gratifyingly, been reduced to a hostess for their cell's meetings. And here, spring of '47, was the site of Rose's first living-room trial, the one that mattered, that changed everything. The meeting where, with classic party perversity, Albert, wrongly accused of spying when he was only an incompetent blabbermouth, was made a spy. The trial in which Albert was aided and abetted in flight from his family, his wife and seven-year-old daughter, by the party.

Where was Miriam? Right there. The daughter Albert was abandoning was the whole while in Alma's bedroom. She sat through the trial as she'd sat through previous meetings, gobbling the foil-wrapped Mozartkugeln Alma always provided the granddaughter with whom she couldn't converse in English, only coo at, to the solitary child's increasingly evident boredom. Miriam sat amid a litter of the unwrapped foil, playing quietly with her rag doll, likely smearing it with the German chocolate, and understanding, God help her, who knew how little or much of the things she overheard. The expulsion that would reverse-exile her father from New York, from America forever.

As for Rose, her voice wasn't for once available to be overheard.

Knowing, that day, that if she spoke she'd scream, Rose never said a word that would have given Miriam, as she listened from the next room, the least alarm. Nothing to alert her that this meeting was out of the ordinary, that the party men were handing down anything other than Albert and Rose's next irritating errand, the next recalcitrant shop steward or union chief to pester with their pamphlets and talk, the next cultural gathering to uselessly infiltrate. If anything alarmed the seven-year-old girl, it would have been the *absence* of her mother's voice.

The voice that crosscut through every room and situation, the voice never stilled, for once stilled.

If anything alarmed Miriam, it certainly would have been this: the absence of her mother's voice even when her mother paused in the doorway, on a trip bearing the unbearable ashtray from kitchen to parlor, and hovered there, stared at the girl with tight lips, possibly moist eyes though she'd have disclaimed this, then leaned to fondle her daughter's head, to mold her hand along the darling skull to the small hairs at the neck. Spoke not a word, most uncharacteristically, about the minefield of foil. Instead, still clutching the ashtray like a bludgeon, impulsively grabbed at one of the few remaining Mozartkugeln, bared it of wrapper, and grimacing, gobbled it whole, then stepped from the doorway still unspeaking, to return the ashtray to its place before any smoker's ash grew unsupportably long.

If the girl recalled it—unlikely—it would have been the sole instance in a lifetime that she'd seen a piece of German chocolate cross her mother's lips.

From that day it would be just the two of them, mother and daughter, in the Gardens apartment.

In Rose's constellation of memory, this was Ursa Major, the *real* trial. Something of which to be mordantly proud: that the top men in New York Communism had taken notice of Albert and decided he needed correction, needed to be adjusted, from the status of dissolute husband and father, a Commie lush conducting "meetings" at McSorley's tavern—where he'd been overheard by visiting undercover Soviets!—and pressed into service overseas. Returned to Germany, where his courtly manners made him an asset instead of a sore thumb. A dandy Jew with a trace of German accent tainting his English? Not of such terrific value to an American Communist Party looking to get folksy with the workers. A native German with impeccable English and total dedication, willing to repatriate? Of maximal attractiveness to the new society forming in the ragged shadows and rubble.

So Albert was sent to become an East German citizen and spy.

Rose could really savor the pomp and menace of the committee who'd come to Alma's little parlor to drink tea and put the seal on the destruction of her marriage. She could shroud herself properly in this memory, of the trial that had cost her everything, sent her slinking back to her candy-store peasant family to admit that no, you couldn't hold a man, couldn't, at last, keep that posh refugee. See? Rose's marriage, minus God, had flopped. And so she'd been cast into her life's purgatory: Real's Radish & Pickle, single-motherhood, and Queens without Manhattan, exile to that suburb of the enraged. And Albert Zimmer escaped back to Europe. What was Rose's failed marriage except evidence, against the whole fable of American history, that European chains could never be shrugged off?

———

And what, after all, were Albert Zimmer and Rose Angrush but an implausibility briefly entertained? Tolerated for an instant before being demolished, dismantled from at least three directions at once: her family, his family, and the party. The high assimilated German joining up with Rose the Polack, Rose the Russian, Rose the immigrant, second-generation Brooklyn Jew? Unlike every comedy ever devised by Jewish writers mocking class difference from the sanctuary of Hollywood, these were divisions that exactly *couldn't* be closed by the bonds of love. This wasn't *screwball*, it was *you're screwed*. Not *It Happened One Night* but *It Happened Never*.

How came it even to attempt happening?

Simple. At a packed meeting hall near Gramercy Park, under a high ornate ceiling echoing with voices, a mole met a mole. Rose seated *there*, on one side, in one creaky wooden folding chair; Albert seated *here*, across the room, in the same sort of chair. Both seeking to take the meeting's floor, to steer its innocence and idealism in a given direction, both eager to run back to their contacts and brag of enlisting the group, and both obstructed, largely, by the other. Oh, it was ripe: Albert and Rose discovered each other because they'd been assigned, by their separate and poorly coordinated cells, to insinuate themselves into the same organization, the Gramercy Park Young People's League. To introduce the possibility of solidarity with the coming workers' revolution into this vague, well-intentioned gathering.

Both therefore forced, at some point, to bite a tongue and hear the other. Until, as they tussled for dominance in pursuit of an identical outcome, some other form of tussle emerged in the thinking of both, and the hall's other occupants melted away into irrelevance. Albert thinking: Who is this young Emma Goldman, this zaftig Brooklyn shtetl girl in the hand-sewn dress, covering the Yiddish parts of her speech with elegant rhetoric, with comical double-feature at the Loew's Britishisms? Rose thinking: Who is this fair Germanic professorially handsome fellow in suspenders and gold-rimmed glasses— and can he possibly be, as he claims in his speech, Jewish? This was, you did have to admit, screwball comedy, but such as no Red-leaning Jew playwright, vamoosed to Hollywood, would ever dare committing to paper: Sent to convert the Young People of Gramercy, the two lost sight of their marks, becoming each other's marks instead.

Their infatuation was above all a meeting of two intellects gleaming with the same exalted certainties, two wills emboldened by the same great cause, and they were still uncovering this extent of their political sympathies (though "political" was too limited a term, insufficient to describe what joining the greatest movement of human history had done for their sense of what life itself was *for*), gabbing a mile a minute, barely able to stop talking to eat the food that sat cooling on the table where she'd cooked it for him in the kitchen of his flat, or to sip the wine they'd poured but in their intoxication with the cause hardly needed, when Albert first unbuttoned her dress and his trousers. So the tussle, begun in full public view, now was consummated behind closed doors.

For a little while, Rose and Albert lapsed in their attendance to all urgencies, except those of a cell of two. Two fronts moving as one. Full synthesis achieved and lost on a nightly basis.

Then, when Rose missed three menstruations, married. What could be so wrong? They were two Jews. Two humans. Two believers in revolution. In the eyes of anyone but their families, a matched pair. Any "real American" would have heard his German accent as close kin if not identical to her parents' Yiddish. He was fair and she was dark, sure. But spiritually, they could be taken for brother and sister. Certainly Albert and Rose found themselves allied utterly, proudly so, in the glance of any hater of Jews or revolutionists. Wouldn't the cause soon erase all such distinctions of class and creed and race, weren't enlightened and secular Communists abandoning inhibition to mate furiously with goyim, female comrade seeking camaraderie with male comrade whether Irish or Italian or otherwise? Wasn't any child seeded across some obsolete boundary or prohibition an ideal mongrel citizen of the future world every comrade ought to seek to bring into being?

Try telling it to the Jews. At their futzed-together, hasty wedding (which nevertheless had no reason not to be as sweet as their own private love still could be in that time) (never mind how soon that time had been destined to pass) (never mind the appetites that had been lit in Rose in that brief interval) (never mind, never mind), Alma and her brother high-hatted the Angrush clan, that whole chaotic array of Rose's sisters and their husbands and their broods, the innumerable cousins, as though the shtetl progenitors had been summoned to populate a Brooklyn they'd been mistakenly informed was *vacant* of Jews. Alma and her brother, the vain and elderly and most probably inverted Lukas, treated Rose's family like the servants they'd been forced to terminate just before fleeing Lübeck. The Zimmers, the progressive, the enlightened, the worldly Zimmers, in the face non-German Jews, semireligious Jews, village Jews, felt their own place instantly: *above* them. This union was not what world revolution was meant to make possible, thank you very much!

Then, as if to prove that the cosmos wanted no such union, the pregnancy lapsed, in the privacy of night leaking out of Rose in gobs and streams, so discreetly she was left to explain it to Albert herself, just weeks after the wedding. That, only after a doctor explained it to her, saying it hadn't been much of a pregnancy to begin with, if five months along it could dissolve more or less painlessly in the night. Something hadn't taken, only tried to. It was a mercy, a mitzvah even. Not to bear any longer the thing incompletely forming within her. Now, girl, eat red meat and salad, avoid exotic fruits such as bananas, and try again.

Try again? She bit her tongue. They hadn't been trying. He'd meant to pull out. Now, married, they'd try.

By now they'd settled, out of Manhattan, but not out of the heart of the world's happy controversies: no. Instead they'd made their home in the official Socialist Utopian Village of the outer boroughs, Sunnyside Gardens. Designed, as they discovered, and ironically, on a German basis, Lewis Mumford borrowing from the Berlin architects' vision of a garden city, a humane environment grounded in deep theory, houses bounded around courtyard gardens, neighbors venting their lives one to another across a shared commons. Yet with such struggles as overtook Rose and Albert in that utopian zone, truthfully, they might wish to be a little better partitioned from their neighbors' overhearing. That first accord between them, had it only been a fever of hormones? Their marriage, only a panic of pregnancy, in the wake of brain-befogging stints of sheer fucking?

A baby would make it right.

They tried and tried.

Synthesis of this sort was denied them.

Four years of trying before his seed would take in her again and make Miriam. The girl arrived at the doorstep of the war, ready shortly to be assigned her own booklet of ration stamps. Born into a new world unresembling that nascent utopia in which Rose and Albert had sought to start a family, against the skepticism of two armies made of different species of Jewish uncles, aunts, and cousins. Would it have grounded the union to make issue earlier? Was Albert unmoored for want of a child at home?

No. Rose could revere, in her morbid way, the Kafkaesque penalty of her first trial because she knew the party was only putting something out of its misery after all. The marriage had failed. Wrecked on reefs of personality, the incongruity and nonsupport of the two alienated families, and on Albert's vanity, his uselessness to the task of anything but distant and unreachable revolutions. He was either above or beneath mere work: Given even a sheaf of pamphlets to distribute, you'd find them stuffed into his suit pockets, Albert's campaign to distribute them among the working classes having ended in some dialectical flirtation over drinks with a fellow pamphleteer he'd just happened to run into. As for the demands of parenting, once the girl came along, forget it. Rose had been a single mother before she was made a single mother.

The fact of which Rose was proudest was that one she'd never utter aloud, not to Sol Eaglin, not to her beautiful policeman, not even to Miriam, the daughter who was repository for Rose's whole self, her insurance against being forgotten. Yet it was her signature triumph: the containment of murder. Rose Zimmer emptied and rinsed the Lübeck ashtray three times during the course of her first trial. Ferrying the granite weapon back and forth through the crowded room, the smoky air, Rose didn't swing it to shatter Albert's cranium. Nor Alma's, which would have surely collapsed as easily as an eggshell, tight-combed and hairpinned white wisps drowning in blood as she fell to the carpet. Nor did Rose crown any of the high party operatives. No, though they made it so easy, leaning in lusciously to plop sugar into their teacups, bending to stuff lit matches into mossy pipe bowls, no, though it would have been so beautiful to watch them riot in fear of her and her granite boxing glove. Nor did she go in and murder the newly fatherless girl, whose small body Rose would still have been able to hoist through the window to hurl down onto the pavement of Broadway, drawing cops to whom Rose would then immediately denounce *the cell of Reds she'd uncovered* (You gentlemen revolutionaries are sidelong-eyeing this peasant-stock housewife for a reaction? Well, *there's* your reaction!), no, no, no, on the night Rose Zimmer had discovered she possessed not only the capacity but the desire for murder, she'd let the most delectable array of possible victims go completely *un*murdered. She'd killed not even one of them. She'd carried the ashtray out filthy and carried it back in as spotless as the best-paid Lübeck housekeeper could ever have made it.

Now *that* was a trial!

———

So here, the night of her real and final expulsion, on Rose Zimmer's back step she and Sol Eaglin were encompassed in a cool and fragrant evening, false escape from that pressurized, oxygenless kitchen. The innocent babble of voices rising through the Gardens wasn't innocent. The whole place was against her. A minor reference in Eaglin's original phone call had sunk in now. He'd said he and his group would be coming to her fresh from an earlier "meeting"—that elastic and ominous euphemism—to be held just across the way. No doubt, the meeting had concerned Rose directly. A neighbor had denounced her again. But who? Hah! The question, more likely, was which of her neighbors *hadn't*, by this time? Rose felt the force of this dead utopia, the whole of Sunnyside Gardens corrupted by the onrush of coming disappointment, seeking scapegoats for their stupid guilt at their wasted lives. Rose supposed she made a fair talisman for wasted life.

The Gardens was cold.

Could get colder still.

None among them there knew American Communism wouldn't wake from this particular winter. Oh, the beauty of it! After all Rose had seen and done, to be kicked out bare months before Khrushchev, at the Soviet Congress, aired fact of the Stalin purges. Bare months before rumor of his words leaked across the Atlantic to scald the ears of the devoted American dupes. Then the words themselves, translated in *The New York Times*. Think how sweet it would have been, to see the hound-eyes of the sober and pretentious executioners waiting inside, on *that* day. But no, exiling her would be their last glorious act, or at least the last she'd have to endure witness of, these superb indignant wraiths, men dead who didn't know it.

Tonight, none of them knew.

Again, Sol Eaglin made small talk, almost flirty now that they were alone. "How'd you meet this policeman of yours, Rose?"

"Unlike some who dwell only in a Moscow of their dreams, I'm a proud citizen of a locality that includes Italians, Irish, Negroes, Jews, and the occasional Ukrainian peasant. Aren't your people Ukrainian, Sol?"

He only smiled.

"My feet when they walk touch the sidewalks of Queens, they don't float above. My beliefs don't deliver me from a responsibility to the poor degraded human souls in front of my face."

"You mean doing your rounds? What's it called, the Citizens' Patrol?"

"That's right, the Citizens' Patrol." The two skated around facts Sol Eaglin obviously knew from her party dossier, the existence of which Sol would deny and which Rose would never be able to prove, yet believed in as a certainty, in the manner with which she had been raised to believe—but failed to believe—in an invisible Jehovah, or that her name was recorded somewhere in the Haggadah secreted in the shul's rosewood cabinet. Her dossier would have told him, undoubtedly, that Rose had begun her affair with the Negro police lieutenant after colonizing the nascent Sunnyside block-watchers' organization and appointing herself the liaison to the Sunnyside precinct house. Perhaps Sol imagined her participation in the Citizens' Patrol was a long ruse, designed to allow her to sidle up to a married man she'd already lusted after. Let Sol think what he wanted. Rose had never glimpsed Douglas Lookins before that day.

She lowered herself to a defense. "A neighborhood watch, Sol. Workers helping other workers, making them feel comfortable walking home from the el after a night shift."

"Some of us can't help being reminded of brownshirts, seeing civilians forming marching societies, whispering on street corners to men in boots."

"You'd like to provoke me into an act of despair or outrage, so you can make a report of my diminished value to the cause. Or more likely you've written this report already and are disappointed I haven't obliged you with a nervous breakdown."

"I haven't written any report." He spoke tightly, as though she were the one who'd crossed a line, referring too intimately to his subjugation to the unseen cell leader. For Sol Eaglin, *that*, rather than bodies meeting in the night, constituted intimacy.

"I'm done inside, Sol," said Rose, meaning the kitchen and elsewhere: inside all the implied philosophies and conspiracies that clung in the air around them, had been belched out when they came through the door like heat and fume when you opened a coal stove. "Take them away."

"You should permit us to follow procedure."

"Procedure for what? Looking at you, old man, I can see what the mirror won't tell me. I'm an old woman. I don't have time for it."

"You're a fine woman in her prime, Rose." Eaglin's tone wasn't persuasive. Who knew whom he didn't want to be heard by, in the nearby bushes?

"I'm a degenerate, to hear of it."

"Come now, Rose."

"No, it's a degenerate world now, so why wouldn't we be part of it, you and I and those idealists in my kitchen?" She stepped into his embrace, loathing them both and wanting him to feel her loathing, as well as to prove how easily still she could squirm her bosom into the palms of his hands. Eaglin gave her boobies a good feel before shoving both hands into his jacket pockets. The act might have fit his definition of *procedure*.

Yet she'd outwitted herself, wanted more than she knew. She took Sol by the wrists, this time forcibly inserted his chill palms within her blouse, let him rediscover how she spilled at the whole periphery of her brassiere. Rose's versatile cynicism was dangerously near to spilling, too, becoming irrecoverable, mercury in a shattered vial. Sol Eaglin knew her better than any man alive. Better than her black lieutenant, though she might die rather than let Sol know it. She and Sol had for nearly a decade suffered identical contortions: the party line, and each other. If she'd only managed to wrest him from the obedient disobedience of his marriage, to a meek woman suffering nobly his claim to free love, Rose might have imprisoned Sol happily. They could have installed themselves as a Great Red Couple, lording it right here in the Gardens—but how these fantasies reeked of conformism! How bourgeois, finally, the aspiration to succeed socially within the CP!

Be grateful, then, for Sol's limpet wife and for the instincts of the body that had led her to seek elsewhere. Rose was beyond Sol's destruction, being larger than Sol knew, much as Communism was larger than the party and therefore beyond the party's immolations, its self-stabbings. By reaching for her impossible policeman, her Eisenhower-loving giant, Rose had practiced a radicalism, a freer love than Sol Eaglin could know. The critique was implicit in the gesture. Yet she wasn't tempted to translate it all into Marxism for him, not at this late date. Rose might be slightly weary, at last, of Communism. Yet Communism—the maintenance, against all depredation, of the first and overwhelming insights that had struck the world in two and made it whole again, and in so doing had revealed Rose's calling and purpose—was the sole accomplishment of her life, short of balancing a pickle factory's books. It was also, and not incidentally, the sole prospect for the human species.

"I'm cold," she said. "Let's go inside."

"You're lying." Now Sol was turned on, getting a little humpy, she knew the signs. "You're not cold, you're hot as a baked potato."

"I won't argue, the world is founded on such contradictions. It's possible I'm all at once cold and hot *and* lying. But not lying as much as you, Sol."

2   The Grey Goose

Hello, boys and girls, this is Burl Ives, and I've come to sing some songs for you. Here's a song about a grey goose, the strangest goose. The year after Miriam's father left she was given an album. *Last Sunday morning, Lord, Lord, Lord / Oh, my daddy went a hunting, Lord, Lord, Lord.* Miriam was forbidden to operate her parents' hi-fi, built into a long rosewood cabinet that also included a radio, the most fantastical item of furniture in their lives, purchased on installment at Brown's Appliance on Greenpoint Avenue, and fixture of contention in any number of speeches on the subject of what her father termed, in grip of one of his baroque and finicky tantrums, their "slavery to commerce." *And along came the grey goose, Lord, Lord, Lord.* Miriam had to request the Burl Ives each time. Rose handled what she'd only call "an album" in a manner Miriam related to the Jewish ritual actions Rose hastened to despise: the slipping of scrolls from a cabinet, her grandfather's tender sheathing of the afikomen within its napkin at Passover, really anywhere Miriam had ever witnessed a Jew handling papers of importance or turning the pages of a book as if unworthy, grateful, ennobled, discreetly defiant, all of these at once. Rose tutored her in this action of handling a long-player like the Burl Ives, or her own Beethoven symphonies, narrating what she'd still forbid Miriam even to attempt getting right: middle fingers paired at the label, steadying thumb at the disc's outer edge. Never so much as a breath grazing the sacred dark-gleaming music carved into its canyons, during the disc's passage in and out of the crisp inner papers. That the papers themselves should ride back into the cardboard sleeve just so. A wrong glance could probably scratch the thing. God knew this was a house of wrong glances.

He was six weeks a-falling, Lord, Lord, Lord / And they had a feather-picking, Lord, Lord, Lord. For what seemed a whole year of life Miriam sat entranced or bored, stilled anyhow, mulling what Ives seemed to have to impart, cheery parables of ducks and whales and goats and geese. Once, Sol Eaglin, making his mysterious visits, dapper bullshitting Sol before he'd been humbled, Sol on the make, stopped in the living room to jape at Miriam and her album.

"What's your kid know from ducks, Rose? You ever been to a farm, doll?"

"She knows from ducks," said Rose. "She's been to a Chinese restaurant."

Animals, in Rose's remorselessly unsentimental urban-pragmatist's views, were for eating, sure. (No filthy pets for Miriam.) Rose frowned at children's books when they veered in directions zoological or anthropomorphic to any extent beyond Aesop, with his iron-clad morals (always, with Rose, special emphasis on the bitterness of grapes, the inaccessibility of tidbits residing at the bottom of a vase). To sentimentalize a duckling or rabbit was associated, for Miriam, with her mother's contempt for Catholic ritual: Easter eggs, bland milk-chocolate bunnies ("Too bad, but I'd never have German chocolate in the house," Rose would say, in irony and sorrow, then following with her regular sighing incantation: "They made the very best of everything, of *everything*"), smears of ash, idiot Irish and Italian neighbors under the knuckle of idiot priests. So what was the anomalous Grey Goose, who wouldn't be made a meal of, meant to signify? *He was nine months a-cooking, Lord, Lord, Lord / Then they put him on the table, Lord, Lord, Lord / And the knife couldn't cut him, Lord, Lord, Lord / And the fork couldn't stick him, Lord, Lord, Lord.* Where was Aesop when you needed him? Of all the songs on the album, this was the one Miriam studied, helplessly. *So they took him to the sawmill, Lord, Lord, Lord / Ho, it broke the saw's tooth out, Lord, Lord, Lord.* At last, one day, Rose took mercy on her daughter and explained. The answer, when it came, wasn't difficult, though Miriam, at eight, could never have guessed it.

Now, tonight, nine years later, on the postage-stamp-size platform in a club so small any table was front and also rear, the grapevines of smoke clinging to the ceiling providing an illusion of distance in a room that cleared of bentwood chairs and voices and clamor and filth, and properly lit and fumigated, would have been revealed as no larger than the parlor where Miriam had memorized her mother's albums, yet which somehow made room for not only a stage and a side bar featuring Italian coffee and red wine but also for a whole and intricate social world that Miriam was just learning to parse and manipulate—here, the tenor folksinger on the tiny platform crooned out Burl Ives's version of the folk song, exactly. Note for note, vocal gesture for vocal gesture, syllable for syllable. *And the last time I seen him, Lord, Lord, Lord / He was flying over the ocean, Lord, Lord, Lord / With a long string of goslings, Lord, Lord, Lord.* Miriam guffawed seeing with what neat sleight of hand the blond raffish singer offered up a version cribbed from a children's LP as if dredged out of some mossy Appalachian music-finding expedition, as if salvaged during some hobo's stint working in a train yard, or begging at the kitchen door of the very farm that had raised the Grey Goose itself. Laughed at how smugly the rendition was gobbled up by those unqualified to know the difference—or those who'd endure fingernail splinters before confessing they were familiar with Ives's version. The boy at her side turned, as he had each time that night she'd laughed for no evident cause, and said, "What?"

"Nothing." All this she couldn't explain, not to him. (Years later it would be his name, among so many here, that she, famous rememberer, resolutely couldn't dredge up.) Then Miriam laughed again and said, "Do you know what the Grey Goose represents?"

"Eh?"

"I'm asking what the Grey Goose represents. I just wondered if you knew."

The song now finished, she'd gained the attention of their whole table, and the table beside theirs as well. Chairs, long since reversed so chests married chairbacks, cigarette-knuckled hands flung carelessly forward for ballast, now squeaked. The margin between different tables, between friends and strangers, those who'd arrived in one configuration and those who might later depart rearranged, in pairs or complicated threesomes or alone, had been lost a while ago.

"Enlighten us, Mim," said Porter, the clever one in horn-rims, the Columbia man. Eyeing her for several nights now but too genteel to pry her from the boy. He might think he had all the time in the world. She might agree.

"Well, since you ask, the Grey Goose represents the irrevocable destiny of the working class." Never had Miriam been so delighted to regurgitate a Roseism.

Leaning in from the next table like a Disney wolf, Rye Gogan said, "Ach, fella, beware—your girl's a Red." Rye, middle baritone of the Gogan Boys, an act too big for this stage (not only reputation-wise but in strict bodily terms, the three Irish louts in their thick brocaded vests would never have fit on this club's riser), was the celebrity among them here, not that any of them would acknowledge it. Rye Gogan was also already famous, though who knew how such fame was exactly circulated, as something worse than a wolf. A drunken shark at an evening's end. The girl farthest from shore at that point was traditionally doomed.

"No, really, she *is* one," said Porter. Porter being one of those who always agreed with you by saying the word "no," as if you hadn't intended whatever you'd said so much as he felt you should have. "Not like us paper revolutionaries, gentlemen. Mim grew up in a *cell*, she's been to *secret meetings*. Tell them, Mim."

"Meetings?" growled Rye. "Who hasn't?" The Irish singer rounded his shoulders, that signature vest like a dank filthy sail hung from the rigging of his chest, and creaked his chair back toward his own party. Likely registering that engaging with Miriam's table entailed simply too much smarty-pants confusion to be worth the bother now, even if he'd tabulated Miriam's presence for some pending shark chase to shore.

"You have no idea," said Miriam to Porter, and Porter's friend, named, she was fairly certain, Adam, and the Barnard girl Adam had brought along, who'd said she was from Connecticut, and who'd been looking sick for most of an hour already. "I have a pedigree. My father's a German spy."

"Can he get us into Norman Mailer's party?" said Adam. Adam knew, or pretended to know, where the real action was tonight. Any crowded smoky basement or throngs on MacDougal or St. Marks to the contrary, all persons visible to their gaze were ipso facto losers like themselves.

"He's not allowed into the United States," said Miriam, surprising herself with where this was going, but then seeing it play like nearly anything from her mouth, in this company: delighted amazement at what the wild child from Sunnyside might say next. Her fiercest sincerities were translated by the male ego, on arrival, into daffy flirtation. For instance, when Miriam said she was bored by jazz (worshipping at its longueurs, its brilliant "passages," induced the same claustrophobia she always felt when sitting hushed before Rose's Beethoven symphonies, being instructed in their remorseless dire profundities) and, instead, liked Elvis Presley (cutting class to hide in Lorna Himmelfarb's basement listening to and gazing at Presley being sole salvation in the final semester of her senior year at Sunnyside High), men like Porter went into paroxysms of delight at how the female could want to provoke them, unstuff their admittedly self-satisfied views on every subject, never grasping how anyone they'd ever be seen squiring, let alone this raven-haired Jewess with a vocabulary like Lionel Trilling, could possibly possess such backward tastes. No one who actually didn't get jazz would ever admit it! And if you got it, man, well, you got it. Miriam, therefore, was a tease, ironist supreme. And with a figure.

"She's dead serious," said Porter now, fingering his frames Arthur Miller–style, again sealing Miriam's words in his only-I-get-it endorsement.

Miriam's original boy had been morosely toying with the red wax pooling in their table's blunt candle, dipping his fingertips so they coated. Then jostling the little inverted fingerprints off to assemble like a series of mouse-size bowls on the tablecloth, or tiny bloody footprints, a mock crime scene. Maybe trying to say someone had placed a tiny dagger in his tiny heart. Truly, Rye Gogan's storm-cloud attentions had altered the barometric pressure at their table, possibly in the whole room. While the folksinger interred his guitar to the mildest applause, a poet or comedian, some Lenny Bruce hopeful, stood waiting to commandeer the wholly unnecessary microphone. He wore a cravat and clutched a sheaf of papers, particularly unpromising. Someone knew him. But someone knew everyone. Miriam believed she could get one or more of her admirers on their feet and outside, possibly even Porter among them, and suddenly wanted to prove she could.

"What the hey. I'll get us into Mailer's party."

"How?"

"With my secret Commie powers, of course."

An hour later they stood braving a cold wind at the gentle summit of the Brooklyn Bridge's rotting-plank walkway, the East River's boardwalk, and surveyed the transistor gleamings of the island they'd exited, contrasting it with the low-roofed smolder of Brooklyn Heights, the murk of their promised destination, *Mailer's party*, down there somewhere, one of those faint flares amid a million darkened bedrooms, the sea of sleepers beyond. Here they halted, stared. Boroughphobia. Fear of Brooklyn. Miriam recognized it in her companions and laughed, but silently, not wanting to compel her unmemorable boy to another automatic, threatened *What?*

Miriam felt it in them, this gaggle she'd manufactured by calling them out of the folk basement: their collective reservations at being dragged to this brink, the bridge's perihelion, the immigrant shores. Statue of Liberty, Ellis Island, the sea. For the moment at least this seventeen-year-old Queens College freshman dropout had called their bluff. The Barnard girls, like Adam's date, Adam himself, and solo, enchanted Porter, interested but too sweet to be predatory, and Miriam's grown-sullen date, too. Miriam's ad hoc committee, her cell.

So forget Rose's secret meetings, her living rooms, her smoky kitchens. This night, right here, New York splayed before them, a banquet they feared to eat, Miriam understood for the first time clearly that her Secret Commie Powers were not actually a joke: Miriam Zimmer understood tonight she was *a leader of men*. Not just men slavering over her curves or astonished at her wit or haunted by her Jewish mysteries or dazzled by fluency with the city's mad systems, the subway lines, the Staten Island Ferry terminal and its pigeon population, the significance of a Dave's egg cream on Canal Street, the parsing of baseball affiliation since Dodgers and Giants were fleeing to California (no, you couldn't just suddenly become a Yankee fan, not while Sandy Koufax and Jake Pitler still lived), the dance of the monkeys and hippos on the Central Park Zoo clock, or her ease with Negroes or her startling ability to suddenly turn and greet a shambling, eccentric cousin—if only they knew!—coming out of a chess shop on MacDougal, her allusions to veiled knowledge, the transparency to her of symbols like the Grey Goose, but all of it, all. Surviving Rose and Sunnyside Gardens, that suburb of disappointment, had made Miriam sublime, a representative of the League of Absconded Kings or Queens. And seeing it she at once saw that it was visible to those she drew to her. Now she laughed aloud, and Forgettable weighed in again with "What?"

"Listen." Miriam's favorite idiot bar bet, in her experience completely impossible to lose in any company, gained a new allure here where they shivered on the bridge. The answer would be staring them in the face and they'd still blow it. "I'll bet anyone here five bucks they can't name an island in New York State that has a bigger population than forty-eight of the fifty states."

"That's dopey," said Adam. "Manhattan, of course."

"*You're* dopey, it's Long Island. You owe me five bucks or your last cigarette."

"But hey, who's counting?" said Porter, leaning in with his own still-plentiful pack, tapping a cluster of cigs halfway out. Fingers mobbed in, and then for an instant the five smokers were melded in physical purpose, clustering to bell-jar Porter's match from the night's wind, each dipping a cigarette's tip to the flame. Ladies first, then, once the match was inevitably doused, finishing with the square dance of touching lit to unlit tips. Night workers edged in darkness past them, heads bent ignorant to the city's splendor and misery, filing toward sour bedrooms. Fear of Brooklyn: There was plenty to fear, Miriam knew, though not what her companions imagined.

"I'm freezing," said Forgettable morosely, evidently intending them to understand him to mean *frozen out*. Miriam's date had given up petitioning with his shoulders and elbows to clutch Miriam to him, as Adam and his Barnard girl were clutched, the girl's shoulder inside Adam's tweed jacket, her arm vanished within his shirt at the waist. Forgettable's last few attempts had been despondent anyhow, as though he sensed the turn things were taking. For here at the bridge's height something else had reached a height: Miriam was changing hands tonight, Porter sweeping her away, if something so completely under Miriam's agency could be granted to Porter's own agency. It surely would be. Miriam being just a girl, after all.

Miriam plunged her cigarette's orange tip into the night. "Charge!"

"Screw Mailer," said her former date. As if that were an option, in lieu of what he'd never get from Miriam. "I've got to get up in the morning. I'm going back."

"We'll walk you," said Adam, whose intrepitude might have fallen victim to a whispered consultation with his fearful girl. This sudden defection sealed Miriam's transfer more absolutely than she might have wished: After a flurry of embraces, she and Porter hoofed it down the Brooklyn slope of the bridge, just the two of them, while the rest retreated to Manhattan. Miriam considered him entirely for the first time, her new courtier: With his funny knobbly gait, embarrassed or melancholic shoulders, and gigantic forehead, Porter was really drawn along Arthur Miller or Robert Lowell lines, though for his labored quipping he might be trying to pass as Mort Sahl. Leery Rose, in the right mood, might give him a chance on the basis of a resemblance to Abraham Lincoln. But then why would Miriam need her mother's approval? She canceled the thought.

"Look," she said, again pointing her cigarette past the bridge's descent into Brooklyn Heights. "Remsen Street, it's one of those, terminating at the Promenade." In her imagining, the glamorous town houses would be visible, a crest of terraces peering back across the water at Manhattan, and one of them declaring itself by seeping out jazz and cocktail clatter, clouds of marijuana smoke, genius conversation. In truth all that was visible there was a dark barricade of greenery, seemingly more than a mile beyond and below them, across the silent river's mouth.

"Which?" Now, committed, Porter sounded nervous, as though Miriam should have the address in her pocket, perhaps an engraved invitation, too.

"It'll be obvious from the street, we'll hear it a block away, I expect."

"If not, it isn't worth going," he bluffed, regaining his confidence. Yet that very bluff only carried them a stride or two more on the

bridge's downslope. Porter's confidence was for some other purpose, now that they'd shed their companions. Only when you'd
finally shaken them free, those couple-disguising little mobs, the self-
chaperoning cocoons that blobbed around everywhere together, were
you reminded of their uses. Porter kissed her. Miriam kissed him back,
just as ravenous, even if strategizing how to delay or undo it, or where
they would go, or what it would have to mean. Every personal possibility not deferred to an unimaginable future was present and urgent,
a calamity sweeping all calm before it. Miriam had never managed to
locate any sweet spot between. Porter's cold fingertips already found
gaps in the buttons of her antique dress at her tailbone, causing some
electrical outline to quiver along the whole contour of her buttocks,
to her feet where they attempted to stay rooted on the walkway's
planks. Porter was tall. Miriam got up on her toes, a half measure,
compromise with an impulse to drop in a swoon to her knees or lift
off into the sky.

Precisely to the same degree she'd been mothered in disappointment, in embittered moderation, in the stifling of unreasonable expectations, in second-generation cynicism toward collapsed gleaming
visions of the future, the morose detachment of the suburbs, Miriam
was in fact a Bolshevik of the five senses. Her whole body demanded
revolution and gleaming cities in which revolution could be played
out, her whole character screamed to see high towers raised up and
destroyed. Every yearning Rose might ever have wished to dampen
had been doubly instilled in her daughter. For all of her quashing
of utopias, for all of her "facing facts," Rose had merely been proving Miriam's innate suspicion that life was elsewhere. For God's sake,
you could see the Empire State Building framed at the foot of Greenpoint Avenue! And for what felt like ten years Miriam had gathered
in the special appearance and attitudes of the girls who had enrolled
at City College but still lived at home, or at least kept rooms in their
homes, in Sunnyside Gardens. The knowledge behind their new cat
sunglasses, the cigarettes they snuck and the gossip they ceased on the
communal back patios when nine- or ten- or twelve-year-old Miriam
wandered up. Miriam knew these girls were telling her her future and
wondered why they bothered to conceal it. They couldn't conceal it.
Miriam could see the Empire State Building now, past Porter's shoul-

der as she pulled her mouth from his and leaned and gasped for air and stalled for time, her cheek against his arm. The stupid beckoning phallic symbol, brazenly named for the nation's criminal ambitions yet paradoxically bearing with it the pride Rose had instilled in Miriam for being an *American* and a *New Yorker*, the dull amazing monument was always there, stabbing the air, calling to her, crushing her like a bug in advance. You're nobody so special, Miriam Zimmer!

Except here on the bridge, upper lip already raw in the high wind from Porter's five-o'clock shadow's scraping, Miriam felt all the freedom accorded to *nobody special* as a power equal to the Empire State's mass and force. Had anyone ever already known what Miriam knew at seventeen? It seemed unlikely. And tonight she would know more. She was going to let Porter be the first to make love to her because he was just special and not-special enough to be the one to do it. *That night beginning on the bridge*, as she'd already half started to call it, could be sudden enough not to be a story she'd owe to anyone at all. It would erase the debt to Forgettable, too, if he'd been brushed off in favor of a significance in her own life that outweighed the difference between one man and another. Not that the discarded suitor would ever know what ledgers of guilt were kept in Miriam's head. "Take me somewhere," she said.

There, with her words, to which Porter panted his grateful consent, began the insane night that had already had so many beginnings. First, withdrawal to Manhattan, not in boroughphobia now, no (and their ultimate destination would be proof of this), but total disinterest in Mailer or the dark roofs or cold sky or anything outside of themselves and their skins. If they could have left their clothing on the bridge, they might have done that. The IRT at City Hall took them to Union Square, where in a high-backed booth at the Cedar Tavern they entwined tongues and fondled until asked to leave. They repeated the performance at the Limelight coffee shop, to which Miriam had with exasperation dragged Porter after he'd expressed a dazed uncertainty as to where else to try—they'd have had more privacy in a corner of Mailer's party, which she'd by now fully visualized as consisting of sultry Bennington girls being serially deflowered in piles of coats. They had more privacy even in Washington Square, where for another turbulent session they settled on a bench. But Miriam was freezing now, whenever they quit walking and Porter's hands resumed inching inside to loosen her already flimsy coverings. She could actually feel a breeze where a trickle of her excessively fervent self had moistened her anus and inner thighs. "Why can't we go to your rooms?" she whispered.

Porter looked at her, not for the first time, with an admiration suggesting Miriam was Wuthering Heights mad. "There's a strict dorm policy."

"I thought you Columbia men were trying to change that."

"Trilling weighed in against us," bragged Porter, proud anytime he could cite that name. "He seemed confused that we'd even *want* women in the dorms, leaving their nylons around, as he put it—"

"So why don't you make a stand?" Miriam shamelessly gave this the Marilyn Monroe treatment, lips at his ear. "Protest for your cause."

"My roommate," Porter said helplessly. "I couldn't—"

The virginity Miriam trailed around with her was an anchor, one she vowed to cast off before dawn. So they rode the subway again, to Grand Central, and she guided him downstairs to the track where the 7 line would carry them back to Queens, then to the rear of the platform. Miraculously, a train hovered, panting slightly with its doors open. They boarded and it took off as if it had been waiting for them. "After the river the train goes elevated, Porter. I'll show you something you've never seen before."

"What's that?" he said dreamily. They'd walked with their fingers entwined, pulling downward to draw each other close, his hip at her waist, her breasts at his ribs, each awkward rubbing step a kind of prolongation of the endless make-out session the night had become. Now they stood against a door, unwilling to discontinue the contact between the lengths of their bodies, letting the train's lurches buckle his knee into a place between her legs. She clenched his thigh at her crotch.

"You'll see. The greatest curve in the system," Miriam teased.

"I actually think I know what you're talking about."

"That's when you can be certain you're wrong."

"Nothing you could show me that was curved could be wrong." What was this talk, so stupidly enchanted, so unguardedly self-beguiled on both their sides, so seemingly drunk on each other's wit and promise? Or should the question be: How much red wine had she unthinkingly guzzled at the Cedar Tavern?

"Hold that thought," she said, whispering again.

"I think I have been holding it, for a while already." This latest of Porter's attempted smutty remarks drew perilously close to nonsense. The Queens-bound train rescued them, with its progress up out of the darkness, scraping moonward into the constellation of streetlights and signage along Jackson Avenue. "Holy heck!" he shouted. "It's like a roller coaster!"

As usual, Miriam's facts had been taken for not-even-double entendres, for beckoning inanities. "No, I told you," she said, styling her formulation after Porter's own manner, and leaning into his ear to put it over above the elevated's rattle and shriek. "That was nothing, brace yourself. The real curve's the next one, watch." She urged him against the door's windows, to take it in fully. The 7's lead cars obligingly jackknifed into Queensboro Plaza; Porter's jaw hung vindicatingly open. "It's the only place in the system where you can watch the front cars *of the train you're on* pull into a station from the rear cars," said Miriam. Hammering the point home, she felt like Rose. Like she'd picked up Rose's hammer of personality to impress the Columbia boy, to bonk against his broad, daft forehead. (How could you go to so much trouble to arrive in New York City, as the throngs at Columbia and Barnard had, and not *ride the system*?) As if Miriam's life-exuberance pointed back toward Rose's punitive ferocity, just the way the IRT screamed in the direction of home. Did Miriam pause at that instant and gander at her motives, bringing Porter to Queens? No. She was randy, had been randy for what felt like her whole life, and now she was going to find out the secret of what it was to make love. This was simple enough. They needed a private room. Miriam had one at home.

She tried to see Sunnyside's Forty-Seventh Street through his eyes, too. The slumbering apartment blocks, the tended shrubbery and flagstone walks, Miriam's home borough some false vision of calm, an immigrant's dull fantasy of American sanctuary that suddenly turned her stomach; she hurried him past. No one apart from the two of them had exited the train at the Bliss Street station, and now, on the sidewalks, they passed no one. The whole journey might have been a dream she'd had from her bedroom, once she'd tiptoed inside through the Gardens and the kitchen door, that being farthest from Rose's bedroom, and swept Porter inside. Only he was still blithering about the elevated's rocket ride, so that she had to hush him until her door was safely shut. She stuffed a towel along the jamb as if enjoying a secret cigarette.

At this point, the dream of night—or morning; she'd glanced at Porter's wristwatch on the street and the time was past three—veered toward squalid comedy before becoming a nightmare. The two of them remaining on their feet, in some shyness still unwilling to commit to her bed, Porter struggling with one or another of her fasteners and buttons, forcing Miriam to add her hands to his and solve whatever problem he'd been muttering over, so that before very long she was entirely nude while he still wore his whole outfit. In exasperation she pulled him to the bed and half tented herself under the spread. "Take off your shoes, at least," she whispered.

"Have you got an, um, pessary?"

"Pessary?" She tried not to snort at the absurd term, which struck her as Midwestern if not actually Victorian. "Do you mean a diaphragm?" What, was he afraid to remove his clothes for fear of pregnancy? Should she lie? Yes. "Yes."

"You do?"

"It's taken care of, Porter."

Miriam flashed on Rye Gogan and his reputation: Where was the masculine devourer when you needed him? Must you swim with sharks to get sharked? Take me, she wanted to tell Porter, yet refused to have to tell him, on the principle that even men in tortoiseshell glasses were meant to transform into animals in the dark. Perhaps especially men in tortoiseshell glasses, according to the cartoons in *Playboy*, Lorna Himmelfarb's older brother's copies of which she'd also perused during Elvis-auditing sessions in the Himmelfarb basement. Something should be swarming Miriam, apart from her desire to be swarmed. She got Porter onto the bed, on his knees before her, as though praying at the entrance to her tent. Pulled him by the belt. Unzipped and researched inside. Oh, Lord, the boy, nicely long and rigid, Chinese-finger-trapped by desire in his too-tight boxer shorts, wasn't circumcised. He also blurted his goop into her palm at the same instant she'd groped the knob and discovered its stretchy hood. Then, sighing, Porter covered her lips and chin and nose with a flurry of seeking kisses, as if both grateful and falsifying the record. *See, I'm ravishing you, therefore I must have been all along!* Instead she'd accidentally ravished him. Like her trail of verbal conquests, Miriam persistently slayed men before she'd begun even trying to.

They kissed as passionately as they had in the booth at the Cedar, embraces that claimed a story was still in the making in the space between their bodies, and meanwhile she cradled his softening self until her awkwardly turned wrist was the only bony thing trapped inside the fly of his boxer shorts. Miriam had gotten more action on the bridge or in Washington Square, more thrill out of Porter's elbow at her breast, his knee nuzzling her lap, than she was likely to find rustling in the shrinkage and stickiness in his pants. And then Rose came barreling in, a titan, Alice's wrathful Red Queen in her quilted robe, her gossamer nightdress beneath it, her expression a storm of reproach, and the story abruptly had nothing to do with their bodies, with Miriam's nakedness and desire and what Porter was or wasn't going to do about it. All that was left of that story was how fortunate Miriam could feel in retrospect that she'd gotten so little of Porter's clothing off. Even knowing Rose had seen nothing, Miriam had time for the stray, absurd thought: Abraham Lincoln wouldn't have been circumcised either, so Rose couldn't object to that, could she?

"Should I call the police?"

"No, Mother."

"*No, Mother* what?" Rose seized any occasion for a mental test, a verbal duel—why miss what was there for the taking?

"Don't overreact, Rose, for God's sake."

The room flooded with light from the living room and foyer behind Rose, every lamp switched on, as though her mother had been awake for a duration of eavesdropping and pacing, and for expert selection of the awkwardest instant to make this confrontation, though truly she'd have had a few to choose from.

"Don't tell me how I should react. Don't tell me what to do. If I don't call the police it's less a mercy than the fear they might arrest me for parental dereliction." Rose's bold, rising, theatrically superb declaration ran over a thin, husky, stuttering sound, something that might have been an effort on Porter's part to apologize or introduce himself or both, even as he juggled his glasses back onto his face and pinched at his zipper and disordered trousers. Rose detoured to a Barbara Stanwyckian quip: "By the way, it's rape, mister, unless you happen still to be in high school yourself."

"Nobody was *raped*," said Miriam, letting her disappointment color the word with scorn for Rose and Porter both. "And I'm not in high school, thank you."

"You ought to be. This matter of skipping a grade makes you think you're a *woman* now? The bosom on you fooled this young man, fair enough, but how can it have fooled you as well? Perhaps you're ready to become parents of a child. It's not as much pleasure as you'd think from the way it begins, making babies."

"Nobody's making any babies." Miriam thought of the word *pessary* again. So long as Porter was present this scene was only comic overture to the crisis, the explosion struggling to begin. It wasn't that Porter wasn't capable of defending Miriam from Rose, or not only. It was that Rose wouldn't unleash what she had, so Miriam couldn't know what she faced and had to defend against, until Porter had been shunted off.

Instead Rose was left playing to some invisible distant gallery of those she imagined might judge her through Porter's eyes: goyim, males, New York intellectuals, strangers generally. So while he stood gaping at her, a hand raised as if he really thought his own contribution would be expected at some point, Rose speechified, rehearsing various guilt-drenched postures. Miriam knew that for all its apparent force Rose's monologue was a placeholder, a form of stalling. "I tried to raise a young woman but apparently produced an American teenager in her place. No doubt the fault is mine, yet it's also the case that the result was sabotaged a hundred ways. First by the father, who couldn't be kept at home. In that the fault is surely mine, we fought terribly, I couldn't keep him fascinated in ways a freethinker like you appears to have already mastered, but what you two lovebirds couldn't imagine is the world I brought this girl into. A battlefield. Not a playground for children in the bodies of adults. You're in a hurry to grow up—we'd given up our childhoods before we knew we'd given them up. I slaved in the back of my father's candy shop. This one, Miriam, ah! Look at the expression! He wouldn't know what a barrel of halvah was if I shoved it in his face."

Halvah! Oh, an intervention was desperately needed, but the difficulty was in how little offense Porter gave, how few grounds for ejection. He stood dopily awaiting his turn, which would never come. As she'd wished for a little more rape earlier, Miriam now wished Porter would make some move, any move, even in panic, to incite Rose showing him the door. Instead Rose, measuring his passivity, latched onto a listener. Miriam couldn't count how many she'd seen frozen on a square of sidewalk at one of Rose's stunning harangues, though she'd never been draped naked in a bedspread while a would-be boyfriend played the part. Maybe Porter was about to begin taking notes as if at Trilling's own feet. Miriam had to do everything herself. She elevated from the bed like a ghost or a muse in her drapery and took Porter's elbow and guided him past a momentarily jaw-frozen Rose, back through the kitchen. Though Porter was apparently properly dressed, he moved as awkwardly as if he wore his jacket backward, his shoes on his hands.

"Go."

"I'm so sorry. When can I—?"

When can I what? Miriam thought, an exact Rose Angrush Zimmer cadence, except Rose would have said it aloud. What in this performance was Porter eager to reflect on or repeat? Well, they'd find each other soon enough, that's if Miriam ever got out of the house again. She craned on tiptoe for a quick kiss, surprising herself by wanting one. She'd after all fondled Porter's secret heartbeat, collected his private sigh. They had, after all, been romancing across a connect-the-dot map of Miriam's city for hours past, hours of what now seemed another night, another life entirely.

The light in the Gardens was morning light. Carl Heuman stood dumbfounded on the lane, sad in a Dodgers jacket that made him look fourteen years old, commemorating or denying the fact of his absconded team, and presumably interrupted in his morning meander to an early-Sunday baseball practice on the diamond of Sunnyside High, where Miriam had polished off her senior classes a year before Carl and her other contemporaries. So Carl Heuman had seen her in her bedspread, shoving the Columbia boy through the kitchen door's gap. It didn't matter. Yet, their eyes meeting for an instant, Miriam now experienced a time-stopped revelation, wholly involuntary: If she died today (why think *this*, to begin with?), Carl Heuman would have known her a hundred, perhaps a thousand times better than Porter had. Just by virtue of knowing Sunnyside Gardens and what they signified, by knowing Rose Zimmer the way any one of their neighbors would have (the boys like Carl Heuman were all terrified of Rose), by being enrolled in the same classes Miriam had evaded, by being from and of these places, forlorn Carl Heuman, whose only living purpose was to become the third-ever Jewish pitcher on a team that *no longer existed*, bore incisive knowledge of who it was Miriam had not yet even begun to escape being, even if he couldn't know he knew it. Porter, on the other hand, could be from Mars for what he grasped of the creature with whom he'd passed the night. Miriam might be altering herself at a furious rate into that other one, the girl Porter believed he'd deviously squired out of the basement club behind the stalking horse of her official date, then halfway across the Brooklyn Bridge and back, then to Queens to find himself more or less raped and accused of rape within a span of minutes, but she wasn't there yet. Miriam was still the one into whose soul dopey, obedient Carl Heuman so effortlessly, if abashedly, gazed. And so, as first Carl and then Porter wobbled along the light-blobbed lanes of the Gardens and vanished, Miriam closed the kitchen door and withdrew to face Rose.

Last Sunday morning, Lord, Lord, Lord / Oh, my daddy went a hunting, Lord, Lord, Lord.

Rose, who reason would suggest might have taken the interval for a chance to invite morning into the apartment, had apparently done the reverse, cinched whatever window shades allowed any margin of daylight, the better to savor the reproving atmosphere of night. She'd then withdrawn to her own bedroom, the darkest room in the apartment. A withdrawal, but not a retreat; she'd left the door open, less invitation than command that Miriam deliver herself into Rose's sanctum.

Of course Rose had an excuse, if Miriam could read her mind (she could), for shuttering the apartment: that of shame at a daughter's nudity cloaked in merely a bedspread. No, Rose's next move might have been spontaneous, not a plan, the drawn shades were no evi-

dence of forethought. Miriam had to grant Rose's instinct for impro-
vised spectacles. This one was certainly special. Rose tore at the sash
of her robe, tore it open, flung it to the floor at her feet. Then clawed
again, at the filmy nightdress beneath, rending the cloth where it held
her vast, soft, pale-yellow, mole-strewn breasts so they tumbled out,
absurd offering, absurd accusation.

"I'd tear my heart out and drop it on the floor if I could, to let you
see what you've done to it. Instead take a look at the body that not
only labored you forth but nursed you and bathed you and in order
to keep you fed and in clothes allowed itself to be destroyed walking
half a mile in shoes with heels every day to the pickle factory because
Solomon Real preferred ladies to appear like ladies even while up to
their armpits in his brine. Hardly a pretty sight, is it? I'm no Botticelli
like you, a sylph in a stinking blanket." So began the real monologue,
the real test. Miriam consoled herself thinking these were essay questions in reverse: Rose wasn't really interested in answers, just that
Miriam meditate on her epic inquisitions. Miriam need only find a
way to endure her mother, posture herself to survive but not submit,
until Rose's forces were exhausted.

A first jab Miriam couldn't resist, though she knew she shouldn't jab.
"I thought you were the bookkeeper—the brains of Sol's operation."

"In the early years I was side by side with the workers soaking
in that piss. That I was the only one who could answer a phone in
proper English or add a column of numbers accurately didn't put me
one step above the delivery boys or for that matter the horses dragging the carts. All so you could have the opportunity to attend the
finest public university in the world, a privilege the historical rarity of
which you couldn't be expected to understand since you've neglected
every chance of learning the way the world works, the way the present world, rather than coming into being unprecedented, is in fact a
product of history. You'd rather learn the way a man's schlong works,
seemingly. You'd rather attend the college of sexual intercourse!"
Rose's speckled chest was aflame with rage and inspiration, a blush
creeping to those breasts barely covered and jostling obscenely for her
punctuation. They now appeared scalded, pink moons in the darkened bedroom. Rose detected their bobbing herself and seized them
with her hands, enlisted them in her tableau. "Here's your result, it's

staring you in the face if you hadn't noticed. He sticks it in you and you become bloated with a child, your body is warped into a battle-field, then enslaved in servitude, the reward for which is a daughter who'll declare herself done with college at seventeen years of age. A finished product, it seems. Look at you!"

If Rose was the Red Queen and Miriam Alice, then Miriam's desired chess move would be to avoid at all costs the squares Rose had titled, absurdly, *intercourse* and *pregnancy*. The nearer to mat-ters of the female body, two examples of which were combustively present between them at this instant, the more irrational (if degrees of *rationality* could even be invoked in this asylum atmosphere), the more combustible Rose would certainly become. No, Miriam had to leap at what looked like possible exits from this territory: Jump to the square marked *college education*. Matters of the mind. Get Rose thinking in abstractions—the illuminations of Marxism, the betray-als of Stalinism and horrors of Hitlerism, the mercy of Lincolnism, the splendors of American freedom, the rapture of public libraries or honest policemen or Negroes and whites together enjoying Central Park—and Miriam might be halfway home. And, while at it, dress one of those two combustible female bodies, the one Miriam had the power to dress. Let Rose be naked, if she so chose.

Therefore even as Miriam began to speak in what she hoped were soothingly reasonable tones, she backed in her Statue of Liberty bed-spread out of Rose's bedroom and began groping in her chest of draw-ers for the rudiments of a fresh outfit. "Mother, I know it's a terrific system but you have to realize that Queens College isn't exactly the same as the Manhattan campus. For me it's like being stuck with the same faces from high school."

"The sons and daughters of other good working-class families to which you're ashamed to admit you belong among?"

"I'm not alone, Rose. It's only the squares who aren't rushing over to MacDougal Street the minute class is over. I learn more in one bull session in Washington Square Park than I ever did at Queens College."

"Ah, only *squares*? Listen to you. Despite the beatnik talk I don't miss your implication for the rest of us. What licenses you to judge so severely?"

"You're telling me you don't sort the world into those with and without a clue, Rose? Would you prefer if I used your word—*sheep*?"

"So these sophisticates flee the minute class is over, yet *you're* the one who couldn't wait even that long. By destroying your studies you've squandered your option to transfer to City, if you're so eager to be away from me, and travel to Harlem to get into the company of the big obnoxious Jews up there. You need a famous atmosphere or you're bored, is that it?" Rose, her robe now tightened again around the ruined nightdress, had followed Miriam to her doorway. She seemed magically calmed, if it was safe to believe it could happen so quickly.

"Mother, where did you acquire all the history you throw in my face? In school or elsewhere—at meetings, in coffee shops?"

"How do you think I became the one who Solomon Real needed to answer his telephones, to repair his double-entry books, to master shorthand for immortalizing his peasant's prattle. Those poor Jews didn't stand a chance!"

"Couldn't I answer Sol's telephone? *You* taught me English."

"I didn't have your opportunities, to throw away like they were worthless."

"You never speak of your school days except for the bewilderment of learning that Yiddish wasn't actually what was spoken there. The shock of realizing you had to start over making yourself American. But I grew up speaking right, because you taught me. The history you want me to recite, you learned it marching in the streets. You learned it reading books they don't have in the Queens College library. I've read those books. Your shelves are better than theirs, Ma."

"*Ma*," Rose scoffed, but she'd been superbly derailed by Miriam's flattery. "You sound Italian. Maybe I should have gotten you out of Queens."

"I can do Italian," said Miriam the Mimic, now looking to make Rose laugh. She simply ventriloquized her schoolmate Adele Verapoppa—too easy. "I can do Yid, too," she said, in perfect Uncle Fred. "I know the difference between Queens and Brooklyn—*Toity-Toid Street. You* taught me them all, a by-product of teaching me not to *have* an accent."

Miriam, her mind a fog of exhaustion, amazed that night had

smeared into this atrocious day without a single blink or nod of sleep, had nonetheless continued to dress herself; the clean dry underwear, the new brassiere and stockings made her feel covered and with some possibility of renewal or escape. But she'd overreached in her flattery. Or something else had turned sour. As she began stepping into a dress, Rose's face contorted again.

"Where are you going?" Rose's voice gripped a lower rung of hysteria. "To *him*?"

"Oh, Mother. I'm only putting on clothes."

"Could it have been me that purchased for you a whole wardrobe of nothing but poodle skirts and party dresses? Was I such an idiot? Perhaps I'm really to blame, perhaps somehow I shoved you out the door to find a man to lay you because I'm finished myself, dry down below—"

"Stop, Rose." Miriam thought better of making mention of her mother's lover, the lieutenant. Who knew what cataclysm that might set off.

Yet why think cataclysm was circumventable?

Rose's hands tugged at the margins of her robe again, but a repeat performance wasn't enough, this wanted escalation. Rose sobbed theatrically and collapsed to the floor, absurdly recalling Jackie Wilson, the soul singer Miriam had seen at the Mercury Ballroom in Harlem, she and Lorna Himmelfarb having snuck up on a dare, their white faces beacons of risk and delight in a sea of black. They'd been tolerated, perhaps indulged or even protected, but it wasn't a chance Miriam would take again without a Negro companion for escort. Now Rose artfully also blocked the door, a grain of pragmatism in her histrionics. The way Rose heaved tears so reminded Miriam of the singer that she found herself issuing a sharp guffaw.

"How could you. If I was dying it wouldn't stop you doing as you wished. No doubt you'd step over my body on your way to Greenwich Village or to a man like that one whose name you won't even condescend to share with me. Step over my dying body on your voyage to where the *squares* wouldn't go. But I hardly imagined you'd shower me with laughter as you went past."

"You're not dying, Rose."

"I am inside."

That's how you know you're still alive, Miriam wanted to tell her. Dying inside was for Rose a way of life. Within her mother was a volcano of death. Rose had spent her whole life stoking it, trying to keep the mess inside contained but fuming. In Rose's lava of disappointment the ideals of American Communism had gone to die their slow death eternally; Rose would never die precisely because she needed to live forever, a flesh monument, commemorating Socialism's failure as an intimate wound. Rose's sisters' unwillingness to defy, by their marriages, by their life stories, the obedient Judaic domestic-life scripts Miriam's grandparents had salvaged from that shtetl that was neither Poland nor Russia but some unholy no-Jew's-land between; this rage too had to smolder eternally inside the radioactive container, the unexploded bomb that was Rose Zimmer. God himself had gone inside her to die: Rose's disbelief, her secularism, wasn't a freedom from superstition but the tragic burden of her intelligence. God existed just to the puny extent he could disappoint her by his nonexistence, and while he was puny, her anger at him was immense, almost Godlike. Finally, if you dared argue, if you needed proof of Godlessness in this vale of outrage, the Holocaust. Each of the six million was a personal injury nursed within the volcano, too.

Rose crawled on her hands and knees to the kitchen. Miriam, in her dress now but barefoot, found a correlative response, a non-sequitur antidote to what was before her: She lifted up a magazine that happened to lie on the foyer's small table, alongside a bowl of keys. *Life*, Mamie Eisenhower in a flowery yellow hat. Miriam padded after Rose, ostentatiously thumbing through the glossy pages, while her mother slithered to the foot of the stove and reached up. Miriam's duty was to witness Rose; this had been required of her for what seemed centuries already, inside Miriam's seventeen years. Witness, confirm, recognize. So: into the kitchen. Lana Turner, in the magazine's culture pages, looked identical to Mamie on the cover; squint, and they were one woman. Rose flipped the gas dial, then wrenched the oven's door open like a black mouth and crawled onto its pouting lip to deliver her head inside.

"I don't want to live to see you put with child and abandoned as I was by that son of a bitch who was your father. My life's been nothing but one long heartbreak since the moment he first laid a hand on my body, now you're walking out the door to finish the job. But I'll finish it for you. It's fine, I've lived too many years past the destruction of everything that once mattered. I can't bear to live through the trials of your stupidity and suffering as I did my own. As if I taught you *nothing*."

"You're not making sense, you put too many things together, Rose." Miriam flapped the magazine under her arm but refused yet to intervene, to take a step in Rose's direction. "My father isn't responsible for everything in your life, he wasn't around long enough for that. My father, for instance, didn't humiliate the Soviet, you know. Khrushchev did that." Could Miriam's scorn embarrass Rose from her demonstration? Rose flopped her arms as though trying to clamber deeper into the oven, a whale going ashore. If Rose could see her own ass from this vantage she'd quit immediately.

"I'm already alone, leave me to die as I should have done the moment that thief stole my life and put me with child. I should have taken the baby in my arms and jumped from a bridge."

"The baby is me, Rose."

"Fatherless a child is worse than dead. We're castoffs, you and I." Rose reasoned from within the oven, absurdly. Yet the room had begun to fill with that cloying, fartlike odor Miriam had been expertly trained to regard as a life-or-death disaster. *Call the gas company! Open all the doors, run out, find a neighbor!* Families they knew hid beyond the walls in both directions, perhaps hearing Rose's moans and shrieks as they sat at morning coffee and newspaper. Rose was off speaking terms with every single member of them.

"Speak for yourself. What lies, Rose. After all this time. If you'd wanted me to have a father you could have told me where he was. You wouldn't let me write a *letter*."

"He tossed you aside without a glance. You think that man had learned to love a child who was barely doing more than combing her doll's hair by the time he vanished? You couldn't give him the satisfaction of making an audience for his great rhetorical postures, you couldn't buy him a drink, you couldn't prop up his vanities any better than I could. What would you say to such a man in a letter?"

"A man, everything that happened to you was done by a man. For a revolutionary your heartbreak is awfully pedestrian, Rose."

"Pedestrian!" It was, admittedly, a peculiar word to throw at the block-watcher, the Citizens' Patroller, the consummate enraged flaneur that was Rose Zimmer. Rose was the Pope of Pedestrianism, scalding all of Sunnyside with her inquisitions-on-the-hoof. The stink of gas continued to expand in the room, a headache with the ambition to cure you of every future headache.

"Rear guard, Mother. Weren't men and women to be equally responsible for their lives in your revolutionary blueprints? Or are those now going into the oven as well?"

Every word Miriam hurled at Rose, as well as the exquisite torque with which it was hurled, came straight from Rose herself. Miriam relished this notion, that Rose must feel she faced a renegade self, the demon memorizer of her inmost hypocrisies. *You wanted a witness?*

"Rear guard?" Rose cried. Like an animal freeing itself from a burrow in which she'd nosed against a hostile occupant, Rose came clear of the oven. From her knees she tackled Miriam to the floor. For one instant Miriam found herself swept into her mother's incoherent embrace, arms of iron, bosom of cloying depths, corkscrewed face corroding her own with its bleachy tears. Then, as if she was and had always been only a child, her body to be handled, limbs shoved through sleeves, hoisted bruisingly here and there, a terrifying slackness came over her, feeling Rose's next intention. Every strength unavailable to Miriam had apparently flowed into her mother's monstrous wrists and shoulders, her wrestler's grip. Rose shoved Miriam's head into the oven. Miriam only slackened. Perhaps it didn't even matter, so much gas filled the room already. Miriam still preferred not to credit Rose with calculation, despite essentially having begun by sealing the rooms of the apartment. One inspiration flowed into another. This was how you earned the right to inflict murder: by showing a willingness to murder yourself first.

Perhaps Rose was testing Miriam. Perhaps Miriam tested her back by the absence of struggle: She anyway wanted to believe she'd been defiant, rather than suicidally helpless, when an instant later Rose's vise clench loosened. Miriam was carried into her mother's lap as they both fell backward, Miriam's crown thudding on the oven's top lip as she came free of it. "You'd do it, you'd die to get away from me," Rose groaned. She writhed loose from underneath, cutting short their mother-reading-storybook-to-child tableau before the flooding oven, to drape herself in a morose, shuddering heap. One breast found the rent in her nightdress and pooled like pancake batter on the kitchen's tile.

Miriam shut off the gas. Then stood, smoothed her disarranged clothing, and went to the kitchen windows, raising the shades to light, the sashes to fresh air. Stepping over her mother without a downward glance, she made the rounds of the apartment's windows, inviting the cool morning to draw the poison out. It would take a while. By the time Miriam circled to the kitchen door Rose had departed to her room, aligned sepulchrally on its high narrow bed like a figure in a marble crypt, Grant or Lenin.

"You're killing me," Rose intoned when she detected by some radar Miriam's tiptoe at her door. Rose's head didn't inch, black curls and gray temples sworls forged of stone.

"A family tradition." Did Rose deserve to be teased? Miriam did it for her own sanity.

"I can't live with you in this house."

"First I'm killing you by leaving, now you're kicking me out?"

"Go to him."

Rose was less a mother than some preening and jealous Shakespearean lover, a duke fantasizing her rivals into solidity. This, in turn, led to an image of Miriam costuming herself as a man, like Rosalind, to smuggle herself into the sanctum of the Columbia dorms. Anything for a night's sleep at this point. It was all too comically impossible to make Rose understand, how the disaster of her arrival on the scene had shipwrecked the tenuous excursion with the college boy. Miriam wondered again whether she'd see Porter a second time. Appropriate to her Shakespearean fugue, he seemed a figure from a dream. Maybe the gas had already done its work, snuck in and muddled her brain, and so she might as well have left her head lying on that oven rack and died. Shakespeare flashed before her eyes because, like any New York City public-school child before her, Miriam had memorized the plays before she stood any chance of understanding them and was doomed to spend the rest of her life seeing how the playwright had detailed every agony and absurdity of the existence to come, from his perch in history. Rose, the fiend for education, would be proud if she knew. Miriam's legs jellied and she sagged into the cradle of Rose's doorway. Rose, on her bed, seemed a mile high.

"There's no him," Miriam whispered.

"Unless you return to college, pack your things and live elsewhere."

"Not Queens." Two mummies, entombed side by side, bargained at the affairs of the living from their holes beneath the earth.

"Then what?"

"The New School."

"You didn't get enough of Trotsky from Mr. and Mrs. Abramovitz and their son who's too good for anything but Harvard, you need to go bask in that hotbed of do-nothing I-told-you-so's?"

"I'm not interested in Trotsky one way or the other, Mother. I want to study ethnic music."

This was good enough for a shriek from the statue-corpse. *"Ethnic music?"*

"You said return to college."

"That's *college?*" No matter how it might appear to anyone less versed in Roseology, the tragic sobbed interval between the first and second notes of this song indicated concession to the inevitable. (A Jackie Wilson sob again.) Achieving this, some butterfly-broken-on-a-wheel part of Miriam managed a smile.

And more: The butterfly raised a wing, tested the sky. "But not this semester, Rose. It's too late. I want you to send me to Germany."

"What's this?" The tones rehearsed *betrayal, betrayal*, but with none of the previous vigor.

"If you want me to go to college, first tell me where he is and buy me a ticket to visit."

"It's too much," Rose attempted. But stopped. The black oven was not so far away, odor still trickling through the apartment. Miriam saw that without conceiving it in advance—two souls can enter a passage like this one, a night and morning like this one, without a plan!—she'd begun extracting from Rose the full and exact price of never mentioning this episode between them again.

"Germany to see him and then I start school in the spring."

"Too much," Rose whispered now.

"No, it's time I had a look at him. You even want me to, so I can tell you what I find."

"You could go get it from your *omi*, from Alma. Anytime you'd wanted, you could have asked your grandmother for that bastard's address."

"Maybe so. But I want it from *you*."

"Leave me alone." The woman on the high bed refroze herself into the carved decoration atop a tomb.

So it was that at last, at the end, Miriam set herself on her own sheets and mattress, still in the fresh dress that she'd worn for her brief headfirst expedition into the oven, the bedcovers, from within which she'd momentarily tugged at Porter's uncircumcised, squirting prick, still flung aside into the corner where she'd discarded them after wriggling into her panties and hose, and lay there, eyes exhausted but wide to the ceiling, and merely breathed. The two of them in their rooms, as ever and always, breathing. The ceaseless arrangement of mother and daughter coiled in fury at each other yet still bulwarked together inside this apartment against the prospect of anything and anyone else outside. Temple and tomb of childhood, armory of Rose's defiance. Before sleep enfolded her, Miriam sensed Rose's fingertip bruises along her soft upper arms. She could nearly count them, eight fingers and two thumbs, where they throbbed. In the next days they'd bloom and fade through purple, blue, banana-yellow, before vanishing.

It had been a trick question, a paradox beyond even Aesop's devising. How could you possibly learn the identity of the Grey Goose *by asking the Grey Goose*? For, after everything, this was at last unmistakable: The Grey Goose—inedible, adamantine, undead, warping any implement that dared glance in its direction, let alone that dared to attack—was none other than Rose Zimmer.

3 Cicero's Medicine

"Do you want to know what I really think?"

The speaker was Cicero Lookins. Or, rather, his head. One of two heads, bobbing in valleys and crests of seawater that refracted in the weighty silent air like a sunstruck chandelier. The atmosphere was noon-luminous, heat-immense. The bowl of sky enclosing the two heads scarcely cloud-daubed, blue almost friable where it pressured the rim of pines the swimmers had left behind. Third week of September and hotter than the hottest day in August, hotter than Cicero felt Maine ought to be, or need be to invite ocean-swimming. Cicero floated vertically, a three-hundred-pound bowling pin barely able to stay below, his toes straining toward those chilled deeper layers.

A fact you knew, if you got in the ocean: The world was getting hotter.

Could get hotter still.

The second head, named Sergius Gogan, had no way to shield its whiteness from noon's blaze, whereas Cicero sheltered under his irregular self-generated umbrella, his lumpy, going-gray helicopter blades of dreadlock. Unmerciful of Cicero, taking Sergius out here. He'd read somewhere that pure redheads like Sergius and his late father went on freckling their whole lives, a one-way progress of melanin from birth to grave, so every sunning niggered their countenances. Sergius wasn't, in Cicero's view, as eye-catching as his dad. He now resembled a helpless pink balloon adrift atop gibbous squiggles of its own reflection. Cicero could hardly convince himself a body extended below.

Sergius Gogan, sad fortyish orphan, had come to Cicero in a rental Prius, after flying up from Philadelphia, in a project of research on the topic of Sunnyside Gardens. Research to what ends? Sergius hadn't said. Fair enough, Cicero knew all those people of whom Sergius spoke. Yet why, pray, should it be Cicero's duty to navigate Sergius through matters of his own blood and kinship, legacies that were, despite all happenstance, *not Cicero's own*? Cicero Lookins didn't want this talk. Being Baginstock College's miraculous triple token, gay, black, and overweight, Cicero usually relied on his ominous aspect to keep the numbers down in his classes and office hours. If only he could take all his office hours in the ocean! But the prospect of immersion hadn't shaken Sergius Gogan.

"Yes," said Sergius now, snorting and gasping in the salt. "Yes. Tell me what you really think. Of course."

"Forget about Sunnyside Gardens," Cicero said. "There's no book in that subject or someone'd have written it already. If they had, nobody'd want to read it."

"I wasn't thinking of a book. I plan to write a cycle of songs. About the Gardens, about Rose and Miriam, and Tommy. About his career, too."

"Ah. Taking after your father." Cicero knew Sergius Gogan taught music to children, at the Pennsylvania Quaker boarding school, the same where he'd been sent when his parents went to Nicaragua, and stayed after they died there. Cicero supposed he'd distantly heard that Sergius's instrument was guitar, like Tommy Gogan's. That Sergius might also compose folk songs was unfortunate to consider.

"I'm trying."

"Concept albums run in the blood, huh?"

"I guess."

"Well, your father had nothing to do with the Gardens, so far as I knew. Anyway, your father didn't interest me." Cicero let the distinction creep in unannounced: that between *familiarity* and *interest*. It was time to become obnoxious.

"Why not?"

"Tommy was sincere in his commitments to you and your mother, and to nuclear disarmament and Salvador Allende. He also struck me as a cold fish. I didn't dig his music, what I heard."

"I'd been hoping you'd tell me about Rose and my mother," Sergius said, now exiling his request in an indefinite past, wilting at Cicero's obstinacy as had any number of young aspirants before him. "And Cousin Lenny."

"Ah." Listen, Cicero wanted to tell Sergius: Cicero Lookins has his own parents and grandparents and cousins, his own dead to get maudlin over, and not one is Jewish or Irish or anything-*ish*. They're black. You, receding-red-haired ghost, with accent blandly neutral, not even tinged with New Yorkese, you are free to melt into the Caucasian Nothing, so why don't you? Cicero's path of grace in life had been to distinguish the saddles he could buck off from the hide beneath and the brands and scars thereupon, those emblems he'd be forced to bear forever. Sunnyside and the whole of Queens, Rose and Miriam Zimmer, disappointed Reds, Lenny Angrush and his various madnesses—enough. These were saddles. Cicero had put them aside. At fifty-six he deserved to.

Why should Cicero Lookins choose to be Sergius Gogan's magical Negro, his Bagger Vance, his Obama to entice him through a "teachable moment"? Well, Cicero was everyone's, he supposed. A career magical Negro. That was his franchise here at Baginstock College, as it had been at Princeton to begin with. A compass for the soul journeys of the straight white folks. Cicero was an expert at pointing the compass's needle where he wanted, knew just how often to use the forbidden word to keep them scandalized and when merely to titillate them with *Negro* or *negritude* instead.

Once upon a time, Cicero Lookins had fled the world Sergius now asked after. Fled from Sergius's grandmother, Rose Zimmer. After high school he'd slipped Rose's clutches, escaped like her daughter, Miriam—Sergius's mom—did before him. Ran from New York City to Princeton, to academia. His scholastic excellence was an offering to gratify Rose: She'd produced a marvel! A black brain! But it also got Cicero away from her, freed him to produce his own marvels to dismay and aggrieve her, perversions of sexuality and theory. One of his minor revenges: Rose's Marxism quit at Marx. When Cicero'd one time popped a little Deleuze and Guattari on her ass, she'd balked.

After grad school, Cicero ran west, to the University of Oregon, propelling himself far from Jews, far from Harlem and negritude, to a place where he could be sheerly non sequitur, an alien emissary on the frontier. The Weirdest Fish in any Small Pond. Then to Bloomington, Indiana, a better gig. Indiana was a little Ku-Kluxian for Cicero, though. He could smell old nooses rotting in the barn eaves. Soon Baginstock College rode to the rescue, offering a lighter teaching load in exchange for being the town of Cumbow's tame bear. Coastal Maine recalled what he liked best in Oregon, that stony libertarian spaciness, the submission of human life to the landscape. So Cicero ran to the town's edge, bought the most expensive house on Cumbow Cove he could persuade the Realtors to show him, to be a fuckyou blight on the neighboring trophy homes. And here, as often as possible, he escaped to the sea. Once, out with him on the waters, a colleague mentioned that in a certain Native American language the word for ocean translated as *the medicine*. Cicero had never wished to look into the authenticity of this fact, he liked it too much.

Now here, immersed in his medicine, off the coast of everything, Rose Zimmer's grandson had come to bother him.

"I hate her," blurted Cicero's smoldering charcoal of a head.

"Who?"

"Rose."

"She's dead." Sergius spoke as if he thought Cicero had led them this distance to sea for fear Rose would overhear them on the shore, and he wanted to reassure Cicero this was impossible.

"Hated, then."

"You were with her to the end."

With her? The word, however seemingly neutral, suggested a certain agency. Cicero'd known people who'd been *with* Rose Zimmer, notably his own father, a choice Cicero might never forgive. Cicero himself was under Rose and endured Rose. With Rose in the sense that the earth was with its weather.

And that was when Cicero heard himself begin to rant.

"It isn't just me, Sergius. All Sunnyside hated Rose. No one could confront her in the smallest regard except your mother. But your mother's confrontations died in Rose's silences, they died before the receiver was back in its cradle. Meeting her as a defenseless child, my tongue was bitten to pieces before I understood it was for speaking. I had to get away to learn to open my mouth, yet if she was in front of me now I'd probably fail to speak truth to power. For don't kid yourself, Rose was *all* about power. The power of resentment, of guilt, of unwritten injunctions against everything, against life itself. Rose was into death, Sergius! That's what she dug about Lincoln, though she'd never admit it. He emancipated our black asses and died! Rose championed freedom only with a side order of death. In Rose's heart she was a tundra wolf, a Darwin creature, surviving on treachery and scraps. Every room contained enemies, every home was half spies, or more than half. If you mentioned a name she'd never heard, she'd rattle out like a Gatling gun: '*Who?*' Meaning, if they were valuable to know, why weren't they *already* part of her operation? If they weren't, why trust them? Why even mention them? She wanted to free the world, but she enslaved any motherfucker she got in her clutches. Now go back to Philly and write yourself a song cycle about *that*."

The trouble with his rant was that time, like a grape blistered by the sun, seemed to Cicero to peel away its organizing skin during the interval of his delivery. The *now*, so oppressively reliable, dissolved. Cicero had become too much the master of this art in the classroom, of unspooling his anger to filibuster any other voice, letting extemporaneous phrases give birth to one another in a kind of generative storm, while his mind voyaged elsewhere.

In this case, what was left of the grape when the skin peeled away was a heartbeat of somatic memory, a moment that had never stopped reenacting itself in some part of Cicero's body: a titanically willful woman of forty-something years clutching the hand of a round-faced, baffled African American child, perhaps just six or seven years old that first of the seeming hundred times she dragged him along on her rounds. Rose Zimmer, his father's lover. She powered with him along the sidewalks of Sunnyside—Greenpoint Avenue, Queens Boulevard, Skillman Avenue—as she made her way spying, gossiping, interrogating, whispering asides, projecting the grid of invisible importances in her brain over the network of streets, onto the apparently innocuous array of semipopulated park benches and barbershops, onto human beings with shopping carts moving so slowly along the pavement that they may as well have been frozen. The boy coming to consciousness from within this disordered moral map, which had overwritten any other. His being granted access to Rose's confidences, her ready faith that he could be the repository for them: first inkling of his own complexity. The fact that she reveled in the dismay and indignation generated by his presence at her side, the outlandish enlistment of the black boy as the righteous Commie-Jew divorcée's right hand: first inkling of his own brazenness. The two of them set Sunnyside aflame, and then visited her favorite soda fountain—whose shopmen and regulars loathed Rose as violently as anywhere else—and soothed themselves with chocolate malteds. Then, having loaded up on comic books and Pall Malls, she delivered him home.

This was how deeply Rose had gotten into Cicero: Within the imposed and immutable corridors of his mind lay an oasis, a microcosmic realm where his present self could converse with her, make fresh access to the single most penetrating intelligence he'd ever known—not that he could persuade her to lay aside the warpages and loathings decorating that intelligence like thorns. These—warpages and loathings—were how he knew it was her. Cicero had no interest in hoodoo. Yet he could reanimate the dead, or one of them, anyhow. It tended to happen at the soda fountain, while seated on twin stools, with malteds before them.

Cicero glanced at the comic books on the counter, one already soaked at one corner where it had rested in a pool of melted ice cream dripping from his straw. *Detective Comics. Tales to Astonish.* He'd lost interest in such things a year or two later and couldn't reconstruct his affection for the garish things now, those amateurish prototypes for the monolithically hellish culture of the new century.

"Rose."

She raised an eyebrow at his tone.

"It's not the child speaking to you now, but the man."

"Some man."

"Every form of human life on the earth, Rose. Those are your words. The feeble and the fags."

"For this I fought."

"That's right. For this you fought."

"Why must I live so long as to regret things I shouldn't even be forced to contemplate coming into being?"

Cicero ignored Rose's lament, too typical to mean other than that he should get to his point. "Your grandson has appeared, darling. Sergius Gogan."

"Surely a homosexual too by this time. He showed every indication."

"Apparently not. Or if so, not apparently so. He's come to ask me to tell him what I know about *you*."

If she'd arched an eyebrow before, now Rose's entirety cocked in scorn, from the upsweep of her short hair, never dyed, still black but for the white at her temples and a streak from her forehead's center, and the sardonic, one-sided smile revealing front teeth's gap, to the attitude of her hand braced on the pantsuit of the one leg that reached to the floor, in her stance of only perching, not sitting, on the soda-shop stool. Rose might avow Marx or Lincoln, but the way her body occupied space was one thousand percent Fiorello La Guardia, sole mayor ever to meet her approval, pure pugilistic screw-you Noo Yawk.

"I've got nothing to hide."

"I never suggested you did," said Cicero. "But it's not incumbent on me to have my brain picked by the ass-end leavings of your posterity."

You could tell she relished at least this part of what her protégé had become.

"You're a teacher, reputedly. So teach him."

"You playing Jiminy Fucking Cricket with me now?"

Rose ignored him. "Here's what I suggest. You say what you know and I don't."

"Meaning what?"

She shrugged. What this signified, beyond Cicero letting his brain be picked, she wouldn't elaborate. If he didn't know, she'd wash her hands of the matter.

"Now finish your malted, I need a smoke."

Rose's words flung him back into his body in the sea.

Well. He'd finished talking. Somewhere during his time-travel reverie, Cicero had ended the nostril-sputtering saltwater monologue. Let Sergius negotiate it. That she whom he professed to despise was his goddamn involuntary spirit animal Cicero wouldn't let on.

"That's the kind of stuff I'm looking for," Sergius said. "The Communist stuff especially, Rose's life in the party. I think it would be terrific, actually, to write some songs about that."

"Oh, songs were written on the subject, Sergius. Your father wrote a few." Cicero began some backstrokes again, his horny feet pointed to the shore. Could he lure Sergius farther out, to where they'd lose sight of land? Could he perhaps abandon the fool there? Cicero beat with fat choppy strokes another distance toward the barrier islands. His house and the others of the cove, their porticoes and sliding glass doors, their decks bearing gas-cartridge grills and thousand-dollar telescopes, were barely visible now. But Sergius, the poor sonovabitch whom Cicero now recalled had been named for Norman Mailer's character from "The Time of Her Time"—did Sergius even know this self-trivia?—Sergius, despite his concave chest and scrawny arms, his scrawny ass, kept pace. His beseeching made him a swimmer Cicero couldn't lose. Sergius had that much of Rose's tenacity in him, perhaps, despite his Irish coloration and Quaker politesse. And so Rose was out here with the two of them. She'd gotten into Cicero's medicine, like a moth, musty creature of the night, plopping into a glass of good water in broad daylight.

"Your mother's friend Stella Kim once told me you had no memories of Tommy and Miriam," Cicero said to him.

"I know, it seems impossible. I was eight when they died. But they'd been away."

"And you can't remember Lenny Angrush."

"No. Just stories."

"Well, your uncle Lenny was the species of motherfucker who'd gratuitously snuff out the chess career of a thirteen-year-old black kid, a kid with very little else in his life to cling to at the time." Cicero was aware he'd concocted this grievance. A reverse sour-grapes maneuver: to inflate the value of that which had been taken from you, merely because it had been taken.

Sergius blinked. "I—I heard he was killed by the mob."

"Sure. Only this wasn't the Martin Scorsese mob you're thinking of. Lenny wasn't involved with the French Connection. He had to find a mob on his own level to get killed by—boneheads from Queens. Stella mentioned this?"

"No."

"You don't know jack about any of the Angrushes."

"You can tell me."

"If I felt like it."

Sergius opened his mouth but said nothing.

"Be free of them," Cicero commanded him. He was out of breath now. But Sergius only stared, helpless to accept this command, his shadow-body wavering beneath his strawberry-hued, bewildered head: a forked radish in aspic, a jellyfish. Maybe Cicero should have attacked Sergius, wrestled his shorts off, attempted to molest the forty-something child who'd entrusted himself to him. The Angrushes had once made a black boy their pet—Rose, and Miriam too. So, for revenge, make Sergius his pet now. Thinking it, Cicero understood that by drawing Sergius out here he'd evaded nothing at all. They were not disembodied heads, no, not free to drift away. Rather, they were heads anchored in a medium. Two American heads barely surfaced from a memory sea, seeking not to be drowned in it, limbs crawling, clawing for life. The sun above for a hammer, beating at fleshed skulls as they stared and blinked in the salt glare. No escape.

4   Accidental Dignity

When he was thirteen years old Cicero Lookins was told, for the first and only time, that Rose Zimmer had once shoved her daughter's head into an oven. Miriam Gogan told him one cool November afternoon, a day unforgettable in any number of arresting specifics.

It began with chess. Cicero had lately been savaging all comers at I.S. 125's chess club, so Miriam, on Rose's counsel, had proposed to bring him to call on Cousin Lenny at the chess store on MacDougal, there to play and have measured whether he might be a prodigy, a wunderkind. Afterward, Miriam promised, she'd shepherd Cicero to a loft on Grand Street, to have his astrological chart professionally drawn for him. So this would be a day of futures foretold.

Though thanks to Rose and Cicero's father's improbably durable affair she might be considered Cicero's de facto older sister, Miriam had artfully ignored Cicero until sweeping him up this day. She'd come and seized him from Rose's apartment, from Rose's grip, and with very little ceremony in the exchange. As though it were graduation day. Miriam in her flyaway hair and long houndstooth coat, hypnotic pattern of the black-and-white squares like some devilishly blurred chessboard, but one you couldn't play on, couldn't see in its entirety at once, because it wrapped around her—Cicero should have known at that moment that Miriam was here to foster revolutions in him, to demonstrate that the chessboard, like the world, wasn't flat but round.

Cicero had been to that point *Rose's Negro boy*. So, Cicero supposed, Miriam planned now to put some check on that dynamic, to insert in Cicero's mind a little healthy skepticism as to Rose's high ideals. Cicero's obedient silences would have suggested the need for such intervention. Outwardly, he was obedient, in the extreme. He'd have appeared to Miriam to be conforming absolutely to Rose's Abraham Lincoln fantasies of the good and proper result of her patient patronage, to her obsession with book-learning the Negro policeman's child by feeding him the novels of Howard Fast, the poetry of Carl Sandburg, and by making him sit, as Miriam herself had had to sit, through repeated listenings to Beethoven's *Eroica*, overlaid with Rose's paeans to its greatness in alternation with her teeth-clenched weeping.

In point of fact, Cicero at thirteen was already a monster of skepticism.

Yet he believed in chess, a secret garden of rational absolutes. On the squares, things swooped or swerved according to their hard-and-fast scripts, bishops and rooks thus, pawns durably plodding, black and white unmistakable foes. Knights, like Cicero himself, had secrets. They played at brazen invisibility, at walking through walls. Apparently looking in one direction, knights killed you in a side glance from another. If you employed them just so, all other pieces seemed earth-mired, sluggish as pawns. To that day, Cicero had been tempted to believe that if you got good enough at a first thing you might never need a second.

Cicero believed in chess, and so though Miriam interested him as a fellow endurer of Rose, one with an advantage of years, when Miriam escorted Cicero into the tiny chess store he forgot about both women. The store, air mucked with pipe smoke, smeared glass cabinets exhibiting exotic sets, and, in the ice-cold mezzanine, the gray obsessive figures, barely human, their coats not even shed, hunched over gnarled endgames. The pale twitchy hands that darted forth from sleeves to clop the wooden pieces forcefully to new squares, and flicked out to punch the dull brass button on the time clocks, then to retract—those hands might have had a life of their own, no relation to the rolling eyes and bunching brows and pursing lips above. You might have no idea, looking only at the faces, which of them was connected to the hands that had made the newest moves. This might be Cicero's first glimpse, really, of an authentically *academic* setting, the destination toward which his life was pitched: a miniaturized world craven with self-regard, unimpressive except to those who read the palace codes, and sublimely oblivious to the outside. And Cicero was here not only to meet, at last, Cousin Lenny, who'd played Fischer once; he was here to play him.

Lenin Angrush bustled upstairs a moment after. "A glass of tea!" he said before greeting Miriam, slapping his palm in mock outrage on the small counter, where the proprietor only lifted his eyebrows slightly. Then the bearded fist of Cousin Lenny's face unclenched, his smile revealing a trace relation to Rose in the gap of his teeth. Behind them, his molars were a disaster area of black and gold. "Bubbelah!" He clutched Miriam in her houndstooth coat, her purse trapped in his embrace, his limbs encasing her like sausage. Then released her to the vigilance of his gaze, which mingled scorn, worship, and guilt. The black hair everywhere on his head was clipped to a weirdly identical length, his Fuller Brushes of eyebrow, his lip-smothering beard, the hair on top the same as that shooting from around his ears, as though he'd been mowed. His spinal curvature tended toward the rabbinical, his eyes toward the heretic. That beneath his stinking black coat he wore some insignias of the hippie—a worn-thin Woodstock T-shirt, bird perched on guitar's neck, a frayed woven sash of rainbow wool for a belt on his stained suit-bottom pants—did nothing to counter the impression of a figure heaved painfully and against steep odds into the present, out of the rank and degraded past.

Miriam's own outfit, once her coat was at last loosened, struck Cicero as a kind of costume, rather than ingenuous clothing: a yellow silk-screened Groucho Marx T-shirt, worn braless beneath her white denim jacket, peace-sign earrings, and tiny, purple-tinted John Lennon shades. Cicero sometimes wondered: Were hippies *serious*?

Anyway, Cousin Lenny clocked her nipples like a hypnotist's pocket watch, a distraction that ought to provide Cicero with an advantage in the coming chess match. Really, though, cousin? A horny, tragic uncle, that's what Cicero thought now, as he stood with his fists dug into the pockets of his Tom Seaver #41 Mets warm-up jacket, staring. Rose had implied Lenny was Miriam's contemporary; he seemed twenty years older, at least. Lenny still hadn't glanced at Cicero, so far as Cicero could tell. When he did, Cicero felt caught, lulled into making a full, slack-brained examination, as though Lenin Angrush was a movie projected on a screen, not a person who could look back.

"So why did nobody mention the black Fischer was a man-mountain?"

Cicero was at thirteen already accustomed to being presented, by Rose, to those who'd shamelessly exclaim over him. There were only so many things they could exclaim. Ready for *man-mountain*, for *black*, for *Fischer*, he picked out only what interested him. "You really had a match with Fischer?"

"One game, a draw." Lenny's boiling eyes consulted Miriam's. "You told him?"

"I'm sure you can imagine that it was Rose who mentioned Fischer to him," said Miriam. "I'll let you explain it."

"Under a tented canopy, Fischer against twenty at once. Opponents seated, he stalking among us, glancing at the boards, selecting his moves carelessly. Like a man brushing ants from a picnic table, that's how the captured pieces flew. He savaged us. I think he forgot a pawn on my board, maybe something got stuck in his eye, who knows, it was a windy day. I was the last alive, my position tenable. Yet when he turned full attention to me I deposited a small portion of diarrhea into my pants. I offered a draw and he took it. Who knows, maybe in his contract it said he shouldn't have humiliated every last man but rather leave a figure of identification for the common rabble to root for. Maybe he wanted to be done with it, maybe wanted a sandwich. In any event, I in my shitted Fruit of the Looms recorded a drawn match against Bobby Fischer. Coney Island, May 1964."

The roomful of players deferred to Lenny, whether out of respect or wearied aggravation you couldn't say. A table was cleared by the window overlooking MacDougal, the glass of tea placed in Lenny's hands. "Play white," he commanded, seating himself at the black pieces.

"He doesn't need to be indulged," said Miriam.

"I'm not indulging, believe me. I want to see his attacking game. If he doesn't have one, he's nowhere. I can see by his outfit he's a front-runner, he likes winners. So let him show me he knows how to win."

"If you want to understand my cousin Lenny," Miriam explained, "begin with the fact that he's the one human occupant of Queens who couldn't allow himself to enjoy the Miracle Mets."

"Hah! The Mets are the opiate of the masses. Make her tell you, kid, how your team represents the abortion of Socialist baseball in America."

"Lenny knew Bill Shea," Miriam explained, obscurely. "Shea like the stadium. The guy who brought the Mets. Lenny had another idea."

"Never speak the running dog's name aloud. Have her tell you, when I'm out of hearing distance. The death of the Sunnyside Proletarians. Your team's a crime scene, kid. No hard feelings."

"Play chess," said Miriam. "Unless you're afraid of him."

"He's playing white, Mim. I await the wunderkind's debut."

Miriam stole one of the bentwood chairs from another table and placed herself beside Cicero, as if she'd be playing for his side. Cicero pushed king's pawn. He needed to pee, said nothing. Lenny, grunting, unhooked a forefinger from his ear long enough to shove a pawn to mirror Cicero's. Then out flopped knights. Cicero centered himself, within this vale of discomfort and disgust, on the possible actions of the pieces, while the large second-story window steamed with pipe-smoke exhalations, burps, and farts. Miriam, not watching the board, waved at the street below, apparently someone she knew, a musician kicking along with a giant case containing either an upright bass or a million dollars' worth of hashish. Outside, the world had colors, and likely sounds other than the lung-rattle of opponents not yet informed of their deaths at some earlier date, possibly in the late 1950s. The interior of the chess shop, apart from Cousin Lenny's improbable sash, was in black and white. Outside, 1970 was more than a possibility, it was a likelihood just weeks off. In here, rumors of *Sputnik* might still have been rash. The present was a gelled substance, like hair pomade, bottled behind this glass. Cicero couldn't navigate it with his knights. In fact, Cousin Lenny now shocked him by trapping one and removing it from the board.

"You're going to lose this game. You like coins, kid?"

"I never thought about them."

"You should discover coins. Numismatics presents a world of fascination and value. Because this, frankly, is going nowhere for you."

"Play the game, Lenny," said Miriam.

"I can play and talk, especially your protégé here. He's got no attack to speak of."

"You know after six moves?"

"You're not even watching. We've played sixteen. I've seen enough. You're a civilian, so you want to see bloodshed. If you demand that I checkmate him, I'll do it for you, but the kid's smart enough to resign already."

Cicero glanced at Miriam, then back at the board. If he didn't study Lenny's decrepitude, only listened to them flicking insults, he could believe they were cousins. Lenny paid as little attention as Miriam. Cicero was left alone to study the position of the pieces, unless you counted the steady gaze, amused and skeptical, of Groucho Marx from Miriam's T-shirt. Cicero thought he still had a prayer. He'd noticed a seam of vulnerability for his surviving knight to explore. But, advancing the knight in this cause, he felt an instantaneous knowledge, spreading like a blush of shame across his whole front, that Lenny had been waiting for him to overreach this last and fatal time. No sooner had the piece landed than Lenny's hand flicked out to push the bishop's pawn a square forward, inflicting on Cicero's ranks three simultaneous disasters. They both knew it. The question was who'd inform Miriam.

"Likely you have a terrific defensive game," said Cousin Lenny. His red, hoary fingertips and weird nubby thumbs scrabbled at remote outposts in his beard, including the beard on top of his head and the beard growing above his eyes and from within his ears, as if something scurried underneath and the fingers chased it. "Flop the pieces from side to side, letting your adversary defeat himself. Playing impatient thirteen-year-olds, this is a consummate strategy. You prefer black, don't you? I spotted this when I first laid eyes on you."

Incredibly, Cousin Lenny seemed to include no innuendo or shame in this remark, but meant it as a cold statement of fact. It was one. Cicero nodded.

"Of course you do. As it happens, this is how I stayed in against

Fischer: circled the wagons, bored him to death. You think you've been playing chess, but you've been playing your opponents, not the pieces. Miriam, the child is a prodigious listener, a watcher of his fellow human animals. I'd be terrified of what information he's gathered on you to this point, as I'm already terrified of him myself. If we can ascertain his sympathies he may prove highly useful to the cause of the workers' revolution. But he'll go nowhere in chess. Now, Mim, tell me, when are you leaving your goyish singer so that we can commence the life for which we were intended? He must be losing his looks by now, and in this I have the advantage, having had no looks to begin with."

"The day you quit jerking off, Lenny, is the day I leave him. You know I've always promised this. But just remember, I can see into your bedroom."

Lenny put his hands over the Woodstock bird, and his own heart. Then he cupped the fingers of his right hand, placed them lower down, and shook them as if they held a pair of dice. "You who've robbed me of my heart's desire since the day you sprouted a bosom, you'll take even this from me?"

"Discipline, Lenny."

He shrugged, arched his Fuller Brushes, beckoned heaven with an upraised palm, evoking the full worldliness of a Yiddish stage ham's rendition of Hamlet or Oedipus. "Then I'll have to jerk in the foyer, where you can't see."

Miriam flipped him the bird. "We've got a date with an astrologer, Lenny. I'll see you another time."

"Wait." With the same hand that had phantom-jerked, he now, horrifyingly, dug in his pants pocket. "Here." He pressed something cool into Cicero's hand. A zinc U.S. penny. Rose's almighty Lincoln, rendered in tinfoil. Cousin Lenny lowered his voice. "Study that coin. If you persist you'll find in it the whole secret law of history. The death of the United States of America rests there in your hand, kid. You can listen to it whisper if you hold your head close."

"I need to use the restroom," said Cicero.

Miriam took Cicero downstairs to the toilet, and then out of the chess shop, that library of souls, that grave of time. Onto the sidewalks of Greenwich Village, where 1969 was permitted to reassert itself, resume its animation and flow. Though as much a confabulation, surely, as that thickened portion of time trapped behind the chess mezzanine's window, the present had the advantage of being still open to negotiation. Cicero had heard that all sorts of people lived in Greenwich Village. The thirteen-year-old secret faggot was ready to meet them.

"I hope you weren't scandalized by that jackass."

Cicero said nothing. Did scandalized include how, in the chess shop's tragic minuscule restroom, his dick was surprisingly hard before he drained it? Crummy, scummy Cousin Lenny—a subject for his fixations? Maybe just the matter-of-fact mimicry Lenny had performed with his hand. Maybe the way he'd wrenched Cicero from his hiding place of chess, reinstalling him in the perplexity of the adult world. That of filthy Lenny and gorgeous Miriam and their unstable relation, and that of Miriam's expectations for Cicero, this day in her Manhattan precincts, this day of something unseen coming. *Nowhere in chess*, that was the phrase Lenin Angrush used, in an action with a result as sudden as pressing a James Bond ejection-seat button. Cicero knew plenty of nowhere, on Queens Boulevard, on Skillman or Jackson or Greenpoint Avenue, in Rose's company or surrounded by streaming schoolchildren, or alone, which added up to the same thing. Nowhere, nothing, nohow: Cicero was still at home only in himself. There, barely. To Lenny's verdict, Cicero now added a vow: Black pieces or white, he'd never touch chessmen again. He fingered the zinc penny, deep in his pocket. American money was a lie. The Mets, a crime scene. Lenny thrilled Cicero by his allusions to secret knowledge, history as a drama of lies. Perhaps it was this that had bestowed Cicero's hard-on.

———

Miriam's missionary zeal was hardly damaged: her fortune-teller would uncork Cicero's destiny. He'd been born on January 20, 1956, at 1:22 in the morning, a fact inscribed on his birth certificate, the double-folded black photostat that Miriam had instructed Cicero to bring along and which that morning he'd palmed into his pants pocket, after slipping it from his mother's drawer of baby keepsakes, rather than try to explain to Diane Lookins her son's multiple errands this day. As they'd gone up the dusty loft-building stairwell to be welcomed inside by Sylvia de Grace, Miriam's heavily perfumed, wizened, and silk-scarfed French (or, possibly, "French") astrologer, both he and Miriam believed Cicero to be an Aquarius. Now came the day's second shock of refusal: When Sylvia de Grace presented Cicero's chart accurately drawn, he was revealed as nothing more than a flat-out Capricorn.

"Still, isn't he on the cusp?" Miriam demanded of Sylvia de Grace, reluctant to surrender the Aquarian delusion on Cicero's behalf. Here in the hot, radiator-clanking loft, Miriam had removed her coat, revealing her hippie garb in full. That costume of hers, as much as Sylvia de Grace's, seemed to argue for a belief in talismans, hoodoo, sacred monsters. *Being on the cusp* might be even more special, Miriam quickly explained, seeing as how it would combine aspects of two adjoining signs—Cicero's would be a stealth sign, then, a spy in the nation of destiny.

But the astrologer only rattled her own elaborate jade earrings and stole Miriam's hopes. Cusps, she explained, were a phenomenon popular with amateurs; for serious astrologers like herself they didn't exist. Worse: Not only was Cicero a dull earth sign rather than one of those transcendent slippery Aquarians, whose age the planet was now entering, but all his subsidiary details were, so far as Cicero could follow them, disheartening: planetary rulerships in disarray, each in houses that signified, according to the increasingly severe Madame de Grace, only to that planet's detriment. "Nothing dignified anywhere?" pleaded Miriam on Cicero's behalf. The word *dignified* apparently held special value here. But Sylvia shook her head. "Not well dignified, no. His moon's in Cancer, but in the twelfth house. We call that *accidental dignity.*"

"Accidental dignity?" repeated Miriam anxiously.

"Placement within this house circumscribes the moon's opportunities to express its benevolence."

"I don't like the sound of that."

To Miriam these facts were important, perhaps even dire; to Cicero not particularly so. Cicero knew his obvious features defined him absolutely in others' eyes. Further definitions—limitations on the moon's benevolence, say—were fictions imposed from without. Definitions unmistakably in error but with which he saw no strategic reason (as yet) to differ. Cicero was still in the information-gathering phase of his life on this planet. Thus everything Miriam revealed to him was good information. The chess shop, Lenny's cipher allusions and black and gold molars, had been good information, even at the price of Cicero's chess vanity. This fake-Frenchwoman's salon, squir- reled into the brick warehouse full of painters' lofts, was full of good information, a cavern of exotica, patchouli pretenses of sophisticated adulthood he could use to fill in the picture he would eventually be fitting himself into. No hurry, though.

Anyway, and more simply, Cicero had never been able to take any mystical shit like astrology seriously for a second. This was true for Cicero even before Rose's influence had reached him. Rose's materi- alist worldview, against which he supposed Miriam's gestures in the faintly pagan direction of astrology were directed as protest. Cicero felt he'd been *born under a bad sign* having nothing to do with any rams or fish or bearers of water. He didn't need another layer to his identity.

Astrology fell into the class of a *fake lie*, one many of its own expo- nents actively disbelieved—not only Miriam, obviously, but most likely Sylvia de Grace herself—and not worth the efforts of the debunking engine Cicero had been born with in place of a brain. Cicero's capaci- ties were reserved for the lies that mattered. Ideology, though that word was as yet unknown to him: the veil of sustaining fiction that drove the world, what people *needed* to believe. This, Cicero wished to unmask and unmake, to decry and destroy. Only, not yet.

Lies of that kind were strewn everywhere. Cicero had strewn a few himself, like adopting the Mets warm-up jacket. For, if a grown-up hippie in 1969 had to care what their sign was, a minimally functional verging-on-teenage male at Sunnyside Intermediate, whether black or white, had to choose from two other constellations of gods. Quick: Who was your favorite Met? And who your favorite Apollo astronaut? Cicero had his answers ready, even if they were for the wrong rea- sons. Tom Seaver had beautiful thighs and an oversize ass, for a white man. In Cicero's study, starting pitchers often had the proportions he relished. The fetishy analysis of a pitcher's windup and delivery justified many hours of active lascivious fantasy on Cicero's part, hidden in the plain sight of the consideration of his father's *Herald Tribune* sports pages, or the exchange of baseball cards with his classmates, or the viewing of Tom Terrific's starts on Rose's prize color television. Seaver was celebrated for the length of his stride, the dip of his knee to the dirt at his delivery's utmost point, the mound-smudged clue left behind on his uniform. Cicero liked to imagine himself in place of the mound when the pitcher's thighs bowed earthward.

Though their costumes were not nearly so flattering, Cicero's taste in astronauts—Buzz Aldrin—oriented along similar lines.

"Screw it, let's go get your fortune told the *right* way," said Miriam, once they'd delivered themselves from the patchouli fog of disappointment and stood in the hustle of the midday Chinatown sidewalk. "Anyway, I'm starving—you like dim sum?"

"Sure," Cicero lied. Whatever global doubts the secretive boy entertained, Cicero felt seduced into awe and gratitude at Miriam Gogan's attentions. "What's the right way?"

"By means of *chicken*. C'mon. But first we'll eat."

Miriam yanked Cicero by the hand into Chinatown, splendidly impatient to move him like a pawn across the mental chessboard of her city. The operation wasn't so different from Rose's, dragging her chubby black ward through her block-watcher's rounds in Sunnyside. Mother and daughter each made a version of Carroll's Red Queen, running to stay in place. Each marked urban spaces like a pinball bouncing under glass, trying to light every bumper before gravity drew them into the trap waiting below. Only Miriam's rounds were animated by exultation, the outer-borough kid's connoisseurship of a Greenwich Village culture that was her inheritance if she demanded it be. Rose, paranoia her precinct, stalked Sunnyside like it was a zoo's cage. Rose kept score. Burned grudges for fuel.

Cicero was already a connoisseur, too, of styles of female power.

Dim sum, at least as Miriam unveiled it to Cicero this afternoon, was merely Chinese soul food. Miriam passed over the trays full of the fussier-looking delicacies, pink pods like saltwater taffy, shrimp in glistening translucent wrappers, in favor of a grease-stained white bag loaded with what turned out to be shreds of pork barbecue, hidden in doughy white buns the size and tenderness and deliciousness of

Cicero's mother's own biscuits. Each bun also concealed a delicious squirt of barbecue sauce, secret incentive to gobble it entire; this was barbecue such as the Apollo astronauts might carry on their voyage. Together, reaching into the white bag again and again as if it might be bottomless, Miriam and Cicero threaded sidewalks narrowed by vendors' stands full of unrecognizable vegetables and cross-eyed fish in tanks, sidestepped the Tom Thumb women with carts. Miriam chewed and talked. Cicero chewed and listened. When they'd emptied the bag, gummed their back molars with dough and threads of pork, Miriam located a dusty Jewish deli hidden somehow in the midst of the exotica and purchased two Orange Crushes in beaded bottles so they could rinse it all down.

Somewhere in this feasting, the dam broke, the last of Cicero's reserve swept away. He fell in love. Cicero didn't find women sexy, but Miriam was the exception, not for her bodily self but for her appetite: She devoured the ripe fruit of the world. He fell in love with the efflorescence of Miriam's details. Cicero's sudden idol had a knack for making what he'd never heard of until that instant sound exactly like the life he craved for himself: *dignified planet, Che Guevara, McSorley's, falafel, Eldridge Cleaver, hashish, the Fugs, Ramblin' Jack, dim sum.*

The chicken was, in fact, a chicken. On Mott Street, in the confusion of the entrance to something called the Chinatown Museum—an indoor court of attractions as decrepit and uninviting as the worst Coney Island parlor, ominous even in daylight—a dirty white hen strutted and pecked in a decorated vitrine that had been wheeled from the shadows to the edge of the sidewalk. "This is Clara," said Miriam. "She's going to tell your fortune. Hell of a lot cheaper than Sylvia de Grace." Miriam purchased a token from Clara's mute keeper, a Tom Thumb man this time, and shoved it into the slot. A winsome jingle played and Clara the chicken began a spinning dance, then pecked at one of several tabs on the interior of the cage, releasing a few grains of corn to the floor of her captivity, and a card with Chinese symbols and English words into Miriam's waiting fingers. "Here you go," said Miriam. "You want me to read it to you?"

Did she think he couldn't read, after all? Cicero, so watchful and adept in the secret chambers of his self, so committed to the path of invisibility, could nonetheless be amazed at how unilaterally his disguise as a fat black boy really worked: *Really?* You think I'm not watching and judging and desiring, not scheming to realize my desires? In certain eyes, Cicero felt granted no more sway in the human scheme than a bulldog leashed to a lamppost or a passing cloud that briefly took an amusing shape. But no. He caught his breath. This wasn't that. What Miriam proposed was that she play oracle, take Sylvia de Grace's place in the thwarted plan to hear Cicero's destiny unveiled today.

"Yes," he said. "Read it to me."

She slipped it into her pocket. "I will, but not here. I've got another idea. You ever had a Dave's vanilla?"

The answer, this time, was actually *yes*. Rose had once taken him to the Canal Street egg cream mecca. Not everything in Manhattan was Miriam's invention. Yet Cicero strategically lied, shook his head, cocked his eyebrows, waiting for her to explain what he already knew. As with letting Miriam narrate the chicken's fortune-telling, Cicero chose to let her believe in his susceptibility to her wonders, his gullibility, even where he wasn't susceptible or gullible. The form Cicero's devotion still took, with Rose, with Miriam, with his own mother, was an *unwillingness to disillusion*.

This would change.

Miriam and Cicero perched together on stools at the counter of Dave's fountain, another timeless zone of men in dented fedoras slurping coffee under Depression-era signage, of glasses cleaned and dried with checkered cloths that were neither clean nor dry. They put their backs to the purring chaos of the intersection at Canal and Broadway and at her suggestion each sampled both a chocolate *and* a vanilla. The white-aproned counterman was only twentyish and had already seen it all in his day, didn't blink at fizzing up four egg creams for a black kid and a hippie chick, never even quit whistling. Beneath the apron the counterman's robin's-egg-blue shirt was rolled midway up his forearms, the sinews and muscles of which thrummed hypnotically as he stirred syrup from the bottoms of their glasses with a long spoon. Miriam held Clara the chicken's fortune-telling card up and then scowled for the sake of drama. "You ready? Hey, Cicero, you paying attention?"

"Sure."

"It's a biggie, I'm telling you."

"What?" Cicero recognized the sound of himself completely taking the bait, felt seven or eight years old and schoolyard-teased instead of the crafty double-digit sophisticate he'd become.

"You have been sent among men to foment revolution and blow manifold minds."

"It doesn't say that." He reached for the card, she lifted it away.

"Sure it does—in Chinese. Let me finish. Boy, this is one freaky chicken. *All roads lead nowhere, choose one with heart. Never look back, something might be gaining on you. She said, Who put all those things in your head*—hey, Cicero, you like the Beatles?"

"What's it really say?" Miriam's evasiveness had now sold him on the urgency of the chicken's censored wisdom.

"Who's your favorite Beatle?"

That was easy: *Paul.* "Ringo. What's the card say?"

Miriam frisbeed the chicken's fortune through Dave's wide opening to the street, onto Canal's sidewalk, underfoot the passersby. "Screw it, it wasn't that great. You know what Rose told me when I played her *Sgt. Pepper's*?"

"What?"

"*I won't listen until they stop screaming.* That's an exact quote."

"Huh."

"You don't think that's funny, that she's placed herself at the head of the anti-screaming brigade? Listen, what's it like with you and her?"

Cicero might or might not have understood the question. "It's okay."

"You can tell me anything, kid."

"Anything like what?"

"Give me a for instance. The single worst thing she ever did in your presence. Go ahead—I'd believe the worst lie you can think of." Miriam drained her vanilla, straw squawking at foam dregs.

Were Miriam's conversational swerves even swerves, or were they explosions? She danced in her own minefield, it seemed to Cicero. Anyway, the worst thing Rose Zimmer had done was done out of Cicero's sight: her possession, and serial repossession, of his father. Worst thing? That Rose existed for Cicero in the first place. Yet this affront was impossible to examine usefully, being the founding astonishment of Cicero's life, the dawning of his understanding that he was born into a world of liars, rather than being born the world's first.

What did Miriam know of the situation? The start of Rose and Douglas's affair, according to Cicero's calculations, matched to Miriam's start of putting Sunnyside behind her in favor of MacDougal Street. Even if Miriam had noticed the disaster, at what point would she have noticed an infant dragged in the disaster's wake? The Sunnyside Citizens' Patrol was founded in 1955; Cicero had been in utero when his father met Rose Zimmer.

"Cat got your tongue? Let me get you started." That's when Miriam mentioned her voyage into Rose's kitchen stove. Her description was accompanied with a bit of convulsive, perhaps involuntary reenactment, fingers seizing Cicero's shoulders to demonstrate Rose's force and suddenness. She nearly jostled herself and Cicero from their stools, arousing the curiosity of the soda jerk.

Cicero, then, in his bafflement at all that had transpired, might or might not have let his eyes again relish those sinewy forearms beneath the rolled sleeves. Something in Miriam's awareness registered this possibility, even as she recovered her poise, the demon impersonation of Rose eclipsed again in her expression. Perhaps it had occurred to her, too late, that nothing Cicero could supply would be any match for what Miriam had revealed: The game was over before it began. She changed the subject, though without declaring what the new subject was, exactly.

"I forgot, there's something else that Chinese chicken wanted me to tell you."

"What's that?"

"*Wear your love like heaven.*" Her eyes flickered to the man behind the counter, even as the sullenly handsome youth had become bored with them again, resumed running his grubby cloth along the silver swan's neck of a syrup faucet.

That's how simply, over what could be regarded as merely a piss-thin milk shake, time could be halted, a life hinged in the middle. Cicero's, specifically. Miriam had seen him for who he was. Unlike the older boys who jeered "homo" at Cicero and a dozen other younger boys in the Sunnyside Intermediate locker rooms, those whom Cicero had no need to fool because they didn't understand what the word meant nor bother to distinguish among those at whom they hurled it. Unlike, too, the haunted, despondent, hungry men, four or five of whom in the past year, passing on a sidewalk, had auditioned Cicero with speculating glances. From those, men he wouldn't care to know, Cicero had no reason to hide. Only glance defiantly back and gather a scrap of knowledge marked for the file on what he'd prefer not to become. Miriam was different. He'd hidden from her, as he hid from his parents, and from Rose, as he'd hidden from those few solicitous teachers who'd noticed his intelligence. Miriam had seen him anyway.

Then, just as wildly, she steered him in yet another direction. Later Cicero would figure she'd meant to spare his embarrassment at being spotted as what was still called, however sympathetically, an *invert*— despite that the soda jerk at Dave's *did* have glorious arms, well worth a lascivious glance between two who'd noticed. The effect, though, was to deepen rather than alleviate his bewilderment. Had the former moment even actually occurred, or was he inventing it? Or, weirdly, did Miriam somehow relate the two thunderbolts? The second of these came when she patted her stomach, stretching Groucho's face with her knuckles as she made circles beneath the T-shirt.

"You know why I craved two egg creams on top of all that dim sum, don't you?"

For an instant Cicero thought she taunted his weight. *Fat faggot.* Then, just as quickly, he landed on the obvious truth. As though she'd flashed on Cicero's thinking of himself in his mother's womb at the start of Rose and Douglas's affair. As though Miriam read his mind and wanted to draw a line through all of it, *I'm pregnant you're homosexual we're linked in thrilling disobedience to Rose who might put your head in an oven too if she knew the truth.* Though Miriam was married to the folksinger and there should be no reason for her pregnancy to seem illegitimate or sinister, Cicero was sure he'd been handed a dangerous secret.

Miriam's talent for worldly implication, the same suggestiveness that had caused college men to swoon over a high-school girl: always that she knew more than what she knew, and that what she knew was that everything was secretly and sexily connected. Her smile said to Cicero, *It's all true.* How could these secrets all be blurted out on the same day, at the corner of Canal and Broadway? Cicero, the sole resister to the outbreak of superstition in his Sunnyside Intermediate cohort, unmoved by the suggestion that if the Miracle Mets could win the World Series and human heroes walk on the moon *in the same year* there really must be something to this Dawning of the Age of Aquarius after all, substance to the rumor that nineteen-69 really was a sex position if you could get some older teen to confirm it! Cicero might have to abandon his resistance to signs and wonders after all.

———————

For, if you don't grant the power of signs, why an *oven*? An oven! Attempt your suicide and filicide with an electrical socket, a bottle of pills, a guillotine, anything else. How many times had Cicero heard Rose mutter or whisper *Treblinka* or *Auschwitz* as the two of them wandered from some encounter (often before Cicero felt they were safely out of hearing) with one or another survivor, one who'd exchanged some words with Rose in clotted, exasperated Yiddish. Ancient souls, even if some were only thirty or forty years old, who had been no more than a kid in the camp, maybe Cicero's age. The survivors walked on tilted sidewalks, barely able to negotiate a bodega aisle or park bench, their refugee life no more than a long postlude to defining trauma. Rose's multivalent tone of grievance somehow also encompassing not only rage against the Germans but admiration for their devilish expertise, and aggravation that she'd now be obliged to boycott their literature and chocolate (the Germans gave us *Goethe*, Cicero!), not only unrivaled depths of sympathy for the suffering of their victims but a dash of contempt for their simplicity, too, their incompetence at not getting out, as well as a trickle of envy for their specially justified postures of misery—Rose, who knew too much, was too complicit with the twentieth century to be merely its victim. Though she was that, too. The century had, in the words of Cicero's schoolyard contemporaries, *ripped her off*. The camp survivors, bearing on their shoulders as they slumped along Sunnyside's pavement among other things the stigma of Stalin's pact, needled Rose at her injured core.

Yet Cicero, seated on a stool at Dave's on a cool November day in nineteen-sexual-position, Cicero at the corner of Canal and Broadway at the dawning of Aquarius yet with not a single one of his planets dignified, Cicero with his head nearly exploding with the reverberations of what Rose Zimmer's daughter has instilled in him in one afternoon—if Miriam was pregnant with the folksinger's baby, soon to be named Sergius, then Cicero's head was fertilized too, pregnant with implications of what leaving Rose and Sunnyside behind could be like for him—Cicero there on that stool was still Cicero silenced. A chubby and *excuse me* BLACK hole of implications unbirthed, reverberations stilled within him. Born a machine for debunking bullshit, he was also a machine for producing silence. Today, the leeriness that Rose, for all her efforts, had only reinforced in Cicero had been somewhat turned inside out—inverted! yes!—by Miriam's drunken, feral embrace of the world. And by her seeing into *him*. If Cicero wasn't invisible, he'd have to consider his next option. Yet today, at last, Cicero did or said nothing that would have quieted the chorus recommending he examine career possibilities as a linebacker or tackle. The habit was too strong.

Forty-three years later, Cicero's dreadlocks were for fucking with minds, his remote-control mental emanations made into fuzzy tentacles. Think of them as chiaroscuro contrails, making permanently visible his head's explosion from all the crap it had absorbed up to a certain point. More literally, the dreadlocks announced the following: Cicero had spent more time than you can bear to imagine *not* cleaning something, not obeying rules every mother teaches every child, to drag! a! comb! through! that! mess! Look ye upon my works and despair. Think of the time it took, how many years Cicero had tolerated being a transparent work in progress. For he'd amassed his head in plain view, just walking down the street weeping hair. Yes, weeping: Cicero felt himself to be some kind of ambulatory grievance. He could have reversed course a hundred times, lopped them off to widespread relief any day he chose. But rather had stuck it out. Already so physically problematic, Cicero had opted to sprout antlers, too. Those obtrusive malformations were meant for getting up in your grille, for taking up airspace. If you'd already suspected you did not want to sit in a movie theater near this black man, here's your justification. The dreadlocks were his brain voice made visible, a silent bellow. Yet with awesome deniability—for they were also merely a hairstyle. How could you be so paranoid as to take offense at a hairstyle?

Whatever it had cost Cicero to stay hidden for so long was matched by the expenditure of effort to throw his silence off. Cicero recognized he was an angry person. He'd become, in any event, a person it was impossible to embarrass. Instead he embarrassed others. That put him nearer to Rose than to Miriam. Miriam was a consoler and inspirer. She embraced social ritual even in its capricious fictions—*all roads lead nowhere, choose one with heart!* Cicero, like Rose in the end, preferred his listeners stunned and bleeding, all masks on the floor, or on fire.

For Cicero, censure of a blatant racist or homophobe was not only useless but fatally boring. The power residing in such accusations was best wielded at random, against the most avowedly sympathetic and correct colleague or student. Cicero routinely dropped a casual "But of course, you realize you're a racist" into friendly interactions. The less evidence on hand, the more destabilizing the result. This was exactly the sort of desire Sergius Gogan had aroused in him in the ocean. Cicero wanted to make himself the issue, on principle. *Do not wish for your nice Jewish family romance without me. It does not exist without me. Blame Rose for that if you want someone to blame. She is the one who put the chocolate in the peanut butter.*

Dignified planets? Cicero hadn't walked one yet.

Part II The Who, What, or Where Game

1 The Sunnyside Pros

"Is he expecting you?"

"Darling, he should always be expecting me. He should be so lucky as to have me appear. Tell Mr. Shea I have what he doesn't know he needs, but needs." Lenny Angrush transferred the thin cardboard box containing the tape reel, pinning it to his briefcase, in order to withdraw his handkerchief and mop his brow. The lawyer's offices were plush and modernistic, for Brooklyn at least, but the reception area wasn't air-conditioned. Possibly some sort of stratagem, to soften up petitioners at the great man's threshold. That being Bill Shea, the glamorous Brooklyn lawyer appointed to bring baseball to the Flushing Meadows swampland.

Lenny'd gotten his foot in the door months ago. Shea sought a grassroots constituency, something he could point a skeptical sports press at. He'd let Lenny organize a few community meetings, corral names on a petition, even thrown him a few bucks for an award in Shea's name, honoring Queens College's Most Promising Future Big Leaguer, which Lenny had landed on his pet pitcher, Carl Heuman. If in subsequent weeks this door hadn't widened, neither had it narrowed, Shea canny enough not to alienate a man of the people. A door needn't widen, so long as a foot remained wedged.

Nobody but Lenny knew how big Lenny's foot was.

Now he flaunted his sacred materials before Shea's secretary, expectantly. The tape reel's box would have fit easily within the brief-case, which held only a small ledger and a Lucite case bearing twin Silver Eagle dollars from the West Point Mint, but Lenny brandished it on the outside. Let the underling be curious. Let her ask.

"I'll tell him you're here."

"Tell him I've got better than an infielder, better even than a pitcher this time."

"Have a seat."

Lenny had a seat in the waiting area. Edged the reel's box into view. Doris? Flora? An attractive dish, with whom on several visits to this office he'd gotten nowhere remotely. He admired her as she rose and stepped quickly in her flats down the blind corridor, devised to keep the sanctum mysterious. Lenny regularly swore renewed efforts to get women into bed more often and in the ordinary way, to seduce a teller or secretary or waitress such as Flora, not require revolution-ary zeal to meet his own, not measure bed partners against the ideal of Miriam Zimmer. There was for instance another Doris or Flora who worked at Carmody's Rare Coin; he might be mixing up the names. He should exercise his manly function, keep his nether por-tions operative. For too long he'd marshaled himself for causes: party, proletarians, Mim. Cousin Rose, recognizing in Lenny a counter-part, counseled him to live as other people do—"Dwell in the world, already!" were her words—yet Lenny knew he ran like a racehorse, in blinders, yoked to purposes, locked in his course.

Coming in dead last, he'd still have run his race.

Today, like a racehorse, Lenny was poached in sweat. The dew of his hairy wrist soaked its trace onto the white cardboard of the tape reel's box. Containing his treasure, the new ball club's theme song, the Irish folksinger's dowry payment. Lenin Angrush had it figured this way: Having leveraged his heart's desire for nothing more than a literal song, the song must be worth something extraordinary. Like Jack's magic beans, the folk anthem's worth would be proved by its apparent worthlessness—*the meek shall inherit, the proletariat shall dictate, the mighty reserve clause shall fall! In Flushing Meadows a stadium of the workers shall rise!*

To each according to his need; Lenny's need was boundless, incommensurate. Therefore the magic beans of the folksinger's baseball song would sprout to produce a glorious mad beanstalk, the consecration of the Continental League's Flushing Meadows ball club, and the shoring of its fate to that of the factory workers of Queens, the indigenous genius and dignity of the borough's laborers and tradesmen. Just for instance, Lenny's first baseman, hiding as a second-generation barrel-humper at Rose's pickle factory. His pitcher, Heuman, lurking in college, studying Gorky and Tolstoy in the original Russian, and who'd eventually need the team to pay for contact lenses in order to better resemble an athlete. Lenny's catcher, the ice-wagon man's son. Men of pavement and cobblestone born. Urban Socialistic baseball would rise to demolish the monopoly teams. The Yankees had Mantle, his jingoistic home runs. The Pros had Carl Heuman's dialectical curveball.

Lenny saw headlines in his dreams, the World Series or All-Star Game, Heuman Whiffs Mantle Three Times! A strikeout's worth of strikeouts!

Fuck Mantle, and fuck the Yankees.

Screw Mim for not loving him, for never having him even once.

Screw being crucially milder than *fuck*, containing as it did some element of tenderness.

Lenny Angrush and Lawyer Shea would show them all. Shea and his partner, Branch Rickey, heroic integrator of baseball, even if Robinson had turned out to be a Republican, one of those Negro dupes who liked Ike. With Rickey on their side, and Senator Kefauver's spotlight on the owners' monopoly tactics, they'd forge a league and a team and a stadium in the homeland, in the bogs of Flushing. All of this, riding on what Lenny Angrush could deliver: a little five-ten pitcher from Queens College with a curveball Mantle couldn't possibly handle. The pitcher, and a team name incarnating the spirit of the working classes. Those—pitcher and moniker—and the song on the reel of tape.

And if Lenny Angrush didn't particularly care for the song himself, who was he to judge?

The Irish folksinger's tune would prove crucial. Miriam, falling in love with the singer, had betrayed Lenny. Yet what were Branch

Rickey's words? *Luck is the residue of design.* The team's theme song was the residue of Lenny's desire. As Marx would have it, *the surplus value.*

When Dora or Dolly or Flossy (he could think of a thousand names for her, why settle on one?) reemerged, Lenny leapt to his feet and seized her bare arm in his hand, spilling briefcase, but not reel, to the floor. "Where's Shea? Is he ready?"

"Let go, you're hurting my arm."

With satisfaction he detected Canarsie in her speech; duress had brought it out, a grain bleeding up through the veneer of elocution lessons. "This can't wait."

"It had better wait. Half an hour at least. He's with a client."

Watching his thumbprint blush to visibility on the flesh of Shea's secretary's arm, Lenny figured to mingle purposes. Fuck Yankees, screw Mim. Carpe diem, grab a little residue for himself for a change. Lenny modulated his tone of imperious harangue. When he chose, he could drop an octave, insinuate, ingratiate, beguile. He did now: "Forget Shea, then. I want you to be the one to listen."

"Listen?"

Had she no eyes? "You must have a reel-to-reel around here, for taking depositions, listening to detectives' wiretaps—"

She scowled. "What detectives? You're thinking of some other kind of lawyer, Mr. Angrush. Bill Shea's on the board of the Brooklyn Democratic Club. He was at lunch yesterday with Robert Moses—"

"One of our more distinguished racketeers, since the whole burg's his racket. Listen, conjure up the tape player, trust me. I'll bring you on the inside, before even Shea gets to hear it."

"Mr. Angrush, what is your ordinary work, when you're not coming up here and bothering us?"

"Bothering you is my ordinary work. I am what is conveniently dismissed as a *provocateur.* I say this with no shame."

Donna's or Floris's eyes widened, perhaps involuntarily. Then narrowed. Seething with suspicions. Good. Let his rhetoric be like the pink imprint of his thumb on the susceptibility of her gray matter. Doreen or Floreen knew Shea took Lenny's calls. He could afford to strike her as improbable—he *was* improbable! Of such bewilderments as he saw in the secretary's eyes now were Lenin Angrush's sporadic seductions made. In fact, she moved as though hypnotized, to a supply closet incompletely disguised behind wood paneling. There, with a little grunt, she retrieved from a shelf at eye level a reel-to-reel player, affording an instant's view of her stocking tops at mid-thigh, flesh bulging snowily above. Bless the new knee-high hemlines. Let only cynics say there was no progress in human affairs.

She set it on her desk, then stood with arms crossed while Lenny took command, unwinding the player's power cord and locating a socket, threading his precious spool past the heads, testing it with a *whrrrr*, then pausing again. He raised his hand. "Preeee-senting the new television and radio theme for the Continental League's linchpin New York franchise, the baseball organization of, by, and for the workingman, the Sunnyside Proletarians—"

"That's got to be the worst name yet," deadpanned the secretary.

"They'll be known as the Pros, of course. What do you mean, worst *yet*?"

"You can't be thinking we don't have nominations coming over the transom hourly, can you? By telegram and telephone, by smoke signals. There's the contingent that wants to call them the Gi-Odgers or Dodgants. I suppose yours isn't actually worse than that. I've heard Empire Staters, I've heard Long Islanders—"

Lenny brushed her off. "Amateur hour. You're speaking of crazies, out howling in the bushes—I've been in to see Shea a dozen times, your daybook will testify. We've had lunches. Shea told me himself, they'll have to field a team from scratch when the moment comes. I've got the players. What do they know of Queens, after all? I'm the bloodhound, I'm their nose on the ground. Flushing Proletarians could be fine, if Shea insists on tying it to the site. Sunnyside is sounding better to me for rhythmical purposes. *Listen*."

Whrrrr. Whrrrr.

"I'm listening, smart guy."

What a tiger was Darlene, now that Lenny'd freed her from her cage! He raised his hand. "Please. It's about to begin." Miriam's folksinger coughed, tuned a string. Then his flat piercing tenor droned through the waiting area, strummed chords giving faint color:

I met a man, a working chap
Heart broken by a team
He grabbed my arm, he held me there
And told me of his dream
New York may hold a million stories
But it's not for million-aaaaires
Our ball clubs fled for western shores
The Yankees win but no one cares—

"You can't do that," said Shea's secretary.

Whrrrr. Lenny turned the dial, stopping the tape. "Don't talk, you'll miss the chorus. Can't do what?"

"Mention Yankees in the lyric. It makes no sense. This is supposed to be a theme song. Don't include the rival brand."

"The team's configured as a thorn in the paw of the plutocrats," said Lenny. "There's not only disappointed Dodgers and Giants fans out there, believe me—there's an ocean of Yankee haters. It's the villain that quickens the blood."

"I'd advise something more upbeat."

"This is what is known as a demo reel. In the final treatment there'd be musical context, trumpets, glockenspiel, fifty-seven varieties of syrup to make the message palatable."

"You sound unpersuaded yourself."

"Shhhh. The chorus." *Whrrrrrr—*

Then from workers' ranks a ball club rose!
A starting nine to topple equality's foes!
Here to salve the people's woes!
The Sunnyside Pros!
The Sunnyside Pros!
Look—away—eeeeeooohhh!

"Why the yodeling?" said Flora. "He sounds like a dust-bowl hick."

"This is the fashion," said Lenny apologetically. He snapped it off there, before what he knew was coming, the singer's additional extraneous flourishes. Lenny's and the secretary's heads leaned together, nearly touching. Lenny might win her by the song's failure, a mixed fate. His doubts about Gogan's tune were enough as it was. To not advance it past Shea's flunky could prove fatal. "This constitutes good singing, nowadays, the voice of the people. Trust me."

Lenny wondered what stink of doubt emanated from his sweat-saturated jacket, undetectable to himself, since he went everywhere in a cloud of the stuff. Instead Doria's sweet tang filled his nostrils, mixing with a certain tweed mustiness that might be her skirt or the office furniture. How long had it been since he'd smelled the body of a woman? Not yet thirty, he mourned his life.

Shea had come through his office's inner doors and now stood watching Lenny and the secretary huddle at the tape player. The tall man in the suit coughed into his fist and they jumped. The strapping, glad-handing Irishman, the mayor's man, Lenny's conduit to Moses and Rickey. Delia or Felicia likely knelt on the carpet and sucked him off twice daily, once before lunch, once after. The carpet being perhaps where Lenny himself ought to kneel, rather than romancing the secretary. Not for the first time, Lenny Angrush bumped into the remainder of his own innocence, a part that had still underestimated corruption. This was nothing to congratulate himself over in a world of pragmatists and price tags, a world as yet unrenovated by revolution.

The song: Had Shea overheard it?

"Mr. Angrush, welcome. Why don't you step inside?" Lenny offered his hand and Shea's palms closed on it like a giant clamshell. No wonder the man had been entrusted with reclaiming baseball for the Dodger-bereft; he wore mitts of flesh. William Shea should have been Lou Gehrig, doffing his cap and silencing millions with a gesture of inner calm, just as he now re-instilled order to his secretary's zone with the minutest nod of his chin. Lenny waddled inside, clutching briefcase. Here was where the air-conditioning was hidden. Canadian gusts reached the great lakes of Lenny's armpits, chest, and belly. He turned to see the girl removing his reel and tucking it back into its box, then reclasping the reel-to-reel's hood, her posture absurdly dainty and obedient. Then Shea closed the door, severing Lenny's view of the scene to which he'd imported a brief measure of music and longing— all snuffed effortlessly. The light glared through shades from behind Shea, silhouetting him like an interrogation cop.

Here, inside Shea's sarcophagus of propriety, the walls lined with handshake photos and gold-seal certificates, Lenny reversed his guess again: Shea would never have fucked his secretary. Bill Shea was the other variety of power animal, a paragon of rectitude, who fucked his wife if he fucked at all. This office was a place of muffled and euphemistic rearrangements of the lives of other men, of amoral solutions writ in legalese—fixes to the crises of horse-betting city councilmen and real estate developers tripped up in their own chicanery. The element of chaos here, the imperative to think of fucking in the first place, was all in Lenny. Shea blanketed the area with uprightness, with Christian notions of normality and virtue, making everyone in range of his signal ashamed of their worst thoughts and grateful to be rebuked.

This was why he got the big assignments and the fat checks. Because Shea got it from his wife or perhaps discreetly in an apartment kept for that purpose on the West Side—here Lenny split the difference between corruption and sanctimony, for *of course* Shea fucked, he fucked hard and like a hammer, a man of his type would have appetites—but never, never in a million years would he accept even a passing blow from a gum-cracking type of secretary from the city's flung-most periphery. It was Lenny, who wasn't getting any, who felt the need to be on the brink of sex and disaster at this instant, in this office.

So it was, that in the seconds before Shea opened his mouth to betray him, Lenny was instilled with a certainty that he gazed on the face of the revolution's worst enemy. Shea had the unflappability of self-certitude, of self-suasion. Lenny Angrush prized special capacities in himself, capacities for the recognition of capitalism's fatal flaw, its undertow of squalor, its keening and clawing, the morbidity behind the sales pitch. These called to him by manner of his own squalorous keening, present always in himself like a high signal, a brainpan whine. Bill Shea didn't register on this index, was something wholly other. Shea was righteous. He believed that bad things could in him be made good.

It was this belief, afloat everywhere in this great land, but occasionally coming home to dwell in a human outline, usually a big beefy masculine template exactly like that before Lenny now, that had prohibited Communism from arriving in the United States of America.

Beefy template dropped a hand mitt on Lenny's shoulder and took measure of his utter smallness.

"Did you hear the song?" Lenny groaned.

"The National League's coming in," said Shea. "It's expansion, just two cities, New York and Houston. Flushing gets its baseball club."

"You're joking."

"What would I be joking about? Rickey and Frick are lined up. Wagner, too."

"You ditched it."

"I ditched nothing. National League baseball returns to New York City. They'll announce it in a week. Under your hat for the time being, please."

"The league, the Continental League." The People's League, though Lenny didn't say the words.

"This is better."

Mayor Wagner and, behind him, always, Robert Moses. Ford Frick, baseball's commissioner. Branch Rickey, author of the Continental League. Lawyer Shea, the fixer. All the dominoes Lenny meant to fingertip-topple, now toppling backward onto him instead.

"What about the other cities?" Lenny asked, not so much caring for the answer as groping for instruments of comprehension: Who'd screwed whom? Was Rickey the Machiavelli, bending Shea to his contrivances? Was it higher up? Or right before his eyes? No matter. Crushing betrayal straight down the line: A life's study informed Lenny Angrush it had nothing to do with him. Nor any other individual agent of history's disregard. That he felt personally screwed, mere faint residue of luck's design. He wondered how he'd break the news to his bespectacled pitcher, scholar of Gorky in the original.

"Let the league appease the other cities. You wanted baseball in Queens. Get happy, son. This is a thousand-percent victory."

"The Pros," Lenny almost whispered. The name, at least. Salvage the name. A kind of dissolving grace was upon him. Waning residue, backwash of unluck. Get him out of Shea's office. He felt light-blinded, invisible. Who knew how many had entered never to leave. The glossy framed handshakes. He might if he wasn't careful be reduced, like Vincent Price's fly, to a head atop a suit. Nauseated smile as Shea knuckle-gripped the life from him. "The Proletarians!" Lenny uttered in protest as he shrank to the door. Outracing the effects of the spell—he needed to be tall enough to reach the elevator buttons.

"I'll take it under consideration."

Shea's token phrase buffeted Lenny's shoulders as he fled. Under consideration, with Gi-Odgers and Dodgants. The difference between Shea's inner office and the outer like stepping into a furnace. Lenny was surprised frost didn't form on Shea's door, now closed behind him. Blinkering himself in shame past the secretary's gaze, Lenny forgot his reel, so she raced to catch him where he poked a button for the elevator. She pushed the white box in his direction. He pinned it with his elbow to the briefcase, adeptly now, locating in despair the poise his enthusiasm routinely destroyed. Let her fall in love with his departing outline. If only the elevator would come.

"I was thinking," said Moira or Maureen.

"Yes?"

"What you want is something more typical of the life of the city. Street-corner music, like doo-wop, which is all the rage. My brother's in one of those groups. If you're trying to find a voice for the workers of New York City, I doubt they're likely to care for that square-dance or banjo-picking sound, when they've never seen a cornfield or a dust bowl in their lives."

Of all indignities. That she should produce a historically apt critique of the Popular Front. What Lenny needed least was what he got. He spoke without turning his combusting face from elevator doors that refused to open. "I'm inclined to agree with you. The progressive's sentimentalization of the rural farmer type who doesn't actually pardon my French give a flying fuck about him, and who wouldn't be worth organizing even if it were possible, is for me a matter of permanent deep distress. We ought to rally around some street-corner doo-wop for a change. I'll take it under consideration."

———————

Lenin Angrush had short blunt thumbs. Unavoidable once you noticed them, lying as they did in hideous view of any observer. Where desire's gaze fell, thumbs went questing next, for a baseball card or cat's-eye marble, for a twist of licorice. Lenny was six when another kid first pointed it out, a difference enough to register with the difference-tabulating engine of the collective grade-school mind of Sunnyside Gardens. In class, handed a pencil for his introduction to forming the alphabet, Lenny accepted it with a grip consisting of four fingers and a big toe. The teacher had to help him cultivate a unique approach. A person's two thumbs, if you let yourself feel it, consisted of the out-grasping claws of the body, forming a pincer hinged right at the heart. Even in the sphere of solitary affairs, a thumb was hung out to dry when you dug in your nostril for a hanger or grasped pecker in fist. You had no option but to maul yourself with your own deformed instrument. So a crucial part of Lenny, industrious, animated, agile, a part defining his human difference from the animal kingdom, fell short. This one fact about himself might have stood for all else in a global account of his failings, had he granted himself that luxury. Some differently constituted person could sit home moping at his thumbs forever. Not Lenny. He comprehensively forgot them, so that he'd blink in genuine confusion if your gaze lingered there, let alone the rare times in adult life when someone remarked.

Why, then, in the presence of Tommy Gogan did Lenin Angrush discover himself persistently sitting on his thumbs? Thrusting them in blue-jeans pockets, masking them behind foam-webbed beer steins? Simple. Tommy's relaxed elegant hand, spidering chords at the top of his Gibson's neck. During kitchen-table conversation the folksinger sat with the guitar like an extension of his body, fingers shifting silently on frets even while his strumming hand gesticulated conversation or waved smoke-bannering cigarette or spaghetti-bannered fork. Miriam Zimmer had fallen in love with the sole profession in which Lenny's small divergence mattered, the sole in which it counted as an infirmity. Lenny, traipsing after Mim through coffee-shop evenings, had been handed a guitar once. He handed it right back, knowing where his mittenish hands could and couldn't go.

So now he sat, thumbs throbbing in concealment, watching Tommy form chords. As evenings dragged on the Irishman liked to lay a soundtrack of changes behind routine conversation, making a strings-damped talking blues of nearly any gibbering exchange, any wine-soaked, purposeless confusion. You hungry? Nawp, I cadged me one of them free cheeseburgers at the Caricature, dum, dum, dum.

Wait, how can you be opening for Van Ronk at the Gate of Horn on Tuesday when Van Ronk got eighty-sixed from the Gate of Horn, dum, dum, dum. Pass the salt, dum, dum, dum. Tommy Gogan, such that Lenny could make out, possessed no wild melodic gift. Those long, nearly double-jointed thumbs, which might have reached for a hundred chords, instead trudged endlessly over the same hoary folk clichés. C-A-minor-G, C-A-minor-G. *It's not as though I have a stumpy prick!* Lenny wanted to scream. Why couldn't saxophones be the craze?

Two of the foam-webbed empties on the White Horse's table tonight were Lenny's own. Having guzzled what he'd usually nurse, on an empty stomach, too, he swam in his beer and his grudges and the bar's sweaty beatnik roar and gloom. Lenny'd worked the conspiracy's algorithm in his head, waiting for Mim and Tommy's spontaneous confab to thin out (See ya lads tomorrow, hey don't stick me with the check, dum, dum, dum). Then, when at last he faced the happy couple alone across the scarred wooden table, Lenny spelled it out for them. Mim's head tipped to Tommy's shoulder, bobbing slightly as he strummed. The formerly bold young woman, the flame of Sunnyside, now seeming to wish to merge with the shoulder of her god, to blend her dark hair into his hoodlum's sharkskin jacket, which he wore over a white shirt and loosened tie, despite the heat, believing himself to be Paul Newman, apparently.

"J. Edgar Hoover made a deal with Wagner and Moses to kill the league."

"Eh, sorry?" (dum, dum, dum)

"Shea's a stooge. Branch Rickey too. The FBI's in bed with the syndicate that runs the major leagues. They coughed up a team to halt Socialist baseball."

Miriam piped up without raising her head from the folksinger's shoulder, voice coming from a frizzy baffle of hair that cloaked her eyes from Lenny's view. "Is the whole FBI required to explain why Shea put the kibosh on your Proletarians?"

"The prospect of a new league threatened them enough that Hoover even stood up to the Yankees, to force the National League into their market. Maybe in fact there was a backdoor deal with the Yankees—

watch, I predict we'll see Shea's glorified farm team sell its best players uptown, like a local branch of the Kansas City Athletics."

"Is there a place for Whittaker Chambers in your scheme? I think he's feeling a little lonely."

"What about Franz Kafka?" (dum, dum, dum)

"Feh to you both."

"He'd make a heck of a stopshort." (dum, dum, dum)

"Shortstop, you uneducated mick. You ought to show some respect for the pastime of your adopted land. And I'd like Kafka better in right field, where his lousy attitude wouldn't infect the whole diamond. Another round for us here, when you can." This last to the bar's girl, who came clearing their glasses onto a tray balanced overhead as she wound through the maelstrom. Lenny needed another place to hide his thumb.

He slurped the top off another ale and then something broke in him, something like a chunk or facing of ice or stone shearing off a cliff and shattering in a valley distantly below. He couldn't catch it before it fell, couldn't issue any warnings to those humans like ants so minuscule beneath. Only watch it fall.

"To see you neo-ethnics cavort you'd think it was 1936 all over again."

"Neo-ethnics?" Dum, dum, stop. The folksinger was at least alert enough to sense when a bucketload of ire was directed at him even if in a language beyond his reckoning.

"You Appalachians. You gaseous yodelers. You plow humpers. The entire fershlugginer diversion represented by the WPA years, when the left fell utterly into Comrade Roosevelt's grip, and every formerly sharp-eyed urbanist went chasing after some oil-rigging cowboy with charcoal and a sketch pad, or shoved a reel recorder under the nose of some illiterate sharecropper clutching a one-string guitar. The party seeking solidarity with the *folk*. Your music is the gasping cartoon the Popular Front left in its sorry wake."

The trigger, the blow that had loosened this cascade, had come hours earlier, when Shea's secretary handed Lenny the box with the neatly rewound reel, the tape containing Tommy's useless theme song. It now lay in his briefcase, with his ledger and the rare coins, at

his feet here in the White Horse. Other shames, pertaining to the secretary's allure, the closing of Lenny's head near to a point where he'd
detected not only her scent but her warmth emanating, that whisper of possibility, these too were tightly containerized, caulked, and
salted like radioactive material in some depth of his recollection's
seafloor.

"My music can do all that?" said Gogan. "I'd sure like to be able
to make a cartoon gasp."

"Sing it with me: Shall We Gather at the River and Drown the
Radiant Future in Its Infancy?"

"I don't really know what you're talking about."

"No, you don't, not personally. Because you're folk music's walking
advertisement for eternal innocence with a hayseed in its teeth. You
don't know, but Mim understands me completely."

"Too completely," said Miriam.

"You prefer Paul Robeson?" asked Gogan, infuriatingly benign.

"Paul Robeson's an intellectual, and I prefer him, yes. As I do
Fletcher Henderson and King Oliver, not for their politics, which are
unknown to me, but for their innate dignity, speaking as it does of a
better world to come. Your preference I suppose is for the barefoot
indigent from the Delta, a moaning teddy bear you can cuddle. You
know, I heard the Yankees still keep a Negro boy in the dugout to
touch for good luck on their way to the plate."

"Shut up now, Lenny."

Saying it, Miriam had raised her head from the folksinger's shoulder. Tommy Gogan stared across the table, his fingers still around the
guitar's neck. Lenny would have liked to have hurt him, but Gogan
might be unhurtable. Lenny reached below the table and produced
the reel from his briefcase, shoved it across between the sweating
steins. "Here, it was useless, less than useless. Write me a new folk
song, when you think of it, called 'Ignorance Is Bliss.'"

"Beat it, Lenny. Go home to Queens."

She could command him to shut up, to beat it, only because no one
was listening. In one of Lenny Angrush's regular milieus—the chess
shop, the coin shop, the City College cafeteria, amid some accidental
confluence of former party regulars in adjacent Sunnyside backyards,
which though newly fenced were helplessly communal, Kropotkin's

Gardens by deep design and which no boundary, no white picket or cyclone fence or high border of roses could corrupt, possibly even in a car of the 7 train as it pulled a horde from Grand Central toward the teetering sun-blazed platform of Queensboro Plaza—in any of these, Lenny's rant, his tone rising to indignation, would have gathered over-hearers. Kibitzers, leaning in to contribute their own grudges, their own angle of attack. Those enmeshed in history and not without a yawp of their own. Giving air to indignities new and eternal, they'd have taken exception to no small portion of Lenny's argument, sure. They'd have also pounded home his point for him, wagged a finger or several at the folksinger for his lack of historical grasp. The point being, Lenny would have kindled a spark. Here, nothing. The White Horse, home instead to drunken painters and poets and teenagers with Trotsky beards who might not know Trotsky's name if they heard it, here Lenny's cascade was just another beatnik word-painting, a splash in the general muddle. If nearby listeners made out any spe-cifics they'd have likely taken it as mere patter. A Lord Buckley or Brother Theodore stand-up routine, something in quote marks. Only Miriam heard him and knew what it meant and that it mattered, and so she was liberated by the lack of dialectical context to command him to put a sock in it.

"It's simply that the naïveté perturbs me," Lenny said, and knew he was sulking. He'd come to be among fellow travelers, seeking consola-tion for the travesty in Shea's office, yet was the cause of a workers' revolution any less dead here in the White Horse than in that office? Likely not.

"I hear and obey," he said, rising, clutching briefcase to chest, a Roman's shield for brazening through the pub's rising throngs to the door. "I return to the homeland, to the solace of my pauper's bed, and to the orange juices and buttered rolls of morning. Remember me when I'm gone. We who are about to die blow you a raspberry, preferably out of the ass." The tape reel in its box Lenny left floating, a vacated life raft amid the shipwreck of beer steins.

"So long, Cousin Lenny. Sorry the tune didn't cut it with the big-wigs." (dum, dum, dum)

Lenin Angrush was eight years old when the swaddled girl was low-ered into his arms. To him still yesterday. Lenny's ma and Cousin Rose sentineled in the general vicinity, rattling teacups, railing. Probably, if considered from a grown perspective, they'd never stepped farther away than from where in a swift gesture they could reclaim the infant from the boy who'd been made to wash his hands and swear gentle-ness. Yet at that moment when the bundle was placed on Lenny's lap, cradled in his crossed legs, it was as though those teacups rattled from distant shores—Lenny and Miriam were on their own island together, that was how it felt to him. Lenny's attentiveness shrunken to pinpoint in the gaze between his and the girl's. The brown of her eyes. Tiny bubble at the corner of her lip. The beaming of her pres-ence, into his. Miriam soothed the calamity Lenin Angrush at eight years old could only understand as the root of himself always, now identified by her effect on him as something soothable, a storming sea of unrest he lived inside but which was not him. At least not when he clung to this girl and they arrived together at this island. The voices distant were nonetheless distinct.

"She's quiet with him."

"And him with her. Oy, this kid. He'll talk your ear off."

"A good influence both ways, then."

"You've got a babysitter, in a couple of years."

"A wet nurse is what I need. I think she wants to take my nipples off. I don't see teeth, but I'd swear they've come already."

A cousin might be *your cousin*, something that belonged to you at last, even as she described your sense of apartness. Your family com-prised a field of night against which you could discern your outlined form. Cousin Rose was already your parents' idol and conundrum, for marrying the impossible German, for embodying the standard of the classless future—Lenny's ma and pa might believe in Commu-nism, but Rose *was* the party-made New Woman, unforgiving in her nature and intoxicating in her demands, her abrupt swerves and vio-lent exclusions. Cousin Rose chipping the mezuzah from her doorway with a screwdriver, gouging wood and scarring paint. Lenny had later quested in the bushes and rescued it, weird token of Rose's disaffilia-tion, her ferocious will to reinvent with the tools at hand. He stashed it with some treasures, shooter marbles and a dud firecracker he'd retrieved from under the el, Aladdin stuff to polish until it produced a genie.

Now Cousin Rose and her German had made this baby. And this baby had been placed in his arms. His new cousin was a girl child, a fact Lenny'd confirm with his eyes soon enough. They couldn't hover forever, not women like his ma and Rose, squabbling at the *Daily Worker* while fucking up a recipe, despairing of some burned ruin and opening a tin of sardines instead. In their distraction they'd left him with the infant alone, even if they'd not yet declared him the babysitter. Lenny's thumbs were not too blunt to insert in the waist of Miriam's diaper and pull. It slid past her dimply ankles easily enough. Lenny pretended stupidity afterward, claimed she'd done it herself. The diaper, left heavy with her piss on his ma's Persian rug, was ripe with stink, but the girl was clean and scentless. Perfect.

Short thumbs were no great curse, not compared to that of learning too soon that only one person existed for you on this earth. The curse of having that thing for which anyone might seek a lifetime, for which anyone awaits, made too utterly apparent, placed too near at hand, too calamitously soon. Placed in your very grasp yet still denied you, as a bullfrog is denied the moon. The years before Miriam Zimmer could organize her teenage personality, the years before she learned she had the right to tell Lenny to bug off, tell him to *make like a tree and leave* or to *twenty-three skidoo*, before she could demand he unmolest her with his attentiveness, demand he make secret his faith, those years might be the best he'd known. A time or three his cousin had occupied his lap again. Once to read a comic he'd brought to her when she was six and he was fourteen. A year later to watch the first television that had come to Sunnyside Gardens, when every kid for blocks around had crowded inside the same parlor to marvel. Those years before he was disallowed from that island he'd begun to know this day when she was first cradled in his arms. Left afterward to drown in his boiling sea. Sometimes she acknowledged him there, sometimes not. But she'd never rescue him. Lenny had loved his cousin her whole life.

Lenin Angrush had been born three times. In 1932 he'd arrived on the earth. In 1940 Miriam had been placed in his eight-year-old arms. In 1956 Khrushchev wrecked the Soviet illusion and it was at that moment that true Communism had floated free of history, like smoke. The weaker ones, that describing nearly everyone Lenny had ever met or heard of, were demolished with the dream. Some flew the coop. The coop, such as it was—the American CP was in tatters.

Lenny's ma and pa, specifically, flew. Zalman and Ida, but to Lenny just ma and pa. They became Jews again and ran to Israel, to farm olives with even more distant Angrush cousins, those putting the Semite back in *Semitic*, building a new Jew world founded on a desert scrap, a few sandy phrases from the Old Testament. A refuge from twentieth-century politics, hiding inside the politics of the sixth century BC—why risk the war of the present when the war of the past was still eligible to be revived? They asked if he wanted to join them. Lenny said no and they departed before he graduated Queens College. Their seats at commencement empty.

Less than a month later an Irish couple took occupation of the Angrush home on Packard Street. Lenny could have evaporated from Sunnyside Gardens then, fled at the sight of his childhood home inhabited, another mezuzah stripped off, the door frame this time sanded and repainted a fresh green so you'd never know. His parents unremembered entirely. Into the memory hole with the whole business, the silence that fell with relief over all that silence could cover, everything but the faces, faces like stoical sinkholes for hiding remorse. The fresh ex-Communists who, unlike Lenny's ma and pa, still lurched around this place, daring you to mention what you knew about their recent affiliations, affiliations held two decades and dropped overnight. Lenny could have dissolved in smoke like so many. At twenty-four young enough to pretend it was all his parents' idea. He was already getting some work in coins. He could have gone to live at the Y, charted some orbit eliding Sunnyside Gardens completely.

In 1956, thanks to Khrushchev, Lenny would have been born a third time in either case. If he'd fled or stayed. One summer night he stood in the gardens, not, for once, his parlor, or Rose's, or some other where a meeting formal or informal occurred, but in the actual gardens of the Gardens, the unboundaried communal patchwork of flower and vegetable beds, some overgrown with ground cover or delegated to the nurture of some young tree, some future shade. He'd gone out to gaze at the stars and enjoy a cigarette—in his unthrift Lenny had become a smoker of cigarettes that summer, a habit he'd soon enough shed, a sacrifice to austerity like so many other vanities, like matched socks, mouthwash, or umbrellas, all manner of bourgeois fancies. He stood among the plots, here carrots and turnips, as if wartime rationing still applied, and over there a bed of dwarf roses, beneath a tire swing lashed to the sturdiest branch of the oldest tree. Stood venting his smoke to the blinking and unblinking stars, the cruciform jets tilting for LaGuardia or Idlewild. From this place, at the center of a city block designed for accord, Lenny heard the voices. The quarreling, the keening despair, the unvowing of vows. From the opened windows of kitchens everywhere, that summer, issued these voices if you let yourself be attuned, took off the mental earmuffs. Despairing arguments with history, with fate, and with the self. American Communism, born in parlors, had gone to the kitchen to die.

One kitchen window was quiet, though a bare bulb shone to show it was not unoccupied. Cousin Rose had no one to argue with. She'd been booted from the party scant months before. Her purebred Communist husband, whether because he was too Communist and too German to stay, or because he couldn't stand her, was long gone. Her black cop boyfriend, home with his family. And Miriam? At fourteen, Miriam had already practiced vagrancy. By sixteen—gone. She'd exported herself from the Gardens, to wherever else the new highschool kid could think to be, Morgenlander's soda shop on Queens Boulevard, or the Himmelfarbs' recarpeted basement, their "rumpus room." Solly Himmelfarb the good Jew who got to lord it over the Commies now—they'd gotten what was coming to them. The same effort of will they'd wasted at meetings, squandered waiting for a new world to come, Sol sank over decades into his furniture showroom on Greenpoint Avenue, selling to Jew and Irish alike. During the war privations, with nothing new to sell, he sold used. He bought back and sold at prices shamelessly doubled. Cannily, not Himmelfarb's but Modern Luxury. Under that name, Himmelfarb earned a bit of luxury for his daughters, the basement room with a phone extension of its own so Miriam could call Rose in her kitchen and say she'd stay at the Himmelfarbs' for dinner again. Lenny at twenty-four probably ate at his own parents' table, before they evacuated for the promised land, more often than the runaway-in-training ate at Rose's. So in this hour of recriminations and torment, any smaller children put into their beds, exhausted souls uncorked at kitchen tables, Rose was alone. Lenny saw her shadow cross the wall. Rose opening the refrigerator to pour a tall glass of tomato juice. Something in the oven for dinner, something previously frozen. Or not. Possibly sardines and saltines, for convenience and despair an equally fine selection.

This scene, Lenny could have fled, that night and forever.

At that moment Lenny became aware he was not alone. He heard a scraping in the dirt, at first thought it could be an animal, God help him, some rat or squirrel about to bolt up a pants leg. No, a kid—incredibly enough, a teenager, on his knees in the dirt of the flower garden, currying over some ground with a little hand rake. Lenny heeled the butt into the dirt and stepped closer for a look. It was that kid Carl Heuman. He was nearly Miriam Zimmer's age, her schoolmate, though at fifteen the girls were women but the boys were boys. Heuman was one of those who was always lingering around invisible, a witness, a sponge. An earnest boy—Lenny had even seem him doing his fly-on-the-wall act at party meetings, helping the kitchen ladies keep the tray of almonds full or pour the tea while he recorded the adult universe with his mind. Now Heuman tended his parents' marigolds in the moonlight while mother and father tore each other's throats out over Khrushchev's undeniable and shattering truths. A slug in the grass, leaving a trail of teenage woe glistening where he'd been. Lenny had been the same, not so long ago.

"Didn't see you down there."

Heuman said nothing.

"You like flowers?"

The boy shrugged miserably.

"You ever contemplate the world of numismatics?"

"What?"

"Coins."

"If I weed the flowers my pop'll take me to a ball game."

"You like Cal Abrams?" The Dodgers had once featured a Jew outfielder, even if not much of a patch on Duke Snider.

"Erskine. I wanna pitch."

Lenny didn't have the heart to tell the kid what he knew: Smart money had the Dodgers absconding. There was a reason Walter O'Malley had sold Ebbets Field: His gaze went West. The mighty correctors of segregated baseball, secret official team of the American Communist Party, now flirted with year-round sunshine. Tanned fat-cat movie-Jews to fill seats, in place of pasty Mitteleuropeans not half Americanized.

The grown men knew and didn't know how to break it to the kids. Not so different from Khrushchev, the grown-up from Moscow, at last forced to break the childish heart of the American CP.

All affiliations slumped into abjectitude.

This whole popcorn stand, Lenny could have blown.

"You throw lefty?" asked Lenny, based on how Heuman held the rake. The kid was not tall.

"Uh, yeah."

"Lefties stick around. Look how many chances they're giving that overthrowing mutt Koufax. Got a curve?"

"I don't know."

"I'll teach you." Lenny hadn't stood on a diamond in ten years—the other kids had learned to throw near his head, he'd reliably go whining down into the dust, and that was that. But he could play catch with the poor bastard. He could coach a curveball out of him, if Heuman had any arm whatsoever. Make a little salvage from the ruins here, where a gabble of voices rained on through the pretty night in June 1956, evening of the day in which Khrushchev's Secret Speech, delivered in February, had been printed in its entirety in *The New York Times*.

From this disaster area Lenny could have tiptoed, with no one saying a word.

Either way, go or stay, a new life. Lenny stayed. This night, encouraging the fifteen-year-old pitcher in the mud of his parents' flower beds, Lenny felt the old Communism, the obedience to Moscow, peeling from his spirit like a thin skin, a covering inconsequential, which dried and crusted and blew away, to reveal the pink new self beneath. A week later Lenny took a job at Real's Radish & Pickle, humping barrels. Cousin Rose, finding him seated in the office there, in collar and tie for his interview, glared at him like he was mad, making Lenny positive it was the right choice.

It was Rose and Miriam who were his compass—if a compass could have two needles, one abiding, the other flying off to parts unknown. Rose, entrenched in the Gardens and her neighborhood, entrenched in her sidewalk Citizens' Patrol, hunkered in local grievances. Behind it all, entrenched, englued by rage, in her beliefs. Too much a way of life to quit now, even if she'd never speak of it. She'd been kicked out, Lenny knew. They took away her membership before immolating themselves in corrupt Moscow directives. Lenny took Rose as his model: the Last Communist. He'd never say to her what he knew, that he recognized her, except to signify recognition with his presence. They were two, a cell abiding. Rose was Lenny's compass needle that never wavered.

Miriam, the bird that flew. Lenny spotted her from time to time, exploding through her high-school years, seemingly grown a new inch of bust each time he glanced. His lap ached for the baby he'd held, for the kid who'd had the time of day for her cousin just a few scant years before cutting him off. Miriam wasn't even sixteen the Saturday she first shocked him with a how-do-you-do where he sat at an open-air concrete chessboard at the corner of Washington Square Park, trudging through an endless endgame with one of those non-resigners. You had to prove to these schmendriks that you'd beaten them, they'd never take your word for it, the point being that every once in a while you hadn't. They'd eke out a draw by stalemate, though that was a term they seemingly refused to learn, perhaps for fear of its general applicability to their whole existences. Miriam and a friend, a Negro girl, came upon him, the distance between Sunnyside and Greenwich Village collapsed, and Lenny, rising out of his question-mark posture there, nearly straightened up completely free of his clothes. She might as well have ridden a horse up and greeted him from its saddle, he was so discombobulated.

Miriam and the Negro girl both wore dark sunglasses. Two teen-age girls, laughing at Lenny before he managed to utter a word. What made him understand immediately that his fly was unzipped? It would have been for hours now. He raised his zipper and immediately resigned the game, to the astonishment of the schmendrik, at whom he merely flipped his palm: You know nothing.

"What are you doing here, Mim?"

"We're going to the movies, if you'll buy us tickets."

"Who's this?"

"Janet," said Miriam. "We're best friends."

If it was meant as provocation, Lenny wouldn't bite.

"You live in Manhattan, Janet?"

The Negro girl shook her head, and Miriam said, "We met in school, Cousin Lenny."

Lenny took a closer look at Miriam's friend, wondering if there was some connection to Rose's cop. But the cop and his wife had a boy, a single child, no elder daughter. This instead consisted of one of Miriam's typical and instinctive rebukes to Rose: Mother hides with her blacks, I brandish mine.

"Terrific, I'm surprised I've never seen you around the neighborhood. Now, why not ride back to Queens? They got movies there."

"We like it better here." The girls laughed together again behind their wall of glasses, which offered Lenny only sun-shattered glimpses of his wondering self. Through the general maniacal atmosphere Lenny surmised that if there was anything at all to this best-friendship, even if it had only been conjured today and would be gone tomorrow, it was an arrangement that could breathe in Greenwich Village as it couldn't anywhere near the precincts of High School 560.

"So, what are you seeing, some kind of Mickey Rooney picture?"

"William Holden. Wanna go?"

"I couldn't possibly sit still for that crap. Opiate of the masses. But I'll walk you."

"Pay our way."

"You don't have enough for a flick, you shouldn't be riding the subway."

"We have enough, just not for popcorn too."

"I'll buy you popcorn. That way, Rose hears I ran into you, I had remotely nothing to do with William Holden—I bought you a meal. I put some food in you and advocated you reacquaint yourselves with the 7 train, which is what for the record I am doing right now."

Lenny, feeling himself expand into the illusion of stewardship over the pair, nonetheless knew it was just this—an illusion. Miriam would apparently have to be allowed to go through a brief beatnik phase.

At twenty-three, at twenty-four and twenty-five, Lenny savored the luxury of believing this the awkwardest passage between them. An eight-year-old could love a baby, sure—it was crazy but undeniable, and nothing could get in the way of it, because it was crazy and a secret. A fourteen-year-old boy could love a six-year-old girl, too, because not only was she contained and presexual but he was still more or less so himself, a handful of wet sheets and furtive jerks notwithstanding. A fourteen-year-old didn't even yet know what he was jerking about. A grown cousin—*once removed*; Lenny clung to this distinction—could marry his grown cousin. When they were twenty-eight and twenty, say. He'd wait that long. But a worldly twenty-three- or twenty-five-year-old couldn't love a new-breasted halfling, one tumbling through all manner of teen rituals of self-becoming. Lenny figured both knew it, though couldn't say, and thus found themselves forced to repel from the whole area, a defensive reaction. Relations between the cousins turned, necessarily, ironic, caustic, sporadic. This would pass.

Lenny in those years went on some dates.

Lenny journeyed a few times up to 125th Street to get his ashes hauled.

Lenny purchased an expensive tailored suit for a dollar from the closet of a man who died ostensibly of woe.

Lenny having proved himself astoundingly inept at the humping of barrels got fired from Real's Radish & Pickle.

Lenny having proved himself to be the leading self-taught expert in five boroughs on the distinguishing characteristics of U.S. coinage, the eccentricities pertaining to the various mints and corrective restrikings of the high and mighty Silver Eagle and the lowly Buffalo Nickel and Lincoln Cent both, and having learned to suppress a general tendency to lecture career coin men with no interest outside their subject on the political and philosophical implications inhering in same, made himself gradually indispensable to the operations of the public counter at Schachter's Numismatics on Fifty-Seventh Street. Following an investment of hanging around the counter kibitzing for

three years, Lenny was grudgingly awarded enough hours as an eval-
uator of collections to manage his Packard Street rent and still find
time for chess.

One night, fondling a girl his age he'd taken outside from a party
at an apartment above a laundry on Greenpoint Avenue, a new pack
of cigarettes proving a useful excuse for a venture, the girl stopped
him and said, "You don't recognize me, do you?"

"What's your name?" It was a way of stalling. She had a high black
hairdo and a pretty body that was making him feel crazy and a nose
and lips that nearly dripped from her face, features years older than
the figure that had arrested him from across the room, from where
he sat on the cold radiator. Her mother's face, most likely, prematurely arrived on the daughter's person—good reason to go out of
the brightly lit room to the dark of the street. Now Lenny was being
asked to concentrate on recognition. He squinted to make a show of it.

"Susan Klein. We went to high school together. You were a year
ahead."

"That explains it."

"You fascinated me then, you know."

"I'd hoped to fascinate you now."

She ignored him. "My best friend dated a kid from Sunnyside Gardens. Moe—"

"Yeah, Moe Fishkin."

"She explained it, it always stuck in my head what she said. The
Sunnyside Gardens boys, they're Jews, sure, but *they don't seem like
Jews.*"

The unnameable affliction of his beliefs. Lenny could only smile. By
1959 nobody said "I am a Communist" except in a Hollywood flick,
either a swarthy heavy making a dying confession, expiring words
from a body riddled with FBI lead, or some tubercular, misguided kid,
maybe Robert Walker or Farley Granger, facing up to consequences of
his treasonous acts. All sympathies, affiliations, anxieties, smoothed
into silence—never say *Rosenberg*, never say *Hiss*, never say even the
word *capitalism* for terror of its implicit opposite. Daily life was a
patient that had survived a hideous and life-threatening surgery, that
of its detachment from history entirely. At any instant the wounds
might begin seeping blood.

"Moe Fishkin signed up to the army, summer of '56." Let Susan Klein wonder why at that moment a promising intellect like Fishkin had thrust himself into the ranks of anonymous service to his nation. Fishkin had had his morale lobotomized by Khrushchev. Lenny clamped his mouth onto Susan Klein's motherly features and inserted his hand through the zipper on the side of her dress, found the small of her back, commenced a forage for her daughterly tits.

Lenny in those years conceived the Sunnyside Proletarians, a place for the truth to hide in plain sight. As the new baseball team would encode the Dodgers and Giants, let what was unnamed be renamed, what was lost be found. Or never actually lost, because it had never yet existed.

True Communism was by definition a prophecy of the future.

In 1958, in 1959, the true Communist hung in blank space, sustained by nothing but going on, shed of illusions. No Trotsky diversion now, for Trotsky, too, had been complicit. No Popular Front, no Wobbly organizer, no This Guitar Kills Fascists, no Communism Is Twentieth-Century Americanism. The true Communist pulled the tab on another tin of sardines in her kitchen. The true Communist put his lips near and issued breath to slightly dampen a gold Austrian 1915 Corona before wiping it with a chamois.

The true Communist was waiting.

Then, at the start of the new decade, Miriam presented her cousin with the Irish folksinger and he said pleased to meet you (dum, dum, dum) and Miriam told her cousin she'd met the man she was going to marry and soon enough Lenny Angrush learned he'd spent his whole life, sunk the dowry of his heart's expectation, that which he'd hoarded since the day the eight-year-old sheltered the swaddled infant in the enclosure of his arms and lap and crossed legs, in exchange for a shitty doggerel tune, not even possessing a melody, anthem for a baseball team that would never exist.

Lenin Angrush entered the bounds of the stadium in Flushing, the stadium named for Shea, one time only. In 1964, the year it opened—he entered it only before an official game was played there, never to return. Tommy's song was by that time mercifully forgotten, the name Sunnyside Proletarians nearly forgotten, Lenny quit with baseball entirely, save for when his eyes wandered against his will into the rat's maze of the *Daily News* box scores, there to savor the residual accomplishments of the Dodgers who'd been Brooklynites and still labored in Los Angeles, those Brooklyn stars fading one by one in the sun's blaze, apart from the ascendant Koufax. Lenny found in himself no appetite for the gimmicky lore of the Mets, under Casey Stengel and from the first a total charade, an advertising hoax. Lenny was by then a chess man and a coin man, a scrivener too, slaving in his off-hours on a monograph on the Gold Eagle. Lenny's premature middle age, a potentiality anyone could easily have spotted in him at fifteen, was now, at thirty-two, in full flower.

Yet an ancient promise to Carl Heuman trumped Lenny's vow never to honor the stadium in Flushing with his presence. The kid had taken to the curveball. He stood only five ten, his fastball likely never topped eighty-five, he wore glasses, but the curve snapped. College hitters chased it into the dust, they flung their bats into the dugout chasing it, Lenny had seen. There was always the bullpen. Carl Heuman couldn't be so much worse than what the Mets featured there in '63—he could mop up losses as well as anyone they threw out there now, right? Returned from two years in the Peace Corps, the kid had also shed his baby-fat cheeks—maybe a tapeworm picked up in the tropics, who knew. Returned, and bullied by his mother into dentistry, Carl Heuman still had a baseball thought. Lenny kept promises.

So he made a call to the corporate lawyer whose power had only grown. The mighty Shea. Could Lenny still get through? He got through. The week the team moved from St. Petersburg up to get the feel of their new digs, Lenny accompanied Heuman to the clubhouse entrance, still not totally believing he'd accomplished it, though he tipped no uncertainty to the kid.

Those manning the doors at the perimeter of the stadium and at the locker room threshold inside were unresistant, if uninterested. They confirmed that the name Angrush appeared on their list, and shrugged the two men inside. A coach showed them where Heuman could change into a gray road uniform, "New York" across the chest, the only thing they had free in his size. Heuman put his glasses to one side while he changed and then put on a baseball cap and only then returned the glasses to his face, as though reluctantly. Then the coach led the two men through the tunnel and up the short steps and they were out under the sky of the big new bitten-doughnut of a stadium, the fortress Shea and Rickey had forced the city to build, and for a moment Lenny felt all grievance depart to the sky where at that moment a jet screamed past. Its engines rumbled in the concrete of the dugout and in the dirt and in the grass. The Mets lounged in the outfield stretching and at the cage and Heuman was ushered straight up to the mound, to stand behind a protective cage allowing him to pitch safe from line drives. The coach drew Lenny back across the foul line, to stand with him in the chalk box and watch. Heuman soft-tossed to the catcher a few times, then a Met in home whites stepped in with a bat. Heuman didn't glance back at his benefactor, remained wholly absorbed in his task, his moment.

"Who's that?"

"The batter? Name's George Altman. New outfielder. Had a nice camp."

"Can he hit a curve?" Lenny couldn't resist saying it.

"Million-dollar question."

Heuman threw five pitches before Altman missed one. Thereafter Heuman found his pitch, making the batter look foolish three swings in a row, but the coach wasn't looking.

"Thattaboy!" Lenny yelled, feeling idiotic but wanting to galvanize eyes to the prospect before them.

Altman hit a long foul, maybe a triple into the corner actually, Lenny couldn't tell from here. A gloved ball boy ran to gather it. The scene, balls peppered everywhere, players running sprints, seemed less than ideal for evaluating anything. Carl Heuman stood centered in chaos, brow furrowed with sincerity and striving, as much ignored as that night when Lenny had found him squirming in the mud of the flower bed, on the night Communism died. He was like a figure only Lenny could see, an imaginary friend.

Another batter took Altman's place. Roy McMillan, the old shortstop. This might be how it worked. A veteran like McMillan, basically a scout in uniform, took measure of the stuff. A batter couldn't look away from the kid on the mound as it seemed the whole remainder of the universe felt free to.

"How long's he want to go?" said the coach lazily, after McMillan had drilled maybe fifteen line drives.

"What do you mean?"

"Up to you."

"The tryout's over?"

"Tryout?"

"That's what we came for."

"Word from the office to allow your son to toss some batting practice. Favor to Bill Shea I heard."

There went Heuman's whole career, that day on the mound under the jets. His day in the sun. The Sunnyside Gardens kid who'd once thrown batting practice to the Amazings. Too bad Lenny hadn't come with a camera. Without photographic evidence the moment misted into legend, the dentist willing to tell it if you asked, never if you didn't. He didn't burnish—I never threw to Kranepool, no, nor Choo Choo Coleman, no, he'd explain patiently, nor Art Shamsky. Shamsky wasn't with the team yet. He'd speak with no disappointment, it had done nothing to shake his National League devotion, no, the dentist was a fan, though any subsequent visit within Shea's walls he'd pay for a ticket.

Not Lenny. The Mets never got one Liberty Dime from his pocket. Lenny Angrush had no need for this team of confabulated Lovable Losers. He knew too many authentic ones starved for love.

2   Cities in Crisis

The Greenroom. The young NBC production assistant greeting Miriam Gogan as she disembarks Rockefeller Center's Studio 6A elevator is an unmistakable freak-in-containment, eyes pinwheel-spinning his pleasure at being recognized as such, above a Vandyke beard and lips as soft and red as a teenage boy's. She supposes the recognition is mutual, for though Miriam has pinned her shoulder-blade-length frizz into a neat castle perched high off her neck, and selected from the depths of her closet the canary-yellow pantsuit retained for appearances at civic forums, public bureaucracies, and bail hearings, also donned modest jade earrings and an unchunky silver necklace, she doubts this straight costume cloaks her own pot-drenched pupils, dilated-to-meet-you at one in the afternoon. The assistant invites her into the program's "greenroom," reminding her as they go that though today is Tuesday, taping has already been in progress—would just now be finishing—on a Thursday segment of *The Who, What, or Where Game*, the quiz show on which Miriam Gogan has been selected to be a Friday contestant. They film—he explains this as they move past reception, through glass doors, and into the corridor— they film the episodes in bunches, two on a Monday, then three on a Tuesday, keeping the host, Art James, from having to work for more than two days to put a week of shows in the bank. This also saves on hotel nights for the episode champions, who reappear on the panel the day following their victory, carrying over for as long as a week before the show resets with three fresh contestants on a Monday. So if they hurry inside Miriam can watch, on a video monitor, Thursday's final round—"Pot Limit," in the show's language—and judge the play of the winner, who'll face her when she steps onto the set. The other new player, Miriam's future opponent, too, is waiting already in the greenroom, but, according to this kid, he doesn't look any too formidable—an accountant, a nobody. It is today's likely winner she ought to worry about: Peter Matusevitch, a hipster advertising man, he'd begun on Monday—yesterday, that was—and had been winning "all week." The goofy bearded boy in a suit babbles this way at her, as he leads her into the foam-insulated and carpeted chambers of the inner studio, his apparent injunction to make the contestants comfortable melding effortlessly with stoner palaver, that droning fascination with everything. Here were the restrooms, Miriam must know a hell of a lot about current events to get selected to be on the program, too bad you can't see the Chrysler Building through this window, did she want some coffee? The weird fudge of days that pertains in this place, Monday containing Tuesday, Tuesday containing all the rest, seems of a piece with the assistant's fog of approximation.

In a more general way, finding the sweet young head waiting here to meet her is all of a piece with Miriam's New York in the new decade. As though she's invoked him, smoked him into being. It was once the case that, in pursuit of such essences, such encounters, you migrated from the drab gray lands that extended in every direction, seeking a small enchanted quadrant. MacDougal Street, Mott Street, Bleecker Street, a brick cellar on Barrow where a jazz trio's instruments lay gathering dust. Hipsterdom's tiny population glommed new members, those days, at an appreciable pace. Anyone arriving on that postcard-size scene had by all appearances grown sideburns just five minutes before, seeking approval of the essential few who'd each personally gotten turned on by either Allen Ginsberg, Mezz Mezzrow, or Seymour Krim. If back then you saw Tuli Kupferberg or Ramblin' Jack Elliott on the street you not only greeted them and were greeted in fond return, you knew that Elliott was as much a New York Jew as Kupferberg, an open secret to all but the squares who paid to see his cowboy shtick.

A decade later, Greenwich Village has exfoliated its vibe outward, encompassing the whole island overnight. Sure, hippiedom had daubed the planet with its paisley virus, doped flower kids adrift and hitchhiking anywhere. But Manhattan's variation is more intricate and compelling. New Yorkers, a strain of the human species too consumed with mercantile striving to brook interruption, have, with typical acquisitive impatience, *turned on* without *dropping out*. Any given old format, like, say, an NBC quiz program run out of Rockefeller Center, now bleeds with dressed-up freaks along the lines of this kid. No fuckups, they carry the city's tasks forward with as much alacrity as the type of go-getter they've replaced, even if in wry quote marks.

Peter Matusevitch, the advertising executive who is the week's champion so far, plainly shares in the same benign conspiracy. Miriam, seated now in the comfy oasis of the greenroom with the assistant and the accountant, studies her soon-to-be-opponent on the video monitor there. Matusevitch is outfitted in a wide-lapelled mint suit, sports an elegantly waxed mustache, not so large as to be silly, keeps his longish hair combed neatly over both ears, and speaks in tones both insinuating and sweet while he eliminates the previous pair of *Who, What, or Where Game* opponents, as though wishing to convert the tiny violence of their dispatch into a kind of seduction. As soon as this operation is completed Matusevitch enters the greenroom in person and Miriam enjoys another easy exchange of mutual recognition, this at a higher level than the older-sisterly affection she'd granted the assistant: Matusevitch really is a fox. Even if Madison Avenue is, basically, satanic.

Not that Miriam is shopping, except in that, yes, older-sisterly way she shops, on behalf of the single chicks of the Grand and Carmine Street communes. Stella Kim, for instance. It is Stella, her current favorite, with whom Miriam has gotten high just before taking the subway up to Rockefeller Center, and Stella who's volunteered to keep an eye on the toddler while Miriam competes on the show. Tommy, the loving dad, having coop-flown again. Reverting to Woody Guthrie, a man of his people who couldn't stay home, he'd picked today to journey by train up the Hudson, to play a set to bolster the spirits of the ragged band of Quaker protesters keeping a death-penalty vigil at the prison in Ossining, a thing Miriam liked to call his Gig of Sisyphus. Though that might actually describe Tommy's last decade. The career that Miriam, having made herself staunch behind, the great everywoman behind every great man, tries not to consider. Stella Kim would for instance dig Peter Matusevitch very much.

And likely the reverse, Stella Kim being a fox herself. Stella Kim being really somewhat special, really quite a lot more than another of Miriam's dopey commune girls. For it is more generally the case that Miriam, having surpassed the dread age of thirty, mother of a two-year-old, collects to herself living emblems of her earlier self, even if they are mostly without a clue, contain barely a notion behind their brush-shined waterfalls of hair. Nevertheless Miriam enfolds them within her sphere, plays older sister and girlfriend, purveyor of good grass and serious knowledge, to the barefoot and thank-Christ-for-the-Pill-not-pregnant lilies of the counterculture. Those subject, if they are lucky enough, to the special ironic burden of the chauvinist hippie boyfriend. At least Tommy Gogan is Irish, is famous, or had been, and has donated his fame and other, more material prospects to great causes—alibis unavailable to the hordes of ponytailed schlubs still looking to their chicks for laundry duty. So many of these are NYU girls, or dropouts from Bard or Vassar or Stony Brook, come awash in New York. Good churchgoers right through high school, members of Monkees fan clubs, tentative abusers of bathroom-cabinet amphetamines, victims generally of the stupefying effects of the suburbs. Miriam, usher to the city, unveiler of its occult corners, would have older-sistered most of these types even at seventeen, fresh from dropping out of Queens College.

Stella Kim, Bronx-born Hunter grad, survivor of another staunch Red mother, and self-savvy hot ticket, has the capacity really to show Miriam to herself eight years younger. Or so Miriam would like to believe. They'd met, a year earlier, at Yippie headquarters, during a meeting for a call to solidarity with Cesar Chavez, Miriam honing in on Stella's fitful intensity even before the girl bummed a smoke. "Waste of time," Miriam told her as they left the meeting early, to snag falafels and amble to the park. "I haven't touched iceberg lettuce for a year now, big news. Boycott's too slow, let me show you." She guided Stella to the Associated on Eighth Avenue, where they smoked dope behind the Dumpster, then, once inside, loaded their hand baskets with heads of iceberg and bunches of migrant-exploiting grapes. Around a corner, when no one looked, they excavated an open-casket freezer and buried the lettuce and grapes beneath pounds of plastic bags of frozen peas and carrots. "Only takes about ten minutes in the ice to wreck the lettuce. They might still be able to sell the grapes, but they sure won't taste right."

"Cool," exclaimed Stella Kim, impressed for certain. "But what's the baby food for?"

"A baby. C'mon." She dragged her home to show off Sergius and Tommy, no feminist shame in the nuclear family, leastwise not on a night when Tommy had stayed home trying to tease into place between the infant's lips a bottle, stand-in for her laden breasts, which began jetting in instantaneous response the moment she and Stella walked through the door to hear the father pleading with the bawling child. Stella Kim, unflappable, introduced herself to Tommy and then with a sly smile produced an extra couple of glass jars of Gerber, apparently booted into her macramé purse while Miriam paid for those she'd taken to the register. There are few tricks you can teach this girl, who conveys a certain Weather Underground vibe she'd acknowledge only in cipher remarks, passing behaviors. It is Stella, in fact, who has taught Miriam to use slugs for subway tokens, matte disks punched from rolled steel, purchased from a maker in Brooklyn—Stella who, with enough of these in that purse to coldcock a policeman, has gifted Miriam with handfuls. Miriam has used one of the slugs to ride the F to the Rockefeller Center studios today.

It was with Stella Kim that Miriam, the famous rememberer, the memorizer of factual nonsense, one day found herself calling out her own long bluff and writing in to the game show to become a contestant. Miriam's absurd ease with dates and names and geography so impresses her cohort, though this aptitude feels to her merely her legacy under Rose Zimmer's nurture, Rose who would barely settle for less, and a skill Miriam truthfully finds less amazing in herself than she finds it amazingly lacking in her husband and his friends and her friends too. It was Stella with whom she sat at home caring for the kid with the television on, calling out answers invariably an instant before each contestant could do so, and at Stella's exhortation—

"Why not win some of their funny money, if you already know all the answers anyway?"—that she jumped for a pencil and scribbled down the address as Art James read it out: "All it takes is a postcard with your name, address, and telephone number to the 3W'S, P.O. Box 156, New York 10019." Stella who understands how badly they could use the green, while Tommy remains stranded in a valley between recording contracts, a valley Miriam secretly fears may not in fact prove crossable in their lifetimes.

That this is Stella Kim's business to understand, more even than it is Tommy's, is for Miriam as unremarkable as is her talent with facts. For Miriam it may always be this way: the male principle a kind of distant banner flying over her life, marking an allegiance unquestioned yet also in some manner fundamentally esoteric, out to lunch. Whereas beginning with Lorna Himmelfarb, or even earlier, and never more than in the instance of Stella Kim, Miriam's lady confidantes are the ground beneath her feet, the earth itself. Perhaps also even the feet with which Miriam feels herself planted on that earth. Root and body of herself in another. So it is Stella whose eyes Miriam feels she sees through, as she sizes up the killer-hipster mustachioed adman Peter Matusevitch, as well as the other, possibly nonincidental competitor there in the greenroom, the stocky accountant who now presents himself as Graham Stone. Stone rises to take Miriam's hand and bow slightly. Knowing the rigorous screening with which she found herself faced to be granted an appearance on *The Who, What, or Where Game*, no opponent ought to be discounted. Stone has plenty of lascivious sparkle in his eye, too, and for that matter a strange, merkin-like beard blanketing the underside of his chin, perhaps masking a double chin, but also signifying the eligibility of an accountant for entry into the Aquarian age. So until Art James joins them in the greenroom, Miriam is the only one present without facial hair.

───────────

Art James. No one being immune to present fashion, the tidily groomed, clean-shaven Art James wears beneath his tailored gray suit a pale purple shirt and a wide tie that looks like it may have been designed by Klee or Kandinsky. Miriam would gladly wear a dress made from the material of Art James's tie. Nonetheless, as he glad-hands around the greenroom making everyone feel at home and confident for their imminent entry onto the show's set, Art James is sheerly a phenomenon of time travel, a sealed voyager from the indefinite moment in the 1950s when anyone Miriam's age had been first introduced by television to a certain dapper, snappily enunciating, and unspecifiably north-Midwestern version of United States masculinity, that of "the host." Host of nearly anything, it didn't matter. The type is characterized above all by its successful sublimation of the disarranging trauma of the generation of World War Two veterans from which the breed produced itself. It has colonized the public imagination to such a degree that the present mayor of New York City, John Lindsay, is, effectively, a "host." What Miriam doesn't happen to know, for all the trivial facts that, blizzarding in her brain as they do, qualify her to compete on one of the tougher of television's quiz shows—and despite her specific curatorial fondness for the secret Jewish or Polish or Russian names of various blandly appellated U.S. celebrities—is that Art James's name at birth was Artur Simeonvich Elimchik.

The Name of the Game. Stepping onto the set of the show she watches five times a week is as strictly surreal for Miriam as it would be to locate her own face among those in the collage of famous characters surrounding the waxworks Beatles on the jacket of the *Sgt. Pepper's* LP, the identifying of nearly all of which constitutes one of the parlor tricks that routinely causes Miriam's friends to gape at her in wonder at the mad panoply of proper nouns at her ready disposal. The *Who, What, or Where Game* set is a kind of florid proscenium on which the three contestants are mounted like products in a display window, seated before a blue curtain woven with twinkling tinsel— why has Miriam never noticed this before? perhaps she has mistaken its twinkle for static on her inadequate television—and beneath the gigantic stylized *W*'s and the players' individual scoreboards. These scoreboards are all set to "$125," the sum the program spots its contestants, at the outset, for making their first bets. The announcer now briefly explains the rules, how each contestant must judge, from the name of a given category, whether their preference is for puzzling at the "Who" or the "What" or the "Where" of the matter, and then, measuring their confidence, select a dollar amount to bet on the result. The studio audience, concealed behind blinding spotlights, is a distant hum, easy to dismiss. Miriam is on the other hand too conscious of her proximity to Peter Matusevitch and Graham Stone—the sole female, she's been seated between them and so, as at a dinner party, feels responsible to the vibrational neediness of the men at either side. While the theme music plays, unaccountably loud, each opponent leans in to wish her luck. Stone does so friskily, baring incisors, compensating for his husky body and brow. Matusevitch with a vulpine mournfulness that pretends to be sorry he intends to eviscerate her as he has all previous opposition. The announcer intones, *"Who? What? Or where? That's the name of the game! And here's your host, Art James!"*

James welcomes the players, introducing them in the standard manner, according to their place of residence and their profession, or, in the case of housewives, with some anecdote obtaining from a hobby or "interest." Miriam, on being screened for the show, had offered herself as "activist," and suggested they mention her having been wrongfully arrested on the steps of the U.S. Capitol during the May Day protests. Though many hundreds were arrested that day Miriam enjoys counting herself as among the "Capitol Steps Thirteen," for it is in a cell of thirteen women that she found herself detained, and with those thirteen freed on bail by the ACLU lawyer thirty-six hours later, having for that time shared a single toilet in full view and proudly, too, and having shared the solidarity of refusing the only food offered them during that time. The guards brought baloney sandwiches and the thirteen prisoners, not so much defiant as giddy, stripped the baloney from the moist white bread in which it was entrapped and slapped the slimy stuff against the glossy gray wall of the cell where it stuck. One or two disks unpeeling to droop to the cell's floor before the prisoners departed, but most remaining glued there, meat graffiti. Political speech formed of animal product and binders, salt and enzymes.

Of course her breasts had been leaking, too, through that whole incarceration, and during the drive back in Stella Kim's hippie boy-friend's black Dodge, which had a chunky fist painted on the hood, and in the backseat of which she and Stella had curled together and doped and devoured a meatball sub and giggled and then slept, but not before Miriam revealed to Stella the soaked disaster of her bra beneath her T-shirt, and told how she'd been daubing her nipples with the cell's rough toilet paper whenever no one watched.

"Fuck the baloney sandwiches, you could have fed the lot of us," said Stella.

"That's revolting." You would think Miriam should be a lesbian and more than a few times she'd joked aloud that she wished she'd been able to explore in that vicinity, but the truth was she met a brick wall waiting for her there. Miriam found breasts in particular quite disgusting. They reminded her of her mother's body.

The great secret glory of her arrest and which she'd not confess even to Stella Kim had zilch to do with B-movie Ladies' Cell Block fantasies but with what it had in common with her voyage just now up to Rockefeller Center: time away from the kid. A nonnegotiable interval in which she could pass Sergius off to Tommy and regain the autonomous contour of her self for an hour or two. Just breathe free of her own ceaseless mothering of the boy-child, the claustrophobia of loving duty, a liberty the hunger for which Miriam would never enunciate fully even to herself. And when she'd been given her one moment with the pay telephone in the jailhouse corridor it was Rose she phoned. Saying get on the subway and go to Tommy and help. Leaving the remainder unsaid, knowing it was as plain as the baloney on the wall. Go take care of my child, you organizer, you subversive, you unusual and ambivalent mother. Because I'm in jail. You Commu-nist who loves cops, look what I've done. I'm in jail, where you dared me to go. I've gone in the name of your own beliefs. You protested Hitler and you put my head in an oven, now go help take care of my kid, because I'm in jail.

Today Miriam finds herself rewritten. Art James says, "Miriam Gogan lives in Manhattan, New York. She's a wife, mother, and community organizer—welcome to the show. You know, when I was growing up, my mother was a sort of community organizer, too, she'd organize the community of me and my brother to school each day, and believe me, it wasn't easy."

———————

Americana: Songs of the 1890s. The first category holds little appeal. Miriam as a student of the program has schooled herself to choose the "Who" question at such moments, the realm of human identities being that in which she regards herself most comfortable, most likely to dredge up the uncommon fact, and so she selects it despite the higher odds attached on the program's board, betting thirty dollars. Graham Stone, who has revealed a "What" bet, also of thirty, goes first. Art James reads from his card: "One song that typifies the 1890s draws an analogy between a girl and a captive bird; according to the song's title, where was the girl?"

Gilded cage, thinks Miriam, and Stone indeed nails the answer. This ought to feel like good luck but feels like bad instead. Miriam is next. "A hit in its day, the 1894 song 'Sidewalks of New York' was even more popular in 1924 when it became identified with a presidential contender. Can you name him?"

Miriam feels distracted again by what ought to seem good fortune: In any category, a clue that included the term *New York* should be her meat, by right of legacy. She hears herself say "Wendell Willkie?" and into the scant interval before Art James's reply comes the pall of certainty she is wrong.

"No. Al Smith."

Miriam's fund for future betting is thereby hobbled at the outset, the double digits appearing barren, flayed, on that scoreboard where she has envisioned bullying her way up to the four figures. In the wake of her blunder, though Miriam can barely attend to it, so nearly does it seem swallowed in the hum of the spotlight bulbs and the audience's murmuring—speak up, you genteel bastard!—Peter Matusevitch knocks down an easy "Where" at even odds for thirty-five dollars: "The Man Who Broke the Bank at"—"M-Monte Carlo?" Was Wax Mustache genuinely uncertain? Does he have a slight stutter, or is he in fact playing to the crowd's rooting interest, which, Miriam grasps all at one instant, is to witness the rarity of a weeklong champion's crowning? There is always this to consider, the world's old easy bias in favor of the familiar over the unknown.

Matusevitch $160 Gogan $95 Stone $155

———————

Alphabet Soup: "*S.*" "Alphabet Soup" being a mediocre category in which the only determinant is that the answer will begin with an *S*, Miriam finds herself retrieved from what she can now recognize had been the onset of a paranoid inkling, in which the quiz show's topics today would all prejudicially favor Wax Mustache's strengths: Barbershop Quartets, Innovations of Ogilvy & Mather, Cabinet Members of the McKinley Administration. She decides to will herself to confidence concerning the letter *S*, an old companion impossible to allow oneself to become alienated from. Irwin Shaw, for instance, or Subsidized Housing, or Students for a Democratic Society. Nina Simone. Jonas Salk. Bobby Seale. Cardinal Francis Spellman. Joseph Stalin. The System. Sex. Schmutz. She bets twenty-five, again on "Who," this time at even odds. Matusevitch outbids her in this same category and thus by the rules she is denied even a question in the round.

With Miriam dying on the vine in plain sight between them, Graham Stone, questing for an ancient language of the Middle East, fumbles away the obvious "Sanskrit," guessing at "Sikh," while Matusevitch scores easily by completing the name of the gangster known as "Dutch"—"Schultz," another reply she could have given in her sleep. Is it possible that her strengths and his are precisely the same? Miriam has never in a decade been unfaithful to her husband, but there is a time and place for everything. Can she beckon to Art James for a time-out and lure Matusevitch back to the greenroom? She may have to fuck him to wipe the smug mustache off his face after all.

Matusevitch $200 Gogan $95 Stone $130

———————

Cities in Crisis. The announcement of this category falls on Miriam's ears as a sanctification of her presence here. She feels herself the deep soul-occupant of a city in permanent crisis, a true home beyond regret. If "Cities in Crisis!" had been the name of a quiz show, Miriam Gogan might be its all-time champion, or perhaps its host. On the F train, journeying here, Miriam had seated herself beside a Puerto Rican or Dominican man, somewhere in his late fifties she'd guessed, dressed in the innocuously tragic best suit of someone who'd not purchased a suit in thirty years, a gray ballroom-dancer's special, the pants with marks where they'd been scorched in the ironing of creases. The man carried a large photograph framed in heavy silver scrollwork, a black-and-white studio shot of a young woman wearing a chunky glistening brooch on a high-necked dress. Dead daughter or dead wife or dead sister—the man and his photograph embodied a shuddering woefulness, transforming his share of the crowded subway car, so that it held some premonitory air of the funeral home of his likely destination.

The F, though Miriam now employed it to hop from SoHo to Rockefeller Center, wasn't in any intrinsic sense a phenomenon of Manhattan, no matter what an oblivious Manhattanite might think. The line threaded far quadrants of Queens, Jackson Heights, Kew Gardens, acres only marshland when those workers' precincts had first been plotted and the stations named. After a bent glance at Delancey, that mire of Jew legend, at the south end of the island the train exited to probe those by-only-the-dead-known wards of Brooklyn, to putter at last to Coney Island, open-air catacomb of leisure, the dirty boardwalk and beach—the F being the vent from Queens to the sea, if you happened to want to reverse the whole immigrant procedure at the last minute. The point being the man with the photograph might have source and terminus at any one of dozens of outposts unimaginable to Art James or to her opponents. He only happened to dwell with Miriam and the others there, in the same passage through the earth two hundred feet below Rockefeller Center, on his way to and from other realms entirely. Had he exited and come to the air with her there at Fiftieth Street he'd have been zapped to dust by the sunlight. As if in that man's name and on his behalf, Miriam, seeing that "Where" is marked at three-to-one odds, selects it for a bid of the maximum she is allowed, fifty dollars. Cities in Crisis? She might not know the names of each and every station of the dead but she has surely mastered any that would occur to the writers of the questions for *The Who, What, or Where Game*.

The accountant Stone has opted for "What" at a lower price and so precedes her. Art James reads a question: "Malvina Reynolds wrote the song 'Little Boxes,' describing the standardization of suburbia and its houses, which she calls 'little boxes.' According to the song, what are the little boxes made of?" At this, Miriam nearly fidgets out of her pantsuit. Naturally anyone who has ever heard the song, as the accountant plainly has, is capable of doing as he does now and blurting "Ticky tacky!," but that is not the point. Upon his answer Miriam leans into the accountant's ear to inform Graham Stone, stage-whispering too for the benefit of Art James and anyone who might care to know, "I've met Malvina Reynolds!" It was at a party at Dave Van Ronk's apartment, ten years ago now. Miriam had paid the aging folkie, an Old Labor type more of her mother's generation, no attention whatsoever.

"Have you?" says Art James. "Well, I wonder if you've also met the originator of this next quote—that would be fortunate indeed!" Art James has not for nothing reached this station in life. "Let's find out. English author and social critic J. B. Priestley gave the following description of one American city, and I quote: 'Babylon piled on Imperial Rome.' To which city did he allude?"

"That's my question?" This, it dawns on Miriam, will be edited out. As will her breach, a moment earlier, of protocol and frame— for, surely, she leaned into Graham Stone's individual shot. Neither will appear when the program is broadcast. *The Who, What, or Where Game*, whose daily smooth unfolding affords such fine narcotic to Miriam as a viewer, is a construction, not a document of reality. The liberating realization is that it is possible she can say anything at all.

Art James's rictus admits nothing. "That's your question."

What is J. B. Priestley doing in Miriam's Cities in Crisis? "Los Angeles?" she says. She realizes she has flashed on the obscene and marvelous illicit book her gay friend Davis Storr keeps on his coffee table: *Hollywood Babylon*, by the unforgettably named Kenneth Anger. She should be presented a quote by Kenneth Anger, or Davis Storr, anyone less antique than J. B. Priestley. But she feels satisfied with this attempt.

"*No.* New York."

Miriam has betrayed the man with the framed photograph on the subway, allowed her category to be stolen from her. She's gone on record flubbing a question whose answer is her very birthright. This will not be edited out. *Which blond singer buys herself a silver bangle at the Conrad Shop on MacDougal Street each time her group has a top-ten hit? Mary Travers of Peter, Paul, and Mary. Weathermen Kathy Boudin and Cathy Wilkerson were the sole survivors of a March 1970 bomb blast that destroyed a townhouse on West Eleventh. Name the political organization that set the bomb. Trick question—the bomb was set by the Weathermen. Or so they say. Attica inmate Winston Moseley participated in the 1970 riots, violently suppressed by the Nelson Rockefeller administration. Moseley was notorious for which 1964 Kew Gardens murder, in which thirty-eight witnesses failed to come to the aid of the slowly dying victim? Kitty Genovese. The murder was the basis of which 1967 song by folksinger Phil Ochs? "Outside of a Small Circle of Friends." Which childhood friend became so insufferably obsessed with the Kitty Genovese murder that it stopped being worth bothering to call her anymore? Lorna Himmelfarb.* But no, the opportunity is impossible to revise or distend. "Cities in Crisis" will not come again. Miriam goes sullenly unprotesting. For the first time she thinks it might have been better not to get stoned this morning. For the first time she considers, and is astonished she has not considered it before, that it is not only her friends who will watch this episode when it is broadcast—in visualizing her triumph there had been only the image of herself with Stella Kim and others at the Carmine Street commune watching in celebration—but that Rose will be watching as well.

Matusevitch $200 Gogan $45 Stone $155

———————

Spanish Expressions. Miriam, returned to actuality, identifies little upside here. Miriam bets twenty-five on "What" at even odds and finds herself, mercifully, outbid by Stone. Rose exhorted Miriam to learn Spanish as a child, arguing how it would serve her to know the second language of her city—in fact, when they wander together in the old neighborhood these days, Rose goes among the Hispanic residents of the tenements on Forty-Seventh and Forty-Eighth, under the el, speaking in her painfully overenunciated and patronizing sidewalk-acquired fragments, inquiring about *"escuela"* and insisting the children call her *"abuelita"* and so forth, a ritual rebuke to Miriam's failure to acquire the language. To meet her requirements in school, Miriam took two years of French. This, a rebuke to Rose, for whom French is the second language of the aristocracy and also specifically of the Vichy collaborationist anti-Semite she suspects is hiding in any Frenchman, whereas the Spanish flavor of Fascism is properly tragic, commemorating noble remorse at the vanquishment of the Lincoln Brigade. Ironic, then, that the language-flavor of so many of Miriam's present and coming causes—Chile, El Salvador, Nicaragua—is Spanish, too, so in her participation in bilingual meetings and protest demonstrations she is continually thrust against the awkwardness and embarrassment of her old resistance to that tongue.

There lay a deeper explanation, one Rose could never be made to understand and Miriam only partially gleans herself: Miriam's recoil from a second language derives from Rose's aspirational exclusion of her own Yiddish, the language of Rose's parents and the life of her childhood, and a language that Miriam hears not in the Sunnyside Gardens apartment where mother and daughter live together, apart from a word or two so common as to be available to the Irish and Italians as well as the Jews, so common as to be heard at times in the movies or on television. No, Rose puts a premium on proper English. No outer-borough accent is acceptable for the girl. After-school elocution classes were not optional—Miriam at ten and eleven years old rehearsing passages from Somerset Maugham's *The Moon and Sixpence* and eventually sent home with a shellac 78 recording to give evidence of successful graduation from the course. Any Yiddish more extensive and authentic Miriam heard only around the fringes, in the shared backyards, and on visits to her aunts and uncles, the wider Angrushes, for whom it was a matter of no shame whatsoever to mingle a steady stream of *fermisht* and *shteigs* and *mishpocha* and *tsutcheppenish* and *ongepotchket* into their palaver, nor to imbue even fully Anglo-Saxon sentences with a syntactical curvature in the shtetl direction.

In other words, it was Rose who, despite herself, imbued Miriam with a horror of second tongues, residue of her own primal and suppressed bilingualism. If, at one level, by refusing Spanish Miriam was trying not-to-be-Rose, at another she was trying to-be-Rose-trying-not-to-be-Rose-who-speaks-Yiddish. What sense can be made of this? For the defiant prole, why struggle so, to talk like one of the swells? For one so eagerly brandishing the wounds of an exiled people, wherefore such revulsion at the native tongues of the underclass? Well, along with a helpless belief in propriety, and a fear of filth and disorder, a grain of the Communist one-worlder resided in Rose's exalting of a pure English. Shedding the muck of Yiddish, you might shed religion and history. You might make yourself ready for the radiant future. Was this confounding? It was. It might even be fermisht, the kind of fermisht that caused your daughter to study French instead of Spanish, then flunk French.

Peter Matusevitch now scores on "Where," naming "La Paz" as the Bolivian city known as "the City of Peace." Miriam's gratitude at being spared the "What" category then suffers injury as Art James poses the following to Graham Stone: "The expression '*Venceremos*,' used by many Latin American political groups, is the Spanish translation of a well-known motto used by many civil rights groups in this country. Can you name that three-word phrase?" Stone, stroking his blurry goatee, smugly replies, "We shall overcome." Perhaps the least-inspiring utterance of this particular phrase to enter the annals of human speech. She could find it in herself to begin hating Stone, too.

Matusevitch $235 Gogan $45 Stone $185

———————

Goodman, Schwerner, and Chaney. The category exists solely in her mind. In the gulf that seems to yawn between transitions Miriam rewrites the show to her preferences, imagining compensation for her shit odds at a comeback, stoking her amusement and outrage. All—compensation, amusement, outrage—are for the moment indistinguishably melded into a tactic for enduring to the next question, should she ever be faced with one. *In 1967 federal judge William Harold Cox of the Southern District of Mississippi sentenced a group of Klansmen convicted under the Force Act in the murders of civil rights workers Goodman, Schwerner, and Chaney in Mississippi, three years earlier. With what memorable phrase did the judge subsequently explain his actions? He said, "They killed one nigger, one Jew, and a white man. I gave them all what I thought they deserved."* If it is not that Miriam had actually gone down to Mississippi during that Freedom Summer, neither is it that she had been indifferent to going: She'd been specifically prevented from doing so. Now Miriam's failure on *The Who, What, or Where Game* (for it is to be failure, she sees now) recalls to her her interview with the Congress of Racial Equality recruiter, at the start of that Freedom Summer.

Goodman, Schwerner, and Chaney were buried in an earthen dam in the woods, and their bodies located only after a massive FBI search of a hundred-square-mile area of backwoods Mississippi. Before their discovery, how many bodies of unidentified black men, presumably other victims of Klan lynchings, were unearthed in the search? Untold numbers, of which no one could bear to keep count. Miriam, having come to fairly regard herself as a whiz at games and puzzles, genius taker of standardized tests and filler-out of standardized forms, master of negotiation with bureaucracies both of the New York civic infrastructure and of the Organized Left, and above all a dervish at one-on-one interlocutive repartee, *at always having the answers, always clearing the hurdle*, thanks to the long ferocious experiment in Rose Zimmer's laboratory of childhood—her collapse on the quiz program calls up that other shameful moment when she'd failed. The encounter in CORE's offices was a follow-up, actually an appeal she'd requested after being stupefyingly denied in her application to join the Mississippi Summer Project. To enlist in one capacity or another was 1964's sensation, after Martin Luther King's march on the Mall, where they'd all been the summer before, Tommy a little burned up to see Bobby Dylan get the gig, but that was how it went with Dylan then—he'd rocketed from the human pavement of their world. You had to get accustomed to spotting his gawky figure, constellation of elbows and harmonica holder, in the distant sky. Tommy took it personally even if he shouldn't. *Andrew Goodman was a drama student at Queens College in the early sixties. For thirty-five dollars at two-to-one odds, did you know him personally? No, I wouldn't say personally, but I did find out later from some friends in common that we'd picketed LBJ together at New York Pavilion at the World's Fair, a couple of months before Goodman was killed . . . Mario Savio, also Queens College, was supposed to be there as well . . .*

Miriam's examiner in her self-instigated appeal was a slim, proud, scholarly Negro close to her age named John Rascoe. At CORE headquarters he'd led her to a windowless, closet-size office to sit in scuffed white plastic chairs, no desk between them, while he paged through her application file as if he'd never read it, though it held nothing new besides a letter of support from Rose. Miriam at twenty-four technically needed no parental waiver, as would have a college student like Goodman or so many other volunteers, but once she'd been turned down she figured a letter from Rose couldn't hurt—Rose pounded out, God only knew, a strong letter on her cursive manual Olympia. Miriam, waiting for Rascoe to unfurrow his brow and ask her a question—much as she waited now for Art James to throw her another opportunity—felt in that small office the ready expansion of her persuasive self, the insinuating worldly aura with which she'd grown accustomed to seducing down the doors before her. Really, who better to go and transform Mississippi? Miriam was a sovereign in the cause of equality, a legacy from Rose. So for the council's error to be repaired, she merely let her certainty be felt by Rascoe. Talk was hardly needed, really, except as a medium for conveyance of this mood. She'd been welcomed to the Corona Park parlor of the Reverend Gary Davis, listening as the blind singer plucked his guitar, while the reverend's wife served them coffee and sugar cookies. To mention such a thing might nearly be unfair to John Rascoe. He looked about as uptight as they come. Now Rascoe coughed into his hand and explained wincingly that the council had "not seen fit to revise their estimation."

"It's sort of crazy, you couldn't find someone more ready for whatever kind of thing is likely to go down down there—"

"Miss Gogan, the council examiner's impression appears to be that you'd be surpassed by no one in your zeal for the effort."

"Mrs. Gogan. I've been on all sorts of front lines."

"Excuse me, Mrs. I don't doubt you've nerves of steel. The conditions for our workers"—he coughed again—"this is a situation where what's sought is a certain temperance, a capacity to abide with the local population, and in many cases precisely a willingness not to assume a position on any kind of 'front line.' Instead one must allow oneself to be led by the black field directors, even to put oneself primarily in a listening attitude with those you meet in the field."

Black or white, a classic bureaucrat in the making. An egghead. She couldn't resist tweaking him. "*Field* is a funny word in this case, don't you think?"

"I don't think it's funny at all."

"Listen, I've lived in all kinds of privations, most recently in secrecy in illegal loft buildings, and in fact my whole life fearing the knock on the door of both the Nazis and the FBI, which I was taught to believe were more or less the same thing. I've attended more meetings beginning before I was even born than you can possibly imagine. As far as a listening attitude, you can consider yourself to be staring at a gigantic walking human ear, like from a monster movie. Nobody's had to do more listening than me."

He said nothing.

"What?"

"I'm wondering if there's more you wish to tell us."

"You could use me is your bottom line here."

"I admire your confidence. But the necessities of this present cause require keeping free of distraction, being capable of blending into a certain environment."

"Is it my last name?"

"I'm sorry?"

"My husband's famous as a singer. Is CORE worried the reactionaries will find out who I am?"

"I see, I see." Rascoe paged through the file. "I appreciate the concern, but no. There's no suggestion that's the difficulty."

"He's written a song or two mentioning Mississippi, of course."

"I'm not familiar with his work."

"Do you know who the Reverend Gary Davis is?"

He stared at her blankly.

Miriam wondered nonetheless if she should have come as Zimmer. Not have surrendered the surname that gave evidence of her place in the fundamental Negro-Jew alliance. CORE was taking Jews all over the place.

"You mention a difficulty," she said.

"I'm sorry?"

"What is it? The difficulty. You used the word, not me."

Cough. "Mrs. Gogan, there's a matter of a certain amount of ill-considered bragging about certain family relationships. A liaison of your mother's."

"Liaison?"

"Of your mother's. A certain excessive pride in the matter. Unbefitting the circumstances of the work we are trying to do here."

"I'm stunned."

"It's mentioned again in a letter just now."

"Wow."

"You do know the great taboo in the region, the great myth with which we do battle?"

"Now you're going to tell me men have died for less, aren't you?"

"Precisely."

Miriam saw abruptly that any expansion of her confidential persuasive self into the space of the little office had been apt, under the circumstances, to be misread. She couldn't win for losing. As in the lingo of the one acting class she'd sat in on, she'd come in "big" when they wanted "small." Rascoe's rectitude contained more than a little distaste.

"Let me get this straight." She was done making her appeal, but not quite done with him.

"Yes?"

"You're telling your people down there to hand out the line that sex between Negroes and whites is a *myth*?"

College Football: The Bowl Games. Miriam might just as well leave actuality unattended for the moment.

Matusevitch $235 Gogan $45 Stone $215

_____

Rose Angrush Zimmer. The second of her imagined categories consists of nothing less than Miriam's life study. *To whom does Rose Angrush Zimmer make love? To Douglas Lookins, police lieutenant. Are they married? Yes, but to other persons. To whom is Rose Angrush Zimmer married? Her first husband was Albert Zimmer. Were they not divorced? They were divorced. Is he still alive? Albert Zimmer still lives in East Germany. Vee vould prefer to pass over zis matter in zilence, jah? Jah. Her second marriage, after divorce from Albert Zimmer, is to Abraham Lincoln. Correction—to Carl Sandburg's Lincoln. Rose Angrush Zimmer is married to a book? Yes, that is correct. A Person of the Book, she has also chosen to marry one. In Rose's utopian scheme you can marry whom you want. Only, a rabbi has to officiate.*

_____

Goats in Fact and Fable. Art James says jauntily, "We'll see who knows their goats!" and Miriam, aware the show is nearing its close, thinks *Fuck it*, bets her remaining forty-five dollars, again on "Who," at the nice odds of three-to-one. When the question comes up, "The novel *Giles Goat-Boy* is a parable about a young man raised as a goat who later learns he is human, and commits himself to learning life's secrets. For one hundred and thirty-five dollars, and at risk of elimination, name the author," she arches her eyebrow and bats out "John Barth," just as if she has been dominating this proceeding as she'd expected to all along. The payout somewhat salves the humiliation the scoreboard advertises above her head, the applause of the studio audience breaks like surf over her head—their relief on her behalf explosive in its fervor—and Miriam, coming down from both the fugue of drug effects and her fury of disappointment, returning to her body under the bright plasticky light, surrendering her hard-won separation from the absurd immediacy of Art James's tie and the boinging musical transitions, measures what she can salvage here. Even losing, she can use the dough. Something better than nothing. Hell, she's *in the game*. Never mind that the others score as well—they all three of them know their goats.

Matusevitch $285 Gogan $180 Stone $265

The Works of Charles Dickens. Graham Stone nails "Fagin." Peter Matusevitch bets too much and falters on "Jarndyce v. Jarndyce." Then Art James presents Miriam with the following: "After a trip abroad in 1842 Dickens published a volume of travel sketches that were well received in England but gave great offense in the country he had visited. Name this country." Miriam lingers for an instant on the resemblance to the earlier question concerning "Babylon piled on Imperial Rome": *You are to be presented with an unrecognizable image of yourself which you must not fail to claim as yourself.*

"Here," she says. "America."

"Yes, that's right, the United States." James's voice savors the words as if they are a steak. "Well, Miriam, you've made a nice comeback from a long way down."

Her losing streak broken, Miriam's cloud of silence breaks, too, and speech rains out. "Funny about these Limeys," she says. She won't likely win this contest but as in her CORE interview she will not go down voiceless. "Coming over here and throwing conniption fits."

"Yes," says Art James, but it is the sound of a page turning in the air between them. Keeping things moving along is James's only real style, the style beneath the tie and the jocularity, a cold formation of military origin. If you proceed with alacrity Monday and Tuesday can be fit into Monday, and Wednesday, Thursday, and Friday into Tuesday, the remainder to be hoarded into resupply.

"Pretty rich—J. B. Priestley coming over here getting all huffy, calling us an *empire*."

"Uhhhryes." But all this will be edited out, she knows.

"We could have a category on dumb shit the Brits say about America. G. K. Chesterton and F. R. Leavis and D. H. Lawrence." But all this will be edited out.

"Uhhhryes. So now—"

"Because no New Yorker has ever *once* equated this place with Babylon, it's just utterly bogus."

But all this will be edited out.

Matusevitch $285 Gogan $230 Stone $315

Pot Limit. Quotes: Words from the Bible. In the final round the fifty-dollar limit is lifted, and so it is technically anyone's game, and Miriam must qualify her crazy desire to claim an improbable victory against the odds that both Stone and Matusevitch would fumble on the same round, an event that has not to this point occurred, as well as against the fact that it would not hurt in the least to bring home a check for two hundred bucks, and it is at the moment of this thought that she is riven by a savage yearning for the child, by a phantasm of his voice, an image of the fair, tear-damp hair at his temples. For the cost of not thinking of Sergius for an hour, it has been proven again today, is that an hour's deferred anxiety and passion may be injected into her bloodstream as if having accumulated in some unknown rupturing organ of her body.

The periodic exits Miriam craves from the cloying auditorium of her maternal life are sustainable only at the extremes of triumph or disaster. As in the arrest on the Capitol steps, and in the jail cell, a day all triumph and disaster both, nothing in between. Sergius in the hands of Tommy and Rose, neither as capable of changing a diaper as Stella Kim, didn't matter in the least. The extremities of the righteous cause, the indignities of the baloney sandwich, these had exempted Miriam from her guilt. This cataclysmic principle may be motive enough for Miriam to wager her whole stake and thus come out of here with something more definitive, to avoid the mediocre middle where too much of life is lived, in which the child is waiting for her to slump home on the subway and rescue him from the Carmine

Street commune where he is likely underfoot while Stella stirs a pot or smokes some pot or talks on the telephone, where he likely clings to her legs in bafflement and need.

Miriam, hedging, bets fifty on "What," at even odds, and Art James reads: "Included in the judgment stipulated by Moses is a famous phrase specifying parts of the body that epitomize simple, one-to-one retributive justice. Tell me this phrase."

"An eye for an eye, a tooth for a tooth?" She speaks this reply as a question, not out of any uncertainty but because Miriam feels all stridency fall from her as she melts back into the conventions of the game, letting it recapture its proper form, the script she has absorbed into her body's knowledge as the show's passive viewer—in this case, a contestant's modest uncertainty that even the most obvious answer will elicit Art James's approval and be awarded the points. She is the mother and housewife and she has placed third, no shame, in a contest with two men. The show's end is a kind of small death, covered in applause and prizes, and Miriam now finds it incredible that Art James and his staff can bear to enact more than one of these in a single afternoon. The upstart accountant has in the end toppled dapper Peter Matusevitch, denying him the distinction of a one-week championship, but that is because he is not upstart but up*holder*, of the status quo, against suspiciously flowery-looking advertising men who speak too softly, who speak in tones nearly sultry, who speak as if placating feral policemen at an antiwar demonstration's front line. Graham Stone has come here in the mild disguise of his merkin-like beard, but his suit, and the girth displayed within his suit, and the trim of his hair around his ears, and the barking heartiness of his voice collude to proclaim his right to seize victory here. Peter Matusevitch turned out in the end to be another skinny hippie, hair smoothed over his ears and collar fooling no one, and the show has been scripted as a delayed rebuke to him—for he fails in the end on a biblical quotation while the accountant aces his own. Miriam, for her part, is real real gone, drifting untethered from the scene by the last dissipation of her hopes, a part of her already on the subway rattling through tunnels downtown to rescue the kid, and she feels now that she has failed not only Sergius but also the mournful man with the framed photograph, for whose honor she'd been playing here today no matter how oblivious he'd be to that fact, even as Art James proclaims "That's right!" to her shamefully obvious answer, and pours patronizing congratulations again on her comeback to this respectable showing. She is to be awarded a check for two hundred and eighty dollars. She has also won a lifetime supply of Adorn hair spray, token of one of the program's sponsors—"lifetime" signified, it will turn out, by the arrival at her address, two months later, of a large cardboard carton filled with twenty cylindrical aerosol cans, along with a certificate avowing her right to demand more.

It is Stella Kim who, in the Yippieish spirit of putting the crappy artifacts of a corrupted world into play as absurdist political gestures— the pleasure they both share in plopping heads of iceberg lettuce into freezers, or shoving Danish five-ore pieces and Trinidadian pennies into the dime slots of pay telephones, or opening a pile of junk mail and removing all the postage-paid return envelopes from odious corporations and sealing within them a single slice of Kraft American cheese, shoplifted earlier that day for this purpose, then dropping the results in a mailbox, to arrive grease-stained and stinking at their point of origin—it is in this spirit that Stella suggests one day when the American Friends Service Committee has sent out a call for supplies to be added to a shipping container that will be delivered to the embattled mountain exiles of Guatemala that she and Miriam gather up the incongruous and already dust-gathering crate of Adorn and ferry it to the AFSC offices and add it to the stash. And, though the wish is hardly in the spirit of nonviolence the Friends espouse, Miriam can't keep from hoping the Guatemalans will be able to convert Art James's gift to their cause into individual flamethrowers. Or a bomb.

3 Sandburg's Lincoln

This is how Rose Zimmer came to live her long decades in Sunnyside Gardens: It was instead of a Jew farm in New Jersey.

Her brand-new husband was two husbands, a Jew and a German. The Jew in him wanted cities. The German wanted forests. The German wanted a farm. The German in him, God save them both, whose father was a banker and mother an opera singer and society wife, the German in him who knew only urbanity and culture, who encountered his first and defining jolt of Marx as one of the appetites of the parlor, served forth with tea and cakes and intellectual conversation, the German in him who'd discovered, when he met his comrades, a peculiar flavor of intellectual conversation that had galvanized his passivity and reordered his life, made him proud with revolutionary possibilities—yet was, nevertheless, an intellectual conversation, a construction of the parlor, like tea cakes piled in a delicate formation on a plate—this German part of him now wanted a farm. Wanted, he said, chickens. Would clean chicken shit, collect chicken eggs, strangle chicken necks when needed.

Thus Rose née Angrush, newly Rose Zimmer, found herself in a Packard riding south beyond all known civilization into the wilds outside Newark to consider taking up a plot of land in what was called the Jersey Homesteads. He'd unveiled the trip quite suddenly, saying vaguely that there were some people there he had to talk to, and adding, as if it were nothing, that he wanted her to weigh it as a future home for their family. Dragged almost screaming by Albert, who could barely steer the dusty, sagging, borrowed vehicle with any competence, who had barely known how to drive before becoming obsessed mere months ago with acquiring his license. As they veered scudding around an ordinary bend in the highway Rose smacked her hand downward to find her copy of Carl Sandburg's *Abraham Lincoln: The War Years, Volume II*, just published, and borrowed from the Jefferson Market branch, and gathered up today as an essential survival option for any outing to the countryside: something to read. She gripped the thick binding as if praying to Lincoln to reinvigorate the union between the Packard's tires and the earth.

"If you pilot your tractor in the same manner as you're keeping us on this turnpike, your—what are they called, furrows?—your furrows, Farmer Zimmer, will come out fercockt and your string beans will all resemble lightning bolts, do you realize?"

"Please, Rose."

The Jersey Homesteads, something impossible, something that couldn't be, but was. It happened under the leadership of a crazed utopian named Benjamin Brown—"a Russian-born Little Stalin" the newspapers had called him, though in fact he was under command of no known cell, was just a shtetl man with a vision, that of wishing to lead tenement Jews out of tenements and back to the soil. Against all odds, except that this was the desperate low pitch of the Depression, when the impossible routinely happened, this Brown had gone to Washington to meet personally with Harold Ickes at the Department of the Interior and come out with a hundred-thousand-dollar check from the Roosevelt subsistence program, with which he'd begun buying up dead farmland from every ignorant New Jersey farmer with his hand out, assembled twelve hundred acres of this nothingness, and then begun to organize Jews. As dubious a plan as Hitler's Madagascar, probably, but Brown had managed it. Here, he'd announced, would be a communally owned factory, a clothing manufacturer employing hundreds of tailors, as well as a communally owned store and a communally owned farm. This Moses of the Tailors roused the sorry Jews of the Lower East Side and the Bronx—those who, in those low days, could assemble their five hundred dollars for a share of the Homelands. Voilà. The future. Rose had heard stories from housewives visiting cousins on their brief return from toil: dust for five months, snow for three, mud for four. In the little concrete-box houses that dotted Brown's utopia, the housewives, when they weren't in the factory or field, did nothing but shovel, scrub, sweep, and polish. That was if you'd dragged with you anything still to polish, if you hadn't sold it all off a cart on Delancey Street in order to afford the five hundred to go live in this glorious future.

Now the scion of Lübeck's bank and opera house, this idealistic husband of hers, would drag Rose to this muddy hinterland because of some lingering Black Forest fantasy of a pastoral agrarian homeland. A scene like something Lübeck Jews had never glimpsed except painted in blue on a Meissen plate.

"Jews come here in buses," said Rose. "Not borrowed automobiles. Those with automobiles get a little fresh air out on Rockaway, or all the way to Montauk, if they're ambitious. Then go back home where they belong." Only a city Jew could want farms, she wanted to scream. Those with villages in their blood knew the depths of ignorance, the suffocating stupidity of the life of the countryside. Only those with the villages still in their blood could understand that the future, for Persons of the Book, was in the cities.

"This could be an answer for us, Rose. You know three wouldn't fit in my flat."

Since the failure of the pregnancy Albert brandished it in every situation so proudly: their invisible baby. That which like the revolution was proven inevitable by its refusal to appear. That which like the inevitable revolution was a solvent clearing up any reservations expressed, any negativity or false consciousness. The day would come, and they'd better make themselves ready. Which apparently now involved a Packard ride to the Jersey Homesteads, if that didn't moot it by killing, instead, the two and the imaginary third.

"Watch the road. Three live in flats all the time. My parents' flat held six." What she didn't add was that babies weren't raised in flats, they were raised in *blocks* of flats. In neighborhoods. Babies were dropped at upstairs apartments for an hour, or for three or four hours—babies, to Rose's understanding, thrived on a density of other babies and their mothers, in rooms streaming with aunts and cousins, kitchens blazing with arguments drowning the radio. Who'd teach you to boil a diaper on a farm in New Jersey? Or, better, boil it for you?

The city at their back, the trees whistled past, a leaf tunnel into incomprehension and fantasy.

"You want to discover the New World, Albert, you should have a bigger map than gets you only to New Jersey."

"What's wrong with New Jersey?"

"The teeming millions come to New York, they either have the sense to stay put in the greatest city on earth or the raw stupidity and courage to go in covered wagons and stake out an Eden of the far horizon, some place with an Indian name, Dakota or Oklahoma. Or to Hollywood, a paradise worth clawing your way across a continent. A place worth getting a few people eaten along the way. Go get corrupted in the sun, like Ben Hecht. To turn your back on New York City yet only go as far as New Jersey suggests, as they say, an impoverishment of the imagination."

Rose found again she had opened her mouth and couldn't quit. After that first year of marriage, it turned out her silence had an expiration date, like a package of butter. Sometimes she marveled over herself as she'd always heard herself marveled over: Oy! Where does the third Angrush sister get this fershlugginer mouth on her? From where does this girl find the material with which she berates her family? Can she be stopped?

She couldn't be stopped. From the day Rose learned to read and converse she'd been assembling the vocabulary with which to animate her own mother's attitudes not by shrugs and moans, not by hands wringing or hovering at her temples, but with lashings of the English tongue. And on finding herself at a Communist meeting, where the new kind of argumentation was being enacted by young persons no different from her in background and temperament, a few even with the mouth and the brain atop a body with breasts and vagina—for why not? wasn't history crying for the arrival of such?—on finding herself at a meeting, Rose's voice was catalyzed. She marveled at herself but would never admit she found herself a marvel. It was merely right to be Rose Angrush. To be Rose Zimmer was no less right. History had commanded she exist. And marriage was, itself, she discovered after a year of foolish fearful silence, a highly dialectical situation.

At their arrival at the Jersey Homesteads, Rose's view of her prospect was in one sense improved and in another sense injured. The place was not exactly as she'd pictured, a place with barefoot Jews with faces like dust-bowl photographs. She and Albert were treated rather royally by the two organizers, evidently party men of the scurrying toady variety, who'd greeted them at the address, a low slab of house identical to many others, where Albert with no small difficulty had been directed and parked the car. The two, one with a sunburned bald spot and in overalls, a *New Yorker* cartoon-Jew farmer, named Something Samanowitz, the other sweating in a black suit and minia-ture tie, a Red clerk of the variety who greeted you at doorways with pamphlets you'd never read but couldn't refuse, named Daniel Ostrow, ushered Rose and Albert first to the garment factory, the shop floor. Here, if you squinted to blur the sun-garlanded pine boughs at the grimed windows, the place could be taken for the Triangle Shirtwaist Company, with the improvement that if you leapt from the window you'd land not ten stories onto pavement but a few feet into dust and manure, the pervasive smell of which intensified as they advanced to the central farm.

Never mind the smell. Their guides might be imagining they gave a Soviet tour to John Reed and Emma Goldman. They were as solici-tous of Albert's and Rose's regard as could be imagined; in her naïveté concerning the day's agenda, Rose first ascribed their fantastic defer-ence to the borrowed Packard. But none of this mattered. It was no good, it wouldn't work. This wasn't Latvia or the Ukraine, it was New Jersey, and Rose's snobbism concerning this frontier's medioc-rity couldn't be assuaged.

Really, the place was wretched, dismal. Political devotion, among those who'd migrated to the Jersey Homesteads, ranged from pro-gressive fellow traveler to the hard-line cell member, but who'd have time to do much organizing while drowning in broadcloth scraps and chicken shit, or while shaving grayish root vegetables, stuff you'd be better advised to toss into the rubbish, in order not even to boil them for broth but to make a "salad"? This was what the Depres-sion had done to them all. This was what the Depression had done to Communism. When it should have stoked the revolution, it had smothered it—precisely because it was in the parlor that the nascent flame of American revolution could be nurtured, and it was in the bovine, calloused imagination of the American worker that it went to flicker and die. In a way, Rose had to revise her thinking: This *was* a frontier as distant as the Great Plains, for even an hour into New Jersey you couldn't detect the throb of European history anywhere at all. The American story, all over again. Set out into the dusty blandness of this starving utopia and you instantly began dying from lack of mental oxygen.

They'd come to the vast central field, where, it now dawned on Rose, some scheduled activity—the occasion for their visit on this particular day rather than some other—was to take place. Not a lawn but a field, one that she felt certain had been not mowed but *hayed*, by a thing dragged behind a tractor, so that the ground on which folding chairs had been set up and blankets thrown down was pimpled and prickly, where fieldstones lay exposed by the sheering away of whatever growth had covered them before, and where a low wooden riser for a band or speaker had been set up. Could the Jews of the Homesteads be so daft as to intend a square dance, to persuade themselves they'd really gone west? Now they emerged from the low concrete houses with baskets, these farm Jews, these forest Jews, these tailors whose wives seemed to her to be begging with their whole bodies for the social sanctuary of a tenement to give articulate form to their suffering, suffering that instead was to fester here in the merciless sunlight. God help them. Around the riser the women straightened their blankets as well as they could be straightened on this broken ground. Then laid out baskets and in the sun-dappled quiet of the afternoon set themselves to the task of what could only be called picnicking.

The little riser with bunting sat empty apart from three folding chairs. What was meant to occur there? Rose hoped to leave before finding out. Anticipating boredom, she'd retrieved from the car her volume of *Lincoln*: She'd lose herself in Sandburg's prose before another car-sickening ride back to civilization. She'd seen enough. The day that had begun with Rose having to take the mad prospect with some seriousness had met its end. The certainty that she would never live in this place she felt as a cord of titanium in her soul.

Albert led her to the blanket occupied by the Jew farmer in dungarees, Samanowitz, and his wife, Yetta. Rose tried to radiate preemptive disinterest in the social niceties. Yetta Samanowitz resembled a
grainy black-and-white photograph of someone's grandmother from
some town neither Polish nor Russian, a figure glimpsed in a frame or
locket, except this gray figure managed to lean toward you and offer
a plate featuring egg salad and pickles and chopped liver on toasts—
God help you, to eat chopped liver in this heat!—and say in perfectly
normal English, "Take a little something. And a glass of tea. You
should have brought a hat for the sun, I can go inside and fetch you
one if you like."

"No, that's fine." Rose's cord of adamancy only tightened like it
was bolted at one end to the heavens and, at the other, to the earth's
core, with this blasted lawn beaded between them. Yet at the next
turn, when Albert and their two escorts, the farmer and the schlepper
clerk, ascended the small stage in the dire sunlight and waved their
hands and she saw that Albert was to speak to the assembly—such
assembly as it was, the scattered souls melting on the straw, these
Jews like insects paralyzed in daylight—Rose felt that cord wrench
itself into a pretzel shape.

Albert and the farmer sat in chairs while the clerkly one stood and
coughed loudly into his hands, without a microphone to gain their
attention, yet finding no difficulty silencing all but the children. He
introduced Albert Zimmer, special guest from New York City, "an
important organizer and speaker." Out here, importance could be
claimed for Albert, Rose supposed, in a one-eyed-man-in-the-land-of-
the-blind sort of way. Perhaps that was the draw. How long after he
relocated here the residue of such borrowed importance would attach
to him was another question. This place being where importance, it
seemed to Rose, came to die.

Albert thanked his introducer, Ostrow, and the farmer Samanowitz, seated behind and who hadn't spoken, then thanked all gathered for welcoming him here "on such a day." Why *such a day* Rose
couldn't imagine, but Albert was graced with a little applause of the
sort managed by an aggregation of human beings congratulating
themselves for existing in the first place.

"The very first thing I wish to say to you may come as a surprise,"

Albert began. "To begin with I want to tell you my high opinion of you, as workers and families, but also as Americans. You are all, seated before me, outstanding Americans, better than you know. Better than many. I say this because I've heard stories, in preparing to meet with you, and even as recently as during my tour this morning, that in the neighboring towns they won't sell to you if they learn you're from the Homesteads. Because, they say, you're Communist here. I've heard the Monroe Township won't let the children attend their schools. Because you're Jewish and suspected to be Red."

"Speak Yiddish!" came a cry from the field. Some scant applause followed.

Yetta leaned in to Rose's ear, startling her. "Someone will always say this, half our public meetings." Her tone was shrugging. "The other half, the meeting's in Yiddish, and someone yells 'Speak English.' You can't win."

"He couldn't speak Yiddish he wanted to," said Rose. Yetta fell silent. Rose, by way of partial apology, and despite her Brothers Grimm suspicion that to eat of this place was to accept the contamination of its possibilities into her body, against every instinct of her refusenik mind reached for a toast smeared with chopped chicken liver and pan-browned onions. It was fresh. She was starved.

"Of course, you may also wonder who it is who has come to you and presumed to affirm your accomplishments as Americans. I hasten to confess I'm nobody in particular, bear no authority before you except that as an American, another citizen of this land but also of the world, a citizen like yourselves of human civilization, and therefore entitled not only to speak to you as one equal to another but entitled to my beliefs. To share my beliefs, against prejudice such as that you've encountered, and beliefs in favor of what we come here this great day to celebrate—freedom."

Okay, thought Rose. Quit setting the table and put out a meal. Albert was a great setter of tables, but the meals were fewer. Still, he somewhat came into his own there, on the platform, high forehead glinting with perspiration but whole frail being also glowing slightly with the regard of the scattered bodies. Their selves flowing toward him and that essence of the lost city that he represented. The citadel of cobblestone and language, dense with intellection and, no matter how poor they had been there, a paradise compared with this squalid sharecropping into which they'd been duped.

Albert had talents as an orator, though this was a different thing, completely, from possessing any powers of looking you in the eye and speaking with conviction, or of going toe to toe with Rose or any other potent challenger to his bromides. In this she ran rings around him. It was only here, in the middle distance, that Albert could resuscitate some measure of Rose's regard. Seated close in the car he'd been too utterly enclosed within Rose's obscuring field of acute and ravening disappointment. Here, up on the riser, she could glimpse his charm, a blend of loquacity and elusiveness.

This was the case in their bed life as well. He'd impregnated Rose trying not to, as she was driven mad by his persistent squirting on her thighs and belly, the indirection of what ought not to be indirect, and so had madly clutched him to her a crucial instant longer. Now, in his attempts to repeat the first accidental success, that which threw them into this panic of a marriage, his diligent wish to assuage her and her sisters and his mother by the dowry of his seed, Albert struck Rose as a man who was invisible when going the main path. Indirection was all he had. Coming at her straightaway she could barely feel him, and the seed reached no target inside her, vanished instead as in a parlor trick.

Albert flickered in Rose's desire like a radio going in and out of signal.

"Let me ask: What nation possesses a richer heritage of revolutionary struggle for human freedom than our own United States? Yet the revolutionary gold in the ore of American history, so rich and abundant, has, like the material treasure of capital itself, been hoarded by the forces of reaction. By default, the revolutionary camp has been unable to claim for itself any continuity with American tradition. This is why your homestead is so heartening a signpost, why you, though you may not know it, though as your head is lowered to the fields you may feel you're merely eking out an individual subsistence, you're struggling for far more than one factory or one farm. More even than one new town forged in the countryside, but rather for a shining prospect of material communalism for the whole people of this land, even for those who suspect and denounce you, those whose prejudices blind them to dreams of freedom. This is why I've come to honor you with my admiration and bring you encouragement from those whose admiration you may not be able to feel from this distance. On this day above all."

Say it, Albert, now, go ahead and say it. Explain that to scrape their potatoes from clods of earth makes them activists.

"Communism is twentieth-century Americanism."

Did anyone, among the sun-slackened arrangements of bodies on blankets, shout out any protest at the tired slogan? Did they interrupt with requests that he speak in Yiddish or for something more nourishing than recruitment ideology? No, they lay paralyzed by his flattery. Though Rose supposed others here might be silenced by a cynicism not unlike her own. For now, as the fulsome arrangement of People's Front clichés were produced, Rose felt herself not only turning off to Albert as she'd been briefly turned on but experiencing a revising revelation about the facts of their mission here today. It was that which caused the cord of adamancy she'd felt within her now to move like a band to her throat, imposing not only silence but a struggle even to breathe.

For she realized now that this speech of his was a party errand, product of a party command. No surprise in that. Ostrow and Samanowitz not merely tour guides but Albert's party contacts.

Albert's sudden learning to drive, bumping into curbs for a month seeking his license, that had been a party errand, too. Which meant, as she followed the logic, that the whole proposition to move here had been a party errand, one originating not in recent days but known to him months before springing it upon her. She could hear every word, as if in a stream the secret dictation now poured into her ear. Consider the situation of a town full of abject Jews, ringed by the yahoo suspicion that they were Reds, as if merely to erect their winsome farm and factory dream was equal to traitorous affiliation with the Soviet. Given this plight, and their terrible weakness, why wouldn't this town choose the strength that came from the party? Why not opt for the support that would then flow from New York, and from farther east than New York. This was a chance to enlist a fully CP municipality, America's first!

And not one word of any of it had been made known to Rose, despite her place, ostensibly at Albert's side, in their cell.

All these specifics suffused into the general knowledge of what she already knew: the things a party cell required of its women. In regular behavior the women were always to avow and affirm the primary myth, which stated that in the gleaming future toward which their efforts all pointed, the divisions and inequities between man and woman would be effortlessly solved. Meanwhile, in the nearer term, the party, with its genius for skulduggery, routinely destroyed the tender trust of a marriage between so-called equals.

As if Albert had ever been capable of inhabiting such a trust in the first place. Rose doubted it.

"On this day, of all days—" What in God's name was he talking about? Then Rose squared Albert's words with the limp bunting arraying the riser on which he stood. All day she'd been seeing the flags, thrust out on poles and draped from porch rails, yet only registered them as a trite irritant, at a level well beneath the range of her exasperation at the foliage. Yet of course, this day of all days. Their Packard expedition rearranged itself one last time and shame flooded Rose's body, both at her obtuseness and at her therefore helpless participation in the most inane of rituals.

It was the Fourth of July.

———————

How then, if it was the party's desire that they live in the Jersey Homesteads, did they land in Sunnyside Gardens instead?

They'd underestimated Rose's strength.

If the cell's intentions had been conveyed to Rose only by the secret telephone of her husband, she'd reverse the charges. Let the cell hear from her by means of the same telephone. *No.* A fairly simple message, requiring no Soviet cipher to unravel.

For Rose, a student of *no*, this was a sort of graduation day, a dissertation in one syllable. A *no* of her own personal devising, no longer merely the *no* of her inheritance, the *no* of her forebears. With it she need be audible not merely to Albert but to some functionary in Moscow, one who could be envisioned as standing with a seashell to his ear, monitoring her husband through oceanic vastnesses. Rose had to make her reply audible against the force of a command she herself affirmed as historical in its imperatives, rather than pretending it didn't exist. To refuse was to say: I exist not only to subsume myself to this cause but to flourish within it, *and I want no chickens*.

Construction of this *no* was under way before they'd reboarded the Packard's long front seat and waved farewell to their hosts. It was under way even before the conclusion of Albert's speech. Rose had lifted herself in full view of her orator husband and all else and gone and seated herself in the cool leaf-shade of the car's running board, to commune with a chapter of *Lincoln*. Let them come and tell her she'd in some way failed *Communism* or *Americanism* by refusing mud and straw and sunburn: No. In Rose's private researches, which converted the glad-hander's shuck of the Popular Front into something true and real, she abided with both Communism and Americanism at a depth no farmer's plow could touch, not of topsoil but of mysterious intellectual root. Sandburg had isolated a passage from Lincoln's message to Congress in December 1861: "Labor is prior to, and independent of, capital. Capital is only the fruit of labor, and could never have existed if labor had not first existed. Labor is superior to capital, and deserves much the higher consideration . . ." This, six years before *Das Kapital*.

The other point, you dummies, was that *The Prairie Years* came first. Lincoln had put log cabins behind him, in favor of cities, of civilization—not the reverse!

So Rose's walkout on Albert's Fourth of July address was mere overture. They rode in silence from the Homesteads to New York, apart from a refreshed attack on his driving.

"You're like a painter, daubing at the thing."

"Which?"

"The automobile's pedal. You approach it with feathery little brushstrokes—add a bit more blue to this corner, Señor Picasso."

"I rather doubt Picasso has a critic standing beside him as he works."

"A more steady application of pressure might be more to the liking of Yetta's chopped liver where it presently resides high in my throat."

"You've got nothing to say about my speech? I thought it went well."

She only looked out the window. Let Albert interpret the force of a *no* chiseled in the stone of Rose's glare, a *no* in smoke signals emitting from her ears. A *no* inscribed, that night and weeks after, in semaphore postures of unavailability in their marriage bed. Let him pass that one along. Comrades, in the contest between the allure of chickens and the prospect of my wife's legs ever again parting, I have reluctantly but with swelling resolve concluded against chickens.

Then, living in the battleground of her *no*, Rose gave Albert a glimpse of a possible accord. An armistice, that was to say, between herself and the unseen presences searching for Albert's usefulness to the party. Look, Rose told him, more or less flatly, if they intend to implant us, make us a party worm in the bud of Utopia, why not Utopia with a skyline? Why not with a place you could buy a pack of cigarettes within walking distance, from those who'd happily sell the cigarettes to Jews? Idealists had already forged a suburb, the city equivalent of Brown's Homesteads, so why be stranded in Jersey? Don't you see that Sunnyside Gardens is where the city Reds go?

As with the Homesteads, the Gardens was populated by history-stunned Jews whose immigrant journey needed a stop. Rose had already gotten familiar with the place. A few distaff Angrushes lived there, including Rose's older cousin Zalman and his wife and their moon-eyed boy named for Lenin. How would *that* go over in the Monroe Township school district, I ask you?

The Gardens were sanctified as a leftist social laboratory by Lewis Mumford and Eleanor Roosevelt. If Mumford and Roosevelt were merely Pink, not Red, wasn't the usurpation of Pink by Red precisely what the Popular Front was meant to accomplish? To ally and align with such progressive sentiments as already floated in American life, in a community such as the Homesteads or the Gardens. Like a man on the make who says he just wants to be friends, then gets on the couch and next thing you know your clothes are off. Nine months later, out pops a proletariat! So why not stay in the city? Sunnyside Gardens could form the simultaneous rejection, inversion, and satisfaction of Albert Zimmer's Jersey Homesteads trial balloon.

The Gardens and the Homestead might really be the exact same place, only tugged inside out like a sock.

In New Jersey the concrete-bunker homes huddled surrounded by road and field and forest, expanse of land dwarfing the blot of attempted civilization, making it puny and precarious.

In Queens the family homes surrounded a communal garden wherein muddy vegetable beds could be given lip service within a theater of urbanity. They also offered a nice whiff of exclusivity, of social arrival. The Gardens were half Kropotkin commune and half Gramercy Park. Like her marriage, even if foolish Albert had mistaken himself for something other than aristocracy!

So what if Rose had wrecked Albert's party career at one stroke? Wrecked inasmuch as he'd bent not to the cell but to Rose, hence was proven weak or untrustworthy (as though bending to them would have proven otherwise!). Better they learn what she knew. Anyhow, Rose knew she'd rescued his career as much as she'd wrecked it, by ending his drift through the Manhattan ranks where his contacts might go on forever imagining that given his loquacity and cuff links, given Alma's apartment—her granite ashtray and Meissen salvage—he possessed either money or deep influence to donate to the cause. He possessed neither. Rose was the stronger of the two, no matter what fantasies about Albert their cell entertained. In Sunnyside *she* could perhaps accomplish something.

Sunnyside then. It was decided, by the end of that July. With help from Sol Eaglin, a party man with a foothold, they had a lease on Forty-Sixth Street by mid-August. Albert's new vehicle operator's license burrowed into his billfold's depths, for safety's sake, before he ever got his leather soles anywhere near the cast-iron accelerator of a John Deere.

Utopia was better when equipped with a subway stop so you could go screaming back to reality for five cents.

The timing? Sublime catastrophe of irony. Rose and Albert and their imaginary baby moved into the apartment the same day the Hitler-Stalin pact was announced, the Popular Front wrecked in one stroke of the pen.

Rose and Albert in the mouth of history, shaken like a mouse in a cat's.

———

The war overturned the life of a recruiting Communist in Sunnyside as anywhere else, the Popular Front's precarious rhetorical line dismantled overnight in the face of the pact. Go ahead, sell Hitler to your typical fellow traveler—he who, emboldened by anti-Fascism, had tiptoed into the party. He who was tearing up his pamphlets the next day, hearing of Stalin's reversal, his expedient embrace of Nazis. Europe, melting in a rain of nightmares, dictated that young men become soldiers on real fronts. And that Reds become Jews again.

Albert, isolated in this way, never took to the life of the Gardens.

Began decamping, by means of the elevated subway, to his old life almost immediately.

There to commit his various unnameable offenses, the offenses of an aristocratic lush with a German accent, running from an unhappy marriage to the barrooms of Manhattan.

"Loose lips sink ships" was the phrase. Well, they could also get you sunk in American Communism.

Meanwhile, Rose stuck. Who'd guess four decades, more, could descend from the strength of saying *no* to New Jersey? Rose Angrush Zimmer, having propelled herself from the rank of the sisters squabbling in a Brooklyn candy shop's back room, had, in marrying Albert, hardly bargained for this outer-borough destiny. Yet entrenched in the vast *no* of Queens, one made a life.

In exile, Albert's letters—not many—came from Rostock, from Leipzig, locations, thanks to *Life* magazine, impossible to envision except as wholly deserving ruins, palaces of rubble. The letters might come from a machine for reproducing German stamps and postmarks, one installed on Saturn or the moon, zones far less improbable than postwar Rostock. The envelopes had obviously been opened and resealed before reaching Rose's mailbox. Albert had seemingly qualified himself for Hoover's watch list at last—he should be proud. The mother crumpled the scant pages into the trash while the girl took the envelopes and steamed off the stamps.

It was a year or so after he fled that Rose erected the shrine, the small, half-circle table in the kitchen, on which the six volumes of Sandburg's *Lincoln* were aligned, and propped in front a small cameo portrait of Abraham Lincoln given Rose by her sisters jointly on her thirtieth birthday. Albert moved out and Lincoln moved in.

Rose's Communism, the core quotient of knowledge and belief, was durable in Albert's absence, durable in the absence of all encouragement. It hadn't required, as had Albert's, a cultivation of vanities, pleasure in pasteboard rhetoric. The crumbling both of her marriage and of the Popular Front left Rose etched in the hard outline of her private certainties. At the next reversal, Hitler invading Russia, Rose was not among those who let down their guard and became intoxicated with public certainties again.

You didn't talk, you read. You worked. Attended meetings but didn't boast of it, took small assignments to visit a tenants' rights meeting, a youth club. Were staunchly for the unionization of the workplace and the nationalization of industry and the education of the masses yet expressed this not in Popular Front braggadocio but in dogged community-mindedness—championing the Queensboro Public Library and the Police Benevolent Association, walking an Irish kid across a street he'd never usually cross and introducing him to a slice of pizza. Rose's Communism in the war years was like the book of ration stamps she'd been issued, with another like it for the infant Miriam, each of which Rose preserved in its own wallet of the softest calfskin, an irony when you couldn't get beef. Like the ration stamps, so with your political self: You tore off a square of your essence and laid it down only when necessary, hoarding the remainder in hopes the supply would extend until the siege was over.

The White Castle on Queens Boulevard couldn't serve burgers during the shortages, and yet the office staff at Real's Radish & Pickle were so accustomed to lunchtime at the counter there, they went anyway and were served hard-boiled eggs. Yet when the war was over and the eggs were replaced with burgers again it was not the world it had been before. Rose's war was different from anyone else's, but in one regard it was the same: It made her more American.

Rose's second cousin Lenin Angrush had caught the Socialist flame but also the sickness, whose symptom was blabbering what you felt to any listener. Lenny was too wide-open, a mind like a gasping pore. Among other things, Zalman's wife, Ida, failed to prevent the pore of Lenny's mind from absorbing the local accent—Rose walked her to the door of the private elocution tutor on Greenpoint Avenue, but Ida wouldn't grasp the necessity. Lenny, despite his advanced and esoteric interests—global revolution, chess, numismatics—grew to talk like a chestnut vendor, an iceman, a head emerging from a manhole. No child of Rose's would ever come of age to speak in the fershlugginer tongue of Queens, distinguished from the stigma of the Brooklyn accent primarily by its nagging and lethargic undertones.

Speaking of icemen, or workers in sewers, Rose had a couple of each.

Yes, men got through her door after Albert. Handsome, heavy of chest, Rose was seen by men and didn't always flinch from being seen. It was her prerogative to feel a man's penis in her vagina if she chose, at this juncture in history, given the catastrophes that had befallen anyone's assumptions, given the stalking horrors of the newsreels. As an occupant of a ruined century you could shrink the world to the size of one woman with one man in the clearing of a lunch hour. Yet were any of these men anything more to Rose than that? Well, apart from Lincoln, barely any. An hour in her bed but not so much as a cup of coffee afterward. Let alone to be there long enough to get a glimpse of the girl returning from school.

In the apartment with the two of them, mother and daughter, no man but Lincoln. Rose was a reverse war widow, divorced but still married to the Jew who'd run back to Europe because he wanted to dissolve his urbanity, his Jewishness, and his Americanness in the solvent of the Eastern bloc. Maybe there he could have his wish—maybe the party would eventually award their spy retirement to a farm with chickens!

Rose was divorced but still married to a century turned on its head.

———————

Were there men that mattered? After Albert, after the war? Just three. One undeserving, but for a time truly possessed by Rose; another deserving, but never hers to possess. And one not of her choosing but Miriam's.

The undeserving, Sol Eaglin. Rose's party fling, perhaps an inevitable tumble. Sol was Albert's own contact, likely the specific assigner of Albert's tasks of acquiring a driver's license and dragging his young wife to New Jersey. Kept for years by party protocol secret even to his operative's wife, Sol had been unembarrassed to crawl out of the woodwork the moment Albert was gone. Sol's was to Rose a familiar face, hitherto anonymous in meetings where others spoke up— his glaring at her over the course of years had suggested no special meanings apart from sexual curiosity. Now, along with admitting his special role in their lives, Sol explained that he had a wife at home but avowed free love, happily declaring the facts that his wife was unloved by him, lately unfucked by him, and completely uninterested in his doings. With that, the eyebrows raised lasciviously on the blank canvas of Sol Eaglin's pate. He had the exaggerated appetite typical of the man who balded in his youth, this according to rumor among her sisters and Rose's own observations. The first time she saw a photograph of Henry Miller she mistook it for one of Sol, though on second glimpse there was no deep resemblance in their features, not apart from the bald dome and the twinkle of an inexhaustible selfishness, disguised as something sublime or idealistic.

What she and Sol did in bed was beyond imagination. For the first year at least this nearly compensated for the dull thump of his rhetoric, his persistent remarking on the subject of himself as if reciting lines from a biographical essay in a Soviet high-school textbook.

1948–1950. Those were the years she'd have carved on the affair's tombstone. In every serious sense, it ended in 1950. Yet in truth, Rose and Sol Eaglin fell into bed a scattering of times before she gave herself to Douglas Lookins, and before Sol personally spearheaded her expulsion from the party. This denied aftermath, the sporadic fucking after they'd broken it off, was analogous to the subterranean kindling of other renounced flames—specifically the Soviet dream.

Navigating Albert's delusions regarding the CCCP, then Sol's equally absurd and stubborn faith, Rose discovered her previously unglimpsed talent for silence.

Let disappointment burn brighter than love, and in doing so let it preempt judgment by those outside the arena.

Let unspeakable go unspoken.

Police lieutenant Douglas Lookins was the lover who deserved her. Maybe the lover Rose deserved, though she wouldn't presume to claim as much. And anyway, she couldn't possess him. What use to concern oneself with the unpossessable deserved? Her black cop, noble enduring grandson of slavery, starved husband and disgruntled father, Bulge veteran, Eisenhower Republican, six foot two and near three hundred pounds of moral lumber, of withheld rage and battened sorrow, embodied cipher of American fate stalking Greenpoint Avenue, rattling kids off doorsteps and out from where they ganged around parking meters, daring anyone to utter a cross-eyed word—the man should have from Rose whatever he required.

What Rose required from him he'd given at first glance, quite completely: to be seen. The galvanic surge of mutual knowledge, occurring instantaneously at the Renters' Alliance meeting, to which he'd been assigned in order to protect the two intrepid landlords who'd actually agreed to come and address the potential lynch mob. Rose had gone planning only to observe but found herself compelled to stand and offer some spontaneous words of global perspective, likening tenancy to Irish serfdom, if only to stick it to the idiot second- and third-generation micks making themselves the most reactionary faction in the neighborhood on this issue as on so many others. She'd barely sketched a few comparisons when met with Douglas's skeptical, saturnine glance, containing more recognition than she could practically bear.

Recognition—of what? What was Rose Zimmer by this time?

Middle-aged, almost abruptly. Mother of a fourteen-year-old giver-of-as-good-as-she-got. Miriam, she of the razor alertness just about to commence wasting itself on boys and Elvis Presley—a hormonal onset that would come almost as a relief to Rose, a needed interruption in the laser beam of a preternatural child's intelligence, Miriam attending to Rose's skirmishes with her sisters and with Sol Eaglin, Miriam sticking herself to her cousin Lenny, making sport of flattering him with her uncanny parrotlike queries on baseball and coins, Miriam burrowing through books, anything on Rose's shelves and anything Rose brought home from the library, anything at hand except she shunned the Lincoln shrine—since toppling it twice as an eight-year-old and being slapped away from the thing, she steered a berth. Miriam unmistakably never forgetting a rebuke or a cuff but silently tucking it into her mental catalogue, no matter whether Rose apologized or not.

Too much a mother. But not here. Another reason to stand and speak at the renters' meeting: to be visible as something other than the single mother in the apartment where every day one grew nearer to desirability and fecundity while the other grew further from the same, to be visible as something other than Real's Radish & Pickle's wizard bookkeeper—one who by now kept her own hours, managed the office nearly effortlessly in passing—to be visible both as a political animal and as a woman. Every day walking on Queens Boulevard she drew a stare less. For each man who earlier would have glanced in her direction Rose felt herself becoming less the woman and more the political animal, or perhaps more the moral scold. For she'd become radiant with disapproval, to trump anyone who'd dream of rebuking her from the right or the left of her unique position as a political exile, a political conundrum. The embattled party wanted nothing to do with her, and the anti-Communist throng didn't know what to do with an unshameable Red. The more she involved herself with civic causes like the library and the Citizens' Patrol, the more impossible and integral she became. Sunnyside's own whatever. Look out, she's coming. Prepare for a civic lecture. Don't litter or make reference to *Sputnik*.

Standing there stuck mid-sentence when she met with it, the mountainous black man's gaze made Rose a woman again. The whole roomful of jostling fools might as well have seen her naked at that instant—she felt as though she were. In his look any number of thresholds were cleared instantly. Douglas was ex-army and wore his police uniform militarily clean, militarily natty. Rose realized at once she'd been living, for decades, in a persistent state of cultivated hysteria about the U.S. authorities infiltrating their meetings, infiltrating their ranks, and what a relief it was to simply acknowledge one such actual authority undisguised, in uniform, and telling her at a glance he knew she was a dirty Red. Anyhow, the authorities hounding Rose were the ones *within* the ranks, always telling her she wasn't Red enough because she couldn't go the whole nine yards of Soviet bullshit. Here was how Douglas Lookins confirmed everything about her in a glance: His appetite said she was still a woman and his disgust said she was still Red.

Everyone thought it was an affair between Jew and black but it wasn't. It was between Commie and cop.

Two competing operators on the same beat, the same circuit of pavement.

Albert had tried to explain to her the shame of being a noncombatant during the war and she'd scowled at his failure to see the manliness, the honor, in pacifism. Now she loved a man in uniform.

If Carl Sandburg had written a six-volume *Douglas Lookins* she'd have not only read it but erected a shrine in her foyer.

But Douglas Lookins had Diane Lookins and Cicero Lookins at home. Too bad for Rose. On this matter he was like a soldier, serving without judgment, obedient to the letter of duty, the spirit having vacated the premises of his marriage however many years before. Rose was prohibited from meeting Diane Lookins. From even asking, after the first round of questions met with clipped replies. Douglas Lookins got to know Miriam Zimmer, barely, for Miriam was less and less at home, franchising herself to the kitchen table and basement of the Himmelfarbs, to the schoolyards and soda shops and then to Greenwich Village and whatever lay beyond the horizon of her sophistication. Miriam had the power to throw it in her mother's face and yet simultaneously inform her not at all of what it consisted.

Douglas Lookins indicated minimal interest. He was not in the market to father a white teenage bohemian. He was not on the prowl for a second family.

Rose Zimmer, however, got to know Cicero Lookins a great deal more. Douglas introduced the two of them at the library, quite deliberately, a day when he knew Rose volunteered there doing after-school tutoring. He presented the chubby Cicero as a problem for a local expert to address: This was a kid who needed books, badly. *Listen now, boy, this lady will tell you how it works here.* It was neither a gesture of closeness between the lovers nor the imposition of a burden, merely pragmatic sense. A child had appeared in the Lookins house with a mind his own mother couldn't fathom. His father had no better luck. Soon enough it was as though this had been the affair's higher purpose, as though Douglas Lookins had been unconsciously seeking this consummation. Every part of Rose's defiant idealism could be enlisted in helping her lieutenant's boy's intellectual apparatus come alive.

Here was what Abraham Lincoln wanted from her all along.

They could start with emancipation and civil rights and then she'd bring him along later to labor and capital.

The revolution was actually a secret occurrence going on just under the skin of the betrayed century. An operation—yes, a *dialectic*—among two and then three persons, of divergent skin colors, of apparently opposed ideological beliefs.

1954–1962. In this case, the tombstone's end date being that of the very last time Rose and Douglas had gone to bed together, a happening which in the latter years of the *relationship*—her word, forget anyone else's—had become scarce, sometimes months between. Rose felt him not so much turning away from her charms, these steadily softened and blurred, nor from his own appetite, which did the same, as she felt him sinking backward from her, into the weight of his own footsteps. Sinking into his life's proper role, responsibilities like slow quicksand, quicksand working over a duration of decades. Diane Lookins was sick. Sick without the drama of death, just slow degeneration, a hastening of the mortality outrunning them all. Lupus. Rose learned the name of her illness not from Douglas but from Cicero and knew that Douglas had never spoken that name less from pity than honor. Not wishing to excuse himself to Rose by offering the unanswerable: a sick wife.

Rose let him sink away.

Rose clung to Cicero.

Rose became ever more the bane of the board of the Queensboro Public Library. One of these days, they joked, they'd have to elect her to join them just to shut her up.

Rose railed against Miriam. She who, like Douglas, left Rose more and more alone. She for whom, unlike Douglas, Rose could locate a voice with which to rail. She tilted as her own mother had tilted at her, only translated from the Yiddish.

Rose never loved this way before or after.

And then, the third and last of Rose's postwar, post-Albert husbands, or fourth if you counted Lincoln. The one *Miriam* brought home. Rose's fate was generic, this she understood. A divorced mother of a single daughter, the provider of a man-absented childhood, such a mother was destined, when that daughter ventured out and brought home a man of her own, to enter into a marriage of sorts with the son-in-law. The son-in-law couldn't merely be approved and tolerated—he needed to be secretly married to the mother in the soul of the mother and the daughter both. Not because the mother desired it, though she might, but because the daughter demanded it, in an unconscious action of correction. The mother was a problem to be solved. *Yours ran from you, Rose, but I've fixed it now. Mine won't run. You can quit bringing home the iceman or outraging the neighbors with Douglas.* It was an action of finishing. The mother's failed enterprise sealed and forgiven. *I've brought one home to you, Rose.*

And so it must be a total fait accompli. The Irish folksinger was never given an audition, never brought around as a boy who might be rejected, a mere date. The first time Rose was to meet Tommy Gogan she was informed she should set a dinner table because Miriam was bringing home someone special, and Rose, falling into the spell, into the script, set a table and prepared a dinner. Absurd command obeyed completely. She found herself worrying over her own dress and comportment, blackening the gray at her temples as she'd only very recently learned to do. Miriam arrived separately, half an hour before their guest. Over a shared cigarette on the kitchen steps—Rose and Miriam suddenly capable of admitting to each other that they *both* secretly smoked!—Miriam slammed the door on any chance Rose could modulate what was to be enacted here this evening.

"Mother, I've met the man I'm going to marry."

"I see." Rose recognized this for what it was, a motto, a banner waved. The words were not to be quarreled with. The way Miriam pronounced them, etched as in flames, defiance masked as jubilation, the only question was what they left her to do besides fall over in a faint when the man in this equation walked through the door.

"You don't yet, but you will when he gets here."

Be unreservedly happy for me, Miriam's triumphalism commanded. *And never have intercourse again!*

Before he appeared, Miriam sharpened her pitch. Rose would be delighted, her daughter assured her, to find Tommy Gogan was no unwashed beatnik, was a folk musician not in the callow college-dormitory sense onto which Rose had heaped such scorn, every time she glimpsed Miriam's MacDougal Street circle, but an upstanding and engaged protest singer, and soon also with a record deal. A deal

was in the works, Miriam promised. Organizer with a guitar, Miriam
called him, her appeal giving form to an expectation that hung thickly
between mother and daughter: that it lay with Miriam to find some
way to bear forward Rose's urgencies, to resurrect them from the
Socialist sarcophagus. By the time their cigarettes were extinguished
and lipstick was reapplied, Rose was malleable as wax, could offer no
protest to the protest singer.

Why not be happy for Miriam?

In fact a folksinger, one either of the unwashed or prep-school
variety, was hardly Rose's worst scenario. After Miriam's trip to Germany, of which she'd declined to make even the most cursory report,
unenunciated dread hovered at the possibility that the girl had made
a crazy alliance with her father's history and was to be drawn behind
an Iron Curtain of the soul.

For years after Albert was gone Rose continued dragging Miriam
to her grandmother Alma's apartment, insisting the girl know where
she came from, never thinking her reward might be to have Miriam
fall into a dream of Meissen china and Niederegger marzipan and
grand pianos and politics mulled over snifters of brandy.

Germany. Let it not steal one more thing from Rose's century than
it already had.

No, the Irish folksinger wasn't Rose's worst fear. So it wouldn't
be a Jew she married—little surprise. Miriam, since graduating from
the Himmelfarb College of Assimilation, had run with the uncircumcised as if in a program of renunciation. Rose had watched as Miriam
shrugged off the petitions of her Angrush cousins—Rose's sisters'
daughters, all marrying well, dentists and lawyers and diamond men,
and whispering with Miriam to ask when she'd do the same, and
how Miriam laughed them off. How Miriam mocked the petitions of
Cousin Lenny to remember where she was from, to think of the promised land even as she prepared for world revolution. In this Rose had
no particular ground on which to stand, no one but herself to thank.
So Rose's sisters would be denied the chance to gloat that Miriam
had found a Jew for herself despite Rose's Godlessness. They'd gloat
instead that Rose had reaped what she sowed—she should consider
herself lucky Miriam hadn't brought home a schvartze! This wasn't a
disaster. This was a kind of satisfaction.

Tommy Gogan came in and kissed Rose's hand. He'd put on a tie beneath his denim jacket and he knew to take off his cloth cap and the tiny burr of his accent was, if a slight put-on, nevertheless a million miles from the slack, thuggish tongue that arose typically in the collision of Irish parents and Queens streets. Underneath, his ginger hair was combed and not too long ago cut—he ran his fingers through to revive it from the pressure of the cap, showing a charming eagerness in presenting himself to his prospective mother-in-law.

Tommy Gogan had, as Rose's sisters would have said of a baby born under dubious circumstances yet nevertheless to be embraced as marvelously adequate, two arms and two legs. He had two eyes, and a nose in the middle of his face. He wanted to marry Miriam. He talked of himself as a fighter for peace and equality, not immodestly. Yes, he came from the ranks of the rather corny brothers and had appeared with them on *The Steve Allen Show*, but his own art was less traditional in the blarney sense, more directed to international themes and American styles, specifically The Blues, which term he pronounced as if Firmly Capitalized. Where had Rose heard this before?

The dungarees and dust-bowl heroes, the fershlugginer blues: The children of MacDougal Street were busy refurbishing the old fantasy. The bumpkin arts, the nobility of the country poor, the redemption lurking across some agrarian horizon just outside the city's bounds. The Popular Front all over again!

Yet Rose allowed herself, the entire evening, one single flare of sarcasm. Really, Rose could ratify falling for Tommy Gogan, a threadbare Lincoln type, a Tom Joad, and no more misguided a choice than the man she'd married. For once let Rose keep her tongue. Expected to pepper the boy with queries, apply the third degree, she merely poured the wine and listened, as Tommy Gogan's slight vanities swelled under the steady application of Miriam's adulation. Rose schooled herself to honor what had consented to appear in her pitiable apartment, with its shelf of library books arranged in the order they were to be returned, with each room darkened apart from the one she moved through, to save on the electricity bill. An old woman's apartment, she understood. The two could have run off together. Instead they'd come calling, as Rose had come to Alma. Let Rose find gratitude that a world still existed for Miriam to dwell in with such innocence that she could make each of Rose's mistakes again. In the miraculous hands of the young these were not yet mistakes. The two were in love.

Rose's grievances momentarily drowned in a sea of time, in the sameness years imposed on every human situation.

Were Rose's sisters, and Miriam's cousins, those dull daughters, those aspirant bourgeois, so right after all? Husband, a life's compass?

The whole thing was a matter of permanent wonder.

Miriam and Tommy spoke of causes and protest. Civil rights, Martin Luther King, for whom Tommy and his brothers had warmed up a crowd of Harvard students. Their politics floated in the air, unmoored in theory or party—a cloud politics. Miriam and Tommy were intent on changing the world, and why not, when they themselves were so readily changed? Brought to boiling by the fact of another. Limbs unable to quit tangling long enough to lift their forks and eat the chicken and egg noodles Rose had prepared. She suspected the lad's guitar was gathering dust lately—well, the better to play dust-bowl songs when he picked it up. You discovered yourself and what really mattered only after you passed through the lens of the fairy tale, imposed on every human female and male alike, that someone existed out in the forest of the world for you to love and marry. So let them each cross that threshold and encounter themselves in the light on the other side. Rose, therefore, only interrogated the courtier once in the manner that had surely been expected of her. It was here that she succumbed to her instant of sarcasm, though was it even sarcasm if no one present knew what you were talking about? The joke was for her alone.

"This is all well and good, young man, but let me ask you one thing."

"Yes, ma'am."

"Don't call me ma'am or for God's sake Mrs. Zimmer. I'm Rose."

"Certainly, Rose."

"Tell me this one thing. How would you feel about a chicken farm in New Jersey, should it come to that?"

4   Tommy Gogan's Second Album

After all, after all and all considered, there is no possibility of saying *no* when Rye calls you at the rooming house where you must use the telephone in the corridor where any other laborer might be listening, not that they'd much care, and says, Little brother, good brother, you had rightly best get the first plane down here because there is something about a halfway-decent Irish harmony act that at the moment has the beatnik girls soaking their underthings wringing wet and it is more than good brother Peter and I can possibly exploit by our lonesome selves. Every night we ask ourselves why destiny should have excluded you from this occasion, however long said occasion should happen to last. Forget bricks, please. Forget Canada. And forget the Delta blues. You are a certified County Antrim primitive, or you will be by the time you get here. We have you fitted for a brocade vest and have in fact informed our manager—that's right, good brother Thomas, I said manager, and he's a strange little Jewish fellow in a turtleneck—that our first recording contract ought to have places for three Gogan brothers to sign (Rye spelled the name out, "G-O-G-A-N, not Geoghan anymore, we've been advised to simplify it") for we've got a third and he's got a high sweet voice that completes our harmonies, and he only happens to be on a hiatus. That's right, I told them you were on a *hee*-ate-us, Tommy, just a *wee* stretch of the *verrrr*-ities, I insisted we'd always been a threesome. If you think

I'm talking funny, Tommy, *cor*, you should see how quickly you'll be talking funny too, when you see the effect it has on the wee *lasses* in their berets and sun*glasses*-o. For there was only one Dylan Thomas around these parts, not enough to go around and he likely couldn't hoist up the old blushing johnson anymore from the way he was carrying on at the end and so poor Mr. Dylan Thomas left his female constituency a *wee* bit unsatisfied. Therefore what he sowed so shall we reap. I said *rrrreap*, brother. For their knickers come off at a glance.

No, it is not possible to have refused Rye at the prospect of that call, and who would have wished to? Not the twenty-year-old Toronto bricklayer—born and raised in Ulster, yes, but then few were the Canadians upon whom no greater claim of citizenship elsewhere lay, whether borne lightly or heavily. No, certainly not this bricklayer, he who to take the call leaned on the wall beside the telephone in the corridor of Powell's Residence for Men, in northeastern Toronto, a mostly Scottish suburb in this vast mosaic of suburbs, where the frowning Scots-Canuck landlady had to her chagrin found herself housemother to a fresh contingent of Irish bricklayers, including himself, and she was not a friendly or forgiving sort of housemother either, least of all when it came to micks. Here in her corridor where he clutched the telephone's heavy receiver with knuckles and fingertips so dry and cracked from the laying-in and smoothing of mortar that he doubted the chances he'd lift up his Silvertone tonight after dinner. Even if willing to brave the shushing disapprobation of Mrs. Powell, rising through the transom into the room he shared with George Stack, should his and George's harmonizing voices drift above a certain volume, a measurement verifiable only by her. Often he suspected Mrs. Powell hovered at their door just waiting, such pleasure did she seem to derive from the action.

Apart from his mate George Stack, Tommy Gogan couldn't any longer recall the names of the other brickies and hod carriers there at Mrs. Powell's. For all he knew they still lived and worked there as he'd last seen them, a scattering of young northern Protestants who, by dint of an uncle's letter or because of a friendly tip from a beaverish fellow at a settlement house's labor office, on being viewed en masse were seen as unemployed men to be sorted into professions according to their birth nationalities and creeds. So the Irish had been fated to assemble the dull brick two-stories with which this young city was hurriedly fleshing itself, and in the process to have whatever was native in them be leached by Ontario's winter light.

For to leap to the Canadian provinces was to shed the lineage of European woes not for the great boorish seduction and mystery of the States. Instead it was to come to reside in a cooling zone, a place for blanching memory and grief in the cheery tolerance of Anglophone Canada. This New World where Her Majesty still squinted at you from the currency when you cashed your paycheck. A function, perhaps, of the ratio of humans to timber, to acreage, there being inordinate quantities of the latter and an incurable scarcity of the former. Such that those settling this expanse appeared to have largely huddled against the young nation's southern border for solidarity and warmth, however unpopular it might be to point this out.

Tommy's secret curse, though it hardly struck him as curse at the time, was how little credible woe he'd imported with him in the crossing. Not even a thrashing's worth. Their father could spare the three of them only a single thrashing, bestowed on Peter at age seven, just to convey the hint of tyranny behind such propriety as that of the Geoghans of Belfast. Coming of age inside the crabbed prospect of postwar Ulster, Tommy Geoghan had at sixteen fibbed his way into the Royal Navy, yet never boarded a ship that went beyond sight of land. Never earned a thrashing there either, nor even witnessed one. Bumped out after a service spent playing cards, reading Conrad Aiken and A. E. Housman and six-month-old newspapers, cooking a little, picking up a guitar. Then trailed his singing brothers to Toronto only to find them decamping immediately to contrive their fortunes in New York City.

Despite residing in Toronto nearly for two prime years of his early manhood, Tommy scarcely recalled anything, short of the ache of his brickie's forearms, the thin bite of the evening beer. The time had been spent primarily in the forgetting of the fact and flavor of Ulster. Two years to forget Ulster, then five minutes, off the train at Pennsylvania Station, there barraged with the vibrancy of his new city, to forget the Toronto suburbs and the names of his fellows at Mrs. Powell's, dim threads of memory he scrabbled now to regather, questing in the name of *material*.

Your material being evidently that which you'd shrugged off grate-fully behind you.

~~"Brickies of Ontario"~~

~~"We Should Have Made a Union (But Made a Disunion Instead)"~~

~~"Mrs. Powell's Breakfast Admonition"~~

No, he thought now in his room at the Chelsea, where the ash-tray was heaped with cigarettes and his guitar lay fallow, set on the bed insufficiently distant from the tiny hotel room's desk, and from where his notebook lay before him on that desk with naught but these absurd song titles scratched out to measure his day's efforts, no, that was merely the life that had in the space of one train crossing been shed. He'd begun shedding it as soon as Niagara Falls, where he'd been taken off the train to present to the immigration officials his passport and a letter from his eldest brother, Peter.

His earlier life, that of the shipbuilder's son, the boy in Ulster, was the life wholly falsified, once he'd arrived and inked his name to their manager's contract, pen's progress halting in the struggle to omit the surplus letters in "Geoghan." Warren Rokeach, their manager, Jew in a turtleneck as promised, issuing a small throat-growl of satisfac-tion, his franchise expanded. Tommy, having donned the brocade vest, having donned the sailor's cap and corduroy trousers, began ascend-ing the claptrap stages of the Gate of Horn and the Golden Spur, lean-ing into bare microphones to harmonize with good brothers Rye and Peter.

Petey, eldest, played their act's endearing lout—their drinker, their brawler. Draining pints onstage, Peter mumbled Celtic nonsense not even his younger brothers could decode. Rye stood as their practical joker and lady-killer, a mick Dean Martin. So Tommy slotted into his place as "the sweet one" or, when he hastily carpeted the pink of his cheeks with mutton beards and began, in their stage talk, to distinguish himself for his sympathies, "the sincere one." It seemed to Tommy Gogan in retrospect he'd been in waiting since his discharge from the British military for the world to issue a clarifying demand, to give outward shape to his hapless impostures. Or else, to accuse him of voyaging into adulthood without the proper paperwork. Now this demand made itself apparent: He was expected to produce a counterfeit of Tommy Gogan. In that disguise to voyage beyond accusation of any authority except his inmost heart.

Still, any peasant Irishman wandering in his exile into a Greenwich Village nightclub would recognize them for Ulster Protestant at one glance.

Tommy'd spent at this point a year and a half sleeping on a spare mattress at Peter's Bowery apartment, while nightly thickening the harmonies on "Old Maid in the Garret" and "The Humors of Whiskey." Afternoons when it wasn't cold he'd dress as a civilian, in slacks and a cardigan, step over the Bowery derelicts, and take with him a paperback and a pack of cigarettes to Washington Square. There he'd sit pretending to read and eavesdrop on the rehearsals of self-invention playing round the clock on that outdoor stage. The flamboyant students, the teenagers dressed as artists, making drama of their agonies as he could never have imagined doing. The unfurtive homosexual men and—more permanently astonishing—the dykes, those who pretended to be men in order to unveil their secret selves absolutely, those who faked to be real. Tommy made friends for a day or an hour with runaways, with drunk-in-the-morning poets, with charismatic Negroes who'd borrow his pocket money and cover him with praise and promises and never return. In that park you only had to open a book to have someone tell you why it was no good and you ought to read another. When an embittered painter strolled him up to a second-story saloon and explained it was where the famous expressionists did their drinking, Tommy wanted to reply that the whole city was naught but expressionists so far as the eye could see.

And you all seem famous to me.

Days spent as a lonely walker in the great mad city, he understood its genius to be that of indifference, the conferral of the sweet gift of anonymity on hordes tormented by a surplus of identity, by a surplus of wounds and legacies, and he felt himself to be one upon whom this gift was quite utterly wasted. No use to confer anonymity on a man who'd already achieved anonymity, a man for whom that was his only achievement. No use to offer absolution to the unguilty or disguise to the invisible.

The brother act's ceaseless gigging, along with Tommy's naïveté at what lay past the perimeters of the folk scene, kept him circumscribed within a handful of streets. No matter. Inside these bounds, its coffeehouses and saloons, its basements and walk-ups, was a world bottomless in its presumptions, a bedlam of fraudulence. If the brothers were faking their Irish, at least some measure of Irish lived beneath the fakery. Performers sold one another on "traditional" ethnic folk songs cribbed from Mitch Miller, on songs learned five minutes earlier or invented on the spot. Stages were booked by cynics who loathed the music, yet then turned around and let the most hapless and broke of the singers sleep in their basements and fed them hot breakfasts in the morning. Singers of hobo chants or Wobbly anthems turned out to be bluebloods, born of Ivy League families. Ramblin' Jack Elliott, the most authentic cowboy singer Tommy or anyone had met, was a Brooklyn Jew. A poshly accented actor who declaimed Shakespearean monologues on coffeehouse stages was arrested drunkenly berating commuters at Grand Central while wearing a dress and wig, a *Daily News* photograph of which was immediately pinned over the bar at the Golden Spur. The Shakespearean's real name, revealed in print, also that of a Jew, an Armenian refugee from a work camp.

Greenwich Village's Jews struck Tommy as better fakes than the rest. Their fakery seemed to derive from a fund of dispossession and self-skepticism that made them each and all exiled kings of this preposterous city.

It occurred to Tommy it might be fairly original to pretend to be a Jew, yet the notion was too odd, each time it arose in him, to ever audition saying aloud.

Nights after shows Tommy nursed his complimentary pints while his brothers got bombed or chased tail, or bragged of getting bombed and chasing tail. Tommy chased no tail. Instead Tommy stalked chimeras of authenticity in the counterfeit world. His harmless observing presence found itself begrudged nowhere. If you asked now, you'd find no one who recalled when there hadn't been a third Gogan, it seemed plain as any Rule of Three. He went where he liked, everyone's fondly regarded kid brother. Tommy examined the singers going on before and after them, sorting as best he could the committed from the ersatz; Tommy spun the Lomax field recording *Negro Prison Blues and Songs*, otherwise untouched in the stacks near Peter's stereo; Tommy unobtrusively haunted the Folklore Center and the office of *Caravan*, nodding along as the protest bards put fresh songs to tape for transcription; Tommy, though forbidden from playing it onstage, ate, slept, and bathed with his Silvertone; Tommy daily battled his limits as a guitarist, driving everyone mad with talking-blues accompaniment to himself, his long fingers if anything too long, leading to a dependence on barre chords; Tommy one day in May '59 in the back room of the Spur debuted for his brothers his own composition, "A Lynching on Pearl River." He'd written a song. He wished them to be astonished as he was. Mack Parker's body was barely dry from the dredging when the lyric came to him—coursed through his scribbling fingers, blunt pencil on a paper sack, with help from the *Herald Tribune*.

Rye scowled. "You been to Mississippi while our backs were turned, brother Tommy?" Boorish Rye disliked Negroes, had once tried to refuse on their behalf an opening slot for Nina Simone, until Peter berated sense into him.

"I can be as stirred as the next man," said Tommy. "Or don't civil rights move you at all?"

"Not one black shiny face has yet appeared at a Gogan Boys show, brother. And show me the Pinko that ever paid to hear a note of music. They don't even drop nickels in a workman's cap if it's passed. They sing the union hymns themselves, so why pay? Somebody brings an ill-tuned banjo to the rally and everybody howls along."

Peter, more damningly, put thumb to upper lip and squeezed his eyes shut, as though the tune had converged with his hangover. "I'm at a loss for the word . . . this type of number, there's a word for it, surely."

"It's a topical song," said Tommy.

"Ah, and so it is. Topical. The topic in question, is it only me that's finding it a wee bit *lugubrious*? That may be the word I was questing for."

"More lugubrious than 'The Lambs on the Green Hills,' say?"

"Fair enough, but 'Lambs' is a traditional thing, then. This of yours isn't our sort of number, is it? It's a fine curious song you've gone and written, Tom. Rather bluesish, without being actually a blues."

Rye, sensing advantage, piled on. "Not a lot of melody there, apart from your relentless strumming on that thing. We need no guitar in our group."

"Up yours, Rye."

"Ah, but your lyrical gift! Our brother has been possessed by the spirit of sheerest prose, Petey-o."

The Gogan Boys, behind cherished egalitarian façade, possessed a ruler—their eldest, stumblebum though he might rather appear. With words like *lugubrious* Petey made his directives known. The fix was in on "A Lynching on Pearl River." By the time Tommy was allowed to face a crowd with guitar in hand, the death of Mack Parker was forgotten, and Tommy Gogan's lugubrious song had been buried, too.

But Tommy learned, in the months that followed. He took care to anchor his lyrics to the tune of one of the mossiest ballads, familiar enough to beguile his brothers into doing harmony on the choruses. Peter made him wait until deep in their set—three deep, if you told time in pints—and prefaced what he introduced as Tommy's "fish-wrap songs" with a harangue out of his own fuddled politics.

So *the sincere one* became *the protest one*. "Topical Tommy," they'd not let him forget. Yet through their chivvying Peter and Rye saw the refurbishment he'd brought their act. As his lyrics debuted in the mimeographed broadsheets, as the Gogans began to appear at benefits for causes, they bridged from their old audience—moldy figs who'd fled the bebop venues, tourist-trap rubes at the Café Bizarre—to the idealists, sit-in sympathizers too distant from any segregated Woolworth's, blue-eyed girls with crushes on John Glenn and Senator Kennedy. They came to hear Tommy sing "Khrushchev's Shoe" and "Sharpeville Massacre" and "Talkin' Gary Powers Blues," these girls. So in a delayed action, needing to make himself the golden boy before he could let any gold shower upon his person, Tommy partook of that which Rye had promised. Tommy chased a little tail. Tommy broke a few hearts. Tommy bowed to the urging of a girl named Lora Sullivan and allowed her by her own hand to artfully trim and shave away his foolish sideburns and then when he caught sight of his own pretty face in the mirror broke with Lora Sullivan within twenty-four hours, an instance of assholery Rye might have bragged of, but which never entirely quit the arena of Tommy's self-recriminations.

Topical Tommy had a year in the sun, maybe that long, before the fish-wrap songs quit coming with such ease. Tommy was soon humbled, by American voices, by songsmiths with a claim and purchase on those materials he merely browsed, men who'd never dream of being photographed in a brocade vest but posed strictly in sheepskin coats while squinting at skylines from rooftops, men in the presence of whom though he was most certainly their elder he felt as tongue-tied and chagrined as the younger sibling he was to his core.

In some excess of gratitude at being there in the first place Tommy couldn't keep from grinning and glad-handing from the stage like the Gogan Boy he was, no matter if the subject was potato famine, busted levee, or electric chair. Out of what his mum would have called *respect* and in memory of brickie days, he still wore a tie, feeling it was an affront to a true workingman to assume a workman's clothes.

The new singers coming along just now felt no such compunction. Wherever they had or had not originated, they donned the cloth cap and the scowl.

These were cool customers indeed.

Tommy wondered if he had what it took to fake himself up yet another outfit and a manner to go with it.

Later Tommy imagined he could trace it all back to a cad's vanity in tossing over the Sullivan girl, and wished or imagined he wished to find a way to telephone her and went so far as to leaf through a Penguin William Blake where he'd sworn he'd jotted her number. A girl from Ohio and rumor was she'd gone back there.

~~"Sideburns Raining to the Floor"~~

~~"I Held the Door, Phil Ochs Walked In"~~

~~"Tried to Visit Woody on His Deathbed Too (But Ended Up in the Bronx)"~~

Yet burnishing private myths, revisiting girlfriends, ruing forks in roads, these too were blind alleys, indulgences of the blocked writer. In his Chelsea Hotel room Tommy Gogan lit another cigarette, his last. After this he'd have to go out into the night for a pack—for night had long since fallen. He knew frankly how Lora Sullivan had bored him. There was no song to be gleaned in recollecting a girl who bored you. That life had been, in truth, another counterfeit, the dry run for a self-devising that could stick. That faltering, sporadically splendid interval while he was still in brocade, still on Peter's pullout bed, that interval during which he'd located a protester's voice yet remained a sibling, one fully and unprotestingly beneath the thumb not only of Peter and Rye but soon of Phil and Bobby as well—that had been a life of mere fumbling postures, of sincerities faked sincerely and passions faked passionately and all of it only preamble, so it seemed, to the day when his whole self would be captivated and catalyzed by Miriam Zimmer.

It was one famous wintry morning in February '60 when he trekked to Corona Park in a famous howling snowstorm in the company of a famous young white blues singer to pay call on a famous old black blues singer, one who was also an ordained minister, and so, as the legend would be carried between them for the rest of their lives, he and Miriam Zimmer ought to have asked the reverend to marry them on the spot. The enlivening fame of it all—of Dave Van Ronk and the Reverend Gary Davis, and the fame of the storm, photographs of which dominated the papers the next two days, halted plows and choked subway entrances and skiers in Central Park—became subsumed into the mad dream of that day and those immediately following, the intramural fame of two lovers' discovery of each other. He'd wonder forever and find no good answer to why on earth he'd braved the storm in Van Ronk's borrowed Nash Rambler to go sit at Gary Davis's feet to witness a tutorial on fingerpicking the riff to "Candy Man," he who fingerpicked (or so the joke went) as if his right hand was a foot, and a duck's webbed one at that. Why he'd overcome what Miriam would later explain to him was his "classic case of borough-phobia" for the expedition to Queens. Tommy supposed the answer was that he and Peter had been clashing, as they did, and he'd sought an excuse to vacate the Bowery loft and just then had run into Van Ronk. Who knew whether Van Ronk was even clear on Tommy's name before then, but in his gregariousness the older folkie swept Tommy along. There was in retrospect something servile in Tommy's apprenticeship—a doggish willingness to follow Bob Gibson or Fred Neil on a trip to buy groceries or to the toilet that might not have been wholly attractive. Yet there was a romance in visiting the reverend. If there were songs to come they should come from recollection of this sort of day.

She'd been at the table with the reverend's wife. The house was tiny, in a suburb of tiny houses on tilted streets, snow piling up like it might bury the whole thing by the time they scraped into a parking spot using garbage-can lids, then scurried inside to warm up their hands. Gary Davis occupied his chair with the solemn posture of a wooden carving, aside from the flurry at his frets and the tapping of his right shoe, wearing shades indoors, for he was blind and likely never removed them, indoors or out.

To enter this sanctum of warmth and coffee savor, such unexpected distance from Manhattan and on a day when the boundaries of night and day, curb and cobblestone, roof and sky were all effaced in white, was a sublime transport. Astonishment to Tommy, forever a seaman clinging to shore, exile but no wanderer, mouse in the Greenwich Village maze from which he neglected even to seek an exit. She sat at the table in the kitchen with the reverend's wife and another couple of Negro women—Tommy was fairly sure there had been another couple of Negro women in the kitchen, dressed like younger versions of Missus Annie, as she was introduced. Daughters perhaps. Another white man had preceded them in their visit here, sat in study with his own guitar on the sofa across from the reverend. Tommy recognized him, Barry Kornfeld, a banjo player, Tommy thought. Tommy felt a stab of exclusion at the belatedness of his arrival in the reverend's parlor as in life itself totally, even before he saw Miriam and conceived the jealous notion that Kornfeld might be her boyfriend. She didn't get up immediately but beckoned in friendly hilarity to see Van Ronk stomping his feet clean at the foyer, hale greeting like that of one pal calling to another across two West Fourth Street subway platforms.

Kornfeld wasn't her boyfriend. Or wasn't any longer. Tommy was never to press Miriam for the facts of her relations before, least of all to any singers or guitar players preceding him. She was twenty years old—well, almost twenty, she'd corrected later—and a MacDougal Street familiar, diaphragm in her purse until she could be among the Pill's first customers. Whatever went on before had been blown away for her as totally as it had for him, or if not he didn't care to know.

He'd learn soon enough from her own lips she was a confidante of both Phil Ochs's and Mary Travers's, also that she worked at the Conrad Shop on MacDougal and Third, piercing comers' ears by hand with a safety pin and an ice cube, radicalizing lobes one at a time. (Lacking her phone number, he'd have to visit the jewelry shop to find her the second time.) He'd learn of Rose the Red mayor of Sunnyside and of Albert the spy. For now he wished to repossess that instant she'd first come into the parlor.

The reverend had been slowing down an arrangement of "Sportin' Life Blues" so the younger men could follow.

Someone placed a saucer with a piece of fresh crumb coffee cake awkwardly on Tommy's knees.

Plucked notes rising to the steamed windowpanes and beyond, to cold heaven.

To hold on, if he could, to that moment she stood from her place at the table with the reverend's wife and entered the parlor where the men sat. To halt that instant and try to see her face as he first saw it. To know what it might be like to have gazed into her eyes before she began talking.

———————

By the time he took anything remotely like full stock she'd donned her own sunglasses, dark Wayfarers, well advised in the pale blare of the storm. Therefore to gaze in the direction of her eyes was only to watch the fat flakes spatter against those dark windshields below her wild unhatted raven-black hair—which, captured in disorganization by a broad mother-of-pearl clasp, collected a bonnet of snow at the outermost, where the heat of her body left it unmelted, as blobs clung unmelted to the shoulders and front of her coarse heavy checkerboard coat. Beneath that only her black-stockinged legs appeared, her skirt briefer than the coat's hem. Becoming bored at the guitar lesson (as Tommy himself was bored, the reverend working the same changes a hundred times over with Van Ronk and Kornfeld, and Tommy'd not brought his guitar and so felt unmanned yet perhaps not so unmanned as he'd have felt attempting to follow the old wizard's fingering), she'd excused herself to Missus Annie and the men and insisted the el would still be working and that she knew her way and maybe Tommy would care to walk her? He would care to, yes.

The two tumbled and staggered together on the clotted sidewalks, the whole sky swirling mad flakes plunging to melt at the heat of their cheeks and tongue and hands or array on her coat. By this time she'd been talking so much he couldn't regain his head, couldn't recapture his ground. Before he'd begun to ask she'd said, *Yes, I know who you are. I've seen you sing.* Had they met before? He couldn't imagine it but feared he'd forgotten her in some passage of stage dizziness, the bewilderments typical in the company of his brothers. No, they'd not met, not exactly. But she knew him. And now he knew her. Miriam Zimmer.

She said, *I know who you are.* As if to know Tommy Gogan's name was to possess knowledge of some definite person who bore it, knowledge he lacked himself.

And then by acting as if it were so, she made it so.

Beginning that famous day in the snow when she drew him back to Peter's loft and they shared some reefer and then brewed a pot of coffee for the derelicts and she explained to him why the Bowery was called what it was.

The el barely slugged along its rail where snow had amassed, their car entirely empty though the trains tottering past on the opposite track bulged with the snow-fearful workers fleeing the island at three in the afternoon while they could, as though Manhattan had been hit by the hydrogen bomb and only fools would go in the direction they did, and as they inched into the tunnel the skyline was effaced, white turned to black, and still she wore her sunglasses, and for all he knew he'd missed forever his chance to see her eyes.

———

He'd had a puff of reefer two or three times before and found it not a revelation, not like this day, but which was chicken and which egg on such a day of revelation? In defense against the onslaught he'd picked up his Silvertone, shoring his fumbling tongue with a few barre chords, no advantage in putting his fingerpicking against the reverend's. Thank Christ, Peter was out, no sign where. The dark fell almost before they'd gotten upstairs, but they did nothing but light Peter's candlesticks. She arranged both their shoes on the clanking radiator then found her way to the cabinets and uncorked a bottle of red wine she discovered there, filled two juice glasses halfway. The reefer came out of her handbag as if she'd planned it, this absconding, this near kidnapping. She lit it on a candle. They'd kissed already once, everything else not delivered but promised, in the snow-smashed route from the subway, no saying who'd initiated what as their plunging footfalls arranged collisions. Not so once indoors, where couch, armchair, man's body with coat removed, woman's body with coat removed, table between them, door for possible entrances or exits, all stood at a concrete and painful distance to be navigated with deliberation or not at all. His skin hived with risk, supersensitivity to her presence, the soda prickle of frozen extremities reclaiming life, dread of the clock's advancement to some outcome.

"Here's the first song I ever wrote," he said, and began strumming the opening chords of "A Lynching on Pearl River." Tommy hoped to authenticate the impossible Jewess's attentiveness by retracing his steps, the tenuous construction of a persona independent from the Gogan Boys. Though she must be a fan, she acted like no fan he'd met before. Anyhow, at this moment, in the flood of marijuana feeling, *he* wished to hear the song, which encrypted a defiance against his brothers he'd barely tasted before it had been rebuffed. So, finishing the first instrumental pass, he sang out the lyric for all he was worth.

"That's the first, huh?"

"Yes—yes."

"Then play me the one after that."

She leaned forward, not missing a thing. He almost wished she would—miss a thing, turn aside. She'd shed her Wayfarers now, with the result only that he couldn't look at her directly. Her attentions had seemed to him like a glorious bottle into which he'd hope to slip himself and then expand, like a model ship, sails tucked until the moment they rose to occupy every corner. Instead, he felt like a lightning bug, zooming inside only to be swallowed, rebounding against the impassive glass, pulsing a small light so as not to be lost inside.

Oughtn't the reefer have make her distractible? It hadn't. The world was close around them, eye of the storm, dark fallen entirely outside the windows. Tommy had gone from finding it difficult to imagine Peter staying away a minute longer to a willed certainty that his brother had anchored himself at the bar of McSorley's or the Spur and would ride out the night laid upon or beneath a wooden bench. Or had Tommy forgotten a gig? The prospect was incredible, yet injected him with fear. Then he considered how any gig would be scotched in this blizzard. Miriam Zimmer went on talking whenever Tommy paused in his playing, and he at once drank her talk in and missed it entirely, besotted as he was with interior murmurings, now vain, now flagellating, now quizzical. The difficulty in beholding another person was how you stood in your own way. To be struck open, as Tommy had just now been struck, was to wade into a mire of self-beholding.

"For an Irishman you sure sing an awful lot about blacks."

He'd just unspooled a slack rendition of "Sharpeville Massacre." This recital might be veering into something more resembling a pleading audition, as he scraped the bottom of his own small catalogue. If her remark was provocation, nothing in her expression gave it away. He couldn't quite think how to answer her, not in her own language. He didn't possess any other.

"Did I make you uncomfortable? Would you rather I said 'Negroes'?"

"I suppose I do sing of them a lot," he managed. "Maybe just to harass Rye."

"South Africa, Haiti, Mississippi—hell, Tom, have you traveled to any of these places?"

"I'm defenseless to the charges, which you're hardly the first to lay down. My way of composing is to plunder newspaper headlines."

"You should visit the South, I hear it's a head trip."

"I've thought I'd like to, but minstrel trios aren't so much in demand."

"I mean without your brothers."

"Ah. Maybe I should. Peter keeps us working, though. There's scarcely an interruption."

"What's missing are *voices*, Tom."

"Missing from what?"

"The songs." Her words were neither chiding nor gentle, just laid as level and irrefutable as a brick set into its proper place. It might be that no one had ever listened to him sing until this instant, not even himself. His mother called him Thomas; his father, son; his brothers, Tommy. Nobody'd ever called him Tom.

"We've got blacks—Negroes—of our own," she said. "I mean, you only have to go *downstairs*." They'd stepped, as a matter of necessity, over and around huddled figures making nests in the storm, just to arrive at Peter's doorstep. The men littering the Bowery were black by definition (it was at this moment that he resolved to join her in exchanging the one word for the other), whatever the shades of their faces. They were blackened by condemnation, in wretched black tattered cloth, in shadow. Tommy never saw them if he could help it.

He schooled himself to see *her* now, gaze past her blinding allure, her decorations and aura, the several bracelets clanking as she waved her hand, her beatnik's wrinkled plaid skirt and thin turtleneck, the raven cackle of her hair, instead to meet her seeking hazel eyes beneath thick-arched brows, to address the twist of her wide lips, which at their infrequent rest formed a smirk so perpetual, so embracing in its implications, it absolved its recipient of individual judgment: By pronouncement of this woman's look you were swept into a condition of universal exasperation and forgiveness at once. And then her nose, so thick and bowed it was like a Jew's nose in caricature. You half expected it to be lifted off when the sunglasses were removed. This prole nose sat unenchanted by the enchantment all around it, a blot of humanity.

"Let's brew them a pot of coffee."

"Who?"

"The guys downstairs, if they aren't frozen into statues already. Come on." She leapt up, began shoveling grind into his brother's percolator.

"Served in what?"

"We'll bring down cups, collect them after."

"We can't serve them all."

"Who said all?" She hunted in sink and cabinet. "What say we serve four? You guys are awfully skimpy on china. Not expecting more than two overnight guests at a go, huh?"

He could only gape.

"Nothing more in storage?" She put on her coat and shoved ceramic cups into its two big pockets.

"Here," he said, ducking into the bathroom and taking Peter's meerschaum shaving mug from atop the sink. He chucked the brush aside and rinsed it clean. "Five."

Miriam goggled at the meerschaum mug's beard and scowl. "Holy shit, talk about your gruesome clichés. This is the last household that ought to feature leprechaun tchotchkes."

"That's no leprechaun. He's the Green Man."

"You say po*tah*-to, I say po*tay*-to."

Reclaiming shoes not dried, but now poached and reeking from their spell atop the radiator, Tommy and Miriam ferried the fresh pot and the five cups down two flights, out into a storm trickling to a conclusion. Under windless streetlamps the creaking white hand blanketed the world's contours, each sill and lintel, all God's immobile windshields and volcanic trash cans. The sole exception the human figures who struggled past, punching out of caverns with their knees, huffing steam into fingerless gloves. Miriam found her five huddling in a fleabag hotel's entranceway. She distributed cups and poured the first service, then planted the pot in a mound at their feet, where it scorched a hole for itself to rest in. The Green Man was shoved into the chafed hands of a black derelict with leathery, pitted cheeks, gelid eyes yellow as corn.

"Top yourselves off, there's enough to go around. We'll return in fifteen minutes to collect the utensils, gentlemen."

She tugged his elbow, and they slugged in the tracks others had forged by now, toward Houston. "C'mon, let's get a tattoo."

"I don't think they're open."

"I'm kidding. Look, up there's where Rothko paints."

"Is that what you wanted me to see?" Pollock and Kline and de Kooning were, like Dylan Thomas and Jack Kerouac, names sticking to Village chimeras sighted only instants earlier, further evidence you'd arrived to this great party too late.

"No, look." She pointed across the wide intersection at Houston. "*This* is the Bowery, right here." Gesturing at the air.

"I don't understand."

"I didn't expect you to. Know why it's called the Bowery? This used to be where New York *ended*." She directed his attention behind them, the direction they'd come. "The Dutch, they had this footpath, leading to the farms and woods. There was a bower here, like a giant arbor." This, she drew in the mote-strewn air above. "You pass through the Bowery, you'd exited the city, into the wilderness."

Tommy saw what she wished him to. The phantasmal cityscape above Houston might revert to wild before the snows melted off.

"I've been living here, with no idea at all."

"Nobody knows this stuff," she bragged.

"Somebody could write a song about this."

"Somebody could write a *great* song about this." These words, she whispered. If he could he'd have used his scarf to bind her mouth to his ear, to hear again the electrical hush of her voice in the canyons of the halted storm.

"See, if you think about it, that's probably the reason the bums and old sailors stack up here. They're waiting to pass through, even if they don't realize it. Petitioning for entry, like in a Kafka story."

"Yes."

"Entry to the gardens."

"Yes. To Eden."

"Sure," she said. "Or else up to Fourteenth Street in hopes of a cut-rate fuck."

Nothing in *The Pelican Anthology of Love Poetry* had prepared him remotely. That Tommy could see the girl sought to topple and outrage him was no help. He was toppled and outraged. She was a child-woman, with the eerie savage preternaturality of a ten-year-old, the sort that stared at and through you on public transport. Yet with the self-possession of someone older than herself, a worldly spectator. The *mother* of the child on the bus. Having evidently skipped the raw stage between, where he'd stuck. *Older sister I never had.* He was mortified by the cruddy predictability of the expression. And the presumption of *had.* Was he *having* her? Did he *have* her? (Rye would undoubtedly say no.) After this storm in which the sun had been blotted out, the clock destroyed, what should happen? Was he supposed to take her to bed? Did love at first sight mean you weren't to let the person out of your sight once you'd spotted them?

"You don't need to pretend you're in wherever, in *Algeria*, Tom. Or the Delta. I mean, look, even the Reverend Gary Davis moved to Queens. Those guys down there, they're the real thing. This shit is all *around* us."

This proclamation she'd made on the stairs, as they returned bearing the cups and coffeepot collected from the destroyed men huddling in the flophouse entranceway. The derelicts had drained the coffee and then handed over the cups in mute crushed gratitude, except Miriam had pushed the meerschaum shaving mug back into the crabbed claws of the one who'd held it. "Keep it, buddy. That's a good luck charm. They call it *the Green Man*." He'd moved his mouth in reply, yet nothing was audible apart from his address to Miriam, as "miss."

"You really talk to these guys, you find out they riveted girders on the Empire State Building, or got a Purple Heart at the Bulge, or played cornet in Henderson's band. They're always about a thousand percent more interesting than whatever dumb pitying story you've told yourself—*that's* what some genius ought to get into a song."

Before Miriam Zimmer's vision could be further developed it met its nullification in the form of Peter Gogan, slushy tracks of his unremoved boots demarcating his beery suspicious perambulation of the apartment. He'd been examining the condition they'd left it in when fleeing in their bolt of inspiration, candles guttering, red inches in juice glasses, smoking traces in the ashtray.

"Someone's been . . . sitting . . . in . . . *my* . . . chair," Miriam whispered.

"Why, hello, good brother," said Peter. "Some weather we're having, eh? Be a gentleman now and introduce me to your lady friend."

While Tommy sought his voice Miriam pushed the snow-streaked coffeepot into Peter's hands, then began unloading cups from the pockets of her coat, as in a magic act. She barely entered the apartment, arranging the cups on the shelves nearest the door. "My name is Miriam Zimmerfarbstein, I'm from Students Against Kitsch, and I'm horrendously sorry to have to announce, Good Brother Gogan, that my colleague and I have just taken it upon ourselves *to liberate your unicorn*."

"My unicorn, you say?"

"She means . . . your leprechaun," Tommy managed, and at the word he and Miriam collapsed in shambles of hilarity there in the doorway, skating into a puddle of their own melting shoes and trouser cuffs. Their limbs glided together, coats like a tent collapsed, brains dissolving in a fever of mirth, whole selves liquid except now in the tangle between them for the first time Tommy felt his hard-on like a brick unlaid, a brick burning for the cool balm of mortar, and then Miriam was on her feet abandoning him there, not even straightening her hair or coat or uncrossing her wild eyes but said, "I've got to go, good night to you both, Gogan Boys," and was down the stairs and gone.

––––––––––

"Your brother knows about this?" Saying "brother," Warren Rokeach meant Peter. Rye could—would—care less. They sat on woven mats in Rokeach's office, where Tommy had been just twice, first nearly three years ago, whisked from Penn Station to ink his new name to their general agreement, then again a few months later to meet the A&R man from Vanguard records and sign the contract for *A Fireside Evening with the Gogan Boys*. The place was considerably changed. Then, it had been a hive of professional evidence, walls pushpinned with flyers commemorating Rokeach's roster of acts at career highs, playing Carnegie and Town Hall, glossy head shots, mock-ups for album covers, gunmetal filing cabinets with bulging drawers, wide metal desk heaped with papers and tape reels. All gone now, replaced with a low table of simple blond wood, around which Tommy and Miriam and Warren Rokeach sat cross-legged, sipping, from cups without handles, tea that smelled of carpenter's glue. Rokeach had been flying to the coast; Rokeach had befriended Alan Watts; Rokeach was "getting heavily into Zen Buddhism"; in favor of Japanalia Rokeach had divested his office of evidence of striving, preening, or neurosis, aspects reduced to making testimony from his as yet un-Buddhafied person. For Warren Rokeach's face and voice and mannerisms remained entrenched in decades of self-regard, of laying it on the line, of being he whom after a handshake you counted your fingers. Equally un-Buddhafied, the tension-worm of vein at his flat high temples. Rokeach's fingertip visited the worm, then scratched at the periphery of his neat-trimmed salt-and-pepper beard. "You gotta decide now what your intention is in this deal, because in my opinion this isn't a thing where you can go just partway."

"My thinking was to have you hear the songs," said Tommy. "I want to do what's best for the material."

"Best for the material, that was your thinking, huh? What I'm hearing is you want me to do your thinking for you." Rokeach's eyes shot to Miriam. "Your girlfriend here is biting her tongue. She wants to jump in on your behalf—*she's* done some thinking."

"We're to be married in December."

"That's great, because you've already got a manager. Relax, I'm joking."

Tommy, seated rather awkwardly on the mat, his guitar braced high across his tensed knees, had played "Alfonso Robinson," "Bernard Bibbs," "Howard Ealy," and the album opener, "Overture to Bowery of the Forgotten," those four songs from *Bowery of the Forgotten: A Blues Cycle* that were finished enough to play. "To Pass Beneath the Bower," the finale, was not complete enough to audition. Warren Rokeach had sat nodding, sometimes with his eyes closed and kneading his temple, and then he'd begun to ask questions and Tommy had explained it all to him in an adrenaline rush like that in which Tommy'd written the flurry of songs, like that in which he'd lately been living.

The songs, Rokeach was made to understand, were named for men, actual living men Tommy and Miriam had gone and interviewed in their rooms in the flophouses of the Bowery, a calamity of inspiration extending directly out of their first day together, at the reverend's parlor and on the subway and after, upstairs at Peter's and down on the street. The day of the storm. Tommy further explained: These songs were not merely documentary cameos of the discarded men inhabiting one particular flophouse but an allegory for the individual caught in the grinding gears of the American machine, that which in an allusion to Henry Miller Tommy had in one song referred to as "the air-conditioned nightmare." That Tommy and Miriam were in love wasn't concealed—their hands rested on each other's knees, their bodies grappling in each other's direction like vines to sunlight. That Tommy and Miriam were stoned out of their gourds most days by noon, not excluding here in Rokeach's office, Rokeach needn't be told. He could observe what he wished.

Tommy had acquired his own flat now, on Mott Street. Miriam returned so infrequently to the railroad apartment she shared with two students that, really, it was as if the new place was theirs together. Tommy had never lived completely on his own, gone from boarding school to navy bunk to Mrs. Powell's to Peter's pullout before the shared bliss of Mott Street. Could he be bothered to regret it? A footnote. March into April he and Miriam had stalked his subjects, bargaining their way past ill-tempered managers behind glass windows, up to rooms astounding in their decrepitude and stench, where aluminum pots of beans sat charring on Sterno cans, where the corridor toilets sat barricaded in junkie occupation, leaving only back windows and fire escapes for pissing and even apparently shitting. They bore with them gifts: White Castle burgers in grease-spotted sacks, packs of Marlboros, clean socks or plastic combs, other minor articles of daily necessity, trading raw sustenance for fantastical conversation. Miriam's intrepitude took them where Tommy couldn't have dreamed of going. Her charm opened guarded hearts to inquiry, while her ear for the vagrants' shambolic, fractured dialect translated what he'd never have fathomed as he sat jotting phrases into his notebook.

The men were both white and black and in no case ignorant of the difference. However much wrecked together like Robinson and Friday on the reefs of the Bowery, one set of outcastes still proved capable of prejudice against the other, the other of bearing the deeper stigma. Tommy and Miriam distributed hamburgers and cigarettes fairly to all comers but, when it came to the project of collecting life stories, favored scions of slavery. *We've got blacks of our own.*

The Bowery a Delta at your doorstep. Into the muck with the Jew and the blacks.

The wallflower at last entered into the dance!

Howard Ealy had said he was descended from Ethiopian kings and was the first black member of the IWW and that he had once personally tailored a suit for Theodore Roosevelt. Alfonso Robinson, a short-order cook and proponent of phrenological science, gifted them with figures of men he carved from used matchsticks, featuring tiny splintery penises. Bernard Bibbs, going one better, arranged after their interview to expose himself to Miriam in the corridor, but his material was too good not to use and they didn't hold it against him.

Tommy wondered if he'd ever explain to Miriam how the Ulster boys called Catholics *niggers*.

It was always your guilt, wasn't it, blocking the way to the life before you?

But no more, not with her.

"So the songs are given the true names of these hoboes," Rokeach mused.

"Yes," said Tommy. "The songs *are* the men. There's meant to be no distance between the two."

"I get it, I'm just wondering if there's possibly going to be some legal angle and you ought to change them. But"—Rokeach raised a Zen or perhaps a Hollywood Apache hand—"we can address this later."

"It's a form I call *the living blues*," said Tommy. "The point is to leave my own voice aside, to bear witness instead."

"I like the way you're talking, from my perspective this is very attractive material, very committed material, and I sincerely want to work with you on this, Tommy. So I think we just need to proceed in a deliberate fashion vis-à-vis your brothers, if you understand. I look at your intended here and I see she does. Maybe she's already said to you what I'm thinking."

Miriam smiled.

"She's going to make me say it. She's making me nervous, Tommy, I mean in a good way. The silent partner. In negotiation that's a widely underestimated technique. You let them come to you."

Never mind the small framed watercolor of Mount Fuji, Rokeach was Zen's utter opposite. The shrewd man was unnerved because Tommy had brought a Jewish girl to his office. I brought a Jew to the Jew, Tommy thought, I brought my *own* Jew. Never mind solving the Conundrum City, rather marry its exemplar, its spirit creature. Miriam Zimmer was to New York as the Green Man was to the forest, was to Sunnyside Gardens as the unicorn to its walled garden. *I wed the Jewish unicorn!* He placed his fingers to his frets and without

strumming put words to changes in his head: *Brought a Jew to you,*
now you don't know what to do. All speech, all thought, was song
to him now.

"You gotta dump 'em."

Perhaps not all speech.

"Assuming it's not taboo to say aloud what we're each of us thinking here."

Miriam spoke for the first time since they'd been introduced and
seated. "Mr. Rokeach means you should quit the Gogan Boys, Tom."

"Warren, please. You see, I knew I had another functioning brain
in the room. I heard you talking but I heard her thinking every time
you talked. You should listen to your young lady, Tommy. I couldn't
be happier for the two of you, incidentally."

Tommy felt he was in a kind of delirium. Of course this is what
he'd come to this office to be told. Or had been brought by Miriam,
since, as Rokeach plainly saw, it was she who'd egged Tommy into
requesting this private audience.

"The Gogan Boys are hands down the corniest act in my book,
Tommy. I keep them on because of loyalty and amusement and
because I book them reliably, which brings good karma on all sides,
but the routine is going exactly nowhere. The minute you joined the
act you were the best thing they had. What was corny in 1956 when
Peter and Rye walked into my office was nonetheless the good kind of
1956 corny—Eisenhower exotica. Ireland was as bohemian as anyone
could stand at the time. In 1960 Ireland is as hip as a crutch. The
Gogan Boys might as well be a rock-'n'-roll act."

What lately was exempted from new states of delirium? Tommy
was drunk on what went on between his bare body and Miriam's on
the bare mattress on the bare floor, windows without curtains but
since they lay below sight at the level of the floor it hardly mattered,
the barely furnished Mott Street flat constituting a minimalism less
strained than that of Rokeach's Zen offices. Tommy was drunk, too,
on the particulars of the derelict men in the flophouse rooms, on the
texture of their sorrow and what it had done for his art. Such gifts
weren't given mistakenly. For the first time Tommy felt himself to be
not a performer in a musical act but a musician. He was in the right
hands with the two Jews here. If Tommy's talent was of a passive

nature, if he was less a generator of his own intensities than one making of himself a prism for the intensities of others, he was nonetheless the talented one. He would be married. He would be managed. So let him be split from his brothers by the craft of these two, a craft he couldn't have conjured on his own behalf. This was their Jewish art. He absolved himself of the unspeakable stereotype by the blessing of his total and awestruck admiration.

"The appetite now is for these committed issue songs that galvanize young listeners who want to believe what they're hearing is performed with conviction by someone less hoary than Pete Seeger, God bless him. This thing of yours is terrific with the blues refrains, I want you to stick with this and I believe I could place an album like this in a serious position with a serious company immediately. You have no idea who comes sniffing around. I had a guy asking if I've got anything like a white Odetta in my books. A bunch of alter kockers sitting around dreaming of *a white Odetta* if you believe it. Just a question, have you by any chance debuted any of this material with the Boys?"

Miriam shook her head. "They haven't heard these songs. They don't even know they exist."

"Good. That'll make extricating you just a degree or two easier. Look at her, sitting there. What are you, fifteen? She's contemplating what's best for you from a very definite perspective. She could have my job, Tommy. When I go live on a mountain she's welcome to it. Did you know that I'm buying a mountain?"

"No."

"Not cheap. I'm buying it for Watts, who demonstrates no practical sense whatsoever. The bottom line on this, Tommy, is the separation ought to be total, between this material and your former activities. You're right coming to me, because if someone else tried to break up an act in my book I'd have their balls in a vise. This way, I do it myself."

The nearest Tommy and Miriam had come to a fight was when, after her urging him to find himself the Mott Street place, after forbidding him mentioning the new songs, after a series of snubs and curt remarks at gigs—Miriam borrowing a cigarette from Rye only to turn her back and shower attention on one of his discarded petitioning backstage girlfriends—Tommy had, in a hot twist of distress that he might be meant to choose between them, accused her of hating his brothers.

Miriam's look had been unsentimental. "Let me tell you a Rose story," she said.

"What's that got to do with it?"

"Listen to the story. When I was about twelve, there was this man who lived in the Gardens, Abraham Schummel, and Schummel's wife had died, and he lost his job, and then he sort of went crazy, began writing all this schizophrenic gibberish on the walls of people's houses, and ended in a breakdown. They came and took him away and his house sat empty. And a bunch of the neighbors were raising funds to engage a private doctor and to help Schummel get back in his house and Rose refused. And you have to remember, my mother at this point defines herself as *the* most community-minded, neighbors looking out for neighbors is her constant refrain, and I at twelve am still innocent as to what grudge she bears for Schummel, I see him as a victim too because of the misfortune. And Rose said, I'm quoting exactly, *He was a bastard to begin with.* If you fix Abe Schummel's mental illness, she said, you get yourself a mentally repaired bastard. If you put him back in his house and job you've got a bastard with a house and a job. Because some things can't be fixed."

"I'm to draw from your fine parable that my brothers are like this man Schummel. Unfixable bastards."

"This is what growing up and having someone else dislike your family is *for*, Tom. So you can quit thinking it's your personal burden, some problem you alone can solve. It frees you to see them as plain workaday assholes like the rest."

Ah, and then Rose. Speaking of the unfixable. Rose, the wonderment of Tommy's new life. Rose, the unmistakable point of origin for Miriam's intractability, her cynicism and ideals, her New York native's expertise, and yet again, the point of origin for the force Miriam brought to the struggle *against* her point of origin—against Rose, who occupied the ground Miriam had had to flee from. Against the dead utopian Gardens. They spoke on the telephone every single day, mother and daughter, often for as much as an hour. Sorting grievances, intricate politics of the living and dead, the exclusion of blacks from the Queensboro Public Library's board and how to weigh Stalin's starvations in the Ukraine against the ovens of Hitler.

If Miriam was the Jewish unicorn, she whom Tommy had sought without knowing she existed, Rose might be she whom Tommy had hoped not to find waiting (without knowing she existed, either): the toad in the unicorn's garden.

What if the toad knew something the unicorn didn't?

Schummel a bastard to begin with.

Some things can't be fixed, but *which* things?

Tommy and Miriam rode the 7 out to Bliss Street to visit Rose and as they walked from the el Miriam excitedly sketched the years of her youth, indicating sentimental touchstones of the borough from which she'd run screaming. Yet as they grew nearer to the Gardens, Tommy felt he was plummeting, on beyond Rose's youth, to his own. A portion of him hurtled backward to Belfast, the mysteries of Europe.

When Miriam and Rose spoke on the phone and Tommy sat in the flat's one comfortable chair, scavenged from Houston Street, pretending to tune his guitar, instead trying to make sense of their talk, thinking of the laundry trucks decorated with swastikas he'd seen on a visit to Dublin, and his secret uncertainty as a boy as to what side of the war an Irishman was on.

Miriam's ascent in Tommy's sky was to free him, then, from the leaden orbit of Peter and Rye. Mounting revolution against the Gogan regime was prerequisite to gaining an adult life. How, then, to navigate Rose Zimmer? On the one hand, Miriam could be said to have broken from Rose at fourteen, a matter of sheer psychic survival, like clawing out of a bomb crater. On the other, Rose had never even begun to be overthrown. She loomed monumental, a dark tower, a ziggurat. The toad might not merely be bigger than the unicorn; the toad might be bigger than the *garden*. Of Tommy she demanded nothing specific in the way of behavior or attitude, in exchange for his steady contemplation of that which wasn't to be solved by any man. Look ye upon my works and despair.

When Rose laughed up her sleeve, the sleeve was the twentieth century. You were *living* in her sleeve.

Was Tommy to love Rose? She'd brought Miriam into being, a point in her favor. Yet the prospect was terrifying and he wouldn't have known how to begin. Was Tommy to hate her? Miriam hated her mother enough for both of them—little margin there. And then again, again and at last, Miriam shared with her mother a depth of affection such as to make Tommy jealous as a lover and as a son. His own mother wrote letters, one a month, folded into blue tissue envelopes boundaried with red and white stripes, her fountain script flowery and microscopic and barely worth the strain, so humdrum were her homilies. Tommy wrote back, into the uncomprehending Ulster past, that which refused to grant that it was past, a storybook from which he'd graduated.

His mother wrote to ask Tommy if he had warm socks in winter. She wrote to ask him to petition Rye please to send her a note. She wrote in every letter that the music shop on Burdon Lane still did a tidy business with *Fireside Evening*.

Which made it the sole music shop on the planet doing so. And he wouldn't be shocked to hear that for every copy sold his mother brought the proprietors on Burdon Lane a warm gooseberry pie— made, of course, by the housekeeper.

When he wrote to say he was going to marry, his mother cabled immediately to ask if he would be "bringing the girl over." When Tommy wrote explaining a visit would have to wait because of career opportunities, and that in their happy rush they would be wed in a small ceremony in the front parlor of a minister in Queens, New York, with just a handful of friends and needless to say his brothers in attendance, it was with measurable relief that his mother gave her blessing. (The check enclosed in this letter made a useful fund for Chinese food and marijuana the night of the day of the ceremony.) Though there was, as he expected, no consideration of his parents crossing the pond themselves (in which case it would need to be clarified that the minister in question was a blind black singer), suffice it to say they looked forward to meeting the girl, and any photographs Tommy might send would be greatly enjoyed.

"Yes, certainly," Tommy said to Warren Rokeach now. "I must be severed from the Boys as neatly as possible."

"Strictly for the sake of the new work."

"Strictly for the sake of the new work."

Yes, yes, it must be this. If it was to come to anything, this Chelsea night, "the Night of the Short Cigarettes," as Tommy was inclined to dub it now, watching his last Marlboro dwindle, soon to join the butts raining ash on the cracked linoleum tile of this dire hotel's floor. *Tommy Gogan's Second Album*, if it be animated by wellsprings deep within him, as he knew it ought, must gather its force and substance from the Tommy Gogan that had sprung into being that day of the snowstorm, that found its beginning in the reverend's parlor. He must regain that essence of selfish munificence, of benevolent egotism, in which his guitar had never left his grasp except to be replaced by Miriam—Picasso days, when guitar and woman's body, waist and hips and neck, and the way he played on both, became mixed up and entirely one thing. Those days when for him song seemed to flow even from the speech of passersby—a black in argument with a shop owner, a Dominican cabdriver's paean to the Statue of Liberty—or from the calamitous roar of an el plummeting below ground, from the barstool revolutionary's rumor of a gunpoint eviction or a forced confession, from Cousin Lenny's insane baseball scheme, practically from a dog's waning bark on a distant fire escape. Tommy had briefly possessed this city and been vehicle for its secret song, and the city seemed to want him to sing of it, all proceeding from the certainty he was wanted by Miriam. In her eyes the city had stopped to behold him. For that same instant he'd been keen to behold himself. Himself, himself, it was in himself that he must quest for the songs that wouldn't come, wouldn't permit themselves to be made. His cold guitar pulsed guilt from the bedspread.

~~"Had She Ever Lain with Rye? (Wouldn't Wish to Know)"~~
~~"My Mother-in-Law's the Real Thing, Comrades"~~
~~"Call Me Not a Tourist's Irishman"~~

He knotted his shoelaces and thrust himself from the room, leaving the guitar but taking the notebook and pen along just in case. The Chelsea's corridors were as vast and wide as the rooms were cramped and oppressive, though no better appointed, the carpet oiled and ratty with a thousand years' worth of footfalls. Still, the size of the corridor seemed to mock that of his room. The lobby even worse, absurd chandeliers and walls thick with paintings and the furniture bobbing everywhere as if at sea. New York hotels had a certain Potemkin village aspect, a false front meant to impress—whom?—with fulsome public space. Meanwhile, quarters narrow as a coffin. Tommy's room was a place to die, not to compose an LP's worth of confessional songs, as he'd been commanded by Warren Rokeach, who in desperation at his client's blockage had booked him five nights in the hotel, drawing against Tommy's advance from the record company to pay for it, Warren having bankrupted himself in the purchase of a mountain. Perhaps this was Warren's disguised intent: Enter your room there and die. A second album will never exist and Verve Records wants free of the contract and is willing to front you a suicide room at the Chelsea to be shed of you.

The evening was cool, summer air cleansed by a brief shower, the weather outside an improvement on that inside his room. He found cigarettes at a newsstand at the corner of Twenty-Third Street and Sixth Avenue and noticing his hunger purchased a Gabila's knish from a hot-dog vendor there. Then embarrassed by the notebook under his arm returned with his smokes and knish to the hotel. Outside the entrance a panhandler beckoned, requesting "a quarter for something to eat" and Tommy nearly handed him the tissue-enfolded, steaming, greasy knish but thought better of it, and passed over a dollar instead.

There's a wide canyon between, on one side, the revivalist folkies and New Left topical songwriters and, on the other, the newly emergent and likely more important school of songwriters channeling the transformative currents of the contemporary scene. Emboldened by Bob Dylan, many believe this canyon one that can be nimbly leaped—alas no. Aesthetic responsibilities and a utopian sociopolitical integrity seem arduous if not impossible for most of the New Guthries littering the scene. Among those committing lemming-leaps into said canyon, none could be more poignant than Tommy Gogan's Bowery of the Forgotten, *a nauseous amalgam of keening country-blues ingratiation and arch poetry, larded through with platitudinous pity toward its subject matter. One can hardly picture the actual Negro Bowery vagabonds who donated their names and life stories to the project actually listening with any pleasure whatsoever to the wincingly meticulous enunciation and baggy verbiage of the so-called "blues" that resulted. Gogan exports the liberal condescension of Alan Lomax to the lost island of Manhattan, but hey, at least Lomax had the decency to drag a tape recorder along with him. Is my objection that Gogan drapes himself in the skin of a Delta bluesman? No—to entertain that objection I'd be obliged to reject an awful lot of what's best in the work of white singers in the recent mold, including Dylan. My objection is that Gogan drapes the bluesman's skin over so little that's his own. He drapes it on a pious dressmaker's dummy—or, more specifically, a tourist's Irishman. In a recent number like "Spanish Harlem Incident" Dylan's got the brass and, yes, the respect to want not only to suffer like a member of the underclass (Gogan's great wish) but to fuck like one too. People call Dylan arrogant, but I'll take that over Gogan's sob-sister hand-wringing any day.*

Bowery had at last been released in '64, following months of arduous composition, too long a search for a sympathetic record company, then last-minute wrangles with a Verve lawyer who'd discovered a clause in the Gogan Boys' contract requiring a duration of six months of noncompetition on the part of any solo recordings by individual members. Too late to beat certain others to the marketplace, if it could have mattered. "Who's this fellow P. K. Tooth?" Rye had growled the night they'd gathered in whiskey commiseration and spaghetti supper at the Horse Shoe. "Seventeen-year-old kid, I heard. I say we storm the offices of *The East Village Other* and knock his teeth down his throat." Miriam, who ordinarily took the opposite of Rye's view in any matter, seconded this loudly, then suggested something in a more nuanced vein, involving kidnapping the critic and locking him in a room with the Spanish Harlem hooker of his presumed fantasies.

When Tommy had sobered up from their binge Warren Rokeach told him to forget it. To go back to work. A year later he had accomplished neither. Tommy could recite long sequences from the review that had murdered his album, but he'd failed putting those, or any other words, to song. Now, reentering the hotel faced with his fourth and penultimate night of fruitless woodshedding, he felt incapable of returning yet to the measly room, to the guitar he'd not touched today.

He settled into a love seat in the cavernous lobby, devoured his knish, and wiped his greasy hands on the seat cushion. Then lit a cigarette, deciding to play hotel detective for a stretch, study the comings and goings, the Chelsea's incoherent population. Here, passing upstairs, the seemly balding Brit who'd introduced himself in the corridor, stammering to Tommy that he was writing "space fiction" as if in defense against some misunderstanding. At the desk, demanding mail the management had seized in lieu of payment, the rumored exiled Warhol girl, if she was a girl. Of that, no guarantee whatsoever. Occupying the corner by the lobby's front window, decorated with sneers of boredom, two with Beatle haircuts and nighttime sunglasses, at their feet a case for electric guitar and a small amplifier. Tommy supposed they might even be Stones or Animals or some other benighted subspecies of Beatles. Waiting at the telephone booth, having presumably given out the lobby telephone's number to some uncalling caller, the permanent-resident poet with the mien of a pickpocket. Tommy had the opposite problem, a phone number in his pocket he was trying not to call, for fear no one waited where it would ring.

Miriam had taken this opportunity to convene at a planning retreat, upstate in Kerhonkson, a war protesters' party in the woods. He would have liked to be there with her—it wasn't as though he had nothing to add to the peace movement. Miriam's nose ever to the dissident weather, she'd early that spring enlisted Tommy's voice and guitar for student teach-ins at City College and the New School, at Queens College, all her phantom alma maters. By the time of the April march on Washington Tommy'd even written a set of songs for the occasion. "Sunrise Village," "McGeorge Bundy, Not Me," and "A Student Movement Can Derail This Train" weren't meant for an LP, nor even for a slot at the microphone at the April gathering in D.C., where Tommy hadn't in any case been asked to perform. Rather, with their simple refrains and chords, the songs were calibrated to those seated in circles, for teaching to lads with ill-tuned guitars and less talent, for kindling local solidarities. Tommy hadn't even taken his instrument to Washington, instead marched with Miriam in the astonishing throng, a body among millions, the movement sprouting into being around them.

Miriam knew everyone that day, or did by the time of the bus trip back. She gathered up bosom friends with a rapidity that spun

Tommy's head. The first years, he'd had to work to understand that Miriam wasn't somehow fucking her new friends, or wanting to fuck them, whether man or woman. It was a great deal worse, in fact, to understand that Miriam's appetite for populating their lives with acolytes no less in awe of her than he'd been himself was nothing Tommy could justly forbid. Her ability to plunge into commonality with others made Tommy's gift look paltry. Miriam's was the higher music, cast in his direction less and less. Faultless in affection and support, hilarious and companionable in bed, she'd withdrawn the deep Jewish fire poured over him so copiously at the start. Tommy's guitar was a barricade he'd never learned to climb over, a needless ornament on the plain speech by which Miriam achieved routine communion with anyone: teenagers, blacks, suspicious cops, the cowboy-hatted gas station attendant where they'd come off the highway at Kerhonkson, five long days ago now.

Consummate New Yorker, she'd no driver's license, no aspiration for one. It was just the day before taking residence at the Chelsea that Tommy ferried her to the retreat, in summer rain, highway maps crumpled across her lap in the passenger seat. Kerhonkson, when they found it, was tucked into the disconcertingly named Ulster County. As if he'd never gone anywhere at all, only conjured the mystic Jewess to his father's Opel, on some teenage excursion from gray Belfast. No matter that he held the wheel, Tommy felt himself a teen beside her. Why not follow her inside? But Warren Rokeach had with magnanimity bestowed the Chelsea room; Warren Rokeach had brushed off Tommy's half-assed tape of the teach-in songs; Warren Rokeach had said it was time for Tommy to write a love song, a memory song, something "sensual," something "cinematic," something "groovy."

So Tommy had released her from the car. He helped her with her bags to the door, there greeted by the hosts. The center was run by amiable Quakers who had, Tommy suspected, no grasp of what was about to hit them, what amplitudes of reefer smoke they'd soon involuntarily ingest. She'd taken her bags and kissed him and wished him luck and he'd turned back to the humid mercies of the island in August, to the hotel from whose lobby he'd by this point phoned and left her messages four nights in a row, not once speaking with anyone who could locate her, though those he spoke with were *groovy*, they were *cinematic*, they were even *sensual* in their willingness to pass along his messages.

He wouldn't call tonight, bless the sepulchral poet for standing as an emblem of the pay telephone's uselessness. The pay telephone nothing more than a device for ridiculing human solitude.

Without doubt Kerhonkson was where the action was. In contrast to this bogus bohemia. So far as a lobby detective might care, the morose human specimens arrayed here appeared disastrously unthreatening. Supposedly some kind of creative hothouse, the Chelsea felt instead like a desultory station, a place where insolvent pretenders washed ashore or were like Tommy installed by their managers. Tommy wondered how many other failed singers were entombed upstairs. He should tour the upper floors and take depositions. His second album, *Chelsea of the Soon-to-Be-Forgotten*. Or, *Chelsea of the Forgettable: A Sob-Cycle*. Tommy's talent was, he'd begun to suspect, a load of bricks. He was growing exhausted at not being permitted to set it aside.

A man possessed by the spirit of sheer prose.

The clerk, weary of negotiations with the Factory girl, snapped on a transistor radio to drown her out. "Mr. Tambourine Man." The summer's first inescapable song, it had lately been overtaken by Dylan's own electrified vitriol. The Byrds, another false-Beatles, softening up the world for Bobby's rant. Dylan's psychedelic weariness was now rendered amazing, apparently, even to teens who'd never heard an honest folk song in their lives. Tommy's own weariness amazed only himself, and then only a little.

For two weeks now the new Dylan had poured from every radio in Greenwich Village, from parlor windows thrust wide as if to draw the last shreds of oxygen from the suffocated sidewalks, the track's sound mercurial and seasick, its scorning inquiry forcing each lonely person to give account, if only to themselves: How *does* it feel? Tommy suspected Bobby hadn't a clue in this case, for Dylan had never, like Tommy, been married and felt his wife's attention slip away. Whatever Dylan's qualifications for being its author, or lack thereof, the despicable song seemed to magnify loneliness: Each time you heard it, it acted as a mirror bringing your face disastrously close, forced you to study gray-fleshed sockets, to encounter the red-threaded yolks of your eyes. It did this, even as it declared its listener, officially, *invisible*.

Was this, at last, Tommy's woe, his grievance? Only if he kidded himself that his art reached deeper into his life than he presently suspected it did. He was disgruntled less on his own behalf than on that of Van Ronk, Clayton, so many others, all swallowed and disgorged, all eclipsed, all savaged by the splenetic fusillade pouring from the radio. For, what was it to believe yourself part of a cadre of voices, a zone, a scene, *a field of engagement* defined by its range and relevance— for what was it to be a *folk*? If not, well, *what*? What, that wouldn't frighten Tommy to put in words, even to himself?

Yet the thing that had just now collapsed was also a sketch for a better world that might be. Tommy did believe it, however appalling to confess. And so, to think yourself defined, however cursory one's own talent, by immersion in a collective voicing deeper than that of which any sole practitioner could be capable, and then to have every third remark be did you ever open for *Dylan*, did you ever meet *Dylan*, was *Dylan* there is *Dylan* coming was it like *Dylan* I think I saw *Dylan* he's a second-rate *Dylan* he's no *Dylan* at all and why don't we just pull down the signs and rename all the streets here *Dylan*. The corner of *Dylan* and *Dylan* where I first saw *Dylan* but you never see him anymore, do you? Not the likes of you. Was it better or worse, to have been there at the princeling stumblebum's invention? To recognize the communal property embedded in Bobby's every utterance, or to be blissfully ignorant of all he'd devoured?

"We Didn't Open for Him, He Opened for Us (You Cunt)"

Yet even antipathy was beyond Tommy's range. He found in himself no conviction that this vanished world—one he'd entered merely as the recipient of Good Brother Rye's summons to Greenwich Village to partake of beatnik pussy—was his to enshrine or defend. To be so affronted might be Phil Ochs's prerogative. Not that of a Boy gone wrongheadedly solo. The situation was simple. Tommy had purchased a ticket. Tommy had been granted admission. Now the show was closing. Tommy Gogan was twenty-seven years old and simply needed a new gig. His next might as soon involve bricks as guitars. He heard nothing of what others did in the new music, and suspected they were pretending to hear it. The raw-scraped sonic travesties with which Bobby himself was now complicit. All commitment was gone from the songs. The poetry flayed out, too. As he sat watching the two Animals or Swine snickering behind their shades Tommy felt a certainty come to him: Their strength was numbers. The plural form, Byrds or Weasels. Now he saw the answer to the folk scene's collective riddle, as to why Bobby was cluttering up his music with Mike Bloomfield and whoever was brutalizing the electric piano. Rather than a sincere musical epiphany, the choice revealed the hunger for mates, a Beatles of one's own. Dylan, having shrunken an entire world to his sole person, was terrified by the isolation.

It shouldn't take *a complete unknown* to see it, but Tommy had an advantage in his power of recognition: He was lonely. He should have stayed a Boy. A phrase of Rose's drifted now into his thoughts. It had never, since his hearing, been too distant from them. A phrase enigmatic, or perhaps he only wished it so: "The true Communist always ends up alone." Rose had left the motto unexplained. It explained itself. Tommy left his pen in his pocket, for he couldn't wish for even an instant to sing those words, nor form them with his script, not even to cross out like the rest. There were no second albums in Tommy Gogan's notebook.

Part III   The Wit and Wisdom of Archie Bunker

1   The Guardians Association Scholarship Award

There was, first, always, this unbearable production of self: Cicero's return to the scene of the crime. The seminar room—excel too much in there and be incarcerated, be lifetime painted into the corner of your scholastic habit. *Those who can't but teach, do.* Cicero preferred to get them out of bed in the morning and get on with it, so ran Disgust and Proximity in the generally abhorred nine a.m. slot. He'd become a connoisseur of their morning odor, unshowered bodies sheathed in clothes they'd worn the night before. Cicero liked to get into what would otherwise typically be the Baginstock College undergraduates' hangover dreams, giving them the simplest reason to assassinate him on RateYourProfessor.com, sparing them the difficulty of casting around for something more esoteric. *He schedules class earlier than anyone else and then berates us for being tired.* This put them in a more receptive state than they knew, sleepy haters lashed to the mast of their Starbucks.

"Good morning, everyone. I think we're all here who are going to make it here today, so let's get under way. I intend to hijack today's class but let us first get some of the syllabus material addressed, keep this silly bus on its course. I know we have ready among us Mr. Seligman—yes? good—with his presentation on the *Journal of Personality and Social Psychology* article, that along with the chapters of Aurel Kolnai and the Hilton Als formed this week's assigned reading.

You are all keeping abreast of the reading, I hope? Just now in my idle time before class I was poking around on the blog and didn't see jack shit on the Kolnai or Als." This elicited a ripple of nonsemantic utterances, distant moans, and choked giggles. "Are we not turning the pages or is there some other problem? Are we finding the material difficult? It's too early in the semester for coasting to the finish line."

"Some of it is difficult," said Yasmin Durant, one of Cicero's lovely defiant ones, a repeat customer. Sticking up for the groggy team, yet only as adjunct to her deeper strategy, that of positioning herself as Cicero's echo and sister, his call-and-response partner in this room. Nominating herself for discipleship, Yasmin's head was beginning to cultivate its own little goat-horn nubbins, dreadbumps threatening to take up some space.

"Well, you likely are understanding more than you realize. Stick with it and we'll sort it out in here. But the more you lay down some responses, the greater your traction on the texts is likely to be. It's just a blog, people. You're not going to be graded on the language, I don't care if you comment in emoticons or Harry Potter rebus, Muggle-speak or whatever, just offer some evidence of engagement. Put your footprints on the thing." The September light fractured through tree-tops on the other side of the room's tall windows, and across the big chestnut table, punishing those students who'd lined up on the wrong side. The slant was changed. The heat had broken overnight, breeze like a tide coming in, and where the coolest streams had touched the oak trees they were tainted with irreversible yellow, Maine's seasonal hustle. Cicero might have only a few more weeks' congenial swim-ming. After that he'd have to go in for some uncongenial swimming. It had become part of his job here, to be the ineradicable blemish on the New England horizon. In the seminar room, Cicero had to unfurl pedagogy, make something occur on a weekly basis. Other days, he taught by merely existing.

In the seminar room, an incumbency. A pregnancy, even. Cicero was here to birth something each time. A secret part of him never failed to glimpse terror in the seventy-five minutes laid before him, as if he'd not destroyed such intervals successfully at least a thou-sand times previous. Actually, it was not so unlike contemplating the cold sea before immersion, then stepping off to remember he belonged there, would not dissolve there, was something the damn sea had to deal with. In fact, in the seminar room he taught by merely existing, too. Cicero was adequate simply as an exhibition, a subject for contemplation, and lately he had come to consider the production of awkward classroom silence as an alternative pedagogical implement. Say less and less. Let them plummet into that abyss of the inexpressible where the truth lies, where the action is. Telling himself this, the words always then came in a brutalizing flood. He hammered their bodies with his language and as ever the seventy-five minutes were destroyed in an eyeblink. The cream of the nation's preparatory schools limped out the door crippled by the onslaught of him again. Cicero's silence was mostly theoretical. Fuck actually sparing them, life was too short.

"You'll have noticed we have a visitor today. Sergius Gogan— welcome, Sergius, to Disgust and Proximity. These are my best and brightest here. Sergius isn't a spy from the administration, people, so you don't have to tighten up. Just an interested observer. Now, I'd like to open with a reading from the Kolnai. Page sixty-seven, if you want to follow. '*Thus disordered sexuality represents for the sense of disgust, above all what is disorderly, unclean, clammy, the unhealthy excess of life. Even spirituality in the wrong place may to the best of our knowledge arouse something like disgust. There is something disgusting in the idea of everything on earth becoming pasted over with musings and broodings . . .*' Let me skip down here: '*. . . there exists here the danger that intellectual dallying and raking about may itself come to form part of sexual life, on the strength of the enormous capacity for inflection and amalgamation with alien spheres which the sexual drive possesses . . . It belongs to the total disgust reaction that it is a matter of an essentially cumulative, infectious process, of something which lacks . . . restraint or hold, something which hones in on everything, something putrefied, and at the same time still undirected, undynamic, swirling about in its own dank atmosphere.*'"

Cicero allotted a measure of gravid silence.

"Anyone going to weigh in? Too early for you? Well, don't let it get too late. We'll keep this passage in the background for now." Next Cicero cued the student who'd prepared a ten-minute capsule for the others and leaned back in his chair. The text in question detailed a study in which volunteer subjects were made to confront their sensations of disgust at being asked to don a series of woolen sweaters ostensibly tainted with either physical or moral corruption. Cicero interrupted after the student's paraphrase became unreasonably labored. "Very good, thank you, Mr. Seligman. So what's the *point*? Is anybody surprised that these people didn't want to put on the sweater that they associated with the cockroaches or the tuberculosis even if it was steam-cleaned, even if it was *boiled*. Who here doesn't relate to this kind of magical contamination anxiety?"

Silence.

"What about the murderer's sweater? Point being, is that a different reaction? They got even fewer people to put on the one they claimed came off a murderer."

"It seems mixed up." Yasmin again. "You can't study moral revulsion like it was the same as fear of disease."

"Good. Maybe it is mixed up. If so, who mixed it up?"

Nothing.

"Mr. Seligman, I was hoping you'd mention which item topped their list of aversive sweaters—the one nobody would go near even worse than the cleaned-up-shit sweaters and so forth." His second *shit*. Cicero semiconsciously tallied certain utterances in seminar.

"Yeah, uh, the researchers found that the highest aversion was to a sweater they claimed had been worn by Adolf Hitler."

"Right. So."

Nothing.

"Adolf Hitler is an *easy* one, right? They were going easy on themselves. Or need I confirm this? Is there any lack of consensus among us on Adolf Hitler?"

The uneasy susurrus he got back was enough.

"Anyone thinking of some sweaters they *didn't* try out? You all read the paper. Some sweaters that some people might feel as sure about as you're sure about Adolf Hitler?"

Too much. Or the presence of the unwelcome guest, the Person from Porlock.

"Slow morning for y'all. Well, I'm letting you off the hook because I told you I had a hijack in mind. In the spirit of the Hilton Als book, which we will *not* address directly today because I want to see some reactions up on the blog so that next week I can call you out by name, today we're going to talk about *mothers*. Not mothers in books, because the real point of this class isn't that this stuff is trapped in books. This stuff is trapped in *bodies*, the books are for letting it out. I mean to say your own bodies, adrift through space and time, sitting there sucking on breath mints and whatever else they're doing right now."

He paused. The clock told him fifty minutes remained—the customary short hour of analysis. By Cicero's measure, nothing as yet had actually occurred. Nobody had been put on the couch. That could be okay. Let the remainder trickle, as had the first twenty-five, into the deep bank of unmemorably undisturbing classroom moments for these children of privilege—they'd meet that outcome only with a shrug of relief. *What was Lookins on about today? He called us "bodies adrift"? That could be a cool name for our band.* Nothing was required of Cicero in any regard. Not, except perhaps by that woman he'd encountered again in the midnight hour, voyaging through his special time tunnel, his reverse birth canal, the ghost at the soda-shop counter on Greenpoint Avenue jonesing as always for her next Pall Mall and yet with enough time to spare for fucking with Cicero, tearing him down to his turbulent quintessence. Had he talked with Rose for fifty minutes from the couch of his dark bed?

Cicero, the evening before, had taken mercy on Sergius Gogan, offering the guest room downstairs. After the two swimmers paddled in, dripping from the sea, Sergius dragged his duffel in from the rental car's backseat and Cicero sent him to shower, had him throw the wet cutoffs he'd used in lieu of trunks into the dryer. Then told the stray to find his way down Main Street, past the campus, instructed him to go find the second-story porch of Poseidon's Net, where he could drink a pint of beer and eat a lobster roll or haddock basket. At that, Cicero joked unhumorously, you'll have exhausted the limits of local culture. They'll have baseball on at the bar downstairs, he added, but you're stuck with the Red Sox. And, fair warning, it's also the townie pickup scene. Fresh meat gets plenty attention 'round here.

Having discharged Sergius to Poseidon's, Cicero got into his own air-conditioned car and drove beyond the town's limit to take his usual table alone at Five Islands Grill, there to enjoy a glass of cold sauvignon blanc, dine on a preliminary of oysters and a plate of their pretty fair foraged-mushroom gnocchi, and read a few chapters of *The Man Without Qualities*. The Grill, apart from department junkets with visiting speakers or job candidates, was Cicero's preserve; his colleagues were too cheap to eat there without institutional reimbursement. Cicero felt no interest in extending any ocean conversation with Sergius to dry land. Returning to find the house empty, he tuned his satellite dish to the Mets game and, pouring himself another cold glass from a bottle in his refrigerator, deep-sixed his mass into the couch.

The Mets were improved this year. Though the names grew indistinct, the players increasingly resembling Cicero's red-cheeked students, fandom was native and indissolvable in Cicero. It might be by now simply a matter of the colors, the scripted name with its dropshadow, the skyline logo—*rooting for laundry*, he'd heard it called. Contemptuous of the pull of tribal nationalism in the human psyche and, for that matter, of Ivy League narcissism in scholars ostensibly steeped in Deleuze and Guattari's view of hegemonic dominions, Cicero could humble himself contemplating his own irrational lifetime affiliation with the Mets. A thread of Fascist susceptibility lay in how Cicero fought the pull of sleep each summer night, blood quick to the chance of seeing men triumph in the same orange and blue that had limned Tom Seaver's thighs. Leni Riefenstahl, alive and well on DirecTV. Still, most nights he passed out around the seventh.

When Sergius reentered and found him asleep there, Cicero grunted and heaved himself upstairs. Possibly the wrong night to have a gander at the Mets—was it that which had invoked Rose? Well, too many reasons to need to blame the Mets. He awoke in a coil of sheets, sweaty despite the conditioned air, both arms trapped beneath his body and prickly with blood deprivation, alien companions in his bed. He had to roll to work them free, then beat his palms together to gain use enough to knead his wrists and forearms to life as well. It was before six, September light just animating the lawn's glisten where it curved to the sea. A doe and her fawn tiptoed through the window's picture, soft-footed and surely inaudible even if not drowned by the putter of the central air.

Cicero dressed, got free of the house without pausing to find out whether Sergius Gogan might be stirring in the spare bedroom, only first jotting a kitchen-counter note suggesting his houseguest visit the nine o'clock seminar if he woke in time, and giving directions to the classroom. Driving to Drury Hall, Cicero met more deer on the campus roadways, flushed from Indian-summer woods by the cool dawn, each slender as a slice of toast. Signs and portents, or global-warming symptom? In either case, he didn't hit them with his car. Arriving sooner than even the secretary, Cicero was left to brew the department coffee before he could hole up in his office. There he reinstated his professorial comportment with caffeine and another fifty pages of the Musil, unconcerning himself with the matter of his overnight guests, corporeal or otherwise. He glanced at the morning's texts, selected the paragraphs from *On Disgust*. Checked the course blog and chest-grumbled disappointment at what wasn't there.

Now, having blurted *mother*, Cicero understood he needed go through with something, even if he couldn't know exactly what. Needed to for the sake of Rose, the midnight mover. It was she who required refutation. But Cicero should be cautious. Sergius Gogan only seemed innocuous. Turning up here in Cumbow, the unprodigal son had rattled the box of savage boredom Cicero walked around inside. Yet there were others in this room beside Sergius and Cicero and the phantom of Rose in Cicero's head: his charges, his wards. In loco parentis and all that. Cicero's task was to play neutron bomb, destroy them but also leave them standing.

"There's a passage from Doris Lessing's *The Four-Gated City*, I wish I'd brought it in, but basically, this character who isn't Doris Lessing, or maybe is, but anyway, like her author she's an ex-Communist— what she says is that the problem with all utopian ideologies is they pit themselves against the tyranny of the bourgeois family, and that it's basically hopeless. It's overreaching. The deep fate of each human is to begin with their mother and father as the whole of reality and to have to forge a journey to break into the wider world, or even to begin to understand what, beyond their parents, *exists*. The exact nature of the battle might be particular, with various social determinants, genetic fate, happenstance, et cetera, but the lot is universal."

"Sounds pretty Freudian."

Lewis Starling, among Baginstock's media studies majors their callow post-humanist. Cicero was adviser to the kid's jargon-slippery thesis, concerning *search engines, Turing tests, zombies, contagion*. Starling mouthed "Freudian" with ten-foot-pole distaste, scorning the collapse of his mentor's critical framework into banality. Cicero could, if he wanted, byway through Heidegger or Gramsci to rebuke him. But no need to take it personally or waste the time. Instead he said, "No doubt, Freud was a major stakeholder in this matter of progenitors. Point being, what theorist with any regard for what we're calling 'affect' wouldn't be? *Remember the body*. Any thinker's first sustained effort in interpretation is the same one, that of unmaking our makers. Something like *Mom and Dad: A Critical Stance*. Question is, whether it'll be our last."

"I don't understand what we're supposed to be talking about." This, from Mister *Just Tell Me What I Do to Get an A in This Class*—Cicero had blocked the young pedant's name. Yet for once the kid's characteristic petition for simplification was welcome, seeing as Cicero hadn't halfway satisfied himself. His need, equally, to wreck their evasions and his own. "Listen, boys and girls, young adults, what I'm talking about is the project we're always already engaged in and will never conclude, that of unsuffocating our minds with the basic falsehoods known as everyday life. Put aside your pens, quit writing down what I'm saying. Let's talk about your mothers, *fuckers*."

Fair enough. Cicero usually allotted himself at least one. A scattering of laughs absolved him. But now he'd best reel it back in a couple of notches. "Let's remind ourselves of that term Christopher Bollas calls 'the unthought known'—the recognitions we refuse to fully articulate precisely because they are too much with us at every present moment. Say something here you know about your mother but have never said aloud. It doesn't have to be anything earth-shattering. Mr. Starling, you willing to open the floor?"

"I'm not sure. You want me to talk about something like catching my mother watching Internet porn? Not that I'm saying that actually happened, because it didn't."

"Cute, Mr. Starling." More curdled giggles around the table. This act of defiance had required more of Lewis Starling than had the earlier chafing at *Freudianism*. It had also cost Cicero more, but he tried to ignore that. "But perhaps we should turn to someone else first, yes?"

Nothing but blank faces. One girl left the room. Potty break, protest, or mere indecipherable vanishing? Cicero would be lucky if he ever learned, unless he found her staking out a complaint at his office door after class. He glanced at Yasmin Durant, but his acolyte's gaze was lowered to her lap, against the difficulty of following Cicero to this crossroads. The silence, if not deafening, was unenlivened, a baker's dozen brains in a vacuum pack. Cicero found he was slipping down the glassy face of his own mountain, to which he had addressed himself with no grappling tools whatsoever. He refused to glance at Sergius Gogan.

The children—he had, in a few effortless gestures, reduced them to children, incurring a grave responsibility too casually—could never be capable of meeting his request. Before the mountain he couldn't ascend Cicero now felt the tug of the abyss behind him, the bottomless vale between his syllabus and the ineffable lectures he *wished* to deliver. The gulf yawning between his drab duties here and the impulses that had set him on this life path, his rebellion against the ordinary thoughtless procedures of the here and now. That rebellion begun at his inability to control salivation at the sight of Tom Seaver's ass.

Why expect the nineteen-year-olds to speak intelligibly of their mothers? Most of them likely still spoke with their mothers on the telephone on a regular basis. Or Skyped. As according to Foucault, one can only be able to name a thing after it has begun to die or disappear. Political institutions, the postcolonial subject, or, for that matter, your childhood. Cicero had blundered, once again mixed up living and dead, the Frankenstein affront. Now came the pitchforks and torches, even if only those of his own mental village.

"I see," Cicero said now. He spoke as if someone among the silent students had offered up one of those clarifications that lay solely inside of his head. "Why don't I begin, in that case. You can join in as you are able. What's on my mind today is the stories that don't find themselves getting told, the questions that don't get around to getting asked. The secret people hiding behind and inside the ones that insist on being known instead. I said I would talk about my mother. *My mother is almost entirely impossible to think about.* In truth, I doubt anyone during her lifetime thought seriously about her for more than an instant or two. If I am more truthful, what little thinking about her I do even to this day consists largely of raging against the fact that barely anyone ever spent a concerted thought on her, including herself."

Another walkout. Melinda Moore, one of Cicero's most capable, who the semester before had continuously surprised Cicero and herself as she produced good close readings in her sorority voice, exiting now in a scuffle of closing laptop and pushed-in chair to make it apparent she wouldn't return. Indeed, this assembly threatened to shape into a shoe-leather vote of no confidence. Could Cicero push further, trump disaster? He could try. "What I did apart from decline to give Diane Lookins's life as a person any kind of real consideration was mostly to wish she'd go away. To wish she'd *die.* I wanted her to make it more convenient for my father, so he could go off with a white lady from the neighborhood, whom my daddy was *fucking.*" Cicero knew he was right at or just over his morning's quota for that particular word.

———————

From his earliest impressions, the family's home took for the child the shape of a field hospital, one stationed within the battlefield that was the city. Cicero was fairly certain this had nothing to do with the matter of Diane Lookins's burden of physical ailments, at least not at first. Nor was it solely because of the parents' literal professions: mother a trauma nurse (albeit only in some hazily referenced past), father a daily operative on the urban front, a policeman carrying a soldier's rank.

Instead it was a worldview, or two worldviews intricately dove-tailed out of mutual necessities. The urban soldier must recuperate somewhere, must find a place where he can be nursed—a place to offload injury, insult, grievance of all kinds. The nurse, in order to be a nurse without ever leaving the sanctuary of the apartment, needed a supply of patients, or rather the same patient every night, bearing home diverse unfleshly wounds that neither killed him nor healed. The hospital ethos that was conjured, when a person crossed the threshold into the dark, neatly kept rooms, was the function of an attitude of *triage,* directed toward the permanent emergency of being alive.

The child's sensibility and sympathies, on coming to first awareness from within that threshold, were allied with the outlook of *her*,
the nurse-who-was-also-a-patient, the woman fluttering in the dark
rooms, not the lieutenant muttering grimly home from duty. This,
because the battlefield outside was only a matter of rumor and conjec-
ture, for interpretation from minimal clues, from Douglas Lookins's
bitter snippets of reportage, flares routinely doused by his wife's plates
of food and snapped-on television, by her soothing and hushing and
not-in-front-of-the-boy, by her attention-revamping swoons, every
manner of daily thing that made sustained talking impossible.

Ailment came later, with its inadequate ritual cures, half-drained
bottles of quinine water, bitters recommended by a knowledgeable
cousin down South, shades drawn in vampirish prohibition of the sun,
the diagnosis confirming everything the child and mother already
knew. Her affliction was elusive, phantasmic, sneaking across the
threshold with a wolf's name, efflorescing in moods and colors as
much as in medical conditions. Even prescription bottles of hydroxy-
chloroquine, when those entered the scene, were drawn out of the
realm of medicine into the irrational twilight of the lupus aura. Cure
could be a mood, too, the seductive and submitting odor of Diane
Lookins adhering to curtains and bedspreads, to the telephone's heavy
receiver, to sandwich bread in a lunch box he'd open midday at school.

The dangers of the world beyond the apartment's limits were the
subject of the interrupted talk, transmitted in a series of fragments
worthy of Sappho or Pound. They suggested a world for which the
child felt himself unsuited—at first helplessly so, soon enough defiantly. Still, they had the appeal of opening the cloistered apartment
to something beyond its humid atmosphere of pity and apprehension.
The allusions to a policeman's universe of treachery bore the appeal
of mental intrigue, in a language of seductive opacity. *The Wandering Boys and the Four Horsemen. The Guardians Association. The
Payne Brothers. The James Barber Incident. The William Haynes
Incident. Reefer. Horse. King H.*

On the Take.

*Vice, Harbor, Housing, Motorcycle, Patrol, Internal Affairs,
Transit.*

One Hundred Twenty-Fifth, Convent Avenue, Twenty-Eighth Precinct.

Or simply *Harlem*, name to an abhorrent chapter in his family's life, one recent enough that the child's earliest memories flowed from it. Another home in another city, where everyone was colored and where he and his mother still occasionally journeyed to call on aunt and cousins. A time before they'd come to settle in the rooms venting to the concrete inner courtyard of Lincoln Manor, on Fortieth Street and Forty-Eighth Avenue, south of the el that overhung Queens Boulevard, south of the greener districts of Sunnyside Gardens (despite living among the white Irish and Italians and just a scattering of Dominicans and Puerto Ricans, the child gained a sense of the wrong-side-of-trackness in which they'd landed, an ache in the whole neighborhood to be *over there* instead).

On the take named a policeman's cardinal violation, and the undertow of the wave that had driven Douglas Lookins from Harlem—a wave of recriminations, of barely suppressed scandal. Of unnameable former friends and phone calls with no one speaking on the other end. From the start, on foot patrol, Douglas Lookins had been fixed in these crosshairs: the black policeman's irreconcilable crisis. Hemmed by prejudice in the wider ranks while taken by the street as a betrayer and informant, house nigger, Uncle Tom. Walking that tightrope, between a sky of distrust and a canyon of scorn, you reached out to those like you, those hunkered down and bearing up, in the same fix: your fellow black shields. You formed an *association*. There had been many of those over the decades, many now dissolved and only rumor. The black policemen's support networks, meetings conducted in basements for purposes of pooling expertise and salving disgruntlement, then also gathering, under cover of sociality, to get the wives together, to give out some award for outstanding service, like an Elks Lodge. Always, in any event, to stanch the isolation. The loneliness.

These associations, past and present, provided some of the strangest and most evocative names to be hurled out like swears from Douglas Lookins's lips: the Centurions, the nearly mythical Wandering Boys, later the Buffalo Soldiers. Above all, the Guardians Association. The sole black cops' guild to be not merely tolerated but sanctioned by the NYPD, therefore by far the lastingest and with the widest reach. So it was that Douglas Lookins, who'd skirted participation as long as he could, could feel forced, being a decorated patrol veteran and one of a paltry contingent of black lieutenants citywide, to accept an honorary post in the Guardians. He attended the ballroom ceremony to accept the honor and then turned his back on them.

Why? What could be so wrong with the beleaguered Negro policeman seeking solace among his kind?

This: Three-quarters of black cops, like any cops, were dirty. Numbers according to Douglas Lookins; go check it yourself if you want. So to make allegiance with the Guardians was to avow a brotherhood of omertà with so many hundreds of brothers *on the take*. Taking utmost seriously the height of promotion he'd reached, Douglas Lookins understood himself answerable to the brass, specifically to the deputy commissioner who'd come calling a week after promotion, coffees not even cold on the desk before he'd started asking for names.

A white deputy commissioner, and Douglas Lookins's commanding officer.

Walk a tightrope between a sky of distrust and a canyon of scorn and one of these days even that tightrope might rise up to form a noose around your neck, if it consisted of your fellow black cops keeping vows of dirty silence under auspices of the Guardians.

Having achieved your lieutenancy in Harlem, squelching black-on-black crime, walloping the shit out of kids in order that they *not* have records, breaking up picket lines of Black Muslims boycotting the Amsterdam News Building, escorting Mayor Wagner for *New York Post* campaign photographs, his tall head beside yours even taller in a sea of black kids half of whose hides you'd tanned and might again, distinguishing yourself painstakingly within *the community*, where worth and stature might be measured in what tidal floods of bodies crossed the street upon catching sight of your high, buttoned-up sentinel's form easing down the sidewalk, one week after promotion you named a bunch of names in return for the transfer to Sunnyside, there to spend your pavement hours knocking Irish kids with screwdrivers off vending machines and hearing *nigger* stage-whispered down every block you strode.

But fuck it, the beat was behind you, those dues paid. Let them disembowel every vending machine from here to the Whitestone Bridge and each other in the bargain.

The child took years understanding that his father wasn't actually the only clean black policeman in the history of the NYPD.

A few years beyond that for it to occur to him that Douglas Lookins wasn't certified stainless himself, that some shred of guilty overcompensation might lie behind all the righteousness. But no way to ever do more than wonder whether his father had once had a packet of cash thrust at him and not thrust it right back.

The child took years gathering some sense of it all in the first place, puzzling the policeman's lament out of Douglas Lookins's volunteered and unvolunteered fragments. The inescapable truth was that it was Rose who provided the keys, Rose who aided in the puzzling. This might be the core of Cicero's slavish fury at Rose: that he'd learned more about his father from an hour with Rose than from seventeen years locked inside Diane Lookins's domesticity. Their home was an institution devised *not* to understand Douglas Lookins. Not to receive his testimony, inasmuch as the last thing you wanted in a hospital was for the patient to *talk*. You wanted them to eat, yes—and you fed them to shut them up. You put on the television, fluffed a cushion, and ceded the whole couch in order that the patient stretch his long form out; you remarked on the remarkable vividness of mountain ranges behind John Wayne on the latest color set; you starched and pressed the sheets, all in favor of their comfort—and to entice the patient to slumber.

And when that didn't do the trick, you could begin dying.

Cicero used lexicon and streetwise attitude and an appetite for paradox all derived from Rose Zimmer in order to understand his father. The project was enabled because it was a mutual one, Rose herself trying to get closer to Cicero's father by means of Cicero. So the two of them could work together on that. It was from Rose that Cicero understood that his father was a strict Eisenhower–Nixon Republican—well, no shame there, loads of cops were, as was Douglas Lookins's avowed upstanding hero, Jackie Robinson (who'd even endorsed Goldwater). For that matter, James Brown was a Nixon man; Republicanism was a disease common to the self-made, the self-willed Negro.

James Brown was Douglas Lookins's surprising musical hero, acknowledged to his son once, while in a disreputable mood ("Louis Jordan's natural heir," he'd claimed). But it was from Rose that Cicero understood even to inquire about his father's music, since they owned no records and Diane controlled the kitchen radio's dial. It was from Rose that Cicero learned to imagine Douglas Lookins mourning his regular use of free seats at the Apollo, offered gratis by a Harlem bigwig, or to picture him instead listening with solitary pleasure to the radio in a police cruiser resting in the shadow of the Grand Concourse—it was from her he understood to imagine his father as being capable of taking pleasure, rather than just being out there all day brutalizing and being brutalized. It was when Cicero and Rose began comparing notes that Cicero's view of his father changed, from one derived from Diane's image of him as a monolith rumbling home needing to be dealt with and endured, fed, and eased to bed, to that of a monolith cavernous on its interior, swirling inside with *appetites*. (There was nothing wrong with the food Diane Lookins cooked, but you didn't consume it with appetite, you bovinely fed.)

Of course, it was by failing to disguise her own appetite for his father that Rose led Cicero to extrapolate his father's. For, among other things, Rose. Seeing Rose's appetite taught Cicero that appetite existed—appetite beyond Cicero's own, which might otherwise have struck him as a unique property, shamefully defining his isolation from the whole of humankind. His mother's appetite was cloaked in deference and debility, his father's in stoical fury. Well, Rose demolished the image of stoicism, among other things! Rose let herself be transparent to the child, exposing every kind of raw loneliness, and defiance against loneliness, that had fallen over her in losing Albert and the CP, and in surrendering her daughter to Greenwich Village. And then, exposing to him how loneliness and defiance produced themselves as hunger—an active process of devouring that thrilled Cicero even as it threatened to devour *him*.

Is anything more unforgivable than what a child learns about his parents from their lovers?

And who the unforgiven? Not the parent but the lover.

If Cicero had been thrust at Rose Zimmer, thrust by his father, in order to collaborate with this crazy Jew in the study of his father, who was designated to make a study of Diane Lookins? Who'd etch her legend into the world? The fact excluded, in this scheme of Rose and Cicero puzzling Douglas together, was, merely, that of Diane Lookins's entire existence. She didn't fit in the puzzle. Diane Lookins had no witness apart from her own child. He who, if he contemplated this duty, that of entering into her abjection, of fully grasping it, could only run screaming. Diane Lookins's existence was too heavy and too light, both at once, for a child to assume as a mirror of his own possibilities.

Yes, Cicero studied his mother—once he located the pleasure in study, Cicero studied *everything*. And yes, Diane Lookins in fact had a language of her own, had, even, appetites. Even after she was sick. Cicero discerned this in eavesdropped phone calls, the sultry plea-sure of her gossip, items picked up and savored in slavish delight. The sex lives of others. The *deaths* of others, which confirmed that she still lived. Cicero discerned this too in her use of newspapers and magazines, the nature of those she brought into the house, the care with which she read certain sordid items of confabulated scandal. She didn't want to hear what her husband dealt with on a daily basis, but so long as the crimes were committed by film stars, Diane Lookins *enjoyed* crimes.

What Cicero didn't and couldn't do was give one single indication to Diane that she was visible to him. Not that he studied her, or that he registered what he studied, or that it touched him. Instead he put up a mask of boyish obliviousness to his mother's dimensions—to do otherwise would have been too costly. He studied her in mute glances, while wolfing a sandwich and letting her scrape the crusts, while needing to be ordered to wash his hands and ordered to mutter thank you, while dropping his schoolbooks with only a grunt to say he'd handled his homework already during recess, then left the family home, went to Rose Zimmer's to study the art of opening his mouth.

Today, though, Cicero wanted to think just for once not of Rose, always and endlessly Rose, but of Diane Lookins, the woman cut to drift in the vacuum silence of her distress. Today, with Sergius Gogan here at his side petitioning for more of the dynamism and strife of Rose, more of Rose and Miriam, please, than Sergius had been allotted, a larger share if you will, sir, kindly surrogate grandson—Cicero wanted to say, no, motherfucker, *no*. No more Rose. Diane instead. Cicero wished he were teaching an entire course on Diane Lookins, stuffing the invisible Negress down their throats, except he was too complicit in making her invisible himself, he knew.

Anyway, Cicero kidded himself. Rose had helped him comprehend Diane Lookins, too. For in demonstrating to Cicero the nature and enormity of his father's appetite, Rose had caused Cicero to understand that Diane Lookins relied on the policeman's lover—unknown, unseen, unnamed—to drain off this unruly surplus. By fucking Douglas, Rose acted in concert with Diane Lookins and her hospital necessities, her program of pacification. Someone had to tear Douglas down that way from time to time, to catalyze with Diane's steaming platefuls of food and color television and shushing, to free him to pass out on the couch. The women handled Douglas Lookins in tandem. And Diane Lookins didn't need to be told to know her tag-team partner existed.

There was just one time, so far as Cicero knew, that the three, Diane, Douglas, and Rose, had been in the same room. Even then it was a large public hall, and Cicero had no evidence that they'd come within direct sight of each other, let alone spoken. The Guardians Association Scholarship Award gala, the Renaissance Ballroom in Harlem, June 1973. Less than two years later Cicero's mother would be dead. This ceremonial banquet was the last time he'd see Diane Lookins out in any public setting, short of the dayroom of Mount Sinai Medical, where she passed, or the open coffin at her funeral.

A night of firsts and lasts, then. For it was also the first and last time he'd see Douglas Lookins amid the mythic Guardians, who'd swelled in Cicero's imagination to some kind of Harlem Mafia, *The French Connection* remade as blaxploitation. Imagine his surprise at discovering the homey, aspirational clan of patrolmen's families filling the hall, filtering through the lobby clasping one another in a hubbub of reunion, policemen's medals tangling in rhinestone brooches to great laughter, drinking sweet wine and flipping open wallets to show off graduation pictures, until needing to be urged to go in and be seated, as if at a wedding, around floral-display banquet rounds. Piped through speakers with no low end, the Delfonics and Donny Hathaway. Lining the room, long tables bearing framed photographs of uniformed association members, their reward for being killed in the line of duty during the previous year to be dwarfed by a florist's masterpieces even more garish than those covering the rounds. An emeritus association officer, accompanied by his withered-apple wife, hobbled on two canes to the lip of the riser, wanting to personally shake hands with the new crop of college scholarship winners, the dweebish, oversize, Department of Health–tortoiseshell-eyeglass-wearing threesome among whom Cicero Lookins himself stood foremost, the top winner, and already accepted at Princeton, too. The runners-up (one of each sex, and destined one for Howard, the other for SUNY Purchase) flanked him like the silver and bronze winners on a pyramidal stairstep—Cicero considered suggesting they conspire in a fist-clenched Black Power salute, but thought better of it quickly. So this was the garrulous, familial Guardians' world, the black cop's utopia of solidarity, that Douglas Lookins's naming of names had barred them from, exiling them to Queens.

Or perhaps not. Perhaps if he'd tempered his pride Douglas Lookins would have been readily forgiven. One of their own after all, a decorated top cop who'd appeared in that pic with Mayor Wagner, and, yo, any brother know what it takes to make lieutenant's stripes in a stone racist system. Perhaps dozens of these men had at some point chosen rank over race and named a few names, played a little ball with Internal Affairs, and only Douglas Lookins had made a federal case of it. No way for Cicero to know what sealed his family's exile destiny, really. For, look now: The Guardians had welcomed Douglas Lookins back, they'd given his son the top scholarship. So why couldn't the Lookinses have stayed?

Well, if they'd stayed, who knew where Cicero might be standing instead of atop this pyramid. It was Rose, waiting for them in Queens, who'd pushed Cicero up onto this riser to receive the Guardians' check. Not merely in some general sense, egging Cicero to his school record of excellence, but specifically, by demanding he go around his father's objections and write in for the application form that put him up for the Guardians' scholarship. Rose filled out the paperwork and Diane signed it, her silence an assent to son that was also a mutiny against husband, as well as another remote collaboration with her husband's lover. Douglas, if he even saw the papers going out in the mail, said nothing. Maybe Rose had discussed this with him. Except he didn't see a whole lot of Rose these days.

Now they sat, while Cicero stood gazing out, facing all three from the riser. Douglas and Diane Lookins grim and rigid up at the front, at a table with the parents of the runners-up and a couple of members of the Guardians' board. All dressed to the nines, yet their table seemed laminated in gloom, the shade cast by Douglas Lookins's indignation at being dragged back here by, of all things, his effete boy being given a handout. What a trap they'd set for him! What a trap his whole existence had become: dying wife, Queens political machine proving as depraved with ethnic nepotism as anything he'd met in Harlem, and his know-it-all ex-lover, to whom he'd ceded sponsorship of the child only to have confirmed any suspicion he'd harbored as to the incurably queer underbelly of Communist belief. He'd said *Help him find the chess books* and been handed back a boy who if you put him in great seats behind home plate and tried to settle in to enjoy a game began asking if you'd read *James Baldwin.* Diane and Douglas and the rest of their table, as still and glazed as Dutch burghers by contrast to the jubilance and funk all around them.

In the back of the room, unmissable as one of three white faces scattered around, Rose Zimmer. She wasn't going to be denied the chance to see the triumph of her workings, and so had called in some civic favor, pulled one of her innumerable strings—for a woman as lonely and reviled as Douglas Lookins might take Rose Zimmer to be, as much frozen like Mrs. Havisham in her 1956 betrayals, Rose sure had a lot of strings to pull, a regularly updated Rolodex of the Obliged. No doubt had beaten out some how-do-you-do on her cursive typewriter and gained access. (*White* access it was, too. Imagine some negroid Mysterious Lady trying to crash the Irish or Jewish equivalent of this clan's affair.) So there she sat, making God-knew-what small talk at her table, emanating loud-silent waves of surrogate proprietary esteem in Cicero's direction. Could Douglas and Diane judge the plane of Cicero's gaze, to know for certain that he looked over their heads to see Rose applaud? Through his Department of

Health spectacles, not likely so. Did they know she was back there? Undoubtedly. How not to?

Day of firsts and lasts. It was the last day Cicero Lookins, on the verge of making his prodigal, seventeen-year-old, grade-skipper's departure to the Ivy League, could kid himself that his father's congratulations for this or any subsequent achievement were anything but a tissue-thin disguise on revulsion. For Cicero, seeing his father bilious with rage, understood that it was not only at being forced to congregate with the Guardians. Cicero understood that in his body and person, he, Cicero, was *disgusting* to his father. Could never be other than. Cicero's intelligence, his achievements, the embrace of this scholarship, and his acceptance to a college to which his white classmates wouldn't have dared even apply—none of this mitigated his father's disgust. All of this made it worse instead. Cicero's brilliance, the dawning boldness of his inquiry and his skepticism, all ensured that Douglas Lookins would be forced to confront his son's deviance not as some facet of a subnormality, one pitiable aspect of the pitiable spectacle of a boy who'd sadly not come out right, but rather as something akin to, and borne upward by, the intellectual brashness Cicero'd begun to demonstrate. The queerness would be part and parcel of an *assertion*, coming from a fifth column of Douglas Lookins's own paternity, of shit Douglas Lookins simply did not want asserted.

Cicero knew he also disgusted his mother. In the months before she fled this vale, in the grip of the late mercies of the wolf, Diane Lookins had begun to falter in her pretenses to herself and to Cicero. She couldn't veil her own revulsion with her son, attained by proxy. She was disgusted with Cicero for disgusting his father, as, axiomatically, she'd been disappointed in Cicero for disappointing Douglas, disgraced by him for disgracing Douglas, et al.—even as she had once been delighted in her child *because* he had been, long ago and too briefly, delightful to his father. Douglas Lookins's word might not be law—in practice his words were a conflagration to be doused—but his emotional weathers were the Ten Commandments.

If they numbered even ten. Cicero wasn't sure he could name that many.

Firsts: Cicero Lookins had gotten his tongue around its first dick just six weeks earlier. This miracle, manifest in a onetime act of perfect, double-blind secrecy, Cicero nevertheless felt certain must be worn on his face, as evident as his blackness, as arresting as his mother's cheeks' florid lupus rash. So some part of him accorded with his father, looked out from Douglas Lookins's eyes upon the stage and was revolted, too, to see what Cicero'd suddenly and irreversibly become: one who not only wanted what he wanted but might risk *having* it. A much greater portion of him, however, dwelling as it did in the subterranean ethical sense of the appetites, was delighted and righteous and at this very instant sailed free of the Guardians' ballroom stage, oblivious of time and space (racing well beyond a terrified virginal first two years at Princeton, in which time he'd not get hold of any dick again beside his own), into a future where no aging policeman's censure could damage it even faintly.

Wear your love like heaven.

Meanwhile, Rose Zimmer beamed on him from her place in the back of the ballroom, rising from her chair now to holler with the black folks, streaming undiluted pride, like she'd built the pyramidal stand and the riser with her own hammer and sickle, like she'd picked every flower in the room with her teeth, like she'd signed a proclamation and freed the slaves.

———————

The creak and scuffle of the last exits from the seminar room left Cicero where he'd not wished to find himself again: at sea with Sergius Gogan. No one to blame but himself for extending the invitation to witness the detonation of the three-hundred-pound African American neutron bomb. Even on a good day, Cicero's clientele filed out under a funeral canopy of hush—it wasn't like he awaited applause. A strange thing, the professor's art, the esoteric transaction at the heart of the whole bureaucracy of curriculums and committees: to decant yourself before them, to dare them to wade into the bog of your thinking, what was called your "pedagogy." Colleagues arrayed along a department's corridor like rival churches on a Main Street, no two alike in their ritual methods and occult origins. Yet the students, entering the churches, weren't like congregants. They browsed like shoppers at a mall.

This wasn't close to a good day. Yes, high school's basic training in keeping ass in seat had stanched the room, after the early desertions. And yes, a number had opened their mouths. Cicero was only half able to listen as they turned out their shallow pockets of woe— the standard-issue divorces and institutionalized retard siblings and menopausal tetchiness they discovered when peeking beneath their Band-Aids. Their banalities only made him feel the banality of his own grievances, in the form he'd aired them. Stranded from historical superstructure. Context, always context. Baginstock College's young adults shouldn't have been invited to burnish their gripes, not before reading a thousand pages, or ten thousand—*Another Country* and *A Thousand Plateaus* and *Human, All Too Human*, Jane Bowles and Lauren Berlant and Octavia Butler, stuff still months ahead on Cicero's Disgust and Proximity syllabus, and further stuff too much for any syllabus. They shouldn't be called to indulge such self-importances, and he'd been in error to set himself as a permitting example. Cicero's gripes meant nothing to anyone but himself. Wishing to detonate in their minds, he'd instead done so behind a transparent blast shield, melting himself to slag while leaving them untouched: If he be the neutron bomb, they were buildings. Cicero might as well have torn open his clothes and displayed his belly and dick. *Guess what Lookins put us through this time. Can't believe I set my alarm clock for* that.

"Can I take you to breakfast?"

The morning's unnamed context now opened its mouth. Rose had commanded Cicero to teach Sergius. Well, he'd at least dragged him to school. Innumerable sardonic replies suggested themselves, but Cicero, bile momentarily drained, found he lacked the impetus to select one and deliver it. He *wanted* breakfast, even if it had to be with Sergius. Quarts of coffee had his veins wriggling, but it had gone cold in his stomach.

"You got time enough before you catch your plane?"

"Sure."

A yellow alert. The Portland Jetport was a three-hour drive, and Sergius would be needing to return his rental. Cicero wanted breakfast, but he also wanted Jiminy Cricket out of town, out of the entire state.

To his credit, Sergius caught the note of inquiry in Cicero's silence. "I got on a later flight—later this afternoon, I mean. When I read your note."

Cicero's fault again, for summoning Sergius to class. Or Rose's fault. "Fair enough," said Cicero. "Let's breakfast."

"Do you like the Lyrical Ballad? We can walk there."

Another arched eyebrow. "Who put you onto the Lyrical Ballad?" The little patisserie was a sort of professors' secret hive, tucked behind Cumbow's sole rare-book store. A better shield for repelling both the typical Cumbow townie and the twenty-first-century college student could hardly be devised.

"I sort of made a friend last night, actually. She mentioned it."

"You go working the bar at Poseidon's Net?"

Sergius shook his head. "No, I met her somewhere else. C'mon, I'll show you."

They crossed the lot, past Cicero's car, Sergius seeming unduly proud to have gained his little flaneur's knowledge of the campus footpaths and of the scattering of back streets and alleys that comprised the collegiate side of Cumbow's miniature downtown. In this, and having acquired his enigmatic "friend," Miriam's son for the first time reminded Cicero in any way of his mother, the maven of MacDougal Street. Cicero felt a stir of panic, as if he'd made some irreversible error unleashing Sergius the night before. *This town isn't big enough for both of us.*

No part of Cicero's dread, however, could have predicted their destination. Occupy Cumbow, such as it was. Three little tents staked out on the expertly appointed lawn in front of city hall, a card table bearing leaflets and a Dunkin' Donuts box, a few propped-up signs denouncing Pentagon budgets and bailed-out towers of Mammon. Inasmuch as the encampment had gone from a momentary curiosity to an established nonentity, something to pussyfoot past, Cicero was confident his low opinion stood for the general one.

On a clear morning like this the little outdoor theater was fronted by a rotating cast of three or four trimmed-white-bearded retirees in fleece jackets, Old Lefties who'd otherwise be home penning letters to the *Times* that were never printed. The actual residents of the tents, however, were younger and skulkier, a couple of dingy young hitch-hiker types in darker and ropier beards, with skateboard-stickered laptops draining city hall's public Wi-Fi, and a girl—woman?—in striped tights, cutoff shorts, and filthy down vest, seated cross-legged holding an acoustic guitar, one stickered like the laptops. Half bundled under her watchman's cap, blond, chunky, unappetizing dreadlocks. It was these that made Cicero certain he'd not seen her before.

"Good morning, Lydia."

"Hey, Sergius!"

"This is my friend Cicero. Cicero, Lydia."

Cicero mumbled and stuck out his hand.

"We were heading to the Ballad," said Sergius. "Wanna come along?"

Sergius, in the great tradition of the wan hetero, was serially addicted to the Actualizing Other. Now he wanted his magical Negro to befriend—what name was it Cicero's students gave the archetype? His *Manic Pixie Dream Girl*. Though this one was a little worse for wear than Zooey Deschanel, her function was clear enough. Cicero had wished to leverage Sergius into some kind of encounter with the missing body of Diane Lookins, or at least force him to behold her chalk outline and puzzle over the crime of her absence. But Diane Lookins couldn't compete, couldn't get into the picture at all. Even raging Rose and blazing Miriam, avowed subjects of Sergius's inquiry, were faded, voiceless ghosts by contrast to what Sergius suddenly had before him: a real live pistol-hot protester chick.

Lydia, though so far unspeaking, wasn't shy. She'd shoved her guitar into the mouth of her tent, then leapt up and inserted her small hand into Cicero's mitt—it was ordinarily with grinning men in suits, deans and trustees, that Cicero recalled the imperative of a forceful handshake a moment too late, his dead-fish offering an unbreakable lifelong habit—and squeezed hard. This, not something every white person could manage. She met his eye, too, twinkling in a conspiracy of the dreadlocked.

"Sergius said you're almost his cousin."

"Something like that." Cicero turned on the pavement and slouched, as if toward Bethlehem, in the direction of the Lyrical Ballad. He felt incapable of anything but putting distance between himself and the tiny spectacle of Occupy Cumbow. Though he couldn't say why it so outraged him, the encampment was like a splinter in his eye. Of course, Occupy Cumbow slumped along the pavement with him now, Sergius and Lydia falling into step at his side. Well, breakfast, at least, was an unimpeachable good. Cicero envisioned shoving one of the coffee shop's mammoth, twelve-toed, icing-drenched bear claw pastries across his teeth.

Sergius now babbled. "I wandered down here after dinner last night, Cicero, it was cooling off and I wanted to explore downtown. You didn't tell me Cumbow had an Occupy. They cleared everyone out in Philadelphia, but I guess it's in the small towns where the people are still making their presence known—anyway, when I walked up, you'll never believe what I heard."

"What?"

"Lydia was playing one of my father's songs. I mean, can you believe it? 'To Pass Beneath the Bower.' I had no idea anyone remembered that record, let alone somebody half my age playing it at a, um, rally."

Half your age indeed. But Cicero kept mum. "There was a *rally* here last night?" This much he couldn't resist.

"I've played it at rallies," said Lydia, not troubling even to put defiance in her voice. The secret of her weightless certainty might be that to her it was a rally anytime she lifted her guitar. Anyway, who was Cicero, that she need defy him? "It's one of the great anthems, people take a lot of courage from that song."

"I wasn't aware."

"There's a bunch of verses to memorize, but the changes are simple, you can teach others to play it really easy."

Cicero was truly uninterested. They'd passed the bookstore's front, ducking into the alley where the coffee shop's entrance was hidden. It wasn't the wrong hour to mutter a hopeful prayer for seclusion; a majority of Cicero's colleagues ran classes in the morning's second slot and so would have vacated the Ballad until lunchtime. Sure enough, the three of them assumed the corner table in a room otherwise bare of familiar faces. Nor was the barista one of Cicero's kids, as had been his ill fortune at least once before. Cicero, at the counter, tapped the glass on the other side of which, nestling in a bed of powdered sugar and slivered almond crumbs, lay the morning's last bear claw: Things were looking up. Sergius and Lydia got lattes and heaping square portions of coffee cake. Lydia spooned additional sugar into her coffee, the American addiction to sucrose being apparently not covered in Occupy's otherwise wide-ranging critique.

"The thing is, Lydia and I were talking, and I realized my father's *Bowery* album really is in this wild sense a precursor to the movement. The Forgotten are like a rough draft for the Ninety-Nine Percent, right?"

"Tell me more," said Cicero, then gagged himself with bear claw before he could further betray his own interests.

"Well, if you'd been to Zuccotti Park, or with us in Philly, you'd see it instantly. Whatever anyone intended at the start, once the camping began the movement was all about making the, you know, *urban homeless* visible again. Showing what the typical citizen has in common. Except first we had to learn it ourselves, by living on the streets."

Tom Waits growled on the Lyrical Ballad's stereo, offering his art-school paraphrase of the lament of a hobo, larynx scarred by reflux—the exact vocal equivalent of blond dreadlocks. Cicero suddenly felt he might drown in recursions of minstrelsy, blackface of a very particular kind: appropriations of the Negro vagabond. *Black bum*, hot cultural ticket at last. If only Tommy had lived to see it. The youngest Gogan Boy had never, so far as Cicero'd heard, ever spent a single night "living on the streets"; Cicero wondered how many nights Sergius had, no matter his claim of acquaintance with Occupy Philadelphia. Lydia, on the other hand—Cicero could *smell* the girl.

She interrupted plowing through her coffee cake to speak up now. "Sergius was obviously meant to walk by at just that moment. I mean, I know about a *billion* songs."

The ironies sank in through a certain dawning panic. Sergius had arrived at Cumbow seeking familial inspiration. Failing to drag it from Cicero, he'd scraped it off the sidewalk anyhow. This a direct result of Cicero's non-invitation to Sergius to share in sauvignon blanc and gnocchi at the Five Islands Grill: Cicero's reward for not din-

ing with Sergius was to breakfast with Sergius's new girlfriend, aka
the Ghost of Tom Joad. A girl whose frank and unapologetic gaze,
whose precipitous familiarity, whose *braggadocio* reminded Cicero of
no one so much as, yes, a grade-Z Miriam Gogan. Not that Cicero
was inclined to offer Sergius *that* comparison. Let him live in blind
pursuit of his mother. Only let him please not persist in this sport in
Cumbow, Maine.

"I went to Cicero's class this morning," Sergius told Lydia. "My first
time sitting in a college classroom in, hell, twenty years." If Sergius
ingenuously emphasized the distance between his age and the girl's,
this didn't prevent Lydia from shining steadily in his direction. Cicero
supposed that if Lady Billion Songs had a hard-on for the corpse of
Tommy Gogan, then this handy substitute was youthful by contrast.

"Cool. So what do you teach, Cicero?"

She was the first person her age to address him as other than *Professor Lookins* in a while. "Why don't you ask Sergius to tell you
about it." *And close your mouth while you chew.*

"Well, I hadn't read the texts, but it didn't seem to matter." Sergius's tone was jaunty—he and his Occupy girl seemed incapable of
other than moonish chirping in each other's presence. So the fact that
he was organizing a rebuke was slow to register with Cicero. "I was
expecting some kind of Marxist-influenced literary theory, but this
was more of a kind of sob session, honestly."

"It was political in the highest degree," said Cicero, fierce now.
"You might want to acquaint yourself with what's known as the 'affec-
tive turn' in the humanities, Sergius. What you're disdaining with the
word *sob* is as political as it gets, the passage of exiled sentiment from
one subject's body to another's. The transmission of affect." This was
truth and no good at all. Armoring himself in hostility turned Cicero's
sincerest allegiances to jargon and junk, to ash in his mouth. Besides,
he hadn't attended well enough to his students' testimony, had walled
himself from their sob stories behind the tempered shield of his own.

"Well, I'm surprised to hear you defend it, because I thought you
pretty much went down in flames. I figured it was all some kind of
perverse demonstration on *my* behalf." Cicero saw that inside the
crimson theater of his red hair, freckles, and sunburn, Sergius's cheeks

had flushed with hot adamancy. "I felt sorry for your students, and then at the end I felt sorry for *you*, which is the only reason I invited you to breakfast, but I guess that was a mistake."

"You invited *me* here?" Cicero had to work to keep himself from exploding.

"You're pretty patronizing, Cicero, but you seem to forget I'm a teacher, too."

"I had thought you were here as a songwriter. But I notice you didn't even pack a guitar. A teacher, then, sure, I'll take it on faith. But today you visited my classroom, which put you in the role of student."

Lydia said, "I've gotta say, it sounded cool as *shit*, to me. I keep meaning to audit some classes in one of these college towns. I should've started with yours."

Sergius accepted diversion with plain relief. "Lydia and I wondered if you knew—have any of your students gotten involved with Occupy? She was saying they aren't a real presence at the camp."

Cicero ignored the question. His students regarded the movement, to his knowledge, with the agnosticism they'd feel toward a social media website from which no peer had yet sent them an invite. "What is it that brings you to Cumbow in the first place, Lydia?"

"New England has twelve Occupy encampments still going strong. It came to me in a dream that me and my Gibson should occupy in all of them, at least for a few nights, so I am, which has been pretty crazy but it's also been this totally incredible experience which I wouldn't have missed for the world. It's *exactly* like you said, Cicero: Bodies carry messages from one place to another. I actually have to get down to Portland today, so that's another reason it was such perfect timing that Sergius came along."

"You're driving her to Portland?"

Sergius disregarded Cicero's scorn with no seeming effort. "Yeah. In fact, we'd probably better get on the road, Lydia. Because first we've got to pick up your stuff."

"Ready when you are," said Lydia through a mouthful of crumbs. "Nothing but my ax and my bedroll."

"I'm already loaded out of your guest room, Cicero. I left the house unlocked, I hope that's okay."

"The whole state of Maine is unlocked."

"Great. Well, thanks, then. I'll catch you later." Sergius offered Cicero his hand—dead fish, meet dead fish. So the romance was for Sergius concluded, the feeling between them, at last, mutual: Chalk up another triumph to *affect*.

Still, though it wasn't yet eleven in the morning, one further mortification awaited Cicero this day. Now standing above them, wholly unbidden but undeniably *there*, Vivian Mitchell-Rose, the associate dean of students, Cicero's fellow person of color in Cumbow's desert of same, and, more than once in a while, his kvetching partner, in tones as scalding as could have been worst-feared by white folks seeing them lean their big dark heads together over a restaurant table or behind a half-open office door. Fellow member of the unacknowledged Guardians Association of academia—or perhaps they more resembled the Wandering Boys or Buffalo Soldiers, since blacks in academia threw themselves no ballroom galas or Fourth of July picnics, worked in general a stonier side of the street. The associate dean had been approaching to greet him, then, at absorbing a blast of their corner table's shitty vibe, halted. The Lyrical Ballad was too small for a full and covert retreat, however. You'd barely hope to pull off one of those within a mile radius of campus. So Vivian had frozen, mid-floor, giving a raw checking-out to Cicero's breakfast companions.

The sensation drew him cascading back again. Though not, for once, to the soda-counter stools. No comic book, no egg cream. This time he was out in the blaze on the pavement, Rose at his side, monologuing on who-knew-what civic outrage, the two in full stride as they passed a schoolyard on a Saturday morning. There, on the other side of the cyclone fence, laying out of a stickball game, fingers through the mesh to stare as Cicero and Rose went past, a black kid Cicero knew. Fellow person of color in Sunnyside's desert of same, etc. One of Cicero's occasional-almost-friends—it did happen from time to time, before Cicero's fey bookishness canceled the hope that this hefty cop's kid might be useful to have at one's back. The look that crossed the gap between them that day, through the cyclone fence, was one that said, *What's this company I find you in today? What have you got yourself into? And will I make things better or worse for you if I open my mouth, if I even admit I know you, in front of the crazy-ass white folk?* He only had to blink away the involuntary fantasy to see the same script scrolling as if in teletype across Vivian Mitchell-Rose's eyes. Maybe, it occurred to Cicero only now that Sergius had quit asking, maybe Cicero'd blown his chance to offload Rose from his brain, shunt her into another's. Maybe he should have tried. Yet how could he believe it could be accomplished? Rose Zimmer was an affect beyond Cicero's powers of transmission.

2   From the Stasi Files

14 October 1958, Werkhofinstitut Rosa Luxemburg, Dresden

Dear Miriam,

Imagine my surprise to receive your letter and discover that the girl I remember has been transformed into a young woman capable not only of making such astute and forthright inquiry of her long-silent father but of proposing to undertake to visit here so that we might come to know each other. Or, less to know each other again, truly, than to meet for the first time. Let me begin by saying with delight that, yes, you must come. I'll not burden you with an account of my decision not to interfere with you and your mother, after the silence enforced by the first phase of my repatriation. Let me instead say that the happy shock of contact has now unloosed a reserve of hopeful feeling. May we close the gap of years, and of national boundaries, that has divided us for too long! For now I'll reply to your questions as directly as possible in such a letter as this, while knowing that a fuller understanding will be possible when we sit together and talk, as we must.

Our striving on behalf of international Communism during the years leading up to the war was, however sincere, deeply naïve. How could it be anything other, given the situation of a Communism attempting to bring itself into consciousness from within the American atmosphere? Each of us working in the U.S. party felt the sway of a seductive individualism, one not so far from a kind of drug or sickness—or, perhaps, a messianic religious fervor. (Possibly this may only be viewed clearly from a vantage such as I've attained in Europe.) The brutality of the period of the blacklist and McCarthyism, which I was mercifully spared, represented at least a kind of scales falling from the eyes, for any honest Socialist operating under the American system should understand himself destined to be persecuted as an enemy of that system—such enmity being the precise measure of his honesty. This, your mother and I lacked wholly.

It was during my period of reeducation that I discovered, for the first time in life—late, but it's never too late!—my passion for history. And more, a passion for scholarship: both for working with first sources, with my nose to the earth, in constructing a People's history, and a passion for teaching others. Americans are a deeply (or should I say "shallowly"?) ahistorical people. This luxury no European could afford. My immediate subject, and a tragic one, is that which lies to hand all around me: the near-complete destruction of Dresden in the conflagration. Like citizens of every nation, the German civilian population found itself the victim of Nazism, but it was Dresden's special "honor," alone in Europe, with only Hiroshima and Nagasaki for company, to be on the front lines of the Cold War, and to serve as a horror-tableau of Allied might.

So you must understand, dearest Miriam, your father has in a manner returned to "school"—history being that school from which we never graduate. I am as much a student as you. I must also explain to you how this is in one very literal case the truth: This institute, where one comes to be debriefed after a border crossing so unorthodox as my own, and in which one is typically expected to dwell for several months of orientation and preparation for a fully integrated life in the East, has in my case become a permanent home. It was my fate not only to discover my avocation here but to choose to stay and impart it to others. This place, pleasantly located on the eastern outskirts of Dresden, is an old campus, its grounds comprised of elegant eighteenth-century buildings, a rare instance of those spared, by dint of the countryside locale, during the firebombing. The Werkhofinstitut Rosa Luxemburg, though it goes among those of us here by a nickname, Gärten der Dissidenz, which I suppose one might translate as "Dissident Gardens," however droll this may sound to you. It is not a solitary life, but one I share with Michaela, my second wife. We became acquainted when Michaela came to work here in the administrative offices; she is a number of years younger than myself—another sense in which I remain a student of life! Please know you'll be made welcome amid my new family.

Your plan to visit elsewhere in Europe before crossing to Dresden by train is a good one. If you stay first with your friend's family in London, then cross by ferry to Belgium, you'll be easily able to visit any number of cities by international rail. May I request, only, that you arrange to make a stop in Lübeck, and visit there the "Buddenbrooks House," made so famous by Thomas Mann? As you surely have been told, in the house next door the opera singer and the banker lived in great innocence and splendor—I mean, of course, your grandparents, as I prefer to remember them. In that house I was born. Lübeck was among the first cities to receive Allied air fire, the opening act of the nightmare destined to reach its climax here in Dresden. In that way your journey may serve as a pocket allegory of our family but also of the subject to which I've dedicated my research, and prelude to everything we'll wish to talk of.

Please write again when you have an exact date for your arrival, so that Michaela and I may prepare your hospitality.

I wish you well.

"Dad"

_____

2 March 1961, Werkhofinstitut Rosa Luxemburg, Dresden

Dear Miriam,

I send my heartiest congratulations on your marriage! I suppose I must accustom myself to being continually surprised by your news and I will admit that despite everything I am still adjusting to your maturity. No doubt next you will declare that you have made me a grandfather. If so, as suggested previously I'll arrange a journey to Canada so that I may meet the child, to spare your new family a longer journey. I am also gratified by the swiftness with which you rebounded from the awkwardness with the German boy, into a next romantic adventure. I'll venture that you remind me of myself! I am holding you in my arms as not only a daughter but a newfound friend.

After the admonishments I received from you both in person and by post I should hardly dare mention your mother, but as I'm certain you're aware the scene you present in your letter is an irresistibly comical one, however discomfiting it surely will have been to undergo. The image of Rose's abrupt appearance in the home of the Negro minister with a rabbi in tow, in order to demand that your nuptials be legitimated at the last possible instant in the Jewish faith, has the quality, I must say, of a poem. For Rose everything was always, by its nature, its own opposite. This sudden fawning before religious authority, a legacy she had by her own account overturned sometime in her teenage years, is rather priceless evidence. Yet in the truest sense Rose would have been the only authority in the vicinity, the rabbi and your Negro officiant notwithstanding. You do not say (and so leave it for me to assume) that you consented to your mother's wishes and were sanctified in the bosom of Abraham, etc.

The record album you posted separately has also happily arrived, and I accept it in lieu of photographs of the occasion—I wonder if the brothers all sang together at the ceremony, and also whether the rabbi joined in? Your red-haired boy possesses an ingenuous vitality in both voice and features, I can very much understand your delight in him. Keeping in mind again certain criticisms of my condescending attitude, etc., I will pass over any remark on the "political" nature of the songs you say he has been writing subsequently.

Please let me know, even if merely by postcard, that my package to you arrives. Michaela and I send blessings to you and Thomas,

"Dad"

————

23 May 1961, Werkhofinstitut Rosa Luxemburg, Dresden

Dearest Miriam,

I write in haste to make the sincerest apology, for giving offense by what you call my "flippant tone"—I was delighted by your letter, and wished only to share my delight with you. I'm aware that your visit here was not entirely simple for you, and in no way intended to diminish the seriousness of your feelings, nor of your new union, with the word "adventure." As far as other matters less intimate than ideological, let's please brush those aside for future talks, and rely on such opportunities being plentiful. Please accept a father's repentance and let me know if the T. Mann book has arrived safely, I worry about the mails!

Your loving "dad,"

Albert

———————

12 December 1968, 5 Vitzthumstrasse Dresden

Dear Miriam,

It seems it needs the shock of your report on Alma to overcome the block I've had to writing you. In fact this is the fourth attempt and I hope this will be mailed finally. Not that I find it so difficult, on the contrary I still have a warm and close feeling every time I think of our too-brief reunion, and have frequently hoped it could be repeated, but what I consider a "real" letter takes time and leisure, both at a premium in the rather hectic life I still lead. Though I try to take it more easy, the work still takes a lot out of me, which just can't be helped. As it happens, I have been able to travel recently. In September my researches brought me to Spain, to visit the site of the widely known Guernica "terrors," which Western propaganda, you will likely not be surprised to discover, has exaggerated and distorted. Afterward, Michaela and I were granted a holiday at Lake Garda in Italy, where I did a lot of swimming and generally was very lazy. Then, for my birthday, we went to Verona and saw <u>Aida</u> in the

huge old Roman amphitheater, the singers' voices carrying in the
open air without amplification. The Italians love their opera, and I
really don't know what I enjoyed more, the performance or the audience. Both belonged to each other and complemented each other; life
in Italy seems not as horribly serious and heavy-handed as it is in
Germany.

So, when you say I should not delay in making a visit to North
America if I want to see my mother again, I admit it is possible that
I would gain this dispensation. Probably I could find a number of
rather valid excuses as to why I can't come at this time—Michaela's
pregnancy, financial, business, and whatnot—but, you know something, I really don't want to come. I don't think I want to see Alma
again, for a variety of reasons. First of all, I find it easier to lie in a
letter than stand before her and lie to her straight in the face, concerning so many details of my present life which have been concealed from her. More, I fear the emotional strain involved in saying
goodbye. There would be something so completely final about a
farewell certain to be the "last." Then, too, I notice from her letters that Mother is approaching senility rather quickly now. I would
rather like to hold on to the picture I still have of her from her last
visit here, ten years ago, when we still went hiking together and
could talk about many interesting things. This is perhaps terribly
selfish, but there it is. This letter must get on its way now. I hope
that the interval to the next will be shorter. For you and Thomas I
send my very best wishes for 1969.

Yours,

Albert

————

24 June 1969, 5 Vitzthumstrasse, Dresden

Dear Miriam,

Belated thank-you for the postcard reproduction of Picasso's
Guernica—needless to say that image is familiar to us here, despite
the fact that we do not have the privilege of seeing it in person as

you do in New York, but I assume your reference was "tongue in cheek"—and for your congratulations on Michaela's pregnancy! Well, she has now ferried into the world your new half brother, Errol, of whom a pink and nevertheless rather delightful photograph is here enclosed. I hope you'll have a chance to meet each other soon, please let me know if there's the remotest chance of another visit to us here.

Sending love,

"Dad"

_____

8 November 1969, 5 Vitzthumstrasse, Dresden

Dear Miriam,

I write to thank you for the fourth in what I fear may be an inexhaustible sequence of <u>Guernica</u> postcards, and while I find these brief and rather cryptic messages not unfriendly, I do feel concerned that I may have missed a more substantial letter from you these past months. Please write and reassure me that nothing has gone astray as I fear! You probably understand that I worry about the mails.

Fond regards from Michaela, and from Errol (whose exact time of birth, since you have requested this information twice, was according to the certificate at fourteen minutes past the hour of three, in the early hours of the morning of 26 May).

"Dad"

_____

3 August 1971, Dresden

Dear Miriam,

If you will permit me, my daughter. Your keen intelligence has perhaps been betrayed by the tiny quantity of historical critique one can fit onto the back of a postcard. I find you susceptible to thinking in images and symbols, in Madison Avenue–style cameos and slogans. Yet a few of your assertions demand a response, concerning as they do what has become my life's work. You mention Coventry, you mention Rotterdam, and of course you again and again with your postcards "mention" Guernica. You write (in boldly illuminated hand, decorating your script with flowers and "peace signs" as if wishing to impart some kind of medieval biblical enchantment to your words!), "Suffering is suffering." All this, in dispute of the truth to which I've been documenting: that the Allied firebombing of Dresden was a unique moral and cultural catastrophe, on a par, in the final human reckoning, only with the atomic bombs dropped on the Japanese cities (more died in Dresden, I remind you, than at either of those targets). Dresden also mirrors the Nazi Party's own atrocities, those which have come to define twentieth-century horror in the popular imagination—most understandably, I add!—even to the detail of so many families roasted while huddling together in bunkers into which they entered docilely or were enticed by promises of safety.

There is no precedent for Dresden. Coventry was the center of the U.K. arms manufacture. To overlook this is to overlook the essential facts. The civilian death toll in Coventry, while horrendous, was the by-product of a valid military target. Inquiry into the circumstances at Rotterdam, equally, reveal an episode in "military history"— rather than, as in Dresden, the annals of "terror." A division of the Dutch army was encamped in the city, and indeed, the bombing resulted in the surrender of the Dutch military forces. The Luftwaffe even attempted to call off the attack when they learned of peace talks. Their failure is evidence of the chaos of war.

This leaves your postcard's face. Would it astonish you too much to learn that von Richthofen's fliers aimed their bombs almost exclusively at Guernica's bridges and arterial roads? Again, a military episode. "Suffering is suffering," but the special exaggeration of the tragedies in Spain is a fetish of those who, thanks to artists like Picasso and George Orwell and Rose Angrush, accord a special sacred moral value to the minor scuffles of the "Lincoln Brigade." I was once quite under the spell of such artists myself, so I feel rather indulgent of this error. Yet it is one.

Why have I allowed myself to become so tendentious, when I'm sure it will be irritating to you? My wish, Miriam, is for you to understand that we are on the same side. You say I am "obsessed" with German suffering. Yet to deplore the U.S. actions in Vietnam without grasping napalm's point of origin in the Dresden fire is to lose sight of the trajectory of history. In that, Dresden, like Hiroshima, was not the final phase of the previous imperialist war but the opening shot of the next, and one even more successful in its employment of terror than Hitler's. We all of us live here in the flickering shadow of that fire which has in fact never been put out. To gather and sift testimony as I've spent more than a decade doing is to enlist in what any lover of peace such as yourself must see is the task of assembling human voices against the terrible universality of oppression, and of death.

You say that travel is impossible, and I reluctantly understand. I do nonetheless hope that our Errol and your Sergius will someday play together, and more, that they have the chance to live in a world freed of the destructive legacy of national boundaries—if these sentiments do not seem too optimistic, after my letter.

With my fondest regards,

Albert

P.S. Now that I have begun my long-delayed "paternalism" toward you I find myself incapable of stopping; forgive me. The astrological mysticism in your letters strikes me as sheerest gibberish, and I wish I could make you think better of it. Little Errol is no more "a Gemini with a moon in Mars" than I am a centaur. In fact, it looks from my perspective like a reversion to some kabbalistic superstition, not so far from your mother's hysterical and self-loathing reversions to folk Judaism, as when she imposed a rabbi on your wedding party. The world we dwell in, my daughter, is mysterious enough for us not to wish to veil it in metaphysics! But enough.

---

19 March 1972, 5 Vitzthumstrasse, Dresden

Dear Miriam,

If I consent that the horse in the painting cannot "by definition" have been a political or military target of importance, will you grant in return that the depiction of a horse in oil paint consists of not an account from the historical record but rather a poetical interpretation? Or better still, if I acknowledge what you wish, might you please cease sending me the postcard? Doubtless you've enriched the gift shop of the Museum of Modern Art sufficiently by this point.

Yours,

Albert

_____

15 November 1977, 22 Franz-Liszt-Strasse, Dresden

Dear Miriam,

Into long silence I hurl this communication, in a spirit of beckoning to what lies unfinished between us, and was briefly resumed during your long-ago visit to me, and which then subsequently went fallow—very much my own fault, no doubt. I shall, in any event, now tell you what has made me wish to defy the fear you will discard this letter unread, or even, more simply, some concern as to whether I still have an address at which to reliably find you! It is that I was, January a year ago, operated upon for a cancer of the gallbladder. Originally the doctors gave me little hope of living more than two years. But after two operations and more than three months of gamma rays I have a completely normal life, except for injections every other day, of a special preparation which supposedly mobilizes antibodies. As I can give myself the injections the whole thing is very little trouble. Suffice to say I am practically without pain and at my last checkup, two months ago, the doctor felt that there was only a one percent chance for a new growth.

Naturally my illness gave me quite a jolt and made me realize I could not continue to live in the same way any longer. When I thought that I had a short time to live I felt that whatever time I had left I should live consciously and fully and not negate myself and my own personality. I thus decided already in the hospital that I had to separate from Michaela and for almost a year now have had my own place and am free of tensions and have stopped suppressing my real self. This decision has probably helped the process of healing and regeneration. Living a lie for so long probably also made it difficult for me to write to you. You must promise never to live dishonestly and with regrets.

Maybe you would feel like telling me about yourself and how you live. I would be happy to hear from you. Needless to say I wish you well.

Yours,

Dad

————————

1/19/78

Dear Dad,

I'm generally the first one up. This isn't a moral stance but a habit I can't break. I do like drinking my first cup of coffee alone before I have to deal with anyone else, and I like an hour or two before the phone rings. It rings a lot. All through the day once it starts, and sometimes after I've gone to bed, some guy pining for one of the young girls crashing here. Or girl for guy. It gets dark and they're alone and they call. But I like to be alone in the morning, I'm not lonely at all. So I make the coffee for everyone and drink the first cup or two. You could picture me here with a fresh hot coffee and everyone else sleeping. The hour when I'm starting this reply. The frog-shaped trivet is broken, one leg broke off, so I set the coffeepot on a manila envelope full of your old letters. It was lost for a while but I found it again. All those pale blue envelopes with the red and blue bands. I was looking for it a year ago, actually, but I couldn't find it, and then last night I found it in the back of my desk, all your letters going to back to before I visited. I was looking for it then because Sergius started a stamp collection, even though his uncle Lenny told him coins were where it was at. You remember Lenny, I'm sure. He's actually Sergius's cousin, but we call him "Uncle Lenny" just to needle him. Sergius prefers stamps. And it's a lot cheaper for us, even though Lenny gave him these penny books. You can gather up incredible canceled stamps from a million different places if you're willing to soak them off the envelopes. All brilliant colors and a free tour of the world. I've torn the corners off all your envelopes and I'll soak them for Sergius this morning, what a great surprise: East Germany, wow. The Iron Curtain. I'm not sure I'll tell him where they came from, at least not yet. If he asks I'll tell him, but Sergius is stamp-mad, he has a kind of blindness for anything else, and I'll bet he just ignores the folder, or pokes through it to see if I missed any stamps. Strange thing about your letters, you always type. You even type your name and the word Dad. You and Rose still have that in common, constantly smashing out letters on a typewriter. I read them all this morning again. That's what I do while I'm alone in the kitchen, read and drink coffee and listen to the radio, WBAI. What the pigs did to Angela Davis lately, some other news about El Salvador. It's a good station. Nobody listens to it. Later they'll play jazz or run one of those Alan Watts lectures. I met him once. After a while somebody else gets up, often one of the girls, or maybe Stella Kim, or Tommy or Sergius. The guys always sleep longer than the girls. Whoever it is, I fix them some breakfast. If Sergius isn't up by this point I'll roust him. He has to go to school. Sergius eats like a little old lady, he only wants toast for breakfast, every day. The girls and the guys always want eggs and bacon and pancakes. Sometimes I make them a matzo brei when I can get it and that always turns them on, I have to brew fifteen pots of coffee, and there's this kid dressed for school and munching toast, just sitting there. It destroys me. Sometimes Stella walks him to school if I'm still in my robe. I'll give her my last five bucks and she'll come back with orange juice and a pack of cigarettes and the New York Post, which is a newspaper that's gone completely to hell but it runs a horoscope, which is beneath the standards of the Times. I mention this as a calculated affront to your horror of astrology, of course.

You probably don't know what I'm talking about, in terms of people living with us. You're a Communist only in the sense that you live in a Communist country and you have your long-held Marxist beliefs, if that's what still motivates you. It looks absurd to me now that I've written it down. I guess you must be in the party still. Or again. Is it the same party you were in with Rose, in America? How mysterious. Well, we live in a commune, something I suspect you wouldn't really be familiar with. Honestly, Tommy and I are like the parents, and they're like the children, so it isn't really a legitimate commune, not like the Maoist one around the corner on Avenue C, which has meetings nearly every night, and they go on for hours, and they never figure anything out. Ours is somewhere between a commune and a hostel. We started by letting Stella move in upstairs. Then we had to fill more rooms to afford to keep this place, because Tommy hasn't made any money from his records in a long time, and the money from the ACLU settlement for my wrongful arrest on public property is a distant memory. Did I ever mention I was one of the Capitol Steps Thirteen? We sued their asses, then I spent the money mostly at Pathmark, on bread and veggies and ground beef.

By this time in the morning the phone has started ringing and usually someone has rolled a joint and things are getting a little harder to put down in order. I mean, after the kid is off to school. I spend a lot of time listening, actually, you might not think so from this letter which is all about me, but I do. The phone rings or some-one comes downstairs and the kitchen is pretty much full of people for the rest of the day. Stella asks me who I'm writing to and I show her your letter. She used to help me think of stuff to write on the <u>Guernica</u> postcards and it was Stella who drew the fancy letters with the vines growing on them and the stars and peace signs you asked about. She was just doodling while we talked and then I saw it and thought I'd send it anyway. Stella says I should tell you everyone comes to me with their problems and that I solve them, that I yell at them and make them feel better. She says she doesn't know how I keep it all together. She also says I should tell you that she's the one writing this letter, just to freak you out. Our handwriting really is the same, when one of us leaves a note on the message board here in the kitchen nobody can tell who it is. But she's not writing this letter, I am.

Okay, I'm back. Just got off the phone with Rose, the daily round of complaints about the local politicos. She likes to call them "cro-nies," the local bishops and crooks she deals with on the board of the Queensboro Public Library, Judge Freeh, Donald Manes, Mon-signor Sweeney. These men whose deep Canarsie accents make her feel disobedient, even while she's getting off on their uniforms and titles. Rose is really a crony herself at this point, she just doesn't see it. She's the equivalent of what she used to call a ward boss, a local fixer. Anyway, half these guys were her boyfriend at some point, I can't keep track. But I doubt Rose is actually getting laid these days from the way she talks. Any given mayor of New York is a kind of bad husband in her life, a huge and consuming disappointment. The current one, named Ed Koch, pronounced like crotch, is at least more loud and sarcastic than the previous and gives her some of that Fiorello La Guardia sensation. We call him Ed Kitsch, I don't know why we find that so funny, just the sound of it. I doubt if any of this is going to make you laugh, it's parochial stuff. I always had the feeling that for you politics was a pretty abstract thing. As you may remember, for Rose it's more like a canker sore.

For us it's daily life. The movement has hunkered down and gotten a little fuzzy around the edges, but we're here and Nixon's gone. Did you know Nixon was a Quaker? Tommy's gotten heavily involved in Quakerism. It started with Vietnam. The Quakers were way ahead of everybody with knowing how to apply for conscientious objector status, during the draft. Now it's the death penalty that takes up all our energy, and international stuff, the American Friends Service Committee. They sent Tommy to sing in Africa twice, and now we're talking about visiting Nicaragua, where some really incredible things are going on. Through the AFSC a lot of the guys who live with us are foreign students and dissident and even revolutionary types, how they get green cards I don't know. I guess the Quakers vouch for them, and who doesn't trust a Quaker? We had an Okinawan living with us, Tomo, who threw gasoline bombs at the American base. He used to gobble down raw tofu and sliced green onions doused with Accent, which it turns out is pure MSG. They all keep shakers of it on their table, like salt and pepper. Anyway, Tommy is pretty involved and even wants to send Sergius to a Quaker school. Tommy goes to Fifteenth Street Meeting every Sunday and sits in silence—I don't know if he prays, but nobody pressures you—and he takes Sergius to Sunday school. The elders at the meeting are crazy for seeing younger people show up so Quakerism doesn't die out. In a way their political stuff is a kind of bait to draw hippies in. I don't mean that as cynically as it sounds. It's a good community. They'll even marry two lesbians. The elders say that if Sergius wants to go to certain schools, kept on a secret Quaker list, they'd probably be able to help out with the tuition. The upper grades in our local school district might turn out to be pretty problematic for a stamp collector.

I don't mention Quakerism as a calculated affront to your horror of religion. Actually, the Quakers keep it pretty plain and boring, not kabbalistic at all, you'd be relieved. Very respectable and even kind of German, in a bourgeois Buddenbrooks sort of way. I never told you that I read that book when you sent it, the special dedicated copy with the snapshot of Mann on his patio hinged into the flyleaf just like the way Sergius tenderly hinges postage stamps into his albums. I was so eager to understand what you and Alma were all about, when I was a kid. All those dishes and pianos and all that chocolate, Alma's accent and all the whispering about Lübeck, Lübeck. You probably have no idea that I have that five-ton marble ashtray from Alma's apartment, the one from your father's bank, her one souvenir from the ruins. There's a joint burning in it now pretty much around the clock. The reason I'm going on about this is that for me, that stuff <u>was</u> religious. It was kabbalistic. Being from Queens, the whole High German side of things was to me like some Greek fable about being descended from gods, and then falling into the mortal world. I just want you to consider that your whole idea of yourself as so modernist and atheistic and materialist might not be as complete as you imagine. From my perspective, all the Dresden stuff that consumes you now, all that ruined culture, the stained glass and parapets, it looks from this distance like you're a monk in the Church of Dead Europe. You have this horror of rabbis, but there are different ways of being a rabbi. When I was nineteen and I visited you at that nightmare spy compound that you were calling an "institute" I actually figured out pretty quickly that being a historian in East Germany meant pumping out revisionist Cold War stuff about how German war crimes were no worse than anything else. I didn't get the full picture but I had an inkling. Still, there was something humane about how you went around collecting all those stories, those terrible stories of the fire. You seemed tragic to me, the way your sympathy and your Communist ideals had shackled you to this bogus "scholarship." It wasn't until I realized the flip side was that you had to discredit Guernica to make your case that I sort of lost it. Incidentally, another thing I found yesterday in this file of your old letters were two more blank postcards from the MoMA gift shop. Stella stuck one up on the fridge and I guess I'll enclose one with this letter if I ever finish writing it, just for old times' sake. I really intended to mail you one of those every month for the rest of your life. Sorry if I'm angry.

Where was I? The point was, what I still didn't really understand until just now when I wrote it down was that the unreconstructed Stalinist bit was the least of it for you. What your new life really meant was a chance to climb up the ass of Lübeck again, through Dresden. They bombed your Buddenbrooks, Dad. I'm so sorry. Even Alma was willing to come and live in her welfare hotel on Broadway, but you couldn't hack it in the New World, could you? You weren't too Communist for America, but you were too German. Well, here's the other thing I never really let myself understand until I began this letter, even though I haven't said a thing about it yet, is that my visit to you was one of the worst things that ever happened to me. What you once called "the awkwardness with the German boy" was horrible, and Dirk wasn't a boy, he was a man, one of your weird colleagues or comrades, and the day of the picnic he told me he'd been Michaela's boyfriend before she married you, and what he did to me could, I know now, practically be considered rape, and it seemed like it was some kind of revenge on you for marrying Michaela, and I have always assumed you knew <u>all</u> these things. What you didn't know is that I was also pretty inexperienced at that point, despite my acting, I'm sure, to the contrary. When I came home I couldn't tell Rose about it. She'd said to me for years that the Germans had stolen everything from her—I guess she meant you, and the war, all her dead cousins, and also the revolution she felt she deserved for all her labors on its behalf, and I used to think it was funny that she'd mixed up Nazis and her Jewish ex-husband! And what she always said, at the climax of this particular theatrical monologue, was that it would kill her if it took me, too. And here I was, apparently returned but secretly stolen.

It takes two parents to make a kid, a simple fact I'm sure hasn't escaped you. A missing parent makes the kid, too, either by being missing or by cropping back up. One way or another, or both. Rose taught me, as if it was the most important thing she could teach, to want <u>not</u> to be Jewish. I didn't get it, I didn't see the point of wanting that, because I didn't feel Jewish to begin with. We didn't go to synagogue, she'd pried the mezuzah from the door when we moved into the Forty-Sixth Street apartment where some Jews had previously lived—I could see what Jews did and we <u>didn't</u> do it. My identity was New Yorker, and leftist. An anti-American American, which was complicated enough, a role requiring a constant vigilance. But when I visited Germany and met you, I understood what the German part of you felt about the Jewish part, and what you felt about Rose. You'd taught me, however reluctantly, to feel Jewish. Suddenly I knew that I was, so to want not to be finally made sense to me. I got the information in reverse order. So there you go: It took a mother and it took a father to complete my education.

You two are alike, still fighting the war. Grieving over those charred bodies, some here, some there. Meanwhile not seeing the present world for what it is. I wouldn't entrust a kid to either one of you—but I am the kid who was entrusted to both. I suppose I would have chosen as you did, to leave the kid with Rose, in the New World, despite some particular horrors I could tell you of, not Dresden horrors but involving ovens, a great legacy we share. But really, thank God I remained in the New World with Rose, not that I imagine you entertained any notion of taking me with you. Thank Christ. Thank Sagittarius and my moon in Gemini. Thanks, Uncle Sam, for forbidding the East German spy reentry across our border. I'm reading this crazy letter and it looks like the scrawl of a child, I have no idea if you'll get this far, but in a way it is written by a child, so that's okay. It didn't escape my notice that you've arranged to abandon poor Errol, my Cold War half brother, whose name is completely missing from your letter, at seven, the same age you abandoned me. Please keep the secrets I shared here. Stella's reading the earlier pages of this letter and now she knows. She says I should cross out the word "sorry" I wrote yesterday. But I am. I'm sorry you're sick. And sorry to go on so long, but you asked me to say how

I live. I'm trying never to live dishonestly and with regrets. Please don't write to me again.

Sincerely,

Miriam Angrush Gogan

———

(The preceding materials comprise the entirety of file #5006A, scanned from the Stasi archives discovered at the Ruschestrasse headquarters in Berlin in January 1990, released according to Inter-Atlantic Coalition Freedom of Information statutes upon solicitation by Sergius Gogan. The letters postmarked "Dresden" represent carbons of typewritten correspondence, routinely submitted to authorities by their sender. The letter postmarked "New York City" is represented in original ballpoint-pen holograph, marked by its interceptors with the English-language annotation "Excerpt? Or hopeless?" It presumably remained unseen by its addressee.)

3   The Halloween Parade

The costume fit, beard, hat, black suit, all of it, even if his Adidas running shoes, peeking from below the overlong pants' cuffs, slightly marred the historical gravitas. He discovered the outfit in a shop called, incredibly enough, the Marquis de Suede, where it hung inside a small annex of traditional costumes nearly overwhelmed by disco jumpsuits formed of parachute cloth and tiny leather shorts dripping with brass and aluminum hardware. His tie-dyed T-shirt, jeans, and fringed leather jacket he not only removed but chucked into the shop's trash bin—they were as much a costume, anyway, as this new disguise. Then, after scrutinizing the clientele and any passersby visible through the shop's storefront glass to be certain he remained free of surveillance, Lenny Angrush peeled cash payment off a roll made entirely of the new two-dollar bills—just waving the talismanic bills at the jaded, mascara-and-stubble-wearing Village Person manning the Marquis's register, to say currency's a history lesson if you trouble to examine what rides in your wallet but who ever does?—then descended into the Christopher Street IRT. The MTA operative trapped in his booth there made no remark on Lenny's costume but, unlike the homosexual, attempted at first to refuse a Bicentennial Two. Lenny was forced to harangue him with his responsibility as a city employee to familiarize himself with and legitimate the issue of the realm, sixteenth president defending the third. Successful in this attempt—nobody topped Lenny Angrush for a harangue, and he soon had a long line of irate fellow riders in line at his back—Lenny was granted his brass token. NYC subway scrip, the local currency of Hades, which only a doomed fool collected. Lenny never bought more than one, which he then deposited within a few steps of purchase, refusing to sully his pocket's lint. So he gained entry to the platform to wait with the other decorated losers for a chance to board the uptown local.

Was it just Lenny's imagination that despite the various cretinous bloody ax murderers and sultry Catwomen and Frank N. Furters and Darth Vaders cluttering up the IRT car the black people aboard all seemed to be singling out the rail-splitting lawyer from Kentucky for the hairy eyeball? Was it so wrong to think their gaze ought to fall on this particular figure with gratitude? Or perhaps they found the man beneath unworthy of the beard? Well, joke 'em if they can't take a fuck.

One rider had managed to pass in the costume of a camel through the eye of a subway turnstile.

Here was a fellow in a perfectly subtle Crazy Eddie costume or perhaps it was actually Crazy Eddie himself riding home from work, in this city you couldn't be sure of anything.

Lenny exited at Fourteenth, and promenaded, disguised as a Kubrick monolith in his stovepipe hat, back to Westbeth. Call it a decoy maneuver. Keeping his journey circuitous was as essential as the beard: Lenny tonight wore the whole of the island for his camouflage. The particular mooks on his tail were uncomfortable in Manhattan, a terrific advantage from the start, and on Halloween night the depths of their discombobulation would form his cloak. Probably Greenwich Village in its present manifestation appeared like Halloween to mooks like these on any typical night, inhabiting as they did an inalterable Eisenhower administration of the imagination. Their brains had shut off since, all things subsequent, including astronauts, hippies, metal detectors, minidresses, the Concorde, and the Krugerrand, being modernistic intoxicants they couldn't fathom. Lenny had been commanded not to exit the borough of Queens until the following day, when Mook Prime aka Gerry Gilroy was "to have a word with" him—such euphemism being a Queens-Irish mobster's notion of admonitory subtlety, and the best reason Lenny could think of for taking to the hoof, for going, in the manner of Hoffman and Leary, visionaries no longer finding the decade's waning years simpatico, underground.

Coming out of the subway he passed a coven of witches who hailed him theatrically, black hats doffed to one of their kind.

Lenny liked his own nose. He might be its sole appreciator, but so what? He was equally in the constituency of his own scabbed knees and his blunt but effective thumbs; he enjoyed walking without a crutch and breathing with no jolt of cracked rib or exploded spleen. Therefore don the stovepipe and beard and evaporate into history. Be the man on the penny, the copper face in the couch cushions, everywhere and disregarded—be subliminal money. Rather than go rural Lenny'd hide in plain sight like Peter Sellers in *The Party*, take a room in Miriam's Alphabet City town house and dwell with the painted elephants. He was as much an apostate citizen as any of the roomers there, could probably teach them a thing or two about true Communism and in return be at last absorbed into the routine orgy he'd denied himself for too long.

Lenny'd made it with one flower child in 1974, or maybe '75, in a Stony Brook dorm room, having met her on the LIRR platform after she'd taken in a Pink Floyd concert and likely also a tab of Owsley at the Nassau Coliseum, and while he was returning from a suburban errand for Schachter's Numismatics. Though in bed she called him "daddy," the hobbitish girl's legs were nearly as hairy as his own, truly saying something.

Not that Lenny minded.

Lenny also had a tuft at the small of his back that was increasingly like monkey's fur.

Lenny suspected Miriam's commune was a hotbed of such chicks. Let him have his share. Let him join then in the orgy that would be forgiving of hair in unusual places. In petulant unrequitedness he'd divided himself from his cousin Miriam and her generation for too long. Let him get stoned, since everybody must. He'd been banned, five years before, from MacDougal Chess, for hustling and side bets and too-vociferous lightning rounds that upset the paying clientele, so had said: Fuck Chess. Now he'd been eighty-sixed from Schachter's on Fifty-Seventh—so let him say: Fuck Coins Already. Lenny would help Miriam's red-haired boy steam stamps off postcards, maybe one day he'd find an Inverted Jenny. Now Gilroy's mooks hunted Lenny in Sunnyside, so let him say: Fuck Queens Entirely. Fuck the amnesia of Communists who'd conveniently forgotten they were Communists, of immigrants who'd forgotten they were immigrants, of micks and Polacks who now put the squeeze on the Mongolian and the Korean and the Turk, as if their own food was any better, as if a generation or two had blanched them of history. Perhaps true Communism had gone after all to reside with the Weather Underground. Let Lenny vanish from history himself, into counterhistory. Let Miriam grant him access to her radical commune and they'd blow up a Brink's truck or two, get it out of his system; perhaps: Fuck Even True Communism.

Fuck Everything, Until We Have Nothing to Fuck Except Fucking Itself. Let Lenny be the last aboard the Me Decade before it collapsed, before it was uncovered as a Ponzi scheme of herpes and divorce. Something about the mixture of the Lincoln outfit and the mobster Gilroy's barely masked death threats had given Lenin Angrush the hard-on of his entire life. He had a stovepipe hat on his head and one also in his pants. Nothing to do with the glittering Jayne Mansfield just this instant crossing Hudson Street. The deeper and more persuasive the cleavage, the more certain Lenny was tonight that he was ogling a man.

He found them at the appointed intersection by the gates of the Westbeth complex, the outlet of the Halloween Parade, where the big floating masks and marching bands assembled for their horny trawl through the Village. Revelers swirled: teddy bears, spray-painted Green Giants, headless horsemen, nuns, and the immense sculptural heads held aloft like banners, depicting heroes and monsters of all variety, among them another Lincoln, looming as if he might topple on the humans below, his eyes like empty windows in the black night, his mole big as a half-deflated basketball. Miriam and Tommy were dressed in fatigues and with red berets and heavy black false mustaches. Tommy had, of course, his guitar strapped across his back as if it were a machine gun. Lenny's desire was such that he couldn't look at his cousin directly. Nothing in his pants had abated in the least, but the Lincoln suit was good cover.

"Let me guess," he said. "You're the new Marx Brothers, in a remake of *Duck Soup* with Steve Martin and Gene Wilder."

"We're Sandinistas, Lenny."

The boy stood in their shadow, almost impossible to notice in a gigantic set of cardboard horns garlanded with tissue-paper flowers. Beneath the headgear, the flaming rust of the boy's hair. How a half Jew could look so Irish, a mystery.

"You?"

"Ferdinand the Bull," said his mother. "Sergius is protesting our choice of what he regards as violent guerrilla fighters."

"A bull is protest of Sandinistas exactly how?"

"Ferdinand's the bull who wouldn't fight. He'd rather smell the roses."

Ah. The private codes perpetuated between parent and child, the eternal mystery of hearth and home. Lenny shook his head. What Miriam had needed to explode in Sunnyside Gardens, she'd reproduced in Alphabet City.

"And you, Lenny," said Tommy. "Honest Abe on the run from the Irish Republican Army? I like the incongruity. 'I cannot tell a lie, it was I that tried to hoodwink a leprechaun with fool's gold.' "

"The IRA's not leprechauns, they're fucking mobsters. And it wasn't fool's gold. Contrary to popular understanding, the Krugerrand's not pure, it's eight-and-a-third percent copper alloy. These Kruger medallions had the same ratio, exactly." Lenny felt he'd been incanting these facts into one uncomprehending face after another for five sleepless days now. First, the Schachter brothers, when they'd first come across one of the ersatz Krugerrands Lenny had been peddling under the auspices of their established name. Karl and Julius Schachter interrogated Lenny, first on the showroom floor and then, when from both parties the yelling began, in the back-room vault. There on Fifty-Seventh Lenny had for years been relied upon for his expertise and discernment, his unparalleled knowledge of strike variants, and hence tolerated in his sometimes unwashed state as an eccentric necessity of the business. So what if some dumb mook couldn't tell, in the gloom of an IRA barroom, the difference between an authentic Krugerrand and a medallion, produced in Cameroon, featuring a portrait of the

South African president Paul Kruger and on the obverse a spring-bok antelope? The gold content was the same. *The gold content was the same.* THE GOLD CONTENT WAS THE SAME! You traded in Krugerrands for the gold content, correct? Or did you have some special sentimental dedication to propping up an apartheid nation? Lenny viewed his propagation of the medallions, which, while functioning perfectly as well as Krugerrands for anyone hoarding gold, undermined that coin's malignant authority, as a minor act of righteousness. This episode, he felt, ought to have been folded into the Lenny Angrush legend, not be the end of it. Karl and Julius refused to agree.

After the Schachters hung him out to dry, disavowing to Gilroy's emissaries any knowledge of Lenny's scheme, Lenny'd been reduced to making his case in a tribunal of IRA back rooms. You'd never know how every pub on Queens Boulevard was bigger in its dark hidden area, like the human brain or the universe itself, until you'd been collar-yanked into a half dozen or so. Replace all the medallions with legitimate Krugerrands? Impossible now that you bozos have wrecked my access to Schachter Numismatics! (Not that it would have been possible anyway.) *Ever heard, dolts, of goose and golden egg?* Only maybe he shouldn't have introduced a fable with the implication of *kill*. These being less than allegorical-minded human beings. One had bashed him in the left temple with a pint glass, a soreness aggravated by the stovepipe's brim, even while the purple bruise was veiled in the hat's shadow.

"The gold content was the same," he repeated now to his idiot cousin-in-law. "And furthermore, 'I cannot tell a lie' has nothing to do with Abraham Lincoln, that's Washington and his cherry tree, the father of our country, only I suppose you came over too late for them to reeducate you." At this moment Lenny became aware with a start that he'd undercounted their group. Despite all possible vigilance, peripheral vision had failed—this damned beard. Talk about your *dark matter*: It was Rose's schvartze protégé, from so long ago, now grown mountainous. The black man seemed fearful, despite his size—hunkered against the chaos of the gathering parade, the giant drifting puppets blotting the sky. His costume, if it was a costume, a sky blue dress shirt tucked into belted slacks, over loafers. In his chubby paw drooped a spangled mask on a stick. "The black Fischer," Lenny said. "Still bestride the earth. Let me guess, you're dressed as William S. Buckley."

"Cicero's graduated Princeton, Lenny."

"So I'm not far off. What are you doing hanging around with these schmucks?"

"Cicero's been a very good boy, but we wanted to help him learn to walk on the wild side before he vanishes into grad school."

Lenny met the young man's hard, suspicious gaze. It wasn't so different from that of the blacks in the subway car, only leavened with all the learning Rose had crammed into that fledgling intelligence. Then leavened, too, with bitterness, at having surely run into countless obstacles neither intelligence nor Rose could help him surmount. A six-foot-two, three-hundred-pound black *preppy*? A fag who, on Halloween night in Greenwich Village in 1978, needed to be schooled to discover pleasure? The world couldn't use one of these. Cicero struck Lenny, for all his uncanny characteristics, as nothing more than the typical black man in America: fucked twelve ways from Thursday.

"By 'walk on the wild side' I trust you mean to indicate the coming international workers' revolution that will wipe away all you see before you," said Lenny. The joke was rote, almost exhausted. It called to a lost universe only Miriam even recognized, and Miriam only reluctantly. "You still play at the pieces?"

"Sorry?"

"Chess."

"I've let my game lapse."

"Good, it's imperialistic propaganda, with nothing to teach you except to savor stalemate. Now all you need is to shed that outfit in favor of camouflage, sign up with the Sandinistas here. They might look like a joke, but a getup like that could save your life should the proletariat suddenly seize control of the factories."

Cicero stared. Good, thought Lenny. Employ the black man's silence, I'll employ the Jew's babble. We'll each use what we've got by birthright. Not much, but it can't be taken from us.

"Lay off, Lenny," said his cousin. She looked like a *Ramparts* centerfold in her fatigues. "We've paid our activist dues, now we're more in the market for a revel."

"So long as you recognize it *is* a market. In what sense paid dues?"

"We just came up from a rally for the People's Firehouse. The victory's a year old, but we decided to put Koch on notice by hitting the streets with the Halloween parade."

He waved her off, Lincoln freeing with a casual gesture slavish notions. "It's not for me, to mix up organizing with puppetry. In the thirties, you had murals, in the fifties, dulcimers. Now in the seventies, papier-mâché. I like actual Marxism better." In fact, Lenny held a poor sense of what Miriam's beloved firehouse squatters had fought for or accomplished, and doubted he wanted to learn. Was there anything more goyish than *firemen*? Surely there could be no quadrant of the city more anti-Semitic than the Polish enclave of Northside. He'd heard rumors that the Polish-language daily newspaper there still ran pro-Hitler editorials.

"You should have spent a few nights at the occupation, it was pretty inspiring. A legitimate action, not yakety-yak."

Lenny, unable to stop himself, drunk on unchecked presidential authority, leaned in to whisper and to fondle Sandinista tit. "I'll give you legitimate action."

"Off, Lenny." She shoved him. He staggered back, into a troupe of bearded ballerinas. Tommy remained oblivious to their scuffle— oblivious, or amused, as he always had been at the prospect of Lenny's rivalrous claims on Miriam. Only Cicero watched, his eyes indicting, his face still too good for his spangled mask. Meanwhile the Irish folksinger left Miriam ungallantly undefended, stood gawping instead at costumed performers, pointing out exemplary freaks to his wide-eyed son in horns, the pacifist water buffalo or whatever he represented. More arrived each minute, a panoply like something from Bosch or Brueghel except featuring vastly more men with breasts. Everywhere, men with breasts, all except Lenny—maybe there was the solution, maybe he should grow some of his own, or stuff a brassiere to self-grope. He was going crazy.

"I can't help myself, Mim, the prospect of death has straightened out my priorities." He felt his dick through his pockets. "I'd like to get something straight between us—you ever heard that one, Mim? Get it? I'd like to get something *straight* between *us*." Maybe if he fell to the sidewalk, clutched himself to her leg, and humped like a dog for fifteen seconds he'd relieve himself of a lifetime's torment. If he ejaculated in his Lincoln suit could it qualify as a seduction deferred? Certainly it would appear as nothing remarkable in this bacchanal.

"Prospect of what death?"

"Have you listened to nothing I've told you?"

"The IRA guys?"

"I have to go underground. I survived McCarthy in full view, but these jokers have got my number."

"I don't recall McCarthy sparing you any attention."

"Moe Fishkin signed up for the army, the easy way out. I went the harder route." Everything was a pun in his condition. The titanic puppet Lincoln had veered into the airspace above them, as though magnetized by its twin. Lenny felt as large and inhuman, as perilously obvious even in disguise.

"So with life flashing before your eyes you reaffirm your campaign to rape me in front of my husband?"

"Don't use such bourgeois language. We'll slip away, go climb up a pole at the People's Firehouse, since it's presently vacated."

"I was going to offer you a little holiday reefer but frankly now I'm terrified."

"Please, I could use the narcotic. Especially a cigarette moistened with your lips, as I'll apparently never be."

"Lenny. Don't act so berserk."

"I'll keep my hands to myself, I swear. Indulge me, Mim, I'm on the brink, I'm berserk with *despair*. Get me high."

Miriam had been preparing the joint without delay anyhow, she'd only been taunting him. Now she curled herself around it, to shield her lighter's flame, right in front of the kid and the cops and the black preppy and the bearded ballerinas and the guy dressed as a purple flounder, but in a city where old orders were being disassembled by flamboyance and bankruptcy and derangement they stood tonight at the exact lawless center, this zone flooding in every second with a new freakish phenomenon, some Puerto Rican kids in zoot suits and Mohawks now, and a guy in an improbable bulldozer outfit—a bulldozer with eyeliner, because you shouldn't forget eyeliner—in a city gone berserk itself, nobody cared one whit about a public joint. The miraculous thing was that if the mooks in Lenny's pursuit were to penetrate this throng in their outer-borough mufti, their Members Only jackets and time-machine duck's-ass haircuts, *they'd* be the freaks. They'd leap out like neon. Mim handed the joint to Cicero first and the Princeton grad took hold of it and gave it a good drag, to his credit. The hippies might loosen him up yet. Cicero scowled concentration, puffer-fished cheeks and eyeballs, then passed it along. Lenny accepted it, and had just time enough to flood his lungs down to his diaphragm, to his furthermost bronchioles, when he understood that his vision of Members Only and duck's-asses wasn't premonitory but *preconscious*: mind's-eye hadn't conjured mooks but gleaned them in slantwise vision, through hair's-width apertures in the blinders of his beard. Lenny fruitlessly attempted to raise his voice and coughed spasmodically instead, the noise drowned in a cacophony of mirth and flattery and a marching band's blaring rendition of "Macho Man," and also the adding-machine clatter of blood in his ears. His arms pinned behind him, an elbow's hinge cinching his windpipe, Lenny was muted, taken to ground, beneath the fluttering shadow of his doppelgänger, which now appeared a mournful soul rising to the heavens. He lost compass of Miriam immediately. Forget the father Sandinista and the kid with horns. The last he saw was Cicero staring with helpless inertia. A bodyguard-size figure but every morsel of will trapped in his skull, behind his eyes. Now the Halloween parade had begun. They dragged the lesser Lincoln in the opposite direction.

————

The Last Communist is dreaming. The dream is of a footnote, a new footnote he'll add to his monograph, *1841 Quarter Eagles in Proof-Only and Circulation: A Dissent*. The result he's sought, by means of five years' pestering, has come to fruition, the New York Numismatics Society Press consenting to issue a second edition of his book, in order that innumerable misprints be corrected; now, in the course of making repairs, the Last Communist has inserted *a golden footnote*, one with the power to redeem his whole expedition through planetary time. For it simply isn't allowable that the Last Communist should perish with this monograph his sole accomplishment, not as it stands in its error-ridden and excessively obedient first printing, yet, with the insertion of the footnote, in which he's daringly fused Marx and David Akers to his original scholarship into the occult legacy of the gold standard, he'll die satisfied. *Marx once called money "a veil," yet this is not to suggest, contrary to many readings, that money is only to be looked behind, for the truth it conceals; we must also apply our keen gaze upon the veil, which in a materialist view consists of something in itself.* Thus begins the golden footnote, as it unfolds before the dreamer's eyes. *According again to Marx, "the simple commodity form is the germ of the money form"; what then, is the simple commodity? Gold. That substance rooted in earth itself, and yet with its alchemical binding power upon our senses, tantalizingly suggestive of metaphysical properties; in gold we discover how a veil may be also a germ; gold, medium of mud and stone, a turd or fecal form, may exalt, within the realm of phantasmic hoarding, to become booty of empire and wealth of nations. To grasp what crimes attach hereupon, not merely the suppressed saga of the 1841 Quarter Eagle in its circulating rather than proof-only strikes but also Nixon's abolition of the gold standard, we turn again to Marx, who recalls how, in our disequilibrium between money as a circulating symbol and gold as an aesthetic commodity, we arrive at a crossroads where stands the hoarder, the comical Shylockian miser, whose desire for money "is in its very nature insatiable."* Here the dreamer loses sight of the text, the golden footnote he wishes never to see the end of; something—the pen with which he writes? a Quarter Eagle? a Krugerrand?—sears the palm of his hand, rousing him.

———————

The Last Communist on the last night of his life, maybe, comes to light again with the 7 train as it screams through its improbable curvature at Queensboro Plaza and onto the elevated track, moon and streetlamps piercing the subway's car like Saint Sebastian's arrows. Yet it's not so much the light that wakes him as the tiny arrow of extinguished joint piercing his palm. He'd apparently clutched it while enmeshed in struggle and now finds it has singed the meat of his fist's interior. He opens his hand and lets the roach fall to the train's floor. A film noir clue, prized from a dead man's fingers. His abductors pay no attention. They have the car to themselves, likely have spooked other occupants from boarding as their odd tableau rolled through stations—two goons and a comatose Emancipator. Stovepipe perched on the seat beside him, miraculously unruined. Soreness of half-crushed esophagus suggests he'd gone half the distance to death already and then returned. He wonders how long his brain was without oxygen.

Since 1956, maybe.

Perhaps earlier, from the day he dandled his cousin and his mentality had drained into his lap.

Chessmen, baseball, Krugerrands, the constellation of nonsense with which he's decorated his lonely life. All of it surrounding an abiding mystery: his beliefs. These form a little zone of dark, sheltered and abiding within the Last Communist through decades of incomprehension and scorn, as the 7 train shelters ignorant commuters through passages of dark and light.

The Last is a man abandoned by history. He should have been at the inception, forging a bloody Communism in the teeth of czars. Or lived to participate in its eventual triumph, an H. G. Wells vision impossible to impart to lesser mortals. He should never have been stranded here, in the endless disaster between. Here is only irrelevancy, Miriam's Yippie boycotts and day-care marches; the folksinger's death-penalty vigil; hairsplitting Trotsky dreamers and Frantz Fanon Third World fetishists, French eggheads who'd reconfigured Marxism as mumbo jumbo, a new form of Kabbalah. Or civil rights, which gave way to Black Power, and then see your reward: the hatred of a kid like Cicero. Ha! You might as well, just to pick a random example, try protesting apartheid by retailing ersatz Krugerrands to the Irish Republican Army.

There is no place anymore for the Last and yet if he is honest with himself he knows he is not the Last, he is only carrying a torch for the Last, a torch she hardly needs as she's been out there blazing all the time, waiting for the world to come to her door. She who vanished into the neighborhood: cops, library, pizza parlor, a Christmas card from the borough president pinned on the fridge for her cover story. Sunnysideism is Late-Twentieth-Century Communism.

Lenny should have quit when he got in deep with pickles, should have learned to relish shirts saturated in brine. He was closer then than he knew.

The 7 train idles at the Lowery Street station. Just as the doors begin to close he leaps, not forgetting to grab his stovepipe, and is through, and free.

––––––––––

Rose opened the door and let him in without a word: Perhaps it is the case that a visit from the man in the stovepipe hat is, by this time, her whole lifetime overdue. *Of course, come in, what took you so long?* Lincoln, Rose's Elijah, and why be passed over forever? Just like her, to think that he'd select *her* door actually to come through. "Four score and seven years ago today," Lenny said aloud, and his initial jest was overtaken by the sincerity the words and occasion seemed to demand of him, by the wish not to disappoint. But he stopped. If only he knew the whole speech. Rose stared flatly, her eyes acute and implicitly demanding, awaiting whatever. Her stoical gaze not so different from Cicero's. Yet like the rest of the world Cicero had abandoned Rose, vanished to Princeton and beyond, into Miriam's Halloween parade. Lenny wondered how long it had been since Rose had even heard from the ungrateful protégé.

The whole century had vacated Sunnyside Gardens, quit darkening her door. Yet had it learned anything in the process?

Lenny's lips couldn't from within the Lincoln beard say *hide me* or *hold me* though he desired both. He couldn't think of the words of either Gettysburg or Proclamation and couldn't find his own voice. No assertion seemed equal to the woman before him, from whom his every disappointment had sprung, she alone familiar with the unspeakable Red certainty in his soul because she herself had instilled it, even if barely meaning to. Goonish cousin, he'd been at her table, one summer evening in 1948, and heard something he believed, like others believed in God or country. His parents fed him forkfuls of kugel and Rose fattened his brain with revolution.

Rose in her nightgown stepped back across her kitchen linoleum and stared at the Lincoln silhouette against the moonlit green of the block's courtyard gardens, and he wearing the costume suddenly wondered if she even knew who it was inside, whether she'd made him from his voice or his thumbs, or was fooled. He'd seen no trick-or-treaters while stumbling in through the Gardens. No jack-o'-lantern at her front step. Lenny closed the door behind him. His tongue might be frozen but he still possessed the righteousness inside his Lincoln pants. Or he possessed it again, despite his being manhandled by the mooks and extradited onto the 7 train. This was like the hangover boner Lenny could rely on, at waking after a night of drinking, a force affirming life-in-the-old-boy-yet against evidence to the contrary. Or perhaps like the notorious erection discovered when they cut down and examined the body of a hanged man. Whichever, he'd use it to continue his statement, to make his protest, his filibuster against death. In fact, it encoded its own statement, was a homing device that knew more than he did, one pointing back through daughter to mother, from Manhattan to the old countries of Queens and Poland. A pre-war boner, embodying knowledge of a time when neither Europe nor Communism nor the woman before him had been ruined territories.

"Four score!" he said again, deepening his voice, as anyone would be certain Lincoln's ought to be deepened. He wished to thrill and command her. She retreated through a doorway's shadow, leading him, he felt. The lights were extinguished, Rose's typical fierce parsimony, and by the time he reached her they were two shadows, mysterious to each other in equal portion. Here, the very rooms where Lenny'd first conceived the urge to fuck. The silky layers he tore free of their buttonholes and clasps each held some bulging soft portion of her. The stovepipe had toppled off somewhere behind them, the beard got in between his mouth and hers and had to be ripped free, leaving them each for a moment tonguing gluey fluff, each issuing cat-with-hairball noises before he resumed the devouring effort of lips and tongue against hers, then below, to mumble wonderment at her neck and clavicle and into the sweet fog of her breasts.

The Lincoln slacks were zippered—anachronism, he wondered? He undressed himself with greater care than he'd taken over Rose's night garments. No special reverence for the Lincoln suit, but if he shredded it he'd have nothing else to wear. Their flesh pooled warmly, in regions grown sadly unfamiliar to him over the past years. Not even certain which expanses were exactly hers or his own, until he found the socket. The unmistakable connection, never young or old in its essence. Their root in the animal spectrum at last, such relief to encounter something that dwarfed human history.

Two people more the opposite of nature lovers had maybe never walked the earth, let alone brought into conjunction the sole undeniable natural facts lurking beneath their clothing.

She'd begun scrabbling at his ribs and ass, whether to deter or exhort he couldn't be certain. In either case the effect was exhorting. Small censorious murmurings beneath him turned rhythmic. Decanting himself with what he hoped was a suitably Lincolnesque grunt, Lenny tried to imagine, if cousin impregnated cousin, what wonders might tumble forth? Some dreamy monster of revolution, an American Lenin or Kropotkin? More likely one of history's orphans, like himself, yet more thoroughly cursed, never having even glimpsed the dream. Undrafted backup catcher for the Sunnyside Proletarians, waddling through life in the tools of ignorance.

What a sorry scene he made, by evidence of his own sticky fingertips: now barely able to recontain his hairy potbelly in the Lincoln waistline, as if in dissipating himself here he'd grown fatter, or slacker. His hard-on the last hardness in him, now spent.

"You know who I am?" he said into the dark. Too late, he realized this might be unmerciful. Let Rose have been despoiled by Lincoln, and maybe she'd take it for a dream. On any given night it might be John Reed or Fiorello La Guardia or her black policeman returning—or even Albert returning—so why not Abe?

"You thought you could fool an Angrush from recognizing an Angrush?"

He caught his breath and stood from the bed. "The suit, in the dark—"

"It's true you're ordinarily a lousy dresser, but the black suit is not totally without precedent. I was at your bar mitzvah."

"You're not scandalized?"

"Why all of a sudden be scandalized? My astonishment at you and any number of other developments is a chronic condition."

Was she not human? Or merely inhumanely defended? Some ghost of courtliness stirred in him now, a rarely called-on set of behaviors. "You're a beautiful woman, Rose. I regret nothing. I only thought of our respective ages."

"Don't be a schmuck, Lenny. You've been a fifty-year-old man since you were approximately seven."

Courtliness vaporized in the atmosphere of Rose's feral frankness, itself the intoxicant that had always drawn him to this door. "Ironically it may have been my fruitless love for your daughter that prematurely aged me."

"You know how long it's been since I had sexual intercourse? Spare me about my daughter."

"I saw her tonight."

"And I spoke to her this morning. What are you trying to say?"

He'd backed to Rose's bedroom door. Whether to bar himself in with her or maintain the option of fleeing, he was unsure. No nightlight betrayed Rose's posture, only rustling as she constructed something to cover herself from what he'd left behind. Out beyond these walls two idiots had ridden the 7 train an additional stop empty-handed, presumably exited at Bliss Street, and needed to decide how to explain to Gerry Gilroy how they'd cornered their quarry and lost him again. Perhaps switched platforms and gone one stop back to Lowery, to stalk the streets of Sunnyside.

"Miriam is inadequate to your standard."

"You'll have to be more specific."

"You tried to change conditions for the working class and alter the doomed trajectory of civilization. Your daughter just wants to put LSD in the water supply."

"I beg to differ. My daughter is the greater revolutionary than you and me put together, Lenny."

"You couldn't mean this. You say it to spite me." He was unable to keep the sulk from his voice. "She boycotts grapes and marches for day care but laughs at history. I saw her tonight with her Quaker, playing dress-up as South American guerrillas, like Woody Allen in *Bananas*."

"They're not playing dress-up." Rose's voice, in the dark, took on a dour prophetic undertone, like the Great and Powerful Oz. "They're putting the boy in boarding school and visiting Nicaragua at the start of next year. Tommy's writing songs in Spanish."

"Just costumes, Rose. You're deceived."

"You're the one deceived. Why would they bother telling someone like you, for whom revolution is always allegory of some kind? You're the one who plays dress-up. She got arrested on the steps of the Capitol, she picketed LBJ at the World's Fair, now she's plunging into actual revolution. Where were you? Staring at the mystical Masonic symbols on a five-dollar coin, thinking you're too good to be bothered."

"I saw them, dressed for Halloween in comic-book fatigues. They'd be arrested before they got out of the airport."

"I don't know from Halloween."

"Look at your calendar."

"You look. There is no such American tradition, it's a rumor, a bad dream from the old country, from Transylvania. We came to get away from that horror. Except you, for whom it's Halloween every night of the year. Grow up, Lenny."

"You said I was an old man."

"Also a child."

"This is craziness. We just made love, Rose."

"Get out of my room, get out of my house."

"I've got enemies out there."

"You never made one enemy worth making. Don't after all this time try to hide in my skirts."

She couldn't help provoking and abusing him, any more than she could have kept from inspiring him, long ago and always. Rose was a statue to be studied or ignored, to endure weather and accumulate the shit of birds, but not to be negotiated with. That he was a man in a perilous circumstance wasn't going to impress her.

Better, thought Lenny romantically, to be doomed outright than doomed to such irrelevance. But—not Miriam. Miriam, whether she knew it or not, was under both their protection. He'd come full circle again. Let this be his final priority. "Rose, is she seriously going to Nicaragua? I'm speaking seriously here for a minute, indulge me. After that, if you wish, I'll go. Seriously, they'll get themselves killed."

"For the record, that's my prediction as well, made this morning on the telephone. We don't require a family go-between, Lenny. You're an outlying cousin, which fact explains why your visit here is tolerated, but it shouldn't happen again. Now go."

"If you don't believe in Halloween, how do you account for my arriving here dressed as I am?"

"Because you're a lunatic."

———

They picked him up again creeping out of the Gardens through the Skillman Avenue gate. He broke free, clutched his hat as he scrambled and, thank God now for the Adidas, made for the concrete courtyard of the Cambridge Apartments, where he should have gone to begin with, to vanish into verticality and anonymity, rattle on the door of some kid he'd gone to school with, now grown fat and with fat wife and fat kids, vanish into muddling Queens anonymity where he could park himself until the Krugerrand Caper cooled somewhat. He'd ring fifteen buzzers at once with the flat of his two hands and hope somebody expecting somebody buzzed him in. He only got as far as the dry concrete fountain, in which he sighted irrelevantly a child's abandoned baseball, fluorescent orange, Charlie Finley–style, moldering in webs. Now, there was a man with the iconoclast's outlook. If Lenny'd only been petitioning the office of a man like Finley, rather than Shea and Rickey. Water under the bridge, but maybe Jack Kerouac was right, possibilities for utopian reinvention lay on the West Coast. Maybe Lenny should cross the Hudson, after all this time, Go West, Old Fart, see what was out there. He thought of pausing to scoop the ball, to hurl at his pursuers. But he had a corroded shoulder, doubted he could throw, a cumulative thing he'd aggravated somewhere in the escapade, getting from Village bacchanal to Rose's bed. Fucking was like gym class, like doing push-ups, and he was a long time out of gym. He ignored the ball, dodged for the entranceway instead. The first bullet went through the stovepipe's brim.

The year Rose Angrush Zimmer fell in love with Archie Bunker was the same in which she began attending the funerals of strangers. This was also the time when Rose's perambulations grew increasingly random, her old block-watcher's orbit around Sunnyside becoming wobbly and strange, until it had unspooled completely.

What on earth was her intention, going to the funerals?

It began with Douglas Lookins. Without warning, he'd succumbed to an embolism, just months after Diane's slow-motion passing from her prized array of ailments. In perfect imitation of a loving spouse, as if unable to imagine living on without her. One further brushstroke added to the masterpiece of indignity the affair had been for Rose, but she'd gone to usher him into the ground nonetheless. A policeman's noble interring in New Calvary Cemetery in Maspeth, on a cloud-harassed hillock, there to vanish into the sea of headstones on view from the Long Island Expressway. Rose was the only white face apart from Douglas's commander, a major Rose had come to know. They stood together; Rose might easily have been mistaken here for his wife. No matter. Cicero, now a man, looked something of a stiff himself, in the costume of a Princeton junior, and not glad in the least to be drawn by his father's death back into this universe of hard-ass black cops and their suffering families. Rose offered him a rough embrace, free of tears on either side, and told him to call her, when he wanted, if he wanted. Otherwise, she had spoken to barely anyone. An art she'd perfected on hundreds of former occasions, no effort whatsoever.

Next, the horror of the commune's scattering of Miriam's ashes, mixed with Tommy's, in the so-called community garden on East Eighth Street, beyond Avenue C—a vacant lot. *A vacant lot!* Ground zero for a ghetto childhood, or worse—the pockmarked Lower East Side truly resembled newsreel footage of postwar Berlin. Well, Rose had thought bitterly, at least she made it to Manhattan! Six months later than it should have taken place, the boy absent, being shielded, Rose suspected, from her. There, Rose uttered not a word. The mourners sang and swayed, arms braided together, pot smoke wafting, rumors of the MacDougal Street scene's demise apparently exaggerated. Rose left before the love-in concluded.

Lenny? Shipped in a box to Israel.

So Rose went looking for a proper funeral, which turned out, to her surprise, to mean a proper *Jewish* funeral.

Maybe she'd become meshugah ahf toit, loon-crazy with bereavement. One of those who, losing everyone in a cataclysm, begins seeking situations both anonymous and which exemplify grief. Possibly this wasn't crazy at all, or crazy not like a loon but a fox. The trick might be to diffuse and depersonalize the act of mourning, and also to freeze it, to entrench it as a permanent occupation. *We Jews mourn, there's nothing to it, and also nothing new to it.* Let me attend six million funerals, maybe then I'll be done. By that time my personal dead will be as raindrops in the sea. I'll forget their names.

Funerals in Corona, or in Woodside or Forest Hills or even Manhattan, served one more practical function: They got Rose free of the house, yet vaulted her beyond the immediate precincts of the Gardens, that labyrinth of grudges. For her stores of defiance were running short. The funerals made of Sunnyside a foyer, a lobby, to more important destinations. And she needed, from time to time, and apart from the tasks of shopping or schlepping her letters to the P.O., to get free of the house. Rose watched too much of her splendid new color television. There were days she thought she was falling through the screen, toward the Shea Stadium outfield, a green whose seductiveness mocked her long indifference to green. There were days she spent just adjusting the color balance, trying to modulate the scarlet blare of the actors' cheeks on *Ryan's Hope*.

It was in this mood that Rose stumbled upon the comedy program, curious merely because someone had said it was set in Astoria. She'd thought herself done with love, until she saw him. The doughy bigot with pain all over his face. At first Rose barely listened to his words, heard only the painful music of Archie's accent. He muttered and droned, a caricature of indigenous New York. Her reaction? She should have expected it, yet after a lifetime of such lightning bolts it never quit astonishing her, that her fascination with some human male, whether judge or policeman or mere loading-dock foreman, was wired to her sex. Astonishing that any of her brain's wires still reached that forsaken region! She'd welcomed no man to touch her in a decade, unless you counted her cousin's farcical spasm, the night he was killed. For Rose to respond in the first place, she seemed to require a man whose vanities struck her as secretly absurd—surely this was the only thing they'd all had in common. Perhaps she required that a man's vanities rise high enough to blot her own, to make obdurate stances look reasonable.

So Archie squirreled into her heart and loin.

Edith she could live without—but they always had wives, didn't they?

Other days Rose watched the Gardens as though *it* were the television. If she stared through her kitchen window with persistence enough, teacup turning cold in her grasp, the inhabitants blurred, even those who stood and waved at her, as though Rose took a long-exposure photograph with her mind. She saw just the buildings and the fences and the growth and decay in the beds and along the pathways, saw just time itself. Each by each the new owners had balkanized the commons. A ration of the planet belonging at once to everyone became mere property, a scrap of fenced weeds large enough for a cast-iron barbecue grill or a plastic deck chair, craven assertion of a McCoy-versus-Hatfield view of human rights. Even the walking path had been claimed. You couldn't pass through the Gardens from Skillman to Thirty-Ninth without conducting a square dance of diversions past the new fencework.

The difficulty with permitting the fire of your gaze to melt the humans down to ghosts was this: If Rose then glanced down at the hands gripping the tepid teacup, they'd gone invisible, too. Nobody left to properly mourn it all.

So make of every day an opportunity to read the death lists, put on some lipstick and a black pantsuit and let the body in the casket stand in for everything—body, mind, world, beliefs—going daily into the ground.

Then one day the name in the newspaper was that of Jerome Cunningham, formerly Jerome Kuhnheimer, and known to his family and friends as "Stretch," and she readied herself for the funeral, out in Corona, and when she attended she found that her life inside and outside her apartment, even more specifically her life on the two sides of the television's bowed glass, had gotten mixed up.

———————

It occurred at a generic parlor chapel, one fitted with cursory Jewish disguise, a shawl here, a menorah there. Rose's method was to ensure she'd be unlikely to exchange recognitions, by entering late and seating herself in the back row. There was an oddness to this funeral to begin with, the cohort from Pendergast Tool & Die, Stretch Cunningham's place of occupation, where the poor bastard slaved his whole adult life on the loading dock, mixing uneasily with the Jewish family. The dead man had had either the guts or the stupidity to anglicize *Kuhnheimer*, WASPishly, to *Cunningham*—one single act of boldness in a lifetime otherwise distinguished, if you believed the eulogists standing above his casket, only by Stretch's chimplike foolishness. A resolute unwillingness to be serious about anything: This endeared the man to everyone. A jokester, who'd dropped dead.

Despite Archie's role as eulogist, he came in even later than Rose. He burst in, Edith pushing a yarmulke onto his skull and, with barely an introduction, was drawn up onto the chapel's tiny altar. The portly man was toothpasted into a black suit, one likely in mothballs since some previous funeral, years and neck-sizes ago. Collar and tie looked cinched tight, to stanch rebellion from below; meanwhile, above, his white hair was capped by the ill-fitting yarmulke, containment against the top end's explosion. Between, Archie's face formed a pasty meat-map of his soul. His features showed every type of involuntary pathos, auditioning bovine stupefaction, bearish wrath, and wily self-amusement, without ever disguising that flayed aspect at the corners of his eyes and mouth.

"I worked shoulder to shoulder with Stretch for eleven-twelve years and I, uh, I knew him good. Well, not as good as I thought . . ." Rose, though not understanding how Archie Bunker could intrude on her life in this way, got the gag immediately. Archie, anti-Semite, hadn't known until he walked into the funeral that his beloved friend was Jewish. Archie went on: "Stretch was one of them up guys, one of the uppest guys you ever met, always laughing, tellin' jokes himself, and many a *Jewish* joke he told . . ."

Rose loved Archie even better here, in person, humiliated in front of all these Jews. She felt defiance on his behalf, on behalf of the marvelous innocent resolve that kept the man bumbling forward. He missed his friend Stretch and death bewildered him and yet he found a way to stand there with his foot continuously in his mouth and not flee or begin weeping.

Archie Bunker was, truly, a newborn in the disguise of an aging hard hat. Rose found herself plunging ever deeper into the maze of his charismatic stupidity. And then he finished, and with no one to help him picked his way down from the chapel's riser. "Shalom," he said quietly, glancing at the casket as he passed it, and in his awe at having spoken the alien word it was as if Rose was hearing it for the first time.

Yes, Archie. We have a word for what you want to say to your friend Stretch, a word that doesn't exist in any other tongue and you wouldn't use it if it did. You'd think it was a Commie word and you wouldn't touch it with a ten-foot pole. For what was "shalom"? Not merely "peace." "Completeness"? Maybe. "Reciprocity"? Maybe that, too. But also "hello," "goodbye," and even "good riddance." "All men are brothers, yes, have it your way, now get out of my face, I've got a more important destination." Perhaps truly for the first time Rose felt the abjured power of her Judaism, its sway over the lumpen American mind. Before the onset of the beliefs that had split her from the Jews, Rose was already part of an international conspiracy. Yes. The stateless and ironical People of the Book. Behind all prejudice against Jews lay trepidation and wonder, exactly like that she now glimpsed in Archie.

When the episode was over, her television switched off, Rose had to lay on her bed trembling. Was it possible, what happened at the funeral? Could she make such contact a second time?

———————

Once upon a time, Rose's every footfall on pavement had been a tick on some moral clockface, each encounter a turn of some screw, every polite silent nod of the head burdened with shame in several directions—*I've got my eye on you, buddy, so don't imagine it's you who've got your eye on me! You may appear an upstanding so-and-so to your present cronies but I recall who you used to be seen with in 1952—me!* In the Prisoners' Dilemma of neighborly recriminations, Rose played the warden, jangling keys in the corridor, holding everyone's confession in her breast pocket. Having gone from the party before the party was smashed, never saying how last-second excommunication spared her part in the mass contrition, her authority deriving from who-knew-where. Rose bore nothing more than an arched eyebrow for her badge, her affiliations—with cops, librarians, local pols—as impossible to deny as to explicate. A somersault, from subversive to block-watcher! For Rose, to exit her kitchen and walk to Greenpoint Avenue was to set sail, beneath prophetic colors sooted by a century of remorse. Her banner: lost causes better than any cause that could ever have won. Dragging history's cloud, she'd cover the area for miles, causing witnesses to shudder and fall silent.

Personal grief was another thing entirely. It humbled her to the ground-level gossip of the Gardens. Wearing the mourner's black was unsuitably pitiable, no banner at all. She caught scurrilous echoes even in the hush her old comrades cobbled together just long enough for her to pass on the sidewalk. The glue of political paranoia dried to dust and blew away, and paranoia turned out to be the last thing holding her sense of the neighborhood together. What remained was a bunch of harmless old people gossiping about Florida and death—of the two destinations, Rose couldn't say which was worse. The younger inhab-

itants, for whom Sunnyside was merely a locality in which they'd settled, didn't know her at all.

In her exhaustion, Rose no longer buttonholed, no longer demanded
introduction to each new face that appeared—a momentary lapse that
became a landslide into anonymity. As she awarded her customary
silent treatment to those she'd known for decades, and was unable to
forge a connection to these young couples who'd likely respond with
uncomprehending politeness, a gulf yawned on the sidewalk between
Rose and any other human. The radical basis that had made Rose's
indignation an idealist's warrant had become difficult to recall, even
for her. Lacking warrant, she took on a disconcerting resemblance to
a bitter old lady. Silence once loaded with admonitory implication was
now mere silence. If, spooked by glance or gesture from this lonely figure, a newcomer troubled to ask, the answer came: *So sad, her only
daughter was murdered in South America.* Or, more caustic: *A hopeless case. A Red. The husband ran in the forties, the daughter tried
Manhattan but that apparently wasn't far enough. To find a man to
touch her, she resorted to a schvartze, and even he tiptoed away. Any
other woman would have raised the orphaned grandson, but no. The
boy was shipped off to Pennsylvania instead, into some cult.*

Quakers aren't a cult? Well, you're entitled to your opinion.

At least among the embittered Jews slugging shopping carts down
refrigerated aisles the Holocaust ladies could roll up their sleeves and
show you the numbers inked on their arms. Rose needed a tattoo
reading "Premature Anti-Fascist."

*Listen, I once forced a Wobbly to sit down and talk calmly to a
Kropotkinite. It may mean nothing to you but worlds hung in the
balance at that particular moment in time.*

Amid these ruins, and between invitations to funerals, Rose
walked, and walked far, into the Witness Protection Program of
Greater Queens. Somewhere at the intersection where Forty-Seventh
Road crossed Sixty-Fourth Terrace on its way to Seventy-Eighth Place
and beyond, she should be able to lose herself by immersion among
the numberless humans living, without recognition or mercy, within
the incomprehensible system of numbered pavements. The people, the
people—it was with *the people* that she'd begun, as a sixteen-year-old

who dared contend with her father at the Passover table. If this is a night for asking questions, let me add another: What makes Jewish slavery more compelling, at this late date, and knowing all we do, than any other of mankind's present versions of enslavement? Weren't we all *people*? It was to humankind, living under the false divisions our notions of race and creed had imposed, that she'd dedicated herself. And yet such dedication had led to her disastrous estrangement, not only from her father and his Judaism but from humankind. In obedience to her insight she'd drifted into Soviet-dictated cells half populated by FBI. She'd emerged with a nervous system wired to grasp the world as an arrangement of systems, institutions, ideologies. Now she thought: Enough with policemen and city councilmen! Enough with mayors—you might as well revere the pope! You invested power in any human man, a Jew even, only to see him seduced and corrupted, and in Manes's case to see him unmistakably also headed off a cliff. Considering how Rose possessed a greater intelligence and a stiffer spine than any number of men under whose implausible authority she'd wasted most of her life, it was sobering to think she'd maybe been spared such fate only by happenstance of her sex. Rose Angrush Zimmer had never been elected to anything larger than the Queensboro Public Library board, there to sit, sole woman among judges, priests, and morons of commerce, barely getting in a word for every paragraph of oration she'd been made to absorb. She could as well have been emptying their ashtrays, slicing poppy-seed hamantaschen.

It was only her womb that had relegated her to where she now felt she belonged, in the ranks of history's losers: the People. She'd scoffed at the word *feminism* a hundred times when Miriam had proposed it as a description of Rose's life. Now add this little twinge of regret to the incomprehensible loss, that she should come to see her own life from Miriam's point of view too late for anything but a conversation with her daughter's ghost, on the telephone that didn't ring.

Facing the ultimate loss, the death of an only child, a Jew would customarily renounce God. That renunciation, Rose had achieved decades before.

Therefore, renounce what?

Materialism.

It was in this spirit that Rose walked now, repentant of patrol, now holding herself above no possible solace, and in this spirit that she veered into Kelcy's Bar seeking something other than mercy from the sun blazing on her head and an icy Coca-Cola with a slice of lemon, though she certainly sought those things. It was in this spirit that she again migrated, by the voodoo of longing, into Archie Bunker's world. For Kelcy's was Archie Bunker's bar, located, according to the credit sequence, on Northern Boulevard. Why should Rose not arrive there?

Out of the glare of the tavern, her eyes adjusted slowly, so he resolved from an outline that could have been that of a small circus bear in a porkpie hat: Bunker, seated alone, nursing an afternoon whiskey.

Rose inched between the jukebox and pinball machine, to take a place at the bar. Summoning her fullest hauteur, she took a paper napkin from a pile and daubed at her brow. The five or six men scattered there—two at the bar's corner, heads bent in mulling conference with their drinks, others at the small round tables, marooned on the sawdusty floor—lowered their eyebrows, tamped their curiosity. Bunker greeted Rose with a subvocal grunt. The bartender shifted to face her with a pleasant wordless expectancy.

"Coca-Cola with a slice of lemon, please."

"Pepsi okay?"

"Pepsi."

"You ain't gonna honor the occasion with an actual beverage?" interjected Bunker.

"I'm sorry?" Rose said. Had she stepped out this afternoon in merry ignorance of yet another public holiday?

"I just won a bet with my good friend Mr. Van Ranseleer here—he was sayin' we wouldn't get no women in here on no Tuesday afternoon. Since you won the bet for me, Mr. Van R. owes the rest of us a round, see?" This was directed, Rose saw, at one of the men at the bar's end, who wore dark glasses indoors. "Yeah, that's right, he's blind. We was waitin' for you to speak up so he'd know he was a loser. But don't worry, he's got more dough than the rest of us put together.

So your, what's it called, your Shirley Temple there is covered. But seein' as how you honor us with your presence"—Bunker pronounced this *witcher presents*—"I was just suggestin' there ain't a law against a cold beer, in a spirit of celebreviation."

"Thank you, but I'm not a beer drinker."

"Pardon my assumption—but are you Jewish?"

"Yes, I am."

"Well, you got to admit that you Jewish people aren't known for big spending around a bar. No intents offended."

Rose considered this for a moment. "Is this impression of yours . . . more a matter of the drinking or the spending?"

Bunker raised his hand as if halting a train. "Hey, Scotchmens is much worse."

"My name is Rose."

"Archie. Don't worry, you is more than welcome in heres to drink Pepsi-Cola."

"I know you, Archie. I mean I've seen you before."

"Oh, jeez. Should I'd have recognized you?"

"You wouldn't remember, but I remember you. I was at Jerome—Stretch Cunningham's funeral. I heard you speak."

A series of expressions crossed Archie's face, inventorying the vast range of feelings available on the far side of anything remotely enlightened. Watching, Rose recalled her sense of entrancement that day at the funeral home. "Maybe that's why I got the feeling you was Jewish," Archie said, not untenderly.

"Maybe so."

"Well, that loading dock never was the same without Stretch, I'll say that."

"You're the foreman—yes?"

"For thirty-six years, but they gave me the golden wristwatch now. I got plans, though."

"What are your plans?"

"You're lookin' at 'em." He threw an arm wide and made a canny look to indicate that Rose had unwittingly entered a demesne or fiefdom.

"To sit with your—" Rose skirted *stooges* and *cronies*, conscious of Archie's sensitivities. "To pass the days among your friends here?"

"Are you kiddin'? These losers? Nah, I'm buying this joint so's I can pocket their money. I'm gonna expand it into a little restaurant, bust into the store next door—by which I mean the adjacent store."

"Yes—I understood you." Rose again suppressed a laugh at his incompetent gallantry, a delicate bloom in a shit field.

"I'm gonna make me a fortune."

_____

Now that she'd found her way to Kelcy's, Rose was able to journey back at will.

Archie showed few signs of budging from his barstool, unless it was in agitated proclamation of the injustices done to "Richard E. Nixon." The disgraced president had been the country's last hope, according to Archie, who'd lower his voice sorrowfully to add, "But then we all turned on him, poor bastard." Meeting censure from the regulars there at Kelcy's—men whose faint liberal sentiments were legible only by contrast to Archie's intolerance—he'd blow a raspberry or narrow his eyes and command: "Drink your drink there, and synchronize your tongues to silence." Or, "Skip it. I ain't got no time to, what do you call it, bandage words with you." Then he'd resettle into the sulky pudding he'd been an instant earlier, behind his tumbler of blended whiskey. What implacability!

And of what, or whom, was Rose reminded? Despite every sensible or humane opinion, also the English tongue, having been turned on its head? Her former self!

For Rose had one of these, after so long: a former self. All she'd done was to ride the magic carpet of her darkened apartment's couch, while the illuminated spotlight of the television's tube transported her to Kelcy's Bar, to afterward be whisked direct from Kelcy's into dreamless, amnesiac sleep. In this she discovered freedom, like a painted figure who'd slipped out of a gilded frame, then tiptoed from the museum and into a nearby park.

She'd become a—well, not a regular, not by the standard here. A returner, day after day, her presence barely noted by the others. Their taking her for granted was what Rose came for: to be fly-on-the-wall uncrucial, occupy no role whatsoever. Forty-odd years she'd dwelled, sometimes ruled, sometimes raged like a prisoner, in the Gardens, that urban farm she'd leapt at, in escaping the mud-baked trap of New Jersey. Then one day wandered into Kelcy's Bar and discovered she'd been frozen into oppositional postures, stances at once as defensive as those of a crouching wrestler and as inflated and bogus as an opera singer's.

A former self, shed. Was she, then, at last, an *anti-Communist*? No. That Koestler stuff, *The God That Failed*, was as pompous in its way as its opposite. Another religion. She'd renounced nothing; ideals that had sustained her a lifetime still sustained her, because they weren't ideological nor even really ideals. They existed in the space between one person and another, secret sympathies of the body. Alliances among those enduring the world. You found this where you found it, suddenly and without warning, at a certain meeting or protest. You'd then seek for a similar sensation, at the next hundred such meetings or protests, and be disappointed. It might be found at a pickle factory, in the pleasures of actual solidarity in labor. You found it at the counter of a White Castle, lunching on boiled eggs in a fraternity of those who'd sacrificed their hamburgers to soldiers' rations. And now, at a boor's tavern on Northern Boulevard. The century's great comedy: that Communism had never existed, not once. So what was there to oppose?

Rose existed. Communism, not so much. And for *what* did Rose exist? To talk and read and compel. When young, to fuck. Now, on her downslope, to talk and laugh at inanities and drink. She'd begun accepting the hospitality on offer at Kelcy's, a whiskey and soda water now and again no longer refused, never mind the hideous flavor to which she'd never grow accustomed, never mind the occlusion to razor senses, to the trip-wire alertness on which she'd prided herself for years. No wonder no one trusted the Jews! The Jews refused to be stupid in this pleasant way, where certain lines blurred and dissolved, to form an automatic human amalgamation outside of capitalist exchange, of a kind socialists can only dream. How late in life to discover intoxication—but not too late. She'd tumbled from the party into civic purposes, civic institutions; she should have made for the first available alehouse. She should have let Miriam hand her a reefer, the one and only time Miriam had tried. Dope was like feminism: a gift refused, an opportunity that died with her daughter.

One afternoon Archie, resplendent surrealist poet, gave Rose's secret mood a name. "Comraderism." He'd been trying to name the feeling between himself and the others there, the men whom he lashed with insults when he wasn't driving them into muttering perplexity at his baroque views on the Polish ("People of the Polack persuasion lean toward what you might call a certain lack of drive"), the Italians ("Packed into the subway like sardines we was, with no lights and no fans and me standing next to a three-hundred-pound Eyetalian, half of which was pure garlic"), and eschatology ("You liberals got more ways for the world to end than a dog has fleas"). Rose had grown to be an intimate of the tavern's whole cast: the sepulchral Hank Pivnik, blinking into some unseen distance, perhaps toward his shell-shock's Omaha Beach; Barney Hefner ("No relation to Hugh," he said when he and Rose were introduced, "but we do share certain interests"); Van Ranseleer, the blind man with the dry wit; and Harry Snowden, the beleaguered bartender, who was readying himself against his best instincts to go into partnership with Bunker. For Archie's dream was of scraping Kelcy's off the window and renaming the tavern Archie Bunker's Place.

Right to do it, too, for the place *was* Archie's. The various men who populated the bar were, despite any protestations to the contrary, in Archie's pocket, under his sway, and Rose no less than any of them. More, she had the audacity to believe she was other than invisible to him, to think he might feel something for her. So that day when his stream of talk had led him blundering into the evocative word, she decided she might confess to him, make her stigma known in a humorous way.

"Comraderism," she repeated, moving one stool nearer. "I'm with you, Archie, I don't care what anyone else says. You and me are a couple of unrepentant *comraderists*."

He made the face of a querulous bulldog, raised a chubby finger. "Watch it dere, Rose, don't you go takin' my words out of contrext."

But she couldn't stop. To see Archie on the brink of explosion was Rose's only vice now, the whiskey nothing by comparison. That he might explode in her direction was tantalizing. "My dear Archie, I only meant there's something in the way you or Harry can be relied upon always to be buying rounds for the house, something which somehow seems to testify for a from-each-according-to-his-ability-to-each-according-to-his-need view of things . . ."

She raised her glass and Archie reflexively raised his own, then squinted, wondering if he'd been tricked.

"Dunno if I follows ya . . ."

"The whole atmosphere of the tavern," Rose said, freeing herself to play to the unseen audience hiding in the footlights, letting herself be more than an extra here. "It suggests a sanctuary, from the depredations of the market. What's the phrase? 'After the subordination of the individual to the division of labor has vanished—' "

"What littles I understand in yous gobbledlygook, which is minimal, I wish I *didn't*." Archie delivered the line with restored brio, triumphant in his sacred ignorance. The place exploded with congratulatory laughter, much more than the scattered population of drinkers should be able to supply.

She carried on, into the teeth of the hilarity, but narrowed her target to Archie himself. Forget the room. She'd lost the room long ago. "You'd better face it, Archie, I ought to know a commune when I see one."

"Don't talk that way here," he hissed. The dime on which his rage turned could never be spent.

"Yes, I'm a Communist, take a good look. I'm a woman and a Communist and I got under your skin. I know that look in your eyes, a lifetime's worth I know it."

"Stop dat!" He leaned in conspiratorially close, eyes scanning for the informant, the mole among his drinking companions. In fact, no attention was paid. Snowden, Pivnik, Hefner, Van Ranseleer, they were like switched-off machines, like string-clipped marionettes, apart from those moments when Archie addressed them directly.

"I love you—" she began.

He tugged her by the arm from her stool, his head turned on its exasperated spring, white hair drifting loose maniacally. His lips were drawn back in panic. "Come you! Come into the back, we can't be talkin' like dis out heah." Rose found herself shunted into the bar's storeroom, a place of cardboard crates loaded with bottles, full and empty, and lit by a bare hanging bulb.

"Listen, now, youse."

"Hold me." His mitt had still clasped the back of her arm. Now it leapt as though she were hot.

"Don't get me wrong, youse is an attractive lady, Rose, but jeeeeez I got me a wife at home."

Rose knew all she wanted, more than she wanted, about mawkish, screeching Edith, and the home-truths this man daily fled—the drab recursion of cold bacon and eggs, the sing-alongs at the ill-tuned upright piano, things even his dim sensibility had grown incapable of enduring. How to let him know she'd been around this particular block, had lost all aspiration to remove a man from his wife? She'd be satisfied with a cuddle from Archie. Or a roll in the sack. Yet how to let Archie know it, without razing the little castle he'd erected around his despair? "Now it's your turn to listen, Archie. You think a quarter century of infiltrated cells didn't make me a sorcerer at keeping my yap shut? You think I won't go to my grave with secrets of global import? Sure, I've been an enemy of bourgeois propriety my whole life, it doesn't mean I care to wreck your home. Be orderly in your married life so that you may be violent and original in your adulterous affairs, that's Flaubert who said that. I'll tutor you in doublethink, Archie, just for God's sake and I don't even believe in God take me in your arms."

From Archie came only the slowest of slow burns. His eyes popped, oatmeal with bubbles of steam escaping. She wanted to seize his calf-like cheeks in her hands and scream *Bubbelah!* She wanted to gnaw on his jowls.

"I've chosen you for my final lover. Your lifelong dream, Archie, only you don't know it. Hump a hot Red."

He gaped at her in wonder. "We ain't right for one and the other, see?"

"Why?"

"It's like this, Rose. A Jew and a gentile ain't got a Chinaman's chance."

Archie was alone and never without a choir. Rose needed to accustom herself to this. His invisible studio audience roared with laughter, acclaiming the brutish joke. *Jew, gentile, and Chinaman.* If Archie's sensibility was where melting-pot dreams went to die, this aphorism made a fair epitaph. Yet let it not be the epitaph to their affair, let it not be Rose and Archie's hill-of-beans farewell address on the tarmac. She wouldn't give him up so easy.

"Can you not see that I'm a subversive foremost and a Jew only negligibly? Very well, if it makes you hot, fuck a sorrow-maddened Commie Jew lady."

"Yeeeeeeeze, yers got some mouth on you, Rose, do you think you could stifle it down a percent or two?"

Too easy, he'd only needed to reach for *stifle* to oblige his invisible mob to another sidesplitting crescendo.

"You won't have me?"

"I am *havin'* all of youse I can take RIGHT! HERE! AND! NOW!!!!"

The pileup of agonistic punch lines suggested, to Rose's terror, that the credits verged, the episode nearing its end. Just when she'd gained Archie's attention at last. The consolation being that, should they end here in this back-room cliff-hanger, she'd undoubtedly be central in subsequent episodes. Perhaps a spin-off was in the cards. Call it, simply, *Rose.* Or *Unrepentant!*

Without Rose noticing, the door from the barroom had been nudged open by a small hand. A black-haired girl now slipped inside and called to Archie. The girl wore corduroy overalls and a turtleneck, had hair in braids, might be nine or ten. Archie and Edith's foster daughter; how could Rose have forgotten? No, Rose would never have this man to herself, not long enough to matter. Archie was a planetary giant around which lesser bodies orbited. Whether at home or tavern, someone new always strode through the door. Characters were buried, like Stretch Cunningham, and new stooges appeared, fresh butts for Archie's rage. Rose should learn to live with it.

Archie granted the girl no outward display of affection, only caustic rebuff. "What are *you* doin' in here? How many times I gotta tell you, this ain't no place for a kid!"

The girl ignored his bluster. "Archie, can you buy me some roller skates? McCrory's announced a sale yesterday."

"Yesterday? Well, then, you missed it! And tuck that thing into your collar, for the love of Pete. Just 'cause I bought it for you don't mean I wanna be starin' at it—"

"Sorry, Archie."

"Bought her what?" asked Rose.

"None of your business," said Archie.

"Wait." Rose intervened, stopping the girl's hand where she gathered the necklace dangling at her blouse front. Impassive, the girl unfolded her fingers to display what lay in her palm: a chintzy aluminum Star of David.

A Jewish girl orphaned by fate, sheltered in a cold universe by the neighborhood bully. Of what was Rose meant to be reminded? Anne Frank? Or—? How putrid the heart-tugging shamelessness of it all.

"You bought this for the girl?"

"And what if I did?" he nearly spat.

"You and Edith are foster parents to a *Jewish* child?"

Archie winced, bared his teeth, hoisted a reproachful finger. "Don't youse get smart with me now. This here is a family matter, see? She can't help what she is!"

"No more than—" But Rose failed. The body had requirements of its own, commands among which the language of the mouth was only a minor outlet. Something in the contact broke Rose open. She clutched the delicate hand that held the Star of David to her own bosom, as if the trinket could serve for them both at once. Then, kneeling, swept the girl into her embrace. The girl lay cool and inert against Rose's heaving chest, as Rose's tears now began to pelter her hair. Archie shrugged, screwed up his mouth, rolled his eyes, helpless as ever against the emotional mayhem of Jews. Rose, through the scrim of her sorrow, understood this was no longer her script. There'd be no spin-off.

"Aw, jeeeeeeeez. Will ya look at the two of youse?" Archie's voice grew tender now, almost a whisper. He could afford tenderness, having won again, winning always as he did. "I gotta wonder, lookin' at youse there, why *didn't* youse take in your own grandson?"

Rose didn't answer. She released the girl, who stepped into the protectorate of Archie's bulk.

"Was it some kinda objectivation to the whole Quaker thing?"

You asinine ape, I could care less about any religion. But Rose was finished with lines. Let Archie have the last word. She was done speaking aloud to shadows crossing the room, the lashings of the tube's light and color against the gray inward screen of her longing.

"Nuttin' like dat should get between family, see? It took a little Jew girl to teach this old dog he had one new trick in him, go figure."

Applause. Credits.

Part IV   Peaceable Kingdom

1 The Lamb's War

Was the book about the bull the first book he remembered? If not, then maybe the first on whose glossy cardboard jacket the boy's fingerprints were the first fingerprints, the first whose pages he softened into use by himself. Perhaps there had been some soiled floppy picture books in his room in the commune. Likely so. He'd never remember exactly. Other books encountered at Public School 19, or the library, all beaten to submission by innumerable children before him, cats, bears, tugboats, steam shovels, Sneetches, anyhow nothing making much impression. His mother read aloud to him from her battered Heritage wartime edition of *Alice in Wonderland and Through the Looking-Glass*; he held on to this fact clearly because Stella Kim later visited and brought him that book, along with other keepsakes of Miriam. But the book about the bull had traveled with him to boarding school, been clung to like a security blanket, a minor embarrassment worth enduring when others had moved on to boy detectives and boy scientists and comic books and even stashes of *Playboy*, an embarrassment endurable because he was "the youngest" there at Pendle Acre even when he was no longer the youngest.

To be understood that way, as official baby brother to the entire school, was Sergius's special dispensation. Long before he could grow old enough for it to be questioned, the boy's parents were dead, so anyone who'd have otherwise mocked him for retaining the book about the bull was thwarted. At some other school, who knew? At kindly Pendle Acre, mockery died with Tommy and Miriam. It might be supposed—by the other students and by his teachers, by the resident advisers, by the headmaster—that the book was a talisman of his dead parents. Yet in fact, unlike the *Alice* volume, which he'd keep untouched on his shelf, the book about the bull wasn't a keepsake of his mother, or of his parents generally. It had nothing to do with them. It was a talisman, instead, of the boy's single encounter with Santa Claus.

His birthright: full hippie and half secular Jew. Given that, and with Rose's withering contempt for all ritual and ceremony lurking somewhere in the background, Christmas, for the boy, didn't exactly loom large. No one indulged him, the only child in the house full of adults. It wouldn't have occurred to them. In the Seventh Street commune the mercantile and decorative changes that came over the darkening city in late December made an occasion for exasperation and jokes, for a few temporarily vacant rooms as younger housemates reverted to their distant families for the holidays, and for a few pot-head potluck gatherings. Then for a New Year's party to sweep it all away.

Tommy and Miriam were historical materialists, maybe. Materialistic nohow. Before he understood the word the boy had learned to despise *property*, a series of injunctions as near to commandments as were ever instilled in him: *Thou Shalt Not Covet the Plastic Junk. Thou Shalt Not Request That Which Is Advertised During Looney Tunes. Expect Not the G.I. Joe, Putrid Icon of Militarism. Demand Not the Sugared Cereal. Thine Blocks Be Wooden.* Old stuff was better than new, less was preferential to more, group belongings superior to anything hoarded. All this cut firmly against Christmas and Santa Claus. The boy's world, his room, was not so much devoid of toys or books as it was a place toys or books drifted through. These items, handed down and likely to be handed down again, worn into timelessness, were by this loving use cleansed, even if they depicted commercial icons like Snoopy or Barbie, of their polluted nature as commodities. The nearest to an exception? Tommy did like to blow up balloons. With the boy in tow, Tommy would buy balloons at the Avenue C bodega—thirty-nine-cent packages bright enough to bait children yet not in the forbidden realm of candy or gum or baseball cards—and return to the commune to inflate them, one after the next. The boy supposed the balloons were by definition "new," since he'd seen them purchased. But they weren't presents. Weren't toys, exactly. Weren't even exclusively a child's province, for when the rooms grew cloudy with pot smoke the adults played with them, too.

But at the Fifteenth Street Meeting one December night Sergius Gogan met Santa Claus, or someone dressed as him, and was given a present. The Santa Claus appeared in the middle of a Quaker holiday party, gathered the children around him, reached into a sack, and placed it in his hands: something new and belonging to Sergius alone. This unique status was demonstrated by its wasteful wrapping of bright red-and-green paper, which existed only to delight Sergius for an instant, then be torn aside and forgotten.

Inside was the book about the bull.

The meetinghouse, which wore the name of "Fifteenth Street" but bore no relation to the concrete island's grid, dwelling in a secret gated garden all its own, was Sergius Gogan's sanctuary. It made a place apart from the lawless excess of his daily life, both in the commune and on Seventh Street, where, while Miriam sentried from a vantage on their stoop, he crept sometimes into the junk-laced lots to encounter Alphabet City's feral children. Tommy, drifting into Quakerism as a symptom of his peace activism, had with Miriam's shrugging consent begun taking Sergius along with him for Sunday school. What happened there was more or less impossible to remember even five minutes after it happened: actual Bible study, crafts projects designed to evoke the plight of the Native American, and fifteen-minute sample visits to the meeting for worship, that vast and mysterious room where his father sat with a hundred others to wait in silence for something to enter into them and bring them to their feet to testify, a noble activity regularly interrupted by incomprehensible murmuring speeches on various unrelated topics.

The population there formed an odd mix of young hippies and the Quaker meeting's decrepit core, who greatly resembled those elderly you'd pass everywhere in the city and never consider at all. Yet it was as though both groups had agreed to blur their differences, the hippies dressing less flamboyantly than Sergius suspected they wished to, opting for the drabbest colors in their wardrobes, tucking button shirts into their belted jeans, male and female alike banding their long hair; meanwhile, the elderly made concessions from their end, wearing flowery vests and soft shoes, the men growing surprisingly elaborate beards, the women donning chunky necklaces. They met in another middle, too: All were quiet, unstartling, and cloyingly kind. Everyone in the big silent room, no matter how deep in brow-gnarled contemplation, smiled on the children who filtered in and mostly wrecked the atmosphere. The Quaker meeting was where all kinds of adults who might otherwise reveal their ferocious eccentricity, their unpredictability—the old, the strange, the Jewish, New Yorkers of all former intensities—went instead to practice being innocuous. That was what Sergius liked about it.

The Quakers frequently spoke of the Inner Light—"that of God in everyone." For Sergius this was unavoidably conflated with the notion of a pilot light, the mysteries of which he'd contemplated at the Seventh Street kitchen's battered, enamel-chipped Kenmore range: the Inner Light a thing by its nature tamped and unsparking. A thing, seemingly, quite capable of leaving the outer surface of that which sheltered it cool to the touch and marvelously undangerous. Miriam encouraged him to understand he didn't need to stand on sentry: It was pretty much okay to just forget the pilot light was even there! And a Quaker might even be like a stove with no dials for igniting the jets; you'd leave a kid alone with a Quaker in a heartbeat. When no one at the commune was willing to babysit, this was what Tommy and Miriam did, dumping Sergius at afternoon playgroups within the shelter of Fifteenth Street's high gates, watched over by benign childless meeting "elders" or virginal teenagers with braids and ecology-sign-patched jeans, there to clamber on play equipment in a black-padded courtyard, under the leaf shade of the hidden oasis, eye of Manhattan's storm.

The Sunday evening before Christmas, Fifteenth Street threw open its doors and served a massive bland dinner for itself and for the local bums. Sergius had learned that his father had a special feeling for bums. These street-corner men might not be as urgently heartrending to Tommy as those on death row, but the death-row men were distant abstractions, unavailable to meet and be offered cigarettes, cups of coffee, or White Castles from a massive greasy paper sack. So Tommy had volunteered to help serve the men who wandered in for the free meal, also bringing his guitar in case there was a chance to sing. He encouraged Sergius to come along—Miriam as always taking a pass on the Quaker stuff, but you guys go ahead, paint the town red—and it was there that Sergius had been blindsided by Santa Claus.

Sergius took the book aside once he'd opened it, sealing himself from his surroundings, the stringy men shoveling roast turkey and baked potatoes into their mouths and pockets, the other children thronging the man in the red suit, his father now gently strumming his guitar, beguiling music-averse Quakers with an Irish-tinged "Silent Night." Curled in a chair, Sergius studied what he could of the tale of the calf who became a huge bull and yet refused to do anything but sniff at flowers, even when compelled at swordpoint in an arena of jeering spectators. Then, needing the words, once home he demanded Miriam read it aloud immediately. Sergius's mother was generous with reading, according, however, to her own priorities, imposing the *Alice* book, or *The Hobbit*, which she'd been grinding him through on a nightly basis, one murky chapter after the next. Sergius wanted pictures in his books—now he had them.

"*Ferdinand*, oh yeah, cool. You know, I used to have this book when I was a kid."

No, he wanted to say. It is a new book. It is my book. Not part of your constellation of lodestones, the fog of references it was his legacy to navigate. No. This was given to me by Santa Claus, whom *you* never met. Such sudden anger against her! Had he ever dared before? He touched the smooth clean cover and almost pulled it back from her grasp, but he needed her to read the words aloud to him.

Soon, before he'd learned to read, Sergius memorized and could subvocally incant the whole sacrament of Ferdinand the Bull Who Refused the Bullfight. Ferdinand, who grew strong and handsome and retained the love of his mother, who endured the bee's sting. Ferdinand, who disdained the feistiness of his peers and the red of the cape, who never relented in his love of peace. Of flowers. He who entered the realm of violence yet stymied its expectations, pacified its livid heart. He who, when greeted with the world's belligerent invitations, *preferred not to*.

Sergius understood why the Quaker Santa Claus would appear and give him this book: because the world was an arena. Alphabet City. P.S. 19, the Asher Levy School, an arena. Tommy and Miriam—the inconstancy and chaos of their domestic disarrangements and of their haphazard war with history, their hair-trigger availability for marches and vigils, for squattings and occupations—an arena beyond description, one he'd been born inside. The revolving-door population of the commune itself, this bedazzling warren of NYU filmmakers and Okinawan terrorists and sylph-like women in yoga poses, an arena. His grandmother, seething in her dimmed rooms, straightening the Lincoln relics in her kitchen when the boy bumped them, staring at him too coldly, for too long an interval, before clutching him to her sighing bosom, then stage-whispering to Miriam, "The spitting image of Albert? This is what you bring into the world?" An arena unto herself. Uncle Lenny, horrendous mouth stinking of cigars and pickled herring in cream sauce, ogling Stella Kim, berating Sergius's stamp collection, and scratching his ass—him, too.

The book about the bull was intended to prepare Sergius, twice over. Once, to understand that when he was sent from Alphabet City to the Quaker boarding school in rural Pennsylvania he was being placed, like Ferdinand, in the safe pasture his own essential nature demanded: Sergius was being permitted to quit the arena.

Second, the book prepared him to believe that when Tommy and Miriam flew off to Nicaragua, into the wider and more terrifying arena of violent revolution, armed only with Miriam's training in the art of passive resistance, that judo maneuver of being *triumphantly arrested*, and with Tommy's guitar and his musician's *kinship with the people*, that they would, like Ferdinand, wield the magic armor of nonviolence and return unharmed.

Harris Murphy's flaw, a harelip twisting plainly visible beneath his beard, went unmentioned among the children at Pendle Acre. Even at that Quaker place, the students weren't incapable of cruelty toward their teachers, but Murphy's intensity concerning his charges made it impossible. The music teacher's sincerity was a kind of test, and if most of the students had failed him by the time they'd reached the high-school grades, they'd been forced to do so on his own terms. To mock the harelip would have been to suggest they'd been injured by Murphy's demands on their character, his undeniable insight, his uncanny ability to know when you were high on pot, yet not to betray that knowledge to the Committee on Ministry and Oversight.

Murphy was one of the few actual Friends among the young teachers there. Usually it fell to the headmaster and the board of directors, along with a few older faculty, to maintain the advisory standards: that faculty self-governance operate on the Quaker model of consensus decision making, that the students be led in silent worship for half an hour each day before classes. No matter if those leading the meetings were as little adept in abiding with the Light as the tittering, eye-rolling teenagers. Murphy, the exception, would speak, to students who'd listen, of the private value of silent practice to his own spiritual journey. (If *God*, like harelip, went unremarked, that was only the usual Friendly reticence at an imposition of terms, the sleight of hand that had tempted Buddhist Quakers, Jewish Quakers, even Atheist Quakers to come sit at the benches.) Murphy read George Fox and would insert aphorisms from the great mad founder of the Society of Friends into his teaching, and the first song each of Murphy's advanced guitar pupils learned, before he obliged them by cracking open the mysteries of "Dear Prudence" or "Stairway to Heaven," was "Simple Gifts," in its Quaker revamp:

Walk in the Light, wherever you may be
Walk in the Light, wherever you may be
In my old leather breeches and my shaggy shaggy locks
I am walking in the glory of the Light, said Fox!

That the younger teachers at Pendle Acre were a bunch of neatened-up, rustical hippies went without saying. A teaching job and full residency at the liberal-minded boarding school made a deftly strategic pastoral retreat from the wounds-licking counterculture. They were fleeing the same sort of lifestyle damage familiar to the students, especially those who rode the Greyhound bus home to Philadelphia or New York on weekends. Murphy, though his personal details remained shrouded, was one of these too. Specifically, a broken-winged folkie, another victim of Dylan's mercurial demolition of the acoustic revival. Maybe, though, Murphy'd been too pure even to tolerate Dylan's earlier style. Maybe he'd found modern songwriting itself a bit ostentatious. Murphy strongly hinted so. He'd been half of a duo, Murphy and Kaplon, who'd never gone into the studio, who'd only been recorded once, a single track on an anthology LP called *Live at the Sagehen Café*, performing "The Cruel Ship's Captain." Murphy'd played on bills with Tommy Gogan! Yet he unsubtly hinted to the son that he preferred the sound of the father's voice blended with those of his brothers, on one of those Irish harmony albums Tommy disdained.

Yes, Murphy had known Sergius's mother. A little. Smile tight when he acknowledged it. Murphy being the self-serious type Miriam would have provoked because she couldn't help herself. Yes, Murphy'd known them both. It was no accident, then, when to free themselves for the journey to Nicaragua Tommy and Miriam took Fifteenth Street's tuition grant and installed Sergius at Pendle Acre, the boy came to live at West House, where Harris Murphy was the resident adviser. No matter if the awfully intense harelipped finger-picking observant Quaker music teacher was broken-winged or not, it was his wing Sergius Gogan had been placed under. And no matter who'd first telephoned whom, nor what consultations had gone on previously among headmaster and any number of others, it was Harris Murphy who took Sergius aside in privacy that day and told the eight-year-old that his parents were missing. Then Murphy who let him know, three weeks later, that Tommy and Miriam's muddy corpses had been unearthed, excavated along with a third body, believed American but as yet unnamed and unclaimed, from a hillside, and were due to be flown back to New York City—but that Sergius was, for the moment, staying where he was. As he would, it turned out, more or less forever.

Sergius didn't think that day to ask about his grandmother. Murphy didn't mention her. The surviving Gogan brothers, eking their living touring the western Canadian folk circuit by bus, were no possibility whatsoever. Sergius would live at Pendle Acre. The whole school would parent him. Quakerism would parent him. Sergius, that day, didn't ask questions at all.

Murphy's rooms in West House: the low-ceilinged suite with its basement entrance; the vast wall of jazz and blues LPs, all else modest and monkish, the putrid red shag rug not entirely covering the poured slab of cellar floor; Murphy's kitchenette, the faltering whistle of his teakettle; the crates of Bukowski and Castaneda and Frank Herbert; his two guitars on upright stands, varnish beaten off their wooden faces by his strumming; his stacks of fake books and of old copies of *National Lampoon*, in the photo-collages of which Sergius would eventually first glimpse photographs of a woman's bared breasts (as opposed to the actual breasts of Stella Kim, which he'd glimpsed already, one February night when the commune's radiators howled and sizzled in excess and Stella bewilderingly forsook T-shirt or bra); Murphy's large, water-stained print of the Edward Hicks's *The Peaceable Kingdom*, the official Quaker masterpiece, in which the lamb lay down with all the other beasts of the kingdom, and to view an actual painted copy of which Murphy would one day lead Sergius and a group of middle schoolers on a field trip to Philadelphia; the framed copy of a Village Gate bill proclaiming the night on which Murphy and Kaplon had opened for Skip James, autographed in a red scrawl by James; all of Murphy's paltry vanities and secrets laid bare and which Sergius memorized, he understood later, in compensation and revenge for Murphy having taken him that day down into those rooms to say that his parents were missing, then a second time to tell him they were dead.

Murphy's rooms, those Sergius remembered.

Sergius had cultivated a private science of remembering, in order to understand and absolve himself for what he couldn't. He'd figured it this way: You remembered what was continuous and what was anomalous. The continuous because it stuck around to remind you of itself. The anomalous because it stuck out and so your mind made a Polaroid of the oddness, to gaze at in fear, lust, or bewilderment forever. Stella

Kim's nipples, say, as seamless and purple as the dye-dipped tips of Easter eggs. Those, anomalous forever, he remembered. Santa Claus, that night at Fifteenth Street? Anomalous, unforgettable, enshrined. Dead Cousin Lenny's sneering at his stamp collection? Easy, anomalous, in its almost feral intensity. Conversely—memorable because continuous—were dead Cousin Lenny's "penny books," those rigid, governmental-blue folders into which Sergius obediently thumbed three examples of each year's Lincoln cent: one unmarked from the Philadelphia mint, one marked S for the San Francisco mint, and one marked D for the Denver mint. The penny books were moored in permanent reality and bridged Sergius's New York life and his Pendle Acre bedroom, where he kept them on a shelf beside *The Story of Ferdinand*. So an even simpler principle: You remembered what you kept. You remembered, maybe also, what you wanted. What you couldn't keep or reasonably wish for was forgotten.

By these laws, Sergius forgot his parents.

Tommy and Miriam met no standard for being unforgotten, having been continuous, then lopped off. His parents were an atmosphere that drifted off to space, leaving nothing to breathe.

His parents were unkept. Unlike *Ferdinand* or the penny books, Sergius hadn't imported them to West House. Nor could he credibly wish the dead to resume their lives. No one not in Sergius's position could ever know how little anyone ever actually remembered of anything. Sergius watched the other children with their parents and thought: *You see but you do not remember.*

Strolling cavalier amid the living of the earth, you'd never even know you weren't bothering to press Record. This was what Sergius told himself, in attitudes of torment or shame or simply in wonder at what vast emotional amnesia befogged the first eight years of his existence on earth. His mental dioramas were constructed from hearsay, remarks by Stella Kim or some other Seventh Street housemate, from photographs, and from his tantalized reworkings of what little strobe-like images he did possess: snatches of child's-brain footage grabbed in the tumult of this or that protest at the Department of Health and Human Services or a rainy vigil at the gates of Sing Sing, or of waking astounded to have dozed all night on his mother's raincoat in a corner of the People's Firehouse, where he'd reached up to fondle the weave of a wide flat fire hose spindled above his head. Yet in each strobe-flash or footage-clip nothing of Tommy and Miriam. His parents refused to enter a frame, never spoke a line even from *outside* the frame. They existed by implication, outlines punched in backdrops.

Behind, the outer spaces of self.

If the dead were dead, and in expunged memory unreconstructible, what could the boy reasonably wish to be given in compensation? A mystery.

In any event, on the day Sergius learned of his parents' death, Harris Murphy presented him with a guitar. An emblem of his father, Sergius supposed, though like his mother it made a body he could cling to. The guitar was also like Sergius himself, a shape molded around a vacancy and made easily to cry. In fact, the process of tuning, the endless tuning that consisted of most of his first lesson on the guitar, and his second and third as well—Murphy kept the boy at it, the music teacher's gift for abiding with repetition—sounded like nothing to him so much as the moaning and guttering sounds that forced themselves periodically through his body and for which he was the involuntary audience. Sergius asked Murphy if the guitar was his to keep. It was. It could be kept, could go back to Sergius's room upstairs, to live there with him at night. And so at night Sergius pretended it was the guitar that was doing the crying. Anyway, the interval of crying was subject to a mercy. Weeping for his lost parents was like his parents themselves, an ambiance, in its vastness unspecific, and an ocean that when you stepped dry from it, you wholly forgot.

Sergius was then converted. From what, he wasn't certain. Converted from innocence, perhaps. Yet also from too much unwelcome experience. He was converted from the passive study of chaos, of his family and the commune and the city surrounding it, to Murphy's two disciplines: the guitar and Quakerism. Did the headmaster even require Sergius go to class those first months? He remembered nothing of class, if he'd been there at all. He sat at meals with Murphy and the other students absorbed in the music teacher's penitent, monkish worldview, while the scorning high schoolers blazed around them.

The whole rest of Pendle Acre School was then just junk and noise, needless to consider, at the center of which sat Murphy at his guitar, in the rooms of the half-basement apartment, where were shelved the books from which the reformed hippie read aloud without explanation, nodding his head significantly, breaking the silence with a question or by picking up his guitar again, meanwhile a bag of pretzels open and go ahead, help yourself. Murphy's whole vibe, of abiding in voluntary sensory deprivation, was not unrelated to everyone's whispered certainty that he'd gotten stoned a hundred times more than even the stonerest of the Led Zeppelin–jacketed dudes of the upper grades, no laughing matter actually how many brain cells he'd allowed to float off to the four winds. From this, Harris Murphy's quiet authority derived. Murphy's recovering from the sixties, from the world outside Pendle Acre's walls, was akin to the eight-year-old's getting over New York City and Tommy and Miriam, their lives as unfathomable as their deaths. It made a perfect fit.

Sergius would make himself, then, not only a guitar prodigy but the most prodigal Friend. The Quakerest kid, in a place where there was a fair degree of competition. Meeting on Sunday was optional—perhaps so the weekenders wouldn't be encouraged to feel they'd gotten out of something—but dozens showed up to do, well, *something* in the silence, to feel a part of it, anyway not to scorn. Some kids even rose to give witness, speaking in testimony of the Light. Morning meeting before classes was compulsory, and therefore more rote—plenty of Pendle Acre kids used the time to scribble on homework pages, making up for what they'd neglected the night before. Each opportunity, morning or Sunday, Pendle Acre's little orphan embarked into the Light with ferocious determination, and there was nobody in Quakerdom who'd ever have told him he was doing it wrong. By the logic of Quakerism, at least as it had presented itself to him, first at Fifteenth Street Sunday school, then in paraphrase by Harris Murphy, you *couldn't* do it wrong.

Or maybe there was one way. Sergius, a month or so after his parents' deaths, stumbled into a violation of the Advice of Moderation.

It happened because Murphy had given him a book—not a Quaker book, or not directly, except in that typical Quaker embrace of darker-skinned peoples and their indigenous traditions—*Day of the Dead: Mexican Myths and Folktales*. Perhaps compensating for a certain barrenness in Quaker conceptions of the afterlife, Murphy handed the sorry kid this thing full of jolly skeletons and benign ghosts, of zombie ancestors more often misunderstood than ill-intentioned. The animate corpses in the Mexican tales had a consolingly lumpen quality, stumbling through a droll dusty universe not much different from that of the peasants or shopkeepers they'd been before being put in the ground. Besides, the book seemed to Sergius to say, *Your parents vanished south of the border—they died in the Spanish tongue.* So the book might be intended to reveal to him where exactly they'd ended up.

For some weeks Sergius carried the book with him, the new *Ferdinand*. He'd seized on the tale of a certain Pedro, whose older brother died falling from a burro. This older brother had at his request been entombed with a sort of chimney or speaking tube that stuck out of the grave, in order to give report from the other side. And so Pedro had faithfully gone and on a daily basis communed through the tube with his dead brother, speaking with him of matters secular and prosaic: of earthworms, the crops, and the prospect for rainfall, and of the ironic fate of the burro from which the brother had tumbled—it had been sold into a war, one which the brother had avoided by dying, and which Pedro was now spared according to a local rule that no family should lose both its sons.

Three weeks in a row, Sergius brought the Mexican book to Sunday meeting and, after a certain interval of silence and a spontaneous message or two from a teacher or an older kid, stood and cleared his throat and read aloud the story of Pedro at the graveside. *See*, he intended the message to say, *it's okay*. The dead are still around. And *I'm* okay. You don't have to feel sorry for me.

The first afternoon after he'd offered the story into the silence they smothered him in congratulations. Reading from a book might not be the standard mode of inspired messaging, sure, but for an eight-year-old to give testimony at meeting at all, and more, one in his distinct situation: wow! Murphy took him aside, shook his hand, as Sergius probably could have expected, but also teachers he barely knew, and the headmaster, and a couple of the older girls. It made Sergius a bit of a star, a sacred example of what a place like Pendle Acre was all about.

So the Sunday following, he read it again.

This time afterward not so many remarked, and not with such enthusiasm. Murphy just patted him on the back and suggested they work on some chord fingerings. But why demand congratulation? Sergius was proving himself no longer a sport or novelty but a routine dweller in the Light. Pedro's tale seemed fully as profound the second time aloud as it had each of the dozens of times Sergius read it silently to himself. In fact, the meaning kept expanding. *Death is no big deal!* Let it sink in for all as it had for him.

When Sergius narrated it the third Sunday in a row, the headmaster gathered him up for a little stroll and some Friendly counsel about Moderation in All Things.

Later that afternoon Sergius visited Murphy's rooms to return the Mexican book.

"It's yours to keep, Sergius."

"I don't want it anymore."

"You sure?"

Sergius threw the book against Murphy's couch. It suddenly disgusted him. Not one kid had mocked him for speaking in meeting, as he knew they mocked one another each time one of them conformed to that mild expectation. Not one single kid had pointed out to Sergius how he was unable to speak to his parents through a tube in the earth as Pedro spoke with his brother. No one had censured him, not even the headmaster, and that was how Sergius could be certain he was pitied everywhere he walked. He was the Mexican book's dupe, maybe Murphy's as well.

"I want the ones who killed them to be dead, too."

"I understand," stalled Murphy.

"I want to kill them."

Sergius spoke from behind a hot mask of tears, but just a mask: He only had to accept he wore it because he tasted snot. He felt that if he had a gun he'd fire it at Murphy, not least for instilling him with Quaker shame at his own violence. That the book had bounded harmlessly into the cushions, that the men who'd murdered Tommy and Miriam were cloaked in inconceivable remoteness, that his killer's soul was housed in the feeble container of an eight-year-old, none of these tempered his fury. They concentrated it.

Murphy, seeing what was before him, likely felt he had a test to pass.

"The Lamb's War," said Murphy.

"What's that?"

"Here, sit down, let me read you something." Murphy, as ever lightning-quick with the palliatives, had a plate of graham crackers and a glass of milk set up before Sergius knew it—could he have had them waiting? Murphy knew his place in the book he pulled from the shelf, too, as if he'd been preparing this reading for Sergius, figuring he'd need it. And the half basement's shades were already drawn, so none of Murphy's other pet students would be crouching down and rapping at his low windows.

"'*God hath lost the creature out of his call and service, and the creature now uses the creation against the creator. Now, against this evil seed doth the lamb make war, to take vengeance of his enemies.*' That's you, Sergius. The Lamb's War—that's what *you're* fighting."

"Is it . . . George Fox?" Sergius hadn't heard Murphy use the word *evil* before. Or *vengeance*.

"Nope. This is another early Friend, a guy I haven't mentioned before, James Nayler. Nayler started as a soldier, a feisty guy, and when he met Fox and started running around England speaking of the Light, they imprisoned him and put a hot poker through his tongue. But listen: '*As the lamb wars not against men's persons, so his weapons are not carnal, nor hurtful to any of the creation; for the lamb comes not to destroy men's lives . . . his armor is the Light, his shield faith and patience . . . thus he goes out in judgment and righteousness, to make war with his enemies, not with whips and prisons, tortures and torments on the bodies of creatures, but with the word of truth, to pass judgment upon the head of the serpent, and covers his own with his love . . .*'"

As Murphy droned on and Sergius listened, as Sergius's mask evaporated, caking and crackling on his cheeks and on his sleeve where he'd sluiced it across his upper lip—and Murphy'd known not to demolish Sergius's pride with the offer of a tissue—as Sergius salved his aching gut with a mud of molar-crushed grahams and milk, he came slowly to understand that Murphy was reading as much to himself as to his ward. It was obvious in Murphy's readiness with the passages, the way he now could be seen skipping from one page to the next, stringing Nayler's words to make his case, skipping over who-knew-what and Sergius didn't care to find out. It didn't matter, for what Sergius saw and understood was that the teacher hadn't readied the book for his student so much as uncovered his own Lamb's War to Sergius's view. Murphy hadn't fought his and won, either—he fought it still, fought it every day, that was the message. Murphy's voice was hypnotic if you shut your eyes, and if you didn't, and Sergius didn't, you were hypnotized by the way his elegant tenor formed itself out from below that twisted scar no thickness of beard could conceal. The harelip was evidence enough of the teacher's Lamb's War, it was his serpent-scar, or perhaps a kind of serpent itself, embedded in his flesh. Here was where you encountered the Light: It struck anywhere, anytime. At that instant he and Murphy there in the basement comprised a meeting of two.

Then Murphy put Nayler's book on the shelf, didn't fool around with any offers to loan it out, and Sergius knew that it would be a long time before he spoke again in meeting and that whenever he finally did it wouldn't be a passage read aloud from a book but a true message, like Nayler's, a dire stark communiqué from some remote front of the Lamb's War.

Then Murphy said, "Let's play some guitar."

———

At the start of June Pendle Acre thinned out, summer session consisting of just a scattering of kids. Mostly these were the high-school hippies who'd started the vegetable farm and didn't want to see it die, so signed up for a French or German intensive with not much intention of acquiring a language, nor of even attending the summer classes. More than half the resident teachers hightailed it too, leaving a skeleton crew—though not Murphy. It was three months from the date of his parents' deaths, and a certain question had become unavoidable to the kid who'd been unaware even of any effort to avoid it.

"Am I going back to New York City?"

"Not unless you want to." Murphy talked over chords, reminiscent of something—a Bob Dylan song?—if Sergius could pin it down. "To visit, I mean."

"No, I mean, am I staying in school here next year?"

"You sure are."

"How—"

"New York Yearly Meeting and Fifteenth Street have got you on a full scholarship, not that Pendle Acre would ever think twice about letting you stay if they hadn't, Sergius. You don't have to worry about a thing."

It wasn't much like Murphy to interrupt. Nor to bear upon Sergius with little interrogatory feints, as he did now, the chords continuing all the while. "So do you *want* to visit New York City?"

"I don't know—maybe."

"If you did, who'd you want to visit?"

Sergius shrugged, sensing no right reply. On the tiny menu of names available, he couldn't think which he ought to mention first.

"You remember Stella Kim?"

"Sure." That had been one of the names.

"Well, listen, there's something I wanted to tell you. Stella wants to see you, and next week we're going to send you up to Philadelphia to see her."

"Why not in New York City?"

"Maybe later, but there's something we need you to do in Philadelphia, and Stella's going to be there and help you with it. We need you to talk to a judge, just for a few minutes, and that'll help make it simpler for you to stay here with us, okay? You only have to do it once."

Murphy's *we* and *us* worked like a clamp on Sergius's hundred questions. Sergius managed to voice one. "Are you coming?"

"I'd like to, Sergius, I really would. The headmaster's going to take you up there, and I'll be waiting here for you when you're done."

"Okay."

"All you have to do is say you want to come back here."

"Okay."

"I want you to believe me on this one thing, Sergius, and that's that *I'm not going anywhere*, all right?"

"Okay." It would take Sergius years to sort it out, that what was so reassuring about Harris Murphy was also what was sort of horrible: You too-completely believed him when he said he presented no risk of budging from the postage-stamp universe of Pendle Acre.

———————

In the headmaster's car, on the road to Philadelphia, Sergius ate from a bag of doughnut holes and listened to an eight-track tape of *Fiddler on the Roof*. It just went on and on.

———————

Before going into the hearing room Sergius was reunited with Stella Kim in an adjacent office. The headmaster stood to one side as Sergius and his mother's best friend clutched each other for a long while. Sergius found himself drenched in phantasms of babysitting nights, Stella Kim's scent deep-mingling miso paste, pot, and patchouli. The smell could only carry him back a certain distance; though Stella Kim appeared here in a turquoise pantsuit Sergius didn't think was native to her at all, he couldn't now think of how she'd more typically be dressed. He damped a few confused tears against the turquoise knit. Stella Kim seemed to know to hold him just long enough and then they three went in soberly to sit with the judge. The courtroom was more like a large, dull office than that of Sergius's imaginings, and the judge, equally inadequate, wore no robes and clapped no gavel. He wore a suit, his head was bald, his eyebrows gray and disordered, and he sat not above them, on some podium or tower, but shuffling through a folder of papers at a conference table.

Stella and the headmaster pulled out chairs and seated themselves, indicating Sergius should sit between them. He sat. At the table, too, waited another stranger, who didn't stand and wasn't introduced and, like Stella and the headmaster, barely spoke—the judge didn't wish them to. The judge made it clear at the outset that the adults present were to remain mute on the sidelines in a meeting between himself and *the child in question*, then went ahead to say any number of things plainly meant for their ears. "I've been consternated, *hurm*, by a terrific number of irregularities in this proceeding, not least the simple matter of delays in bringing relevant materials and testimonies to the court's attention, on one side. Yet again, this entire, ah, circumstance is characterized by a puzzling delay at the outset, on the part of the complainant." The words were, to Sergius, a baffling fudge. Yet their tone suggested he was indeed in the long-feared presence of monolithic authority, that against which an elemental orientation had pitted him for life. He was certain, that's to say, that the judge, unrobed and unimpressive though he might be, was likely to now sentence Stella Kim, the headmaster, and himself to the electric chair. They would thereafter be remanded to death row, inspiring a vigil outside the prison's walls, in which they would be referred to as the Philadelphia Three. "As well, there's the whole peculiar matter of jurisdiction, yet, *hurm*, seeing as how the 1973 doctrine for the best interest of the child applies here as fully as in New York, and since the complaint was recorded by the Philadelphia police, and in full consultation with the corresponding offices in New York, *hurm*, it's been deemed that present offices are sufficient to render judgment—" All this, preface to a meeting with *the child in question* that would effectively boil down to a single question.

"Will you confirm for me that you're Sergius Valentine Gogan?"

"Sergius?" Stella prompted, drawing a glare from the judge.

"Uh, yes." Sergius hadn't heard his middle name in a while. *Stranger in a Strange Land*, he remembered.

"Do you understand that your parents are, *hurm*, no longer alive?"

"Yes."

"I'll be arriving at a decision, Mr. Gogan, and I'm not asking for you to make it for me, but your opinion has bearing in the matter, as according to the aforementioned 1973 doctrine. Do you understand?"

"Yes." No.

"Boy, would you like to live with your grandmother Rose Zimmer in New York City, or do you prefer to continue to remain under stewardship of the Pendle Acre School?"

By the end of that summer Sergius's orbit had expanded from West House, and from Murphy's table at the dining hall. The narrowed population of vegetable-garden hippies disguised as language intensives drew him into their precincts—the hovel-like, tie-dye-curtained lounge at East House, the rows of sun-blazed, silk-stinky corn rows, the fire circle out behind the storage sheds. Seemingly a little kid could be elevated to peer status in extreme circumstances like these, the preponderance of empty dorms bonding those who remained as survivors, as on a desert island. Despite three decent meals and Pendle Acre's reasonably plush facilities, the prevailing vibe was that of foxhole-ish endurance, of placement at front lines against an unknown enemy. Cigarettes and hormones might be the common denominators, or the vanishing point where opposites merged. There at the fire circle in particular, feeding brush-cleared tinder and scrap lumber into the crackling flames, then standing hypnotized on the cushion of pine needles and crushed butts, teenagerdom nightly cherished its world's-end unity. The school's rolls weirdly amalgamized privileged kids, those who'd been earmarked for private boarding school from the day they entered Country Day kindergartens, and "troubled" inner-city white kids whose parents had taken advice, from meeting elders like those at Fifteenth Street, to remand their children to the Quakerish safe haven. Weirder still, these constituents amalgamized easily, the chips on their shoulders more or less indistinguishable out there in the woods.

The teenagers had another destination, a two-mile walk to the "town" of East Exeter, which consisted of a pizza joint with a jukebox, a pair of gas stations for purchase of cigarettes, and a small video-game arcade, a foray that was off-limits to Sergius. Fine, he felt no urge to leave Pendle Acre. The fire circle was far enough, and surprisingly far. By firelight the sheds formed a wall of shadow to complete a boundary marked by the dense impassible woods. So the fire circle modeled a tiny realm in which childhood had been left behind while the adult universe was nonetheless securely resisted, a million miles away. One night a stoner kid turned his palm to reveal to Sergius a

half-smoked, sparking joint. "Hey, Serge, you're not Murphy's informant, are you?"

"No."

"Leave him alone," said someone else.

"Hey, man, I just had to check."

———————

In case he needed to be shown how unready he'd feel for any Alphabet
City or Sunnyside ghosts, the music teacher staged an abrupt and horrendous demonstration. One day near the end of that summer Murphy
stuffed a few of Sergius's clean T-shirts and socks into a knapsack and
the two of them got on a train. Sergius fell asleep, with a result that
it felt scarcely more than fifteen or twenty minutes had passed before
he found himself in drowsy stupefaction expunged into Penn Station.
Pulling Sergius's hand, Murphy threaded the commuter chaos to find
the subway turnstiles, and beyond, the downtown platform. Then,
before Sergius could give form to his objections, they ascended the
stoop at Seventh Street.

Stepping inside, out of the August evening's brightness, Sergius
first navigated blind, plummeting through the hard-won, tissue-thin
illusion of his present life into a sensory past he wanted no part of.
Stella Kim had gathered him up again, bearing all her scents—all of
Miriam's scents. Somewhere a musical instrument tooted scales—a
flute, if it wasn't his imagination. Sergius squirmed loose, to find
something more solid, the foot of the stair, the banister he'd learned
once to giddily slide down: an intoxicant memory of the interrupted
life now unwillingly restored. Yet this too was like mercury under his
fingertips, as if the cracked-varnish curves and loose-jointed creak of
the newel post to which he clung formed another impoverished effigy
of his mother.

Adjusted to the dimness, tears now murked his sight. Yet he saw
well enough to notice Murphy kissing Stella Kim, scraping his beard
against her face. They all endured this together for a long instant
and then Stella Kim walked Sergius around the home that wasn't his
anymore. A new housemate occupied the second-floor room that had

been Miriam and Tommy's, a willowy blonde, seated in the room's center, practicing the flute. His parents' large bed was gone, replaced by her futon, slumped into the form of a couch beneath the windows. On the third floor, Stella's room, unchanged, and what had been Sergius's. This was redecorated; no sign of the abandoned stamp collection or those books he'd failed to salvage, their titles now unrecoverable. Others had come and gone from the room, which now served as the commune's spare flop. Sergius would sleep there tonight. It wasn't clear to him where Murphy would sleep—the knapsack had been plopped in the downstairs hall. Sergius tried not to understand. The commune was nothing but pitfalls and trapdoors, zones to avoid, like his parents' LPs, still merged with the commune's general collection, which he'd glimpsed intact where it lined the parlor wall. What was changed and unchanged here: equally disastrous.

He asked if he could go outside. In blazing red evening the street games had been under way for hours and wouldn't stop for the dark. The high darkening rooftops scalded him with their total indifference to his presence. Sergius staggered along until he stood on the pavement at the lip of a vacant lot, there to be met by a kid he'd known before, not unfriendly if not a friend, but after the kid said "Your momma died, your pops, too" and Sergius nodded, language abandoned them utterly. They couldn't even scare up names with which to identify themselves, let alone the terms with which to affix their relation, once the kid pronounced that which had severed the universe and left them standing on opposite ends of it. Someone called the kid back to the game as if Sergius were invisible, which likely he was, or wished to be. A shirtless man sat playing bongos in the backseat of a parked convertible. The gum on the pavement was scorched into blisters, still raw despite the sun's vacating the skyline. Without having spoken Sergius returned inside.

Who opened the door for him he couldn't say. What he recalled the next day was taking the basement stairs to search for the housemate he crossed his fingers remained living there, a curly-haired NYU film student named Adam Shatkin. Shatkin did remain, and was home, and welcomed Sergius gladly into his room. He produced stuff the boy remembered, books and records the student had shared with him when they'd been each other's housemates, including a *Star Trek* cal-

endar Sergius remembered Shatkin thumbtacking to the plaster at the
start of January, its pages now flipped to August, to remind Sergius
how little time had passed. Up in the kitchen, Shatkin cubed tofu for
a stir-fry, which they shared with the flute girl; nobody else was home.
Nobody, that was, apart from Stella Kim and Murphy, whose sounds
too much leaked through the floors, to the parlor level where the three
sat at the commune's long, scarred-oak dinner table: sounds of Murphy's guitar playing and their two voices murmuring and some other
stuff, sounds which soon came to be dominated by Murphy's tone
of injured pleading, which Sergius hadn't exactly heard before but
couldn't mistake. Sergius and Shatkin returned to Shatkin's rooms to
watch Channel 11's nightly reruns of *The Twilight Zone* and *Star Trek*
on Shatkin's small color TV and Sergius passed out there, never ended
up in his own room at all.

The next day, on the subway and into the Penn Station cavern to
find the train to Philadelphia, he and Murphy moved under Murphy's
severe cloud, a silence not Friendly in any degree, and when Murphy
brought his guitar out on the train the temper of his playing was
ungenerous, unteacherly, self-pitying. Sergius didn't take it personally.
He pitied Murphy, too, for what Murphy didn't know and what Sergius could easily have warned him: not to take personally Stella Kim's
quicksilver nature, which Murphy, or likely any lover, could only
know as fickleness. For what it was worth—not that Sergius could
imagine he'd offer this notion to Murphy—Sergius pitied Stella Kim,
too. Unlike Sergius, she'd lost someone she couldn't forget! It was here,
Sergius would later understand, on the occasion of this skin-flaying
plunge into the boiling past, that his project of forgetting had commenced. The visit itself he'd recall, but it drew a barrier in memory,
one he'd never violate. Tommy and Miriam's world, the commune,
bereft of them: so be it forever. Stella Kim and Murphy were equally
fools, and deserved whatever misery they'd discovered together, for
the crime of attempting in her third-floor room what oughtn't have
been attempted: to conjure Miriam and Tommy in absentia by joining
their own bodies. Sergius had no interest whatsoever in some scraped-
up, reheated-miso-soup, harelipped simulacrum.

Back at Pendle Acre for the start of the semester, self-retrieved
from a front of the Lamb's War for which he'd been proven unsuitable,

Murphy returned to his responsible, ascetic self. The dorms repopulated, classes resumed, orange rotting leaves were raked into snaking barricades along the lawns. What might after all have been just a fever dream of New York City, Murphy mentioned only once.

"I owe you an apology, Sergius."

"For what?"

"That visit. It didn't work out as I'd intended."

Sergius shrugged, tuned his strings.

"I meant to take you to visit your grandmother, if you wanted. We should have discussed it on the train going in, but, well, I blew it. Is that something you'd want, Sergius? To see your grandmother?"

Was Murphy *kidding*? Sergius, facing the judge, had been an inch from asking to live with Rose. Yet, that inch left uncrossed, Murphy's offer was grievous and absurd. Sergius suffered a gut-rustle of betrayal: Were Murphy and Stella Kim now regretting that they'd engineered this surrogacy? Had all those machinations, of which Sergius knew he'd been kept in ignorance, been contingent on Murphy's fantasy that Stella Kim would be his *girlfriend*? The two must be idiots, or else intent on his utter demolition. If an eight-year-old knew it, what adult wouldn't grasp that, having betrayed her, it was now inconceivable to visit Rose?

Maybe Murphy just didn't know Rose.

Though Stella Kim would visit a time or two, bringing with her the *Alice* book, a pair of Miriam's earrings, Tommy's LPs, some other crap, Sergius never stepped inside the commune again. And Sergius saw Rose just once again, and only after she'd been taken from the Sunnyside Gardens apartment.

In retrospect, the obtuse question launched Sergius's long, slow departure from faith in Harris Murphy. A tendril of doubt, one seeded, surely, by the Murphy-skepticism he'd picked up out at the fire circle, amid those nicotine, clove, and pot fumes swirling to the galaxies. More than the wretched expedition, the question was unforgivable. Their visit was convulsive, a lightning strike Sergius and Murphy suffered together. The question, deliberate as a reading from Fox or Nayler, was something else altogether. Yet Sergius couldn't immediately let himself feel how badly Murphy'd failed him.

He couldn't afford to.

Sitting there, both hands on his guitar but no longer tuning, exercising recently discovered muscles in his temples and eyebrows and high in his cheeks, those that throttled tears, and wishing also to discover some Quaker super-talent for silently dissolving the query Murphy'd hung in the air, Sergius released a hot stinging quart (or so it felt) of liquid shit into his corduroy pants, and through their weave, into the plaid-upholstered cushions of Murphy's ratty, crumb-infested couch.

_____

What option, for the Quakerest kid at the arcade? First, master *Frogger*. Guide the frogs across the highway, navigate the floating logs, usher them to safety in the bays, a perfectly nonviolent practice involving stewardship of a small quadrant of the Peaceable Kingdom. Presumably the frogs, having earned grace in a world of snares, could go now to nestle at the feet of the lion. *Frogger* made a perfect little Lamb's War of a video game, and while his Pendle Acre friends blasted away tides of starships on *Defender* or *Xevious*, roasting alien hordes in pixel fire, Sergius turned himself into a *Frogger* savant.

The older kids, on their way out to the alley for a cigarette or a covert beer, would come to marvel at the wunderkind's score, on a game they'd been too impatient or slaughter-minded to invest enough quarters to master. *Watch that little frog go, man—he never misses!* They'd buy Sergius some M&M's he'd devour while threading another frog to salvation one-handed. All Murphy's fingerpicking lessons found a fugitive home in Sergius's joystick dance.

Sergius might be more serious about saving hexagonal frogs than any human walking the earth.

He might be the George Fox of *Frogger*.

Q*bert was another option, presenting a universe devoid of guns, bombs, or *Pac-Man* cannibalism: The little surrogate creature, dewdrop or booger or whatever he was formed of, merely leapt and dodged, like the frogs, attempting to stay alive in his peculiar world, a floating pyramidal stairstep adrift in outer space. Q*bert reminded Sergius of the Little Prince, actually, noble orphan on his tiny planet, tending a lonely rose. Q*bert, never able to leap off-screen unless it was to his death, carried a certain secret poignancy. But *Frogger* and *Q*bert* were, at last, too easy and too cartoonish, both games for little children unwilling to confront the universe's starkness even in arcade form. The frogs and Q*berts were Ferdinands who'd never been pricked, nor even led into the arena. For the Quakerest kid, neither made much of a statement.

The search for a video game with a gun button, *but one he chose to renounce*, led Sergius to *Time Pilot*.

The game was simple: Your tiny plane roved the screen's center, curling in the air, rotating three hundred and sixty degrees, as swarms of tiny planes of identical make—but enemy markings—entered from all sides. They shot at you, and you shot at them. You began as a World War I biplane, the Sopwith Camel or some other Allied hero, your airspace steadily filling with sitting-duck Red Barons. *Time Pilot*, as designed, was a massacre.

When you advanced a level, you moved through time. Next, and faster, were the World War II fighters. Level three, modern air force jets. Beyond that and you moved into a sci-fi future, the more typical arcade motifs. Yet the action, though sped up, remained the same.

Time Pilot as played by the Quakerest kid was even simpler. It might approach a Buddhist exercise of some sort. Sergius ignored the flat red button for firing his guns, stayed centered with his whole being on the joystick—on *flying*. His biplane was Silent. Flown thus, attentively, swirling and diving, evading collisions and the intermittent red fire of his enemies, Sergius found he never had to die. The drowsy action of those prop planes, even when they massed, as they did, in uncountable squadrons, was a cinch for him to endlessly evade. Score at zero—*Time Pilot*'s designers had included no reward for merely staying alive, as opposed to points for kills—he remained stuck in Time. (Sergius later considered how World War I made a sensible limit in what he'd converted to a pacifist video game; conscientious objection had, after all, met its horizon in the Nazis.) His enemies or their fire never grew faster, only kept languorously drifting on-screen, until soon Sergius's joystick action drew vast clouds of the unkilled along behind, turning as he turned, yet always more slowly and haplessly.

If his *Frogger* achievements had caught notice, now Sergius drew crowds. His stands attracted townie kids, as well as the Pendle Acre cohort, upon whom he relied to keep those outraged by his strategy from making anti-pacifistic protest of their own. For one thing, a video game *sounded* wrong with nothing exploding, with nothing changing but for the growth of the pursuing flocks. Worse, the affront of the untouched red button. More than one hand reached out in frustration to tap it for him, wrecking the scenario, before Toby Rosengard, Sergius's protector generally on the long walks to East Exeter—and a well-muscled kid behind his Doors T-shirts and bangs, with a little honest-to-God knife scar on his chin from the Columbus Avenue playground altercation that had fated his exile to Pendle Acre—began camping out nearby, presence enough to put out fires before they sparked.

"Shit, he's got the whole German air force on his tail. All you'd have to do now is turn and fire and you'd practically set a record!"

"Yeah, but then he'd move up a level. This way he plays all night on a single quarter."

"He's cheating, you mean."

"Go find your own game and leave him alone."

"What if I want to play this one?"

"Okay, he'll be done in an hour, not that he'll lose, but we've got a curfew."

"You're kidding me."

"Find another game or go beat off in the alley. He's done when he's done."

All the while the red button grew dust. Time's pilot roved immaculate in silence, like Ferdinand the Bull navigating an arena of the sky and trailing a comet's tail of matadors.

———————

Now Sergius resumed his life as a protester. He'd been too young for the 1979 No Nukes march; he and Murphy had helped the upper grades make signs, then chauffeured them in three vanloads to the special bus to D.C., returning afterward to Pendle Acre to practice guitar and listen to live reports on the radio. One year later, at the

reinstatement of the draft, when it was time to march, again Murphy
was still too leery on Sergius's behalf. Sergius pressed the case that
he'd been *born* to demonstrations, citing the People's Firehouse and
a few other things. Still, no dice. Yet maybe these petitions had had a
cumulative impact, or maybe, two years later, Sergius had grown just
another crucial inch. More likely, in the end, it was Toby Rosengard's
offer to be Sergius's chaperone that seemed to put Murphy at ease
enough to let Sergius go and march.

Older kids would be along, too, seniors who thanks to some faltering year in their scholastic background were as mature as college
freshmen, but it was Toby who'd stepped forward with an appeal in
Sergius's cause. Toby, exclusively attired in black concert T's and with
his chin scar and resolute scanty mustache, cut no particular upstanding figure as he slouched toward adulthood; Toby, surely to Murphy's
discerning eye one of the, yes, stonerest of the stoners—but Toby had
something also, to go with that inspiring sturdiness of his frame that
caused Pendle Acre's smattering of jocks always to beckon to him to
stub his cigarette and play power forward when they had something
full-court going. Toby, a New York weekender by train since the age
of eleven, was a born leader, a thing to drive a resident adviser up the
wall when it was applied mostly to leading susceptible peers to skipping classes or once actually arranging a keg's delivery to East House.
In as much, Toby's extending a wing to Sergius might have struck
Murphy as a positive turn for Toby, too. So, when that June morning
came and more Pendle Acre kids than ever before got driven to the
depot, word being the Central Park antinuclear rally could be the big-
gest ever, something unmissable, this time Sergius boarded the bus.

Sergius and Toby had been commanded by Murphy to play
it safe, and you could, in the vast human sandwich between mud-
trampled grass and sky with its distant crust of skyscrapers. The
Great Lawn was celebratory, in delighted agreement with itself, but
Toby felt otherwise, was intrepid in search of a dissident frontier. He
split Sergius from the contingent of Pendle Acre kids. Together they
milled to the park's edge, to feel out the zone where righteousness
met the greater world's enmity or indifference. At Columbus Circle
they squeezed into a front line where a horde chanting to bullhorn
orchestration—*"Whaddoo we want?"* *"PEACE!"* *"When do we*

wannit?" "NOW!"—had wedged to a police barricade, one backed by an edifice of mammoth, flat-eyed horses.

"C'mon," said Toby, and they pressed underneath.

Toby was like Miriam—wild for opposition. This was how Sergius knew his parents anymore, in resemblances, uninvited glances. He found himself swarmed with sense memory now, as if in a reincarnator's past-life terror, the waking dream of time's collapse. He'd pressed too near the horses once before, with Miriam, downtown, at the famous occupation of the Department of Health and Human Services, mothers marching for day care, making allegory by dragging kids into the fray. He knew this creature, its widening, abysmal nostrils, sweat-rivers on bulging breast, jackbooted cop dwarfed in saddle by the disaster of the animal itself, something irresponsibly loosed into the streets, suggesting that in their foolish crusades Tommy and Miriam had overlooked how state power, with its electric chairs and H-bombs, reserved for itself the advantage of nihilism. How could Sergius find words to explain it to them? He'd lost that chance. New York was unconcealed as a holding area for past calamity leaching everywhere into the present, the island flooded with jubilant untold millions witnessing for peace shrunken to the width of one suffering boy and one dreadful, likely also suffering, horse.

———

For his being a ward of the place and having no predilection to venture much from the grounds; for being, more widely, under the stewardship of Fifteenth Street Meeting's Scholarship Committee; for tending never to miss a meeting for worship; for being promoted now to a kind of lieutenant in Murphy's classes, tutoring a legion of younger kids on guitar—for these reasons, at fifteen Sergius was subject to a fond joke around Pendle Acre, that when he finished at some Friends' college, maybe Earlham or Haverford or Swarthmore, he'd return here, to be Murphy's replacement. Not that Murphy was evidently on the verge of retirement, though in his Fox-quoting hair shirt he was ever less sociable with the other teachers; perhaps the joke reflected a nervous wish Murphy would take his intensity elsewhere.

The Quakerest kid wasn't sure what he thought of the joke.

Yet other arenas seemed barely more than theoretical to him.

When one evening he was called to the West House pay phone, to learn from Stella Kim that he might not have exactly forever if he wanted to pay a visit to the nursing home to see Rose—in fact, it could easily be a matter of months—Sergius took the train to New York again. This time, he determined to treat it as an ordinary destination, as opposed to a staging ground for spasmodic episodes pertaining to the irrecoverable past. He'd slay the dragon of his grandmother, discover what dominion she might or might not hold *over* him, what she did or didn't hold *against* him.

In the same cause, he didn't take Stella Kim up on her offer to crash at her new apartment on Jane Street, much as a teenage boy might still nurture images of his mom's best friend's casual way with a Japanese robe. He brushed off Murphy's expectation, too, that he ought to rely on the Quaker grapevine, the elders at Fifteenth Street who'd always offered hospitality. Sergius dialed up Toby Rosengard.

Toby met Sergius at Penn Station and ushered him to his, Toby's, childhood home, a cavernous crumbling brownstone on West Eighty-Second, front corridor lined with Toby's various bikes, for track racing, mountain biking, distance. This was what Toby had shirked college to do: get serious about his biking. With just three souls the house was absurdly empty, a Gothic mansion—Sergius couldn't quit thinking how many dozens of housemates Miriam would've crammed into it. The upper story belonged to Toby and was off-limits to his parents, a couple of shrinks who kept the basement for their offices and mooned around the parlor level in apparent ignorance of the black-light posters and marijuana grow lights above their heads, and to whom Sergius was introduced with a minimum of language on his and Toby's way back out, into Central Park to sit on a rock and get high.

The greens were not filled with a million waging peace, perfectly okay with Sergius for the time being. He and Toby had a whole boulder to themselves, soaked butts and Schaefer bottle caps in its craters the sole evidence they hadn't actually staked out a high perch on the moon. Yet below, a vigil. Sergius, though he couldn't remember his father's face, knew a vigil anywhere. Like one of Tommy's, this involved guitars. *Imagine no possessions*. The singers, barely older than Sergius, their Lennonism secondhand. Sergius wasn't the only Time Pilot. The sixties formed a seaweed gauze through which they all paddled, browsing for opening enough to surface and breathe free.

"This park is my home," Toby said, extinguishing the roach with his fingertips. "I do fifty miles a day." A rare boast. Sergius knew to take it seriously.

"Have you won any races?"

"The competition's with yourself."

Sergius let this sink in. *Nothing to kill or die for.*

"You still hanging around with Murphy?" Toby asked. "That whole Lamb's War bit?"

"Sure, why not?"

"I dunno." Squinting off into some middle distance, Toby appeared to measure how much disenchantment he could want to mete out, then conclude he had little choice. "You figure out who the Lamb is?"

"Huh?"

"Quaker shit seems pretty cool, I mean, I was pretty into it myself for a while, but it's really all about *Christ.*"

"There are Quakers who don't believe in Christ," said Sergius. Though certain of this fact, he didn't sound certain to himself.

"Sure, maybe a few. I looked into it, though. You know most Quakers don't even do silence, right? It's called a programmed meeting, they've got ministers shoving the Light down your throat, like anywhere else. I'm not too into being *programmed*, myself. My parents tried that Werner Erhard shit on me, when I first started getting into fights. The point is, George Fox, *that* dude was *all* about Christ."

Sergius felt the perch shrinking or sinking beneath him. Strawberry Fields might in fact be more bowl-shaped, their granite outcropping lodged at the bottom, looking up. Meantime, Toby volunteered further results of his researches. "Thing is, Christ's the redeemer, right? He's put on earth to forgive us for our sins, because we're, you know, *born stained.*"

Maybe you'd shrunken the world around yourself, narrowed it to what you could grasp or survive.

Shrunk to fit the soul in question.

"So I figure when some scar-face hippie starts pushing Christ, he's really saying he thinks *I'm* evil. I mean, could you look at a little crying baby and think he was born stained? Don't you think that shit's fucked up?"

"I guess I'm more just into the nonviolence thing," said Sergius. *And nothing to get hung about.*

"Yeah, that's cool. You hungry? I know this place on Amsterdam Avenue where you push your money through a bulletproof window, they give you, like, *ten pounds* of chicken fried rice for three bucks—it's crazy."

――――――

The next morning he tumbled downstairs, unshowered and in a cottonmouth fog, to shove his knapsack into the seat of Stella Kim's puttering Fiat, there where she waited double-parked, for the ride out to Queens.

"Late night?"

"Uh, yeah."

She chuckled. "Don't worry, Rose won't know the difference."

They snaked along a Central Park cut-through with the taxis, then vaulted the Triboro into that impossible homeland of steaming stacks and tombstones. Sergius waiting to recognize anything, not daring to guess what trigger lay in his outer-borough DNA, but before they'd descended from the Brooklyn-Queens Expressway Stella pointed out the nursing home. The site bore no relationship to anyone's homeland, situated in no neighborhood or even residential zone, instead nestled hideously in an elbow of the traffic's flow, eight-story tower garbed in a few inadequate hedges, park benches shadowed by the barren overpass. The whole scene was the opposite of evocative of anything, a rebuke to his vanity's presumption that Queens had to do with him personally. Maybe only numbness waited behind his dread of this expedition, making his all-night anesthetic session with Toby redundant. His grandmother in enforced exile, just another chance for Sergius not even to know what he'd missed behind the door labeled Sunnyside.

The smell inside was cruel, cherry Jell-O and urine under a baseline of floral disinfectant. Floor tiles everywhere curled onto the walls, chest-high, as if the whole building were a barely disguised tub for convenient sluicing.

"If you're hungry you can grab a tray," said Stella Kim. "They don't mind."

"No thanks."

She walked him to the room's half-open door, then stood aside. "Last time she thought I was Miriam. I doubt that's going to help you to, you know, get the visit you need."

"Okay."

"I'll see what the nurses are saying. If you don't see me, I'm getting a smoke outside."

———————

He applied to Berklee College of Music, the claim of a single-minded devotion to the instrument his way of letting the Quaker expectation down easy. The elders of Fifteenth Street paid his tuition anyway.

In Boston, two different girlfriends left him because they didn't believe a boy who'd had parents until he was eight years old couldn't remember his parents' faces or voices or touch—at least this was why he felt they'd each left. As if their genial, pale-eyelashed guitarist had revealed some morbid vanity, as if he'd conjured the absence of Tommy and Miriam as a kind of warning, of an emotional stubbornness too unpromising to glimpse in a college boyfriend.

After Berklee he did private tutoring for a while, in Cambridge and Bunker Hill, paying off his loan debt in cash that he walked up to the teller's window to deliver. Some grain of him, though, chafed at entering the homes of the wealthy. He was reasonably sure this was a throb of Miriam's teaching, her message stirring in his bloodstream, like the guilt he felt whenever placing a bunch of grapes in a shopping cart or ordering the wedge of iceberg.

Skills exportable, at one point he got as far as Amsterdam, then Prague. There, among other Americans, he found himself taking the unwinnable side of ongoing political arguments, entrenched in per-verse resistance to an expatriate culture dedicated to trying to out-run the sell-by date of hippieism. As for Europeans, they persistently asked if he was Jewish, and he had no answer. He left Europe.

Six months away, he'd floated free of his contacts, apart from the tutorial service, which set him up in Newport Beach this time. He drew the line at sleeping with his students' moms except for once. He made friends with a black guy who worked on a fishing boat, which answered no question about what Sergius was doing in this particular place.

He wasn't by this time in touch with Murphy. He hadn't attended any meeting for worship since he couldn't remember when.

Yet when Pendle Acre called and said Murphy was gone—the seeker and penitent having presumably finally climbed up some version of his own asshole—and would Sergius want to seriously consider interviewing for the job, he went. A mentor at Berklee had spoken with him once about how the transmission of the gift of music from one person to another didn't necessarily involve taking the stage; this had struck him as pathetic at the time, and yet here he was, career teacher at twenty-six. Even Murphy, paragon of modesty, had ascended a few risers, been the performer once or twice before retiring to the risk-aversion of his discipline, to his student-acolytes' renewable innocence.

The place was superbly unchanged. Since Sergius suspected he was, too, any alteration would have bothered him deeply.

They didn't give him Murphy's basement suite at West House—those rooms were now occupied by a female math teacher Sergius eventually slept with a couple of times, once on the same couch on which he'd sat and learned of Tommy and Miriam's murder, also lost a thousand hours of his life to fingerpicking instruction, and one time shat his pants. Yet even before he'd made the math teacher and visited her suite, Sergius felt he'd come home to the inevitable. He wondered if anyone could have warned him that the day he followed Murphy into the West House basement suite a part of him would never exit again. He doubted it.

The first time he intruded on the fire circle and silenced their talk, Sergius saw himself in their eyes—*that redheaded loser actually went here!*—and knew they were as right as they needed to be.

For what it was worth, Sergius now concluded he despised Murphy. Fuck Murphy, for knowing Miriam and Tommy better than he had. Fuck him for once bedding Stella Kim but not managing to hold her interest. Also fuck him for his fingerpicking, which Sergius had been forced by his advanced training to understand was superior not only to Tommy's, heard on records, but to Sergius's own. Fuck him for his Quaker guilt-tripping, so plausibly deniable, and yet which by its monotonous abiding-with-the-Light had sunk so deep in Sergius he could barely help but broadcast the same variety himself. Fuck Murphy for luring Sergius into a Lamb's War without mentioning the Lamb was Christ, and fuck him, yes, for his unhidable, unfixable harelip, which from the first had been there to teach Sergius to reprove himself for not being able to discount ugliness. Fuck him for being, in the end, all Sergius had, and not enough.

What was despising Murphy worth? Nothing.

Murphy had only been helpless to be anything but himself. Could only teach what he taught, and Sergius hadn't managed to learn it. For what had been Murphy's first lesson, before all the others, if only Sergius had been paying attention? That pacifism and music had flown to Nicaragua and been destroyed. And what had Murphy had to offer him thereafter? Pacifism and music.

For the lamb who lies down with the beasts is devoured.

The bull guided into the arena, refusing to fight, is slaughtered notwithstanding.

The Time Pilot who never fires a shot remains stuck at level one, until his enemies thicken to blot out the very air he requires to breathe.

_____

Sergius had that day entered the room to confront the debris of Rose Angrush Zimmer upright in a chair, clad in a bright-patterned, wide-lapelled polyester shirt and black slacks, costume draped like a puppet's on skeletal limbs. The black of her eyes shone out, only sure live thing in the pale limp flesh of her cheeks. Rose's hair, still black-streaked, was being brushed into an upswept shock by the same orderly who'd presumably dressed her and helped her to the chair—for she was undoubtedly propped there, made ready for her visitor. And now the orderly announced him. "Look, Miss Rose, your grandson's come to see you."

"Hi, Rose. It's Sergius!"

A sound came from her then, a long snorting sigh from deep in her chest, a flicker of dire merriment trapped in there somewhere.

"I'll let you two be," said the orderly. At that he and Rose were alone.

"I'm sorry I haven't visited you."

"Who?" she demanded.

"Sergius. Your—Miriam's son."

"Who?"

The eyes drilled him, her lower lip jutting in a sarcastic smile, no matter that sarcasm might seem beyond her powers. Maybe it was her last power.

Perhaps it would have been useful to have Stella Kim here, if only to be mistaken for Miriam. By the chain of resemblances Rose might have fixed herself to the moment's significance. Sergius and Rose, two blood relatives, each other's last. No, he realized. I've got useless Gogan uncles. And Rose has sisters in Florida, cousins in Tel Aviv. My great-aunts, my cousins, if I knew them. Yet Stella Kim had said they rarely contacted Rose now. Seeing her, who could blame them? What was he doing here?

"I went to school in Pennsylvania, so I couldn't—after they died—"

"Who?"

"Look at my face," he suggested. "You used to say I looked like Albert. Your husband." Desperate to be recognized, he'd risk cruelty.

"Who?"

The bright eyes and sardonic grimace beamed a transmission from the unsalvageable world. The rest, faded and faked, upright like a dummy, her owlish hooting, all might be the price of his amnesiac crimes. The dead thronged in the room between them, unable to supply their names.

Then, in a surprise that jolted the essence of vomit into Sergius's mouth, Rose produced a complete utterance, voice as lucid and commanding as that which had quaked him at four or five years old.

"Have you any idea how long it's been since I had a proper bowel movement?"

"No," he finally managed.

She narrowed her eyes and hissed the punch line. "Nothing but rags." The fullness of Rose's contempt was levied at this inadequate product of the formerly awesome engines of her intent. "I strain, for hours. Rags like you'd blow from your *nose*, Cicero."

The name meant nothing to him. "I'm Sergius, Rose. Your grandson."

"Who?"

They circled this way, as toward a drain. He said his parents' names to Rose, mentioned Uncle Lenny, spoke of Sunnyside, in each case eliciting a horrible guffaw. For that was what he'd decided the grunting sighs low in her chest were attempting to be—laughter. The ghost of a cackling relish at having outwitted her visitor. She'd spoken the unfamiliar name to him twice. Cicero? Was the philosopher her imaginary friend? There were no books in the room. The depths in Rose's gaze were opaque. Or no depths but phantom of depths. Forget not, lest ye be forgotten. His violent need was to salvage a token from her room, souvenir of a tour of the ruins. Maybe she'd have her old Lincoln cameos around, the medallions with which she'd decorated her shrine. Lenny's penny books had kept Rose's fetish vivid for Sergius, alive in his uncle's mockery: "Your bubbie prefers King Abraham, with a crown of thorns. The cent, see, this is the People's Lincoln."

Sergius rifled her bedside. He found only soiled yellow file cards, remnants of some old address system, each entry typed on a cursive typewriter and hand-annotated, Rose's degeneration illuminated in her longhand's descent. The annotations fixed identity, cast judgment, or reported fate: "second cousin," "library trustee," "never calls," "divorce," "hate," "dead." At the bottom of this rubbishy drawer, hidden beneath a few flowery drugstore get-well cards, Sergius's fingers met something soft as flesh. A tattered calfskin folder. It revealed a foxed U.S. Office of Price Administration war ration book (*Any attempt to violate the rules is an effort to deny someone his share and will create hardship and discontent. Such action, like treason, helps the enemy . . .*), hand-inked lines reading, "Zimmer, Miriam Theresa" and "Age 5 months."

Theresa? His mother had a middle name?

Why *Theresa*?

How could it all be so arbitrary?

Sergius fled.

"How'd it go, kid?" He had no idea how long he'd been gone, except Stella Kim ground out her second cigarette, and with her heel now rolled the two butts beneath the park bench where she waited.

"I'm not sure."

"Was she able to talk?"

He thought of bowel movements. "No."

"Did she know who you were?"

"I think she called me Cicero."

Stella Kim laughed sharply. Everyone laughed. Likely the dead laughed, too. "I guess that makes sense," she said.

"Why does that make sense? Who's Cicero?"

She explained.

2   Ferns of Estero Real

What, in this high boot-trampled mountain clearing, at nightfall on her life's horizon, was Miriam Zimmer Gogan's to defend? Only to be the last to know herself and what had happened. To maintain the boundaries and integrity of the self to her private finish line. To mark some conclusive distance from Fred the Californian, now up to who-knew-what in his tent, here in this forest cul-de-sac, under the mountain's darkening torrent of odors and shrieks, the dark's onset. Miriam had felt night pronounce its terrors three times now since their jeep ride up out of León, into the incongruous rain forest of pine and banana riven with sudden pitches of swamp and secret bush-wacked cornfields. She hadn't glimpsed soap or running water since León: How could he even want her? But his stink was worse. Her stink would be swallowed in his. To direct her own scene, then, under the proscenium of leaf canopy and contrails. To recollect her purposes and powers as *a leader of men* and be untenanted by whatever mayhem Fred the Californian wished to visit upon her. To deny the pig Fascist his delight. To perhaps cadge one more American cigarette.

In point of fact Miriam had purchased, with wonder as if excavating from a junk shop some holy relic, a rainbow-bull's-eyed pack of Vantages in León before the benighted escapade into the mountains, before she and Tommy had fallen in with the maybe-CIA botanist. The Guardias had stolen the pack from her at the first checkpoint, and then she'd bummed one back, when on returning to the jeep after their interrogation she'd seen three young soldiers clustering around the treasure. One futzing open the cellophane, the others leaning to snag one and to share a match. Was Miriam about to happen upon a Dave's egg cream or a Jade Palace moo shu pork on this mountain? Not too likely. A Vantage would have to do. To have been, therefore and to her very last, that one who'd after interrogation brazenly divert back to bum a cancer stick from men so young that behind their fatigues and ammunition belts they could as well be the Puerto Rican contingent in the lunchroom at High School 560, she flouncing over to demonstrate to Lorna Himmelfarb how she was unafraid and that *all men are brothers*. New York policemen and firemen appeared this way to her now, ballplayers too, the baby Mets, John Stearns and Lee Mazzilli.

She'd spent her life approaching and confounding groups of men, plenty in uniform, like the phalanx on the steps of the Capitol or the screws in the D.C. jail; now Guardia and Sandinista alike struck her as boys. The exceptions? The exceptions were the problem. The botanist, yes, but worse the two men into whose hands the botanist had by idiocy or villainy delivered them. El Destruido and Fred the Californian. The guerrilla chief El Destruido a gruesome bandy warrior, his whole form like that of a creature enslaved but also strengthened by a sojourn under the gravitational pull of some planet ten times the size of Earth, Saturn or Jupiter maybe: mud-clotted fatigues dragged to earth, bunched at his ammunition belt, the biceps and calves exposed by his rolled sleeves and pants legs sluggishly large and elastic and hairless, glimpsed lengths of a python in repose. El Destruido's drooped canvas hat was worn at the horizon of his eyebrows, baggy eyes masked in permanent shadow, and the mustache framing his comically weak chin was also gravity-enslaved and no more persuasive than those Miriam and Tommy had donned as Halloween props.

"Does it mean 'Destroyer'?" Tommy asked. "Destroyer of what?"

"More precisely, 'The Destroyed,'" said the botanist.

"Tell him I'm going to write a song about him."

After a brief exchange with the guerrilla in Spanish, the botanist said, "He says he expects many songs to be written about him after his death."

"I'll have this one finished sooner than that," Tommy boasted.

Negotiations on this point had faltered, however. As the forest soldiers came and went from the pit fire, afternoon caving to leaf-glade evening, the American whom El Destruido grinningly introduced as *Fred el Californiano* took the botanist's place as their interpreter. It was as if he'd been waiting in El Destruido's camp for them, as if relying on their being magnetized, one American to another. Fred's outfit, drab cliché anywhere else, was disconcertingly incongruous here in the rain forest: serious biker leathers, battered aviator glasses on a band around his neck, and a serious biker's belly stretching a Joplin T. His beard looked either ten days old or like remnants hacked at with a jackknife. The way he'd lurked on the periphery before stepping to the fore made Miriam think of the abstract expressionists in the Cedar Tavern, how they'd mull behind whiskeys until lunging in without warning to brawl, or to try to pick off a Bennington girl. Fred evoked as well one of Rose's mute conspirators, those at a CP meeting who massed contradictions in silence, wallflowers of evil. The botanist himself was now nowhere to be seen. El Destruido, too, vanished briefly from their circle. The boyish soldiers generously shared banana-leaf-wrapped portions of bean gruel and something in tin cups going under the name of coffee. Certainties blurred in the dusk light.

When El Destruido returned, Tommy inquired, by means of Fred the Californian, "You *are* a revolutionary, yes?"

El Destruido nodded happily, needing no translation.

"But not a Sandinista?"

El Destruido's shrug was given elaboration by Fred the Californian. "He says that despite what the Americans believe, not all revolutionaries are Sandinistas."

"Does he know what's taken place down in León? That the factions are now at last united in one purpose?"

El Destruido looked to Fred, who spoke to him in Spanish, then explained: "Not all factions."

"But he is a fighter in the present revolution, yes?"

Fred and El Destruido spoke at greater length this time, and laughed awhile, too.

"What?"

"He says maybe not so much *this present revolution*. He says maybe he's gonna wait for the next one."

"The next one?"

"Sure, there's always a next one. That's why they call it revolution, right?"

Before Miriam herself needed to interfere with Tommy's next question, El Destruido addressed them directly in Spanish, gesturing at Tommy's guitar case, making himself fairly apparent.

"He'd like you to play," said Fred the Californian. "Before you write about him he'd like to hear some of your other songs."

"Sing in English," interjected Miriam. "Play him some of the Bowery stuff."

"Smart lady," said Fred the Californian.

While Tommy aired a rendition of "Randolph Jackson Jr.," Miriam insinuated herself beside Fred. One miscalculation, one small vanity on her part—yet that it might be this which had doomed them seemed unlikely, even in the direst of her self-recriminations. It might only have doomed them to meet their fates apart, like Julius and Ethel. Or not—she might have drawn Fred the Californian's special focus even before the little effort she took now, hoping to make herself sympathetically legible as a fellow cynic, a seeker of the pleasures of irony. For Fred had to be ironic in some measure, appearing as he did, here in this place? Please? Anything less was terrifying.

At least it was the case that Fred caught her vibe. He raised his eyebrows as she moved beside him.

"Odd couple there," she said, nodding at El Destruido and her husband.

"Luck of the Irish held out so far."

"Tommy heard it was a poets' revolution, but I don't think he'd ever seen so many poets with guns."

Fred scoured his beard with a filthy thumbnail. "Heard him mention *Quakerism*."

Miriam was startled, not having seen the other American anywhere near at that point. Tommy'd been dropping the full name of the American Friends Service Committee, as he tended to do everywhere, underlining their sacred status as American *simpáticos* and also fishing for someone to ask, *What's a Friend?* One of the younger soldiers had in faltering English taken the bait.

"Yeah. He's a pacifist." She heard herself strand Tommy with a pronoun; her gambit turned seasick as it inched toward outright betrayal. "I mean, we're not blind to what's going down in León. The AFSC has their eye on what comes after. The revenge killings start and you're basically looking at another Chile."

"You won't find much of that around here."

"What?"

"Pacifism."

"Ah."

"Destroyed's more into what they call *redemption through violence*. Hey, no offense, you mind if I listen to the music?"

Their eyes met, and then Fred's tracked the length of her body and returned. The only irony Miriam read there of the *bitch talks too much* species. Miriam began to wonder how far she'd have to rewind her reel—a few minutes? a few days? to León or Costa Rica?—to do anything but tabulate mistakes.

Fred's next conference with El Destruido no one seemed eager to translate. *"Yo me encargo del cantante, quien me divierte mucho,"* said the forest bandit. *"Quiere ver combate, pero no sabe lo qué es."*

"Entonces, ¿vas a dejar a la mujer conmigo?" replied the American.

"Yo sé qué eso es lo que quieres, mi amigo."

And then they'd led Tommy away.

And Fred the Californian had led her to this clearing where he kept his own camp, a distance apart from El Destruido's men, and where she became very very afraid, and where the last exchange in Spanish between El Destruido and Fred the Californian became as lucid to her as if spoken in English. And why not? She'd been listening to this language her entire life, only not understood because she'd refused to.

"I'll take the singer, he amuses me. He wishes to see fighting, but he doesn't know what it is."

"You're leaving the woman with me?"

"I know you want it, my friend."

Early March they'd crossed, by rickety bus over nightmare corkscrew passes, from Costa Rica, in the company of a group of American Friends Service Committee organizers who wanted to behold León before it fell. Talk was the city would be in Sandinista hands in a matter of weeks. Tommy was occupying the role of the crusading folksinger-cum-ethnomusicologist, Seeger and Lomax in one humanitarian package, and not unwelcome as such. The revolution, apparently, a party with occasional bombings, at least if you didn't know what the city had looked like before all the buildings fell down, or mind stepping past a fly-swarmed corpse in uniform here and there. Once in León, especially, they fell in easily with the company of the poetic-revolutionary Sandinistas, Cuban weapons arrayed under tables full of sweating bottles of cold beer and paper plates loaded with *nacatamal* and *quesillo*. The dissident factions had at last been all painstakingly melted together, the Borgesians and the Pastorians accommodated by necessity and martyrdom, and the people galvanized behind them, ready to make a real revolution. Somoza's influence seemed limited anymore, at least in León, to the embattled National Guard and the planes screeching under the cloud layer, looking as though they might not make it over the mountains.

The night was full of Sandinista folk songs. Tommy immediately learned to sing three or four, memorizing the Spanish phonetically. Muse inert, he might have been leaning to an Englishized cover album of the stuff, until some rough translations forced him to understand that the lyrics largely concerned themselves with how to disassemble and reload rifles stolen from the Guardia. It was then that Miriam nudged him in the direction of *semblanza*—portraiture, so to speak, musical snapshots of people on the verge of claiming their country for themselves. Basically *Bowery of the Forgotten* all over again, only trova-inflected triumphalism in place of bluesy lamentation. He even reworked some of the Sandinista melodies, minus the allusions to Soviet ordnance. Well before they'd set out for the mountains, in search of further guerrilla personalities, Tommy had nearly an album's worth, which he nightly burnished ad nauseam in their hotel room. He spoke of forgoing folk purism this time, instead getting his label to hire Cuban players for accents and coloration, the most musical excitement he'd displayed in ten years at least. Thinking, *What label?*, Miriam bit her tongue.

Getting out of León and into the mountains, where the fighters trained and reconnoitered, took a little creativity, some asking around: Tommy's folksong–army profile wouldn't serve them moving through Guardia checkpoints. They'd met with discouragement and dissuasion mostly everywhere until falling in one evening with a Canadian, one leading, of all things, a botany expedition, cataloguing rare specimens in the Estero Real Natural Reserve. The man was an academic, a fumbler in a sweat-stained linen suit. Impossible to grant his reality except as a figure passing through the backdrop of a Graham Greene novel; Tommy immortalized him in a song the first night. The botanist explained to them he'd exhausted the Honduran side of the range but knew rumors of ferns that grew only on the Nicaraguan. Though most eager to express his solidarity with the people, and to affirm the inevitability of the FSLN's seizing the reins in Managua, the botanist was in possession of papers from the Somoza government authorizing his foray, papers legitimate enough he'd be willing to tough out a checkpoint even in the company of a man carrying a guitar, just so long as the man didn't take it out and begin *playing*.

In fact, while Miriam was interrogated separately from the men, repeating to seeming incomprehension the mantra of *turista* and *científica*, she heard through the murmuring distance of the compound the unmistakable strains of "A Lynching on Pearl River." Not the most auspicious selection, but Tommy later explained they'd demanded he play the guitar to prove he wasn't a spy, the botanist's papers having perhaps not quite the comprehensive sway he'd hoped, and in his panic Tommy'd reverted to his oldest composition.

As for whether the botanist was CIA, in the end that was the kind of argument you could sustain forever if you had the time, which, it appeared now, you didn't. When he first vanished from El Destruido's camp they'd weighed the matter briefly, Miriam exasperated, as so often before, by Tommy's miraculous virginity in matters conspiratorial. Ingenuous Tommy, the least a spy of perhaps any human Miriam'd ever known, also least qualified to spot one. How much or little the old faggot knew about ferns being evidence of nothing whatsoever, unless you thought James Bond was a real example of how agencies worked. You had to recruit from *somewhere*. Enterprises odder than fern botany had been propped up by CIA money, their causes advanced even, whole and accurate botany textbooks written, entire botany conferences attended exclusively by CIA fern moles. There might be nobody who even gave a shit about ferns anymore except those who'd entered the field undercover. Not unlike American Party Communism in 1956.

To win one last argument.

With her mother specifically.

Hell, even to lose one.

The question of whether Fred the Californian was CIA, entirely another matter; at this point she had to pray he was, rather than being what he appeared, or wished to appear, the words for which suggested themselves to her in abundance but failed to string into coherence: *freelance, mercenary, rogue, batshit psychotic*. It was sort of a relief not to have to try to explain what was going on now to Tommy, though of course that thought twisted on itself, Tommy's absence being prerequisite to this present education.

If Tommy was even still alive at this hour.

Unreasonable to ask to go through life entirely companioned, though Miriam had never figured to die in a place where frogs not only groaned but groaned *overhead*. Thirty years readying herself to fight this battle under a Kitty Genovese streetlamp. Go figure.

Having lived her first sixteen years in a dark apartment alone with Rose might be to have been too much companioned in the first place anyhow, Tommy's relatively low temperature representing a lifetime's program of recovery from a primal companionship that was more than enough.

To have been, then, all told, good wife to a good husband, the furthest accomplishment she'd have dreamed of in the Himmelfarb basement or on one thousand revolutionary evenings or out tasting the coffee breath of her Greenwich Village suitors, Porter in his squishy underpants. No more than kisses on the Brooklyn Bridge, on the el, in Washington Square, nothing but kisses and gropings until Tommy made first penetration. Later, on some dozen or a hundred nights she and Tommy might so easily have slipped the bonds of matrimony, into the general polymorphous perversity abundantly available everywhere, including frequently the other rooms of their own house. Smoke a joint, open a marriage. Fall into bed in new formats, in threes or with best friends, including best friends acquired that evening and maybe never to be seen again, say a Sagittarian and Piscean passing through from London on their way to bicycle the length of Mexico and seemingly groovily available with a minimum of consequences (they might be in Chiapas or Costa Rica now, practically shouting distance!). Possibilities touched down like tornadoes in the communes, wreckage that didn't know it was wreckage and sought to swirl you aboard. None of this had ever actually happened. She and Tommy directed any idyllic impulses to their own bed, behind their own closed doors.

Women? No, notwithstanding the lesbian undercurrent in any number of Miriam's consciousness-raising groups, certain wives not only coaching but after hours bestowing on one another their first orgasms—sexual insurrection begun under cover of what might appear to husbands little more than a Tupperware party. Not for her. Plenty of friends had aired their suspicion that Miriam had a hot-and-heavy thing going with Stella Kim. Miriam shrugged this suggestion off, willing enough to leave it mysteriously afloat, though to Tommy alone Miriam had explained how breasts uncannily revolted her. A political embarrassment, but there it was. Probably some kind of maternal trauma—in any event, kissing a woman would have put Miriam in a beyond-impossible proximity to an unnameable dread. Even to frame another woman's unclad breasts in her mind's eye was to begin drowning in some psychic version of nausea. When Tommy suckled at hers, not that she didn't adore the sensations, the reliable wiring, Miriam shut her eyes to keep the ceiling from pressing downward.

She hadn't thought about fucking so much in years as now that she was willing to die to prevent it.

Yet not to die any sooner than she had to.

She didn't think the darkened path back to El Destruido's camp held any possibilities. There was always the forest itself, but no. In this she agreed with Rose. Always opt for civilization's brutalities, for the stupidities of the urbane. Not for Rose or Miriam the primal indignity of nature. The forest was death. Fred's tent was a tiny patch of civilization and perhaps somehow inasmuch a zone of susceptibility to speech and reason. Fred's tent was where she'd go and find her fate as soon as she emptied the pressure in her bladder that had been with her for hours. Fred's tent was where the cigarettes were. *Why did you rob banks, Mr. Sutton?*

To tell one more joke whether anyone got it or not.

The salvaged Vantage, lit for her by those acne-cheeked Guardias, was Miriam's last smoke to this point. But Fred the Californian would give forth with one of his unfiltered whatevers. He'd grant her one in the spirit of the condemned's last request, because even *batshit psychotic freelancers* have a code. He'd grant it under the flag of romance, that being according to *Ms. Magazine* any rapist's self-exculpating fiction. Miriam had never been raped despite a few brushes, a loft's freight elevator, older brother Rye, Dirk in Germany, a scattering of other Who What or Wheres, these accounts all discharged now. To die unraped, then. To live a little more before dying. To taste a cigarette. She smelled him smoking in the tent and the vividness of the American's cigarettes were unlike anything she'd known, little nerve-rewiring tendrils reaching her where she squatted now. In cities the buildings might be made of smoke, Manhattan an ashtray, a bowl of lives smoldering down to crud and every ostensibly clean shirt suffused, deodorant giving way to surges of impatience and nicotine. When they took to the mountain road the CIA botanist had, in his pedantry, as he waded in from the roadside again and again for a sample, insisted Miriam attend to the ferns. In boredom she'd complied, begun learning the names—*Microgramma, pedata, cuspidata*—and then despite herself felt her senses unnaturally heightened. The forest's silence had reached her then, animal dew dripping through the leaves, the scentless uncivilized sweetness of the oxygen. A cigarette was like an acid trip out here. Fred the Californian might be smoking Camels, anyway something unfiltered, or maybe it was that the filters had been removed from her sinuses and forebrain entirely, that she now tripped on withdrawal and uncensored fear. To arouse in him the prospect of a little romance, then, before wrenching his testicles or jamming her elbow into his black-furred throat or raking her already splintered, mud-rimmed fingernails to draw his blood. She'd *taste* the Californian's blood if she had to.

To first live a cigarette's interval and then to die, then to make the man die if she could. To retain the involuntary dowry of her wifely virginity. Tommy at Quaker meetings on passive resistance while she and Stella Kim studied self-defense for women with a martial arts expert who'd gotten boners when they wrenched his arm up and pulled him close for the pretend knee to his real balls. ("Twist, gouge, scream," the self-defense instructor had repeated. Here, she wouldn't bother with the screaming.) Stella fucked the guy, who was later, they heard, arrested for armed robbery, something ridiculous and humiliating about a kung fu "master" carrying a sharpened screwdriver. What she'd give for one now.

What was Miriam's anymore? *To know the kid was safe.* Before they'd gone out of León she'd written to Stella Kim, in knowledge it could be the last chance: *Whatever happens don't let my mother get her hands on the kid.* Miriam's message otherwise convivial, touristic, covering two postcards and then sealed in an envelope on which she'd scribbled the commandment again on the envelope's paper itself, beneath the flap. Let it be found. Let it be seen. *To know she'd lived.* To have reached the high air of the jungle no matter the hands into which they'd fallen. To have gone among the poets and revolutionists when Albert was among the bureaucrats and informants. *To not give anyone the satisfaction,* including foremost this fucker or would-be fucker Fred the Californian now with what a glimmer told her was a pistol in the tent and pretending not to stare through the mosquito netting to watch her squat as the urine flooded from the corroded Brillo between her legs, as she made exact aim at a patch of ferns, tribute to *la Flora de Nicaragua.* To have hand-ushered Tommy to the very limit of his capacities and talents. No one needed to hear *Sandinistan Light,* Tommy only needed have written it, the album like a hologram formed between them, as real as *Bowery.* If he wasn't dead already he'd be playing the songs to soldiers at another campfire, nodding his head in the face of their impassive flicker-lit incomprehension, as if by persisting he'd eventually get them to sing along, *C'mon, everybody this time!* To be, unlike Rose, married to her last instant to the first and only man who'd had her. Yet at the same time to discover, as did Rose, but to bear the knowledge more capably, that *every cell is infiltrated in the end.*

3   Up with God

"Mrs. Zimmer was found walking four miles from her home, after dark."

"Which direction?"

"East, I think. Why should it matter?"

"Just curious. Go on."

"When they took her home there was nothing in her kitchen apart from a few tins of sardines. And in the refrigerator some cans of V-8 juice."

"That's probably about what you'd get if you checked her fridge anytime in the last couple of decades. I mean, since whenever they invented V-8 juice."

"Um, yes . . . I see."

"Which, I'd never thought of it before, must be some kind of war-time ration thing, no? Eight vegetables in a can?"

"I'm sorry?"

"I should be the one apologizing. You were explaining Rose's state when you found her."

The social worker who'd left a message for Cicero Lookins with the Comp Lit secretary had evidently not anticipated being met with he who materialized in her office; never mind his tweed jacket, his navy tie, his penny loafers, never mind his perfect syntax and undropped *g*'s. Never mind his tight-picked, clean-edged, one-inch 'fro, this being years before his dreadlocks—his hairy jargon, his surplus value, his untranslatable self—had belched forth. Erudite sass from a two-hundred-pound black man was enough. So it had gone for Cicero, almost since exiting the Renaissance Ballroom stage for Princeton, stupefaction like this bureaucrat's at the sight of him being serial reward for his excellence in not only reaching the stations he'd reached but for modulating his voice to the local norms. Apparently he'd fooled this particular white lady on the telephone when he'd returned her call. You'd never need wonder how a Clarence Thomas could assemble his shoulder chip in reverse, for it was by Cicero's attainments that he'd gained special witness to the liberals' adjustment to a brush with *actual* equality. Let her saturate in her dilemma; he'd grant no rescue.

"Perhaps you know that her sisters are in Florida. They've been unresponsive. In one of her lucid moments Mrs. Zimmer suggested we contact the Queensboro library board, but it appears her term with them expired a couple of years ago. Her natural daughter is deceased. There's a grandson, just a boy, and a distance away. She identified you as her son-in-law—there may be some gap in our records."

"It's in a manner of speaking," Cicero said.

"If there are other family members you'd suggest we call—"

"I may be her best option at the present time."

"She also mentioned an Archie."

"I don't think he'll be any help to you." It had taken a few phone calls to Rose from his Princeton apartment before Cicero had sussed out who she was on about.

"Is he—a friend? Visitors, even occasional, are a lifeline in and of themselves, especially during transition to managed care."

"I believe he's married and would prefer to be left out of it." Cicero doubted it would advantage Rose with these people to explain her robust occupancy of the imaginary. No, Archie Bunker won't be assisting Mrs. Zimmer with crossword puzzles in your dayroom, no more than would Abraham Lincoln, Fiorello La Guardia, or John Reed. Yet let the social worker be startled, if she needed to be, by the risqué implication that Rose had poached a married man. The bureaucrats should be on notice what a boisterous handful they'd taken aboard here, if and when Rose reoccupied her "lucid moment," and maybe even if not.

Let Rose have enough in her, he prayed, to eat this fucking joint alive and spit it out.

Conflating resentment-at-underestimation on his own and Rose's behalf, Cicero Lookins might be more than halfway toward the commitment he'd no notion he'd shown up in this office to make: to serve not only as Rose's interim power of attorney but as her, yes, surrogate son-in-law, solitary soul advocate, spirit animal. The last of her life's companions, both Douglas Lookins's and Archie Bunker's relief pitcher. *Lifeline*, the social worker's word for it. He'd zero intention at the moment of nominating himself, believing he'd consented only to sign the forms that would permit the visiting doctors here to recommend her for the surgical unblockage of the blood circulation around her lower intestine, which some diagnostician had suggested might allow return of her cognitive function and with it her emotional thermostat, such that she could regrasp the rudder of her own end-time destiny.

Cicero sort of doubted it, but he didn't mind them trying.

He just wouldn't want to be the one who had to inform her that her apartment wasn't there for her to return to. That any hopes of living outside the Lewis Howard Latimer Care Facility rested with the chance of hospitality from one or the other of her married sisters—those whom Rose relentlessly excoriated for the suffocating conformism of their retreat to Florida. Their offspring might be alive, but their sensibilities had perished! No, having been told Rose was little better than comatose, Cicero signed what he had to sign and got out, not accepting the invitation to go in and have a gander at her. He instead went out of the drab facility, put his tie in his pocket, and walked until he found a pizzeria. Ate in Rose's honor a Queens slice with extra cheese—her regular sustenance, between cans of V-8—before finding his way to the F train. Then, taking the occasion of the command visit to the five boroughs to pause in Manhattan before hopping Jersey Transit, he conveyed himself to the West Side Highway to suck a little dick. Or, preferably, a big one.

The moon of his life had two faces, one light and one dark. The sunlit face: his increasing grasp of a vocabulary with which to articulate suspicions regarding the unexamined assumptions dictating the everyday life all around him, the enabling of a savage critical excellence. Cicero Lookins laid waste to a seminar as he'd once laid waste to sixth-grade chess opponents, pulverizing the ranks of their pawns, then treating their major pieces like pawns too. In this bright New Jersey light, in seminar rooms and book-lined offices and in full auditoriums where he stood to fillet a speaker with his intricate qualms, respectfully expressed—in the fullness of this light Cicero seized the attention of his mentors. Under their guidance he began placing articles and presenting at conferences. Then, waiting for no one's permission at all, began his first book, converting his mentors to peers as well.

The dark face? His second life he'd commenced under another mentorship, that of a visiting postdoc named David Ianoletti, a thirty-two-year-old Jewish Italian whose youthful baldness was compensated by a wild swarthy hair suit everywhere beneath his clothes, nearly curling from the neck and sleeves of his shirt, insulating his slippery small body somewhat as Cicero was insulated in his pigmented plushness: undressed, neither was bare. Ianoletti tutored Cicero out of his sophomore virginity, past a foolish trepidation that he wouldn't be permitted to animate anything but a *theoretical* queerness out here in Jersey, demonstrating how his Eden of scholarship needn't also be monastic.

The experiences Cicero'd sampled once, twice in a Sunnyside playground restroom, weren't excluded on this side of the Hudson River. The frontier! Manifest Destiny, get it? What exactly did he think Lewis and Clark had been getting up to, anyway? Or Allen Ginsberg, for that matter? In that spirit, Ianoletti took Cicero in his Toyota Corolla—Cicero, who, in this one way a perfectly average New York kid, wasn't yet a driver—on a tour of the glory holes and other specially appointed toilet stalls of the New Jersey Turnpike: the J. Fenimore Cooper Rest Area, the Joyce Kilmer Rest Area, the Clara Barton Service Area, and the especially fruitful and apropos Walt Whitman Service Area.

Then, and in the meantime, seeing Cicero's problem with driving, on a warm May night, as a parting gift at semester's end, Ianoletti returned Cicero to the city of his youth, in the direction of which Cicero'd turned a chilly shoulder since his parents' deaths. After a nice but judiciously light dinner at an Italian joint on Hudson Street, his generous lover introduced him to the trucks that hid in the shadows of the ruined West Side Highway, parked empty of freight and left open to discourage damage by would-be bandits, and to what went on inside and around the perimeters of the trucks nearly every night. There, Cicero discovered for himself, discovered not as a theory or principle or rumor but discovered with his eyes, ears, nose, hands, and cock, the unashamed homosexual bacchanal that had become possible in the historical margin between Stonewall and disease.

Though from this point he would now be open, at Princeton and while teaching at Rutgers, and while in the company of visiting scholars or at conferences by himself, to encountering further iterations of David Ianoletti—and sometimes did—and though he soon learned to drive, Cicero became for a couple of years a regular denizen of the trucks.

He wasn't in any way ashamed of the dark face. It was merely that it remained dark, even to Cicero while he visited it. An obverse nature defined it: Wear your love like heaven, yes, but what constituted your love might be more than was visible or imaginable from earth. Yet that it was *one* moon with two faces he explored—that was the point. If Cicero's sunlight pursuit was to think with critical acuity, to read literature and philosophy as the record of a species attempting to know itself, what did that represent but an effort to give names to the bewilderments represented by his dark-side glimpses of true human freedom? What was theory, his insatiable sorting through successive frameworks of Nietzsche, Barthes, Lacan, all the others, if not an attempt to hurl the net of language over the splendid other life, that of bodies grappling toward and through their incommensurable desires?

All this had waited for Cicero to be ready, as he could never have been until he'd escaped Sunnyside, public school, the gravitational field of Diane and Douglas Lookins's home. It was only after, place secured in the sun, that Cicero could afford to slip back to the nether surface, to detail the variegations, the craters and outcroppings, the pebbles strewn there to be known only in the dark. That's to say, whether he wanted to think it or not, *he had Rose to thank*! For Princeton, yes, and Nietzsche, but also for David Ianoletti. For the trucks at the West Side piers. He had Rose to thank, and Miriam, only Miriam wasn't around for Cicero to do any return favors.

So now this, what repayment might entail. The social worker called. Rose was sensible again, enough anyway that she badly needed a visitor. A familiar face as a peg on which to hang her remaining self. The social worker made Cicero understand that by turning up in person, by signing those forms, he'd placed himself in the sights of the Foucauldian social services machine. Rose Angrush Zimmer, or this ghost that had replaced her, needed that lifeline in the human world. Fair enough. Cicero would be her lifeline. He'd jaunt to Queens, where he'd thought he'd never need set foot again, on some kind of regular basis, why not? He took the train into the city periodically anyhow. And so his visits to Rose, in the garden of her decline, became enclosed in the dark face of his moon, that part of Cicero's life unknown at Princeton. The convergence was natural, for among his peers and mentors, the various gray Casaubons of his dissertation committee, one would have been as incongruous an explanation as the other.

"You see, there are these trucks, they're left open to no purpose, the men come from all over and no one organizes what happens there . . . for example the other night I was lifted off my feet by a group of strangers, yes, just raised aloft for the strange sensation of entrusting myself to their hands, while another man sucked my penis—"

"Well, there's this old woman in Queens . . . you'd call her Jewish but don't let her hear you say it. She was my father's lover for nearly a decade—"

In Cicero's fantasy interrogation, his dark-side orals exam, the interlocutor continued:

"What's your devotion to this old Jewish or not-Jewish woman—a matter of a certain unaccountable love?"

"No more that than a certain unaccountable hatred."

"You feel obligated, then?"

"My father didn't have a lot to teach me, apart from I was obligated to no man."

"Obligation's the wrong word, then. Sheer guilt?"
"Maybe."

———————

His first task was to visit the basement of Rose's house and sort what remained of her stuff. He bagged the portion of clothing that might still be useful—nightgowns, undergarments, flat shoes, the least ornate of the polyester pantsuits that had in her last years overtaken any other manner of dress. He gathered all papers, the contents of her card file of addresses, a scattering of keepsakes, photographs, and ephemera, a World War Two ration book—the whole compilation more scant than he'd have imagined. He found one school photograph of himself, sixth or seventh grade, teeth cinched in a false smile, shanghaied in a tie his mother had knotted. Not one item gave evidence of his father. No love letters of any kind. Rose's books had been reduced by some unseen helping hand—"a neighbor," explained the uninterested manager who'd already rented the apartment—the preponderance donated, with her classical LPs, to a local thrift shop. Nothing remained of her political books, her Engels and Lenin and Earl Browder, nor of her Lincoln shrine, only five or six volumes someone had decided might be essential: a moldering Jewish prayer book, three novels by Isaac Bashevis Singer, and Howe's *World of Our Fathers*—the Singer and Howe, he assumed, each unrequested gifts from her sisters, only why saved when the rest was gone? Had they been by the bedside? Had she been *reading* them? Or did this express some Jew's editorial hand? He found, too, Moses Maimonides's *Guide for the Perplexed*; it would be too much to credit this last as the selector's joke on Rose's present dementia. Cicero packed the books and other paltry leavings, along with the clothes, into the back of a taxicab, to decorate her new life. The furniture, the massive television, and the cabinet stereo, all useless, and in any case forbidden in the nursing home, he abandoned. When she asked, he knew to lie and say he'd taken the television and stereo himself, rather than offering them as he had to the Polish family that occupied her old rooms, to spare himself her excoriation.

———————

For his first visits they formed an eating club of the most abject variety. At the encouragement of the nurses he always walked into her room carrying two lunch trays. *She won't come to the dining hall*, they told him. *It confuses her.* Maybe, he thought but didn't say, confusion wasn't the primary issue. *We bring trays to her room, but we can't sit and put the fork to her mouth. The trays come out full. Maybe she'll eat with you.* Maybe so; he was willing to try. He'd take the trays in, to where she'd been helped to a seat beside her bed, where she waited fully dressed, hair brushed, eyes glistening with anticipation and shame at his visit. He'd unwrap the day's fare, egg salad on white bread, pasta spirals in Parmesan cream. Take the paper cover off the apple juice, tell her the rice pudding wasn't bad. She'd sample a bite or two, squinting at him, every resource of skepticism and censure still agitating in her smile. The gaze with which she'd cut down American brownshirts, or landlord-corrupted police captains attempting to execute eviction notices, she now levied against Cicero's slight oversell of the rice pudding.

Rose had regained her senses. She recognized Cicero when he came. Rose Angrush Zimmer now mounted a comeback, from the bed of her infirmity—yet you can only come back so far as where you left off. She recovered spite, she recovered disenchantment, she recovered paranoia. Except the milieu and personae that had once organized her reactions were mostly scattered to the winds now. She reassembled her deranged silent treatment of the whole of the twentieth century, but it quit before she could fire it. Ronald Reagan was president, history had toppled into absurdity. She'd kissed the century farewell too long ago. Sunnyside? Malnutrition and derangement having destroyed her block-watcher's authority, she patrolled memories instead, tried to incite against former neighbors and comrades—against her betrayers on the library board, against a misguided Zionist grocer who died in 1973, against a Real's Radish & Pickle shop steward who'd Red-baited her in 1957.

Rose's only daughter was dead. That no one should have to live through the death of a child was a tempting motif, yet so generic that it plainly left her unsatisfied even as she bewailed it. Soon enough, she let it go. After all, who were you accusing in such a circumstance? God? In whom you didn't believe? She was insatiable in search of a better enemy than old nonexistent Yahweh; for instance, the Jamaican nurses. They'd imprisoned her here, they'd stolen cash from her bedside table, they coveted her clothes. Between interrogations of these women who merely changed her sheets and gave her sponge baths and sometimes forced her to move her limbs to spare her bedsores, Rose resorted to ancient archetypes of enmity. She rediscovered Trotskyites: Cicero, when he tried to explain to her the slant of his studies, turned out to be one. And Nazis. In fact, her hunger strike might be against Nazis.

"What I wouldn't give for a braunschweiger on good black rye," she told him, in the course of refusing an ice-cream-scoopered mound of tuna on shredded iceberg.

"You want me to get you one?"

"Are you kidding? I haven't eaten German liverwurst since 1932. Not that they don't make the finest of everything—if I close my eyes I can still taste it."

"Maybe if I hunt a little I can find you a U.S.-made liverwurst sandwich."

She waved her hand. The conversation was defunct. When he arrived next, it was with a liverwurst sandwich. Not German, he assured her.

"What did you pay for this?" she said after one bite.

"Who cares, Rose?"

"Whatever you paid, you were robbed. Only the German is any good."

"But you wouldn't eat the German."

"I'd spit on it."

Nonetheless, the liverwurst went in her. So their eating club was alleviated of the burden of the trays. He ferried in lasagna and borscht and pierogis and pastrami, all according to her whims; he imported cheesecake and licorice and Orange Crush, and everything they demolished together while she complained of its inadequacy to the food of her memory and of Cicero's unthriftiness, his foolish inability to locate a bargain. Given the lousiness of the food, the prices were ludicrous, a crime he'd paid so much!

Cicero recalled her munificence when as a child she'd insist he eat three, four slices of pizza, plunking a ten-dollar bill on the counter, then sending him home to Diane with what change remained from it jangling guiltily in his pocket. He'd never realized what a coupon-clipper she'd eventually become, eking out her years alone after quitting the pickle factory. Now, in this world of shrunken battlefronts, Cicero's perceived extravagance was an enemy at her gate. Like all enemies, it demanded to be shamed into submission. Fair enough. Cicero enjoyed feeling extravagant in her eyes, though his forms of luxury had nothing to do with an outlay of $3.99 for a not-terrible pastrami on rye.

Paranoia, thrift, denunciation—as the backdrop of her recollections paled, these irrational essences took the foreground. She'd spent her life poring over Real's double-entry books, after all; maybe what was left behind wasn't the Communist but the managerial accountant. One day he arrived to discover her in a fury, claiming the staff had stolen a pair of slippers, ones he'd presented on his previous visit. She needed them, had begun walking, making scouting forays to the day-room. His mistake was to have purchased a pretty nice pair.

Cicero looked. The slippers were beneath her bed. He pointed them out.

"No, no, no, listen to me, they *took* them." Her voice was full of real terror. "The moment my back was turned. They'll take anything, I don't dare sleep."

"Those are the slippers I bought you."

She barely glanced, was derailed for not a second. "They resemble them, yes. They replaced yours with this pair of fakes, thinking I wouldn't know the difference."

"That's pretty . . . elaborate."

"They switched them in the night. I gather they found these at some ninety-nine-cent store. Where else would they shop?"

"The slippers look exactly the same to me."

She arched an eyebrow, as if having sprung a trap. "They *are* the same, only made of cheaper materials."

"You've worn them?"

"What choice do I have?"

"Well, then. Despite being surrounded by enemies, you've got slippers."

She breathed heavily through her nostrils, as intolerant of his shortcomings as when at ten he'd failed her demand to help solve a stubborn quadrant of her *New York Times* crossword. "Yes, think of that. You got fleeced again."

"Fleeced how?"

"If these schmucks were able to find adequate slippers, perfectly resembling the pair you bought, *give me one good reason for buying such an expensive pair in the first place*?"

This golem of rebuke may have been the point from the beginning—who knew? surely not Rose!—but it had needed the electricity of conspiracy to get it up on its feet.

_____

The golem, though, was *Rose*, made of parts of her old self. For she was up on her feet these days, in slippers supplied by Cicero, and it was Cicero who'd prodded her to eat, and to think and remember, to gather her forces. Now, in a careful-what-you-wish-for instance, it would be Cicero who had to feel accountable that she'd begun, yes, to competently terrorize the joint. He'd even managed to fatten her up a bit (and himself, too), much to the astonishment of the Jamaican ladies. Heaped pastrami with horseradish mustard, chocolate malteds in Styrofoam cups, trays of eggplant Parmesan—burning this new fuel, Rose regained her snap and bite, took a survey of the dayroom's occupants and found them wanting. Convicted, without trial, of a mass conspiracy of lumpen stupidity. Incapable of debating with her the connotation of a *60 Minutes* segment, let alone analyzing either the miscalculations of the Popular Front or the sinister contrivances of the nursing staff. Relegated to her borough's last holding area, before dispersal of its people to the copious acreage of waiting cemeteries, she declared herself ashamed on behalf of Queens. What she'd give in here for an Archie—what she'd give even for an *Edith* Bunker to wrangle with. Dialectic had collapsed for Rose everywhere, from the disappearance of Miriam from the other end of the telephone line to the loss of the old familiar contest of appetites in the arena of her body.

"I don't want sexual intercourse anymore," she said one day. "I don't miss it."

"Good for you." It was, Cicero sometimes thought, *all* he wanted.

Add this, then, to the myriad gulfs between them, the fascinated unsympathy that bound him to Rose.

"What I pine for is a bowel movement."

He'd bought her a lined notebook, and she'd begun a tabulation, a record of her failures at toilet, in the faltering block letters that had subsumed her script. "The food goes in," she told him. "It must come out eventually."

"I'm sure it has been, somehow."

"No, Cicero. I'm being converted into a block of solid human waste. That's the only explanation."

On this subject alone, Rose recovered her irony. What, short of obsessional disappointment, had ever lit her fuse? Albert had failed and abandoned her; she'd gone to lunch on the ironies for a decade, until Communism came along to displace him. Now it was her shitting.

"There's less of you and more of it every day," Cicero suggested. In Lacanian jargon, a phenomenon such as the cessation of Rose's sexual longing and the replacement of her familiar self with an excremental double bore the exotic name of *aphanisis*: the dissolving subject's failure to identify, in the face of the world's depredations, with the contours of her own desire. But Cicero spared Rose the translation of her potty talk into Latin. Save it for the other side of the Hudson.

"I'm conforming to my peer group," she deadpanned. "I'm getting ready for the dayroom."

———

Early in May, buds on trees and birds actually audibly twittering on the island of landscaped pavement where the Lewis Howard Latimer Care Facility soaked in BQE exhaust fumes, at what Cicero figured to be the summit of Rose's new capacity to tyrannize her caretakers, a nurse pulled him aside, to say, "You must take her from this place."

"*She couldn't possibly live with me,*" Cicero blurted, terrified by what might be his own shadow, unless it was the shade of Diane Lookins. He'd accustomed himself to the waves of disgruntlement emanating from these dark-skinned women each time he strolled through the automatic doors with another grease-redolent paper sack, to visit the white Jewish lady who handled them more imperiously than any other—that, no easy contest to win. From his early flippancy with the social worker who'd summoned him here, Cicero had been humbled by the degree to which he depended on these women to go on tolerantly wiping Rose's behind and to phone him when she'd suffered a downturn. His only tactic was to keep his head low while passing through.

The nurse clucked. "She's well enough to step outside. It's no good for their souls never to leave these walls. I meant nothing more. You do as you like."

The next week, leading her to the subway on a bright gusty Wednesday afternoon, Cicero almost panicked. How tiny Rose had gotten! Maybe the size she'd ever been, except to his imagination. But now, enfeebled. She'd regained vitality by local deathbed standards, such that he'd kidded himself. Here on the outside she struck him— even dressed to what remained of her nines, and emboldened by his saying *Hell yes, let's take in a Mets game*—as likely to be swept off the curb by the least gust of litter-fouled wind. How'd they persuaded him she was capable of a field trip? Why'd Cicero chosen to believe them? Yet he got her aboard a 7 train.

There, like a child, Rose insisted on standing at the double doors to ogle the approaching platforms, each a stretch of sidewalk severed from the earth and propped aloft on girders. She strained for the least sight of Shea, Sterno can in Band-Aids of orange and blue, as it heaved into view two stops before the Willets Point exit. Seeing her alive to the world, Cicero grasped the sense of the nurse's injunction. He'd discounted the cost of Rose's enclosure. He'd himself come to weirdly relish the sensory-deprivation episodes of these visits, his interest passing beyond a kind of cold study, or something penitential, to a bodily savor of what he could only call *the scent of death*. He supposed he was burying his parents in slow motion. Or maybe it was a Pavlovian effect, given how he rewarded himself for each slog to Queens with an immersion in the realm of the West Side trucks.

They walked up for the day game amid only a scattering of desultory regulars and hooky-playing teens, to learn, no great shocker with the Mets these days, that the ticket representative had on offer good pairs and singles in all sections. Before Cicero spoke Rose leaned in and said, "Up with God."

"Excuse me?"

"Upper level reserved. The cheap seats." Tickets in her clutch, headed to the turnstiles, she expanded. "I'd say sneak in, if you weren't too big to hide. If you're unsatisfied with the view we'll finagle our way to field level in the later innings."

"Sounds like a white-people thing. When the black man sits in the upper deck, he usually stays there."

"Then you'll be the Rosa Parks of the upper deck."

"Sounds exciting. But what's with the God talk?"

She shrugged. "It's just an expression. 'Where'd you sit at the game?' 'Oh, you should have seen our seats. We were *up with God.*'"

"Sounds like Lenny."

"Not everything that sounds Lenny stems from Lenny. Lenny didn't invent Lenny, in point of fact. I heard the ballplayers are going on strike soon."

"See, Rose? Labor's not dead yet."

She waved him off, labor being eternal or never having lived in the first place. "The sonovabitch owners are slandering them in the yahoo press. What are you staring at, Cicero? You think I can no longer decipher the sports section of the *New York Post*, the only paper that comes into that place on a daily basis, God help us."

"Just impressed you made the effort."

"Don't patronize me."

He wasn't. The opposite. He was gawping as she revitalized to an almost terrifying degree, like a sponge form nourished with water and whose ultimate size was unpredictable. Next thing she'd have him by the shirt sleeve and they'd be working the rounds of the stadium as if it were the sidewalks and storefronts of Sunnyside.

"There must be an elevator," he suggested.

"Let's walk. I like the ramps." It was as though the el platform had inspired Rose to migrate to highest ground, whether to pontificate to her borough or to try and step on its head. In accord with this speculation, they perched in shade near the stadium's rim, the players seemingly no nearer to them than the LaGuardia jets shearing atrociously low, in a section sparse enough nobody observed how Rose and Cicero sat and yakked through the anthem.

"They're never gonna sell us a hot dog up here."

"You can go and get some, unless you think they won't sell hot dogs to a black man. I'm a naïf, I wouldn't know of such things. Who's this pitcher?"

"Pat Zachry, Rose. I thought you were getting regular with the *Post* sports section."

"Pat Zachry failed to make an impression."

"Yeah, well, Pat Zachry's what happens to Tom Seaver in the age of Reagan."

He left her there, took a census of the gloomy food outlets in the stadium's chilly upper caverns, corralled dogs, soft heavy pretzels, soda. Dave Kingman hit a bases-empty home run in the fourth and thin cheering from across the horseshoe of stadium resounded around to their side, rattling like coins in a cup. Zachry let runs bleed through in the odd-numbered innings, shadows of light stanchions groping over the mound now, the game taking on a lulling rhythm of despondency, pierced now and again by a self-amused jeer.

"It's not much, but it's pretty good," said Rose.

"Yeah."

"Why didn't we do this a long time ago?"

"We're doing it now."

"Take me inside after the next out."

"You cold?"

"I need a toilet."

He dropped her off and found the men's, where, how do you do, some seventh-inning-stretch action looked to be unfolding. Cicero sensed it at his back while he stood at the urinal, more stalls occupied than their nearly abandoned section could possibly demand, the sort of thing that went on everywhere once you knew to look. Another ready partner appeared then, slipping into the remaining stall. Maybe Wednesdays were a regular Upper Deck Reserved situation, reliable as the Walt Whitman Service Area, who knew? Well, somebody. Cicero didn't trouble to zip his fly before slipping in behind him, and his fortyish Irish-dad-looking friend gave up his burden about as quickly as Pat Zachry letting the Giants tack on another run. Cicero was rinsed and waiting, his back propped on the chilly cement wall, before Rose reemerged.

"Cicero?" she began, once they were back in their seats.

"Um?" They'd picked up a couple of ice creams. He spoke with a tiny wooden paddle in his teeth.

"You believe in God?"

A foolish question: What chance had Rose ever given him to sign on for that stuff? By the time Cicero might have tracked down those particular avenues in his own mind he'd found Rose's skepticism waiting around every corner, preformatted for his convenience.

Yet if he had a grudge against her this wasn't it. Of those consolations that Rose's disdain had foreclosed from his consideration there wasn't a single one Cicero would ever wish to have bothered with. Her intervention in his life story, her intrusions on his mind, had represented among other things a significant time-saving measure. From the shoulders of giants, and so forth.

"Why should I suddenly believe in God?"

"I just enjoyed the shit of a lifetime, that's why."

"Me, too," he lied.

"What are we, the Corsican Brothers?"

———————

But it was never like that again.

———————

Six months later he found her in bed, unwilling to dress for his visit, file cards strewn across the bedspread. Her horrendous blockage was back, her world again narrowed to the size of the room, or to the size of the shrinking room within her. The Shea visit had faded like a dream. "*Help* me, Cicero," she said, not a plea but indignantly, as though he'd neglected this effort long enough. Rose's handwritten cards, home for her tattered recall, an address file grown to a Parkinson's-feeble block-letter index of the players under Rose's memory proscenium: Real's Radish sales reps and library board members shuffled together with ancient CP contacts disguised as boyfriends, or vice versa. *Sister*, reminded one card, Flatbush address lined out, replaced with another in Florida. Then, in a shakier hand, *DEAD*. Others held random jottings, Rose scripting cues for every occasion. *Elie Wiesel HATE* formed the complete text of one. If she could somehow read all the notes at once, or project the cards into a hologram of her own head, she'd be restored.

There was no card for Miriam, who therefore went unmentioned lately. Cicero couldn't imagine any sympathetic reason to bring her up. Nor her grandson, who'd been vanished to Pennsylvania.

That Sergius Gogan didn't come up was a mercy to Cicero particularly, a sore spot he didn't wish probed.

"Who you looking for?" he asked now.

"He's a policeman I knew."

"You know a few of those."

"No, no, long ago. He's dead."

"Then why do you care?"

"I . . . want him to arrest a nurse." Always this, the dire bottom line on her plummets: black women thieving what belonged to her. Always this: a onetime revolutionist's fantasies of uniformed men, bringing cold justice.

"How can he, if he's dead?"

She stared as if he were stupid, the primal exchange between them, an eternal principle pointing back to his first uninvited lesson in the Dewey decimal system.

"You looking for my father?" he suggested, just to rescue them from this brink.

She nodded.

"You can't remember his name?"

"I—"

"Douglas. You want me to write it down?"

"Yes."

He flipped over a twenty-year-old file card and used the blank face to commit a fresh tag for his father.

DOUGLAS LOOKINS

LOVED YOU

DEAD

The gaps grew. He did once in a while find her voluble, though. Some days she talked as she hadn't in fifteen years. Cicero dubbed these the Dementialogues, something akin to the deathbed filibuster of Dutch Schultz, or H. G. Wells's *Mind at the End of Its Tether*. Swiss-cheesed with missing nouns, they nonetheless showed flashes of her old cryptological verve, her lunch-line debater's logic. She'd begin without warning. *"It isn't the Jew in me that fell in love with a Negro, Douglas. It's the Communist."*

Cicero lately was finishing a book, growing proudly fat in his carrel. Or say *taking on some stature*, the signature classroom heft and gruffness that he'd come to accept as a derivation from his father. So let Rose call him Douglas if she wanted. Cicero visited less frequently, his New York ritual overturned in any case, the words "gay cancer," once just a whisper going around, lately getting into the newspapers. The West Side trucks had grown nervous, then eerie, and then depopulated overnight. To take the Jersey Transit in was sheerly a sacrifice, at best a chance to grade papers or take a nap.

He made it his duty to keep her talking if she wanted to try. "Why's that?" he asked.

"You can quit being a Jew, it's done all the time. Be absorbed into the parade of American winners. The Communist part, with no choice to be what it is, only to walk naked or in shame—*that's* the Negro in me."

"I like the way you think," he said. "You might want to keep your voice down, though." He glanced at the hallway, where she never ventured anymore. "Don't go walking naked either, okay?"

Yet the fragments shoring her ruins were not all decipherable. When decipherable, not all compelling. She'd begun reminiscing about the Lower East Side, dullish shit regarding icemen and ragpickers, a lover's career on the Yiddish stage, and he'd thought the fragments weren't even *hers*. Rather, it appeared she'd been cribbing from Howe's *World of Our Fathers*.

"You browsing that Trotskyite's book?" he taunted, but she didn't seem to recognize the word, or want to. A late flirtation with not only *father*, or *Cicero's father*, but *the Holy Father* might be overwriting even that baseline sectarian commitment. For she'd been reading Moses Maimonides's *Guide for the Perplexed* as well, preposterous as this might seem in her condition. He caught her at it one day.

"I can bring you some other reading matter, if you like." He unpacked salt bagels and whitefish salad, mostly for himself these days.

"God creates the world by going away from the world," she said.

"I know I'm slow, Rose, but I just don't get it."

"If He's here, He takes up all the room. It's only by leaving that He opens a region of possibility for anything else. For *all this* to occur."

"So what's that meaning to you, in particular?" Cicero braced himself for a translation of Maimonides's terms along the lines of Rose's peristaltic fixation: *To make room for a feast you must first take a dump.*

"This, Albert, is the reason we never had a revolution in America!" She'd called him *Albert* by now a dozen times, *Archie* too, none of it seeming any longer anything too personal. He was content to be the man in Rose's life, her Big Other.

"How so?"

"Capitalism wouldn't get out of the way. We couldn't breathe, we couldn't begin to exist. It filled all available space."

"The God That Refused to Fail?"

"Yes!"

"You did okay, though, Rose. You existed for a while. It's in the record books."

———————

In the upper story of a top-to-bottom house party on Pacific Street in Brooklyn, a slyly renovated fixer-upper with exposed brick walls shellacked and the staircases replaced with spirals, a kind of home that despite his status here as "native" New Yorker Cicero'd never been in but pretended, to the many in-from-the-provinces young fags packing the rooms, that he had, full of framed black-and-white Fire Island photographs, the reclaimed diner table and also the upright piano's bench bearing trays of emptied drinks and strewn with smashed rinds of expensive *fromage*, the whole thing a birthday bash for one of these older queens seemingly half the convivial tribe had bedded and who showed some early signs of the wasting disease, and now someone shushing the crowd and snapping off the Carly Simon on the stereo so that for an instant the storm raging outside and rattling the stale-grouted windowpanes sending a chorus of silly-spooky *whooooo*'s through the party, quieting the crowd not for cake and candles but to raise the volume on the television and cajole the revelers to attend to the spectacle unfolding there, Diana Ross commanding a drenched million picnickers and ghetto boys from the open stage in Central Park, Diana Ross not bowing to the storm but soldiering on, and this now becoming the party's main attraction as though scheduled for their delight, Cicero joining, too, and acting as though he knew these songs other than from his father's well-worn *Supremes' Greatest Hits* double LP with the skip that wrecked "I Hear a Symphony," meanwhile, the dancer Rolando, who'd just half an hour before been explaining to Cicero that in ballet one never so much as lifted one's hand without considering the parallel plane of the corresponding foot, had now slipped the big toe of his own quite beautifully bared foot into one of Cicero's front belt loops, from behind—it was here, in the house party in the July storm, that Cicero realized not only that he never need visit Rose one single time again if he chose not to but, somehow more significantly, that despite having called her the day before to say he'd be coming and having come from Jersey *he wasn't going to visit her today.*

He didn't even know how the fuck you got from here to there on the subway anyhow, and he wasn't going to ask one of these in-from-the-provinces young fags if they could tell him. He simply wasn't going out in the storm.

He asked to use the telephone and he called and got an attendant he knew a little. Not one of the island nurses this time but a younger black from the neighborhood. He thought of her as a girl though she was likely Cicero's age. Hell, possibly a freshman at Sunnyside High when he was a senior and keeping it to herself that she recognized him, and who, it now occurred to him all at once, had been searching, in their previous Latimer Care Facility encounters, for a chance to puncture what she judged as Cicero's excessive air of propriety moving through her zone. When he asked this attendant to explain to Rose that he couldn't manage to get there in the storm, she just barked her black-girl laugh into the receiver. You think she gonna remember you called *yesterday*? The phone wasn't far enough from the hoots and catcalls in the room where the television showed a Supreme on her bravest day, the diva's triumph as if devised as a transmission to this whole insular defiant homosexual group mind, the realm no more native to him really than any other into which Cicero'd insinuated himself, with its secret semiotics like *Ethel Merman* and *Sydney* and *The Trading Post*. The girl surely heard it all leaking through the line, and then Cicero understood that he was actually hearing Diana Ross's voice twinned through the phone, and then the attendant said, *You watchin' the show? Because we sure is, and I wanna get back to it, brother,* and Cicero wondered if the mysteries and inversions of his identity could ever be stanched so long as he set foot in this goddamn city.

And then he was far away from that place, or from all those places. A great number of things and people had begun to die, some of them in reality, some of them only in Cicero's mind. In the recourse of his discipline he could tell himself, and sometimes believe it, that the purpose of his work was to bind and salve what was lost. Critical thinking might merely be another name for triage, the salvaging of what could be salvaged from the continuous ruin of human occasions. Cicero was not so far now from his original vision, home as a kind of field hospital, his mother the nurse in attendance. Only now the whole world was the hospital, and he was the nurse.

By the time Cicero tested negative in Oregon—left to wonder whether he'd escaped infection by happenstance of his preferences or some idiot luck of the body—word had reached him of David Ianoletti's death. The trucks not only were gone but had been swept ahead of a merciless harvest of the regular denizens, a world vanishing like a mirage. Who knew how many from that Pacific Street house party still lived? Half? Fewer? The heyday of a polymorphous bourgeoisie had been such a brief interval, in the end. Its formerly obnoxious ritual songs now hung in the air, strains of party music drifting across some unnavigable body of water.

Cicero was an expert deathbed visitor. Attending to Rose, he'd learned the marks to hit: mainly, get his damn self through the door, into ward or hospice or darkened bedroom, abide beside a dwindling body. Primarily the task was to show up and not demand anything of the dying. Tell a nurse to circle back later, while never doing the same with a doctor; hike up a gown and steady a body over a toilet seat, wipe up after. T-cell count obsessions were a sport not so different from Rose's constipation journals, really. Cicero'd made peace with the odor of certain disinfectants commonly applied at the join of an IV needle to the crook of an elbow or back of a wrist, didn't begrudge the ocher stain these sometimes imparted to his Arrow shirts. Cheated of any chance to visit David Ianoletti, he'd made amends with other lovers. There were not so many of those, putting aside the men at the trucks with no names he could trace—though among his lovers' lovers, and his friends, the times offered plentiful dying men to call on. After a while Cicero told himself to quit. Just because he was an expert was no reason to make too much a habit of it.

The last time, in for a conference, Cicero went without calling ahead, directing his cab from LaGuardia off the Grand Concourse and to Latimer by easy memory, then checking his rolling suitcase with the nurses at the front station. He'd brought Rose a copy of *The Vale of Attrition*, just off the presses, imagining it would mean something to her to see her nappy-headed protégé published. People of the Book and all that. Now he was one.

Well, it might have meant something to her a year earlier. He placed it in the chicken's claws that had become her hands, and she stared, Kubrick-ape-at-monolith-style.

"I *wrote* it, Rose."

All that existed of her was the adamantine skepticism death-beaming through slitted eyes. Her mouth might be fused shut. He'd been away long enough now, and she'd journeyed far enough over her horizon, that it wasn't by any means certain she knew who he was.

He pulled the book from her hands, turned it over, and let her examine the large paperback's back cover. Verso Press wasn't ordinarily in the habit of using an author photo, but Cicero knew the passport-style black-and-white served a purpose of which no one had dared speak: to make obvious, without needing to awkwardly assert in the jacket copy, that diversity had occurred, in case the author's name didn't sound black enough. Cicero'd posed in a Jean-Paul Sartre trench coat and skinny tie in front of a downtown Eugene consignment shop. Through the shop window's reflections a still-life arrangement of tchotchkes was visible over his shoulder, prominently including a dressmaker's dummy, bald but with breasts, its gaze directed out of the frame. Cicero's dreads were under way now, sea snakes still adrift in the current, not yet dragged down by their own weight.

"Look," he said. "That's me, there." Why bother with names? Let her put the picture together with the man before her. It came to him that this exercise meant more to him than he'd admitted. He wanted to impress her.

Rose bore in, obliging him by paying what little she had in the way of attention. "Who?" she said.

"Me. I wrote it. You can keep it."

She scrutinized the photo, maybe putting something together. Then her fingernail, hideously large, clicked on the profile of the dressmaker's dummy. *"Who?"*

"Me."

Rose shook her head, closed her eyes, inhaled through widened nostrils, indignant to be misunderstood.

At last she mounted one more effort to pronounce her objection to what had been placed before her.

"Why won't she look me in the eye?"

———

Retrieving his luggage, the nurse said, "Funny thing. She goes a year with no visit, then two in one week."

"She had someone else here?"

The nurse nodded. "Her grandson, I think, a teenager. With a woman, but the woman didn't go in."

———

All his life Cicero had been in training to open his mouth. To inform Rose in the matter of how it had gone with him, being child-prisoner of her stewardship. Or to make the sole confession the prisoner owed, of the crime committed after he'd served the whole sentence and been freed. Helpless audience, *his* prisoner now, she'd also be self-erasing, impossible to injure. Cicero could say anything, knowing it would slide off the greased façade of her present. Next visit, she'd have reverted to old wars. Yet Cicero'd not found his voice, just fed the next Dementialogue with mild queries, until the last chance was gone.

One day, that was what it was. Gone.

Now, with Sergius Gogan and the girl eight or ten hours gone down I-95, Rose's bemused grandson presumably aboard his airplane while his sexy singer, his Marxist Pixie Dream Girl, tried out her routine in the Occupy Portland encampment, Cicero lay awake on his bed, room lit only by the picture window's imperfect, flat-assed moon, as it gilded the pines and water, this night cooled enough that the thermostat hadn't cut in, no central air to drown the heave and rattle of his own undead breathing. Yet by the same token Cicero lay sweaty in his sheets, unable to believe he'd ever be dropping off, remembering too well in the dark that morning's hell, his bloodless tingling arms like another body trapped beneath him, and dreading the chance that sleeping he'd commune with Rose, the real and restless dead.

Say what you know and I don't.

Nor had he opened his yap and disburdened himself to the grandson. The stupid fact remained lodged inside his stomach all this time, ulcerated into an unwanted secret.

Told to Sergius, it hardly even rose to the level of a confession. Just a silly story of how the young man's whole life came to be arranged—look, kid, here's the radioactive spider that bit you!

Yet Cicero'd withheld, as if in the primal grip of some Lieutenant Lookins *hold-your-tongue-and-let-them-hang-themselves* injunction. "Keep your bullets in your gun." Well, Cicero'd fired one, once. The opportunity had found him, in the form of a pair of hippies making their way to his door one afternoon in Princeton, June 1979, the summer between Cicero's graduate education and his first weeks of teaching, that hinge into his present life.

Stella Kim had been dressed in what Cicero supposed she'd thought
was modest for the occasion, just a string of chunky furnace-glass
beads and a black beret for decoration, over a purple blouse Cicero
was reasonably sure he'd seen before, on Miriam. Well, it made sense
Stella Kim would see raiding Miriam's closet as a suitable memorial strategy—the two women had a *Persona* thing going in the first
place. As for Harris Murphy, he appropriately enough presented as
a poor man's Tommy Gogan in his denim work shirt, tennis shoes,
hair that cleared his ears by way of comb instead of scissors, beard a
foolish way to split the difference between exhibiting and hiding his
deformity—that was to say, a poor thing indeed.

Harris Murphy and Stella Kim insisted on taking Cicero to coffee,
or lunch, before getting to their point. Cicero brought them to a restaurant where he thought they'd be comfortable, where they could get
a sandwich with sprouts in it, and when they asked what he wanted
he said he wasn't hungry. The two were nervous at what they were
doing, and proud, too, and had the heterosexual stink about them.
This whole legal melodrama was enfolded in some humid encounter
left unmentioned, but unmistakable to Cicero. Stella Kim was bound
to dump Murphy—that, too, was obvious. She ran rings around him.

Of course it was Stella who had any real knowledge of Rose, so
it was Stella who did all the talking, and all the insinuating. Murphy
just listened, glowing at her, in love. But Cicero also understood that
it was Murphy who'd be the kid's real caretaker if they pulled off this
maneuver. Stella Kim could take this business or leave it, put it aside
as easily as Miriam's purple blouse. She showed Cicero her prize, the
letter from Nicaragua, with Miriam's poison-pen injunction reiter-
ated within the robin's-egg-blue airmail envelope.

"Why is this all going down in Philly?" Cicero asked.

"Nobody's clear what the jurisdiction is. But Rose called the cops
in Pennsylvania, maybe because the Queens cops told her she had to.
They were probably just trying to get rid of her."

Cicero could see it. He'd seen it before. Rose getting up in the face
of a baffled public-school principal or beery supermarket manager, or
helpless librarian or bus driver even. Rose being wished to be rid of,
by policemen most exactly.

"He is her grandson."

"She didn't even try to find out what was going on with him for two months. We're just doing what's best for Sergius. I mean, c'mon."

"So you want me to see this judge."

"Miriam's gone. Nobody else can say what you can say."

Well, that was so.

Two weeks later came his chance, to be the straw that broke the camel's back. He dressed to impress and appeared where he was asked to appear, in the wood-paneled, pipe-stinking office of an old man who looked as unhappy with the scenario as Cicero felt. Yet, when the questioning began, Cicero also felt the nauseating onset of a mono-lithic hypocrisy, that of an institution that shored its power precisely by leaving every person covered in self-revulsion while abjuring its own sick curiosity. Cicero sat, not meeting the judge's eyes, siloed in his indignation and his blackness and his natty suit.

He could honor Rose or Miriam in this room, not both. If honor anyone at all. He supposed it might just be as simple as choosing the dead woman.

"In this regrettable—*hurm*—unusual—*hurm hurm*—been sug-gested you might provide—*hurm*—never ideal—in full confidence—*hurm*—decision rests with me—any light you might shed—*hurm*—"

"Rose never did me no wrong." In obeisance or revolt, couldn't say which, Cicero descended to Ebonics.

"Been led to believe—*hurm*—"

"Maybe you could ax me in particalur what you wanna ax."

"— something concerning a kitchen stove?"

"Oh, yeah. I can corroborate that shit, yeah. Stuck her *haid* right in the *oven*."

"—*hurm*—"

"You really need more than that? 'Cause I got places to be."

4   Occupation

Lydia stroked Sergius off in the rental in broad daylight, as he aimed the car through the vacuum of towns or traffic between Augusta and Brunswick. Though they'd shared a kiss the evening before, it had been a chaste one, seeming an idealistic extension of his discovery of the encampment and her singing. Indeed, her guitar had been strung on her neck between them, legislating distance like a chaperone's ruler. They'd only begun making out in earnest after getting out of Cumbow, at the last rest stop before the interstate, having pulled in to pee and score more coffee, plus some maple-sugar candy in a little glassine tray, formed into the shape of endangered waterfowl, terns, plover, and loons, and which they devoured in the parking lot—what a fiend she was for sugar! It was like having a pony, the way she bared her teeth to the gums and nibbled it up from his hand!—and then, the gritty sweet still on their tongues, they'd gotten hot and heavy in the car. But he had a plane to catch, a ticket he'd already rejiggered once. She'd begun fondling his thigh through his jeans as he eased into the one-point-perspective task, set the rental's cruise control to sixty-five. They had no music, Maine radio was hopeless, a desert. And then she fondled more than his thigh. And then she unzipped him.

"Whoa."

She laughed. "You gonna be okay, champ?"

"I think so." The four lanes plunged through a tunnel of lonely forest, signs warning only of moose crossing and bridges that flooded in storms. Sergius locked into the right lane, half a mile behind a distant tractor-trailer. He needed a while to steady the thud of his heartbeat and untense the muscles in his thighs before he could stay completely hard, and then, sweet pony's tongue in his ear, her body pressed against his shoulder and blocking any view through the rearview but no car had appeared there in fifteen minutes anyhow, it all happened at once, and he barely serpentined from his lane, and no one would have noticed if he did. No moose were harmed. She daubed him with brown recycled-paper napkins and he ran the defogger to unsteam the interior glass, all the breath that had come pouring from him at the last instant.

"Wow."

"Wow *you.*"

"That's the kind of thing that could get you killed."

"A lot of things go on that only ever make the news if somebody croaks."

They left the car littered with rental agreements and cheapo maps, coffee containers and Wendy's burger sleeves, and the balled napkins she'd used to clean him off her forearm were lost in the pile. He'd failed to stop for gas and so the putty-faced stooges at the rental place charged him to refill the tank at eight dollars a gallon, yet the usual rip-offs now seemed only like the price of entry into a dream, absurd signposts of his distance from this corrupted world of detritus. It was astounding, really, that Sergius could lay down a plastic card and quiet these people asking him questions in voices buzzing like mosquitoes. Not mosquitoes, people weren't mosquitoes, a horrible comparison. Yet having met Lydia, and in the wake of his foolish journey to see Cicero (what an angry man, what a failed human, in his antiseptic seaside mansion! a mausoleum for his radical sensibility, and then to go abuse his students for it!), Sergius felt he'd floated into a new life, one both urgent—in some way unprecedented to his experience, or with no precedent more recent than that of overnighting in his mother's arms in the People's Firehouse—and completely opaque to him. Everything meant something, if only he knew what it was. He had no thoughts of Tommy and Miriam, yet for once they were still presences abiding within him. Could this be the Light? The texture of this new life was nonporous. Like molasses. The mosquitoes buzzed, lodged in their places in the depths of the molasses, and only Sergius, and Lydia at his side, had the privilege of moving through it.

"Hey, where are you going, anyway?" he said. His voice sounded giddy. He was giddy. "For a minute I was imagining you were getting on this plane!" She'd ridden the courtesy van with him the brief distance from the rental lot to the Portland Jetport's sole terminal, which presented another oasis of calm. No curbside check-in, no layers of taxicabs, no cosmopolitan hustle here. One jet had crossed the sky as they circled the off-ramp, but now the sky was still, cloudless too. Possibly Maine was secretly part of Canada. Yet the day had burned off its coastal fog, warmed back to Indian summer; he supposed they'd journeyed three hours south, too, from one zone to another. Hard to believe he'd been in the sea yesterday. A return from a spell of northern confusion to his ordinary life, that's what this was, only he'd dragged this girl out with him. Her guitar case and bedroll were heaped against his lonely duffel, islanded on the stretch of curb where, as the van pulled away, no one remained to observe who or what was being left unattended. Sergius hadn't touched Lydia's guitar, not once, not wishing her to know he was a thousand percent more proficient and yet by comparison exquisitely voiceless, inferior in every way.

"You want me to?" she asked. She took his hand in both of hers, then abruptly—and for just an instant—slid his thumb entirely into her mouth.

"Uh, sure. I—"

"Well, I don't have a ticket and anyway planes are a drag, I never take 'em. Maybe I'll come down and visit you in Philadelphia if you want."

"I'd like that. Though it's not exactly Philadelphia. And we don't have any Occupations that I know of." What did he feel he had to apologize for? His wet thumb cooled in the open air. They'd not spared one word for anticipation of this parting moment, more inevitable than most, writ in the stone of an electronic ticket. "Heck," he said, "maybe we could start one up!" Among numerous falsehoods of the previous evening, Sergius had spent less time at the Philadelphia encampment than he'd caused Lydia to suppose. But then wasn't any participation enough to qualify, by definition? He imagined showing her East Exeter, the gas stations and the arcade, no semblance of a public commons. He could teach her *Time Pilot*, his old trick to make a quarter last an hour and a half. Assuming the game was still there, he didn't doubt he could recover the knack. It wouldn't be. He was reeling, he felt, but it was a kind of happiness, though it discovered no happy conclusion. Maybe it was enough to reel.

"Sergius, that stuff you were saying to your uncle, about the encampments and homeless folks and all that?"

"My uncle? Oh, sure."

"Come on, grab your stuff." She hoisted her guitar and bedroll now, and led him through the glass portal, which slid noiselessly, into the bland atrium of the terminal. "This might seem weird after all I've been saying, but the encampments aren't important."

"No?" Inside, he struggled not to be distracted by the beckoning of the far-off ticketing representatives, those dim sentinels of his coming voyage. Approaching an airplane, your mind prepared by beginning to levitate off the surface of the planet in advance. Airports, even this rinky-dink one, made Sergius feel spaced out, shrunken, strange. Yet he could stow his small duffel in an overhead compartment, needed endure no redundant human contact. He'd only have to play the kiosk, a little video game of its own, until it belched out a boarding pass. But not yet, not yet, for to have it in hand was to part from her. One fact about the Time Pilot was that he never met another, always traveled alone.

"I mean, a little presence like in Cumbow is nice, but at the big ones, one thing everybody learned is, if you're spending all your time feeding the homeless, you're not organizing anymore. 'Cause there's a *lot* of homeless, and some of them are flat-out mentally ill."

Sergius wanted to object. *Aren't you a homeless person?* He said, "Sure, I see what you're saying."

"My boyfriend and I were in Madrid in May last year, we got to be part of the protests there, the Indignados."

"Oh."

"You probably never heard of them."

"No." His claim on inclusion was idiotic. Now Occupy chose to reveal itself to him as another select vocabulary, an occult dialect, not unlike that of Cicero's classroom. And she had a boyfriend.

"I'm touring the last camps before they get shut down, it's a historical thing. You've got to take the wider perspective. We're viral! Where's the bathrooms in here?"

"Boyfriend?"

"He's in New York, I'm supposed to meet him. We're planning the next action, what comes after the camps. C'mon, there they are." She drew him by his sleeve toward the restrooms. Strung with guitar case, sleeping bag, and duffel, the two slogged like some amoeba through the echoing, ammoniac zone.

"So you're in a cell."

"C'mere." Before Sergius could protest, she directed him through the passage to the women's room. The word for the smell was briny, different than a men's, some oceanic or menstrual undertone. They heaped their goods outside the stall she'd chosen—the farthest, sized to accommodate a wheelchair and with bulging chrome handrails on all sides—then latched the door and she clambered over him. "My turn, Sergius." Of course. A woman always wanted you inside her. Sergius was effortlessly hard again. He was met with a bit of a soup, once the tattered cutoffs were at her ankles and he peeled the stripy tights that were her only undergarment. This evidence of Lydia's arousal, the sopping hair and frictionless inner thighs, was enough to carry Sergius along as they rocked together, hands clutching the handicapped rail. The mouth that had savaged the maple-sugar loons and plover drew at his lips and tongue; when she came, she reared, neck arteries bulging athletically, and again displayed teeth high to her gums.

She ended in laughter. "There's no *cell*, you big dummy."

"Sorry?"

"It's wherever you are, right now."

"What is?"

"Occupy. Like a way of being, Sergius. Just living differently."

No longer early for his flight, Sergius at the escalator found himself gathering with other travelers, men clutching laptop cases, a scattering of couples and families embarking for who-knew-where on a

Thursday afternoon through the Logan hub, enough that a line had formed for passage through security. Yet Sergius moved in a field, a splendid bubble extending from his episode in the restroom, that kept all these other human presences in the range of the unobtrusive and inoffensive, the merely pitiable. The Inner Light, that of God in every man, was a dim thing indeed, yet in the afterglow of two orgasms Sergius found the generosity required to grant it. All through the carpeted mezzanine placid travelers un-shoed and dis-walleted, the announcements and CNN feed barely reaching them here, the Jetport's restaurants and shops beyond view; this liminal zone remained unpolluted by commerce, nothing to trouble the murmur of ritual compliance. One of the new backscatter machines stood sheathed in a ribbon of fluorescent tape, an unwrapped Christmas present, while the line fed through the traditional metal detector. *To pass beneath the bower*: Sergius's old private joke in this setting, if you could call the uninvited entrance of your dead father's voice into your mental theater a private joke. Only now he could hear the song's chorus in Lydia's voice, in place of his father's. Somewhere behind him now, in the humid daylight, she hitched or walked into downtown Portland. Being a young hottie, probably the first car had stopped for her, so she was gone from the Jetport already. Sergius joined the other seekers at the belt, prepared his garments, hoisted up his duffel.

"Will you step this way, sir?"

"Huh?" He'd emptied his pockets, set off no alarms. He'd passed.

"Please collect the contents of your tray and if you will step over to the side here, thank you, sir."

The blue-uniformed Transportation Security Administration officer took hold of Sergius's duffel. Other travelers kept their heads down while Sergius followed his worthless possessions, moving sideways out of the natural flow, a salmon flopping ashore. In one hand he grasped both his Nikes, with wallet and keys and coins loaded inside them, in the other his boarding pass, special license to exist in this place. He wanted to show it to someone again, but nobody had asked. The TSA officer wore a thick walrus mustache on his beefy red cheeks, resembling one of those tough-guy '70s baseball closers, Goose Gossage or Al Hrabosky. Their jobs had been taken more recently by a slimmer, darker breed of man; perhaps in some other era this officer would have been an athlete, and so the hint of thwarted destiny fueled his bitterness. But no, that thinking wasn't right, for it was a native resentment that gave athletes like baseball closers their winning edge. They came to the job already bearing their grudges and so, probably, had this man.

"Is something wrong?"

"Please stand right there, sir."

Sergius shuffled in his socks on the patterned expanse, to a place beside the carrel where Officer Hrabosky now unzipped and began rifling through the contents of the duffel. The results were unspectacular but the investigation wasn't concluded.

"We'd like to give you a pat-down search, sir, and you have the opportunity to request a private room if you'd prefer." Bland deference denoted the certainty that every passenger, once jostled from complacency, would reveal as some type of freak on the verge of explosion.

"It's okay."

After the third caress of his armpits and ankles and lower back had confirmed his lack of ordnance or taped-on bomb, Sergius began to understand that Officer Hrabosky was dawdling, and not in a lascivious way. Another TSA officer had arrived now, a female, and, positioning herself some distance away but in unmistakable relation to the problem of Sergius, she murmured inaudibly into her hand radio. Sergius reminded himself that despite the radios and badges and the fake-cop blue of their button shirts, these weren't policemen but slaves of an idiot system, brainwashed workers. He'd be Friendly, meditate on the Light in them, escape in a plane.

"Can you explain to me what the problem is?"

"I'm sorry but you'll have to wait, sir."

"Wait for what?"

"A supervisor will explain. You can put on your shoes if you'd like."

Sergius got his private room now, though he hadn't requested it. A windowless, undecorated, low-ceilinged cubicle large enough for a table and two seats, it wasn't far—you walked right by these places, until forced to notice them. His duffel was whisked off to some other station, apparently for bomb-detecting chemical wipes. Or not; Sergius was given contradictory replies to his queries. The supervisor appeared, a senior citizen who resembled the late-innings closer in mustache and every other regard, only shrunken, denatured of color and vitality, and wearing a zipped windbreaker over the uniform, its puffed form concealing potbelly or shoulder holster, perhaps both. Maybe this was the closer's manager, then, trudging to the mound for consultation. Maybe the supervisor was the other man's father—Maine was a small state. But that was absurd. Sergius shouldn't accord any special wisdom or authority to the man. He was merely old, which made it specially pathetic that his career had culminated here.

"Hello, I was told—"

"Sir, will you stand back, please." The supervisor left Sergius's proffered hand dangling. He gestured with his own radio at the seat Sergius had initially refused, on the principle that *he had a plane to catch*, though he'd checked himself before producing even such faintly intemperate I-am-a-citizen-with-rights language. They knew he had a plane to catch. His boarding pass remained in his left hand. Now he took the seat, revising expectations downward. He was grateful they'd at least left the door open. The younger man left the room, returning to the pat-down area, while the intermediary, the radio-woman who'd still not ever addressed Sergius directly, took up a disinterested pose in the corner. You were meant to find women in uniform erotically fearsome, but perhaps those properties were reserved for the attendants in the sky, or she-cops of the earth he'd left behind. This officer emanated only a fierce gray neutrality, making her seem a feature of the purgatorial cubicle.

"Would you mind answering a few questions?" asked the supervisor.

"Sure, whatever." This came out sounding sulkier than Sergius had intended.

"We're grateful for your patience. You entered the terminal at 1:36, according to a time-stamped security tape. However you didn't make contact with the airline kiosk for an hour and a half, and it was another twenty-five minutes before you made the attempt to clear security."

Sergius's passage had been downgraded to *an attempt*, no matter his innocence beneath the bower. An hour and a half? Once they'd exited the illicit bathroom, he and Lydia had moved their stuff again, to a bank of vacant seats at a high window, there to moon and spoon until he'd reluctantly and relievedly let her go. Teenagers did this all the time, in airports, on train platforms, and so forth.

"I was early for my flight."

"Would you tell me in your own words how you spent the duration of your time in the facility before contacting the airline kiosk?"

"Who else's words would I use?" Idiotic; if, with this quip, he was winning, it was to lose. Undoubtedly a rival account existed, in the form of surveillance video.

"Sir, I'm employed by you the taxpayers to render security for flights departing this facility. We operate on a standard basis with no special predisposition or attitude." The gray baseball manager had seen a thousand seasons, was master of a putty-like jargon with which he painted all outcomes as indistinct and unspecial. "Once you're flagged I have to generate paperwork to resolve the matter, and so, you and me, we're both inconvenienced here at this juncture. I'm seeking your full cooperation now to avoid additional disruption of the screening process."

"*Were you watching us in the bathroom?*" Sergius heard the childish term and was embarrassed.

"Sir, you were automatically flagged by the incongruent time signature. We're just following protocol."

"I imagine—what I did might be some kind of misdemeanor." There was time, still time, to melt at the gate into Boarding Group Six and, as he breached the cloud layers, to mass this interview into the jumble behind him, with Cicero, Lydia, all else.

"I can still get you on your flight, sir," the supervisor said, mind reader now. Or perhaps this was routine carrot-dangling. "I'll need to photocopy your ID and boarding pass, and I'll require for you to answer a few other questions to round out my report."

"Sure."

"The person with whom you arrived at the terminal was known to you, I mean previous to your encounter?"

"What? Of course."

"The distance from the rental lots to the terminal is brief here, sir, but you'd be surprised what folks can get up to."

Sergius told himself this change in register, the unfunny salty humor, was a positive sign.

"No, known to me."

"For how long?"

"A—a little while."

"Did she give you anything to carry in your luggage or on your person?"

"No." Only a lingering scent, an ache, a vision.

"Not a fellow traveler, then?"

"Sorry?"

"She's not to be considered a fellow traveler?"

"What's that supposed to mean? *A fellow traveler?* Is that some kind of code word?"

"Sir, I try to be cautious to use appropriate terminology and if I've offended you, I apologize. I meant that despite accompanying you to the facility she had no travel plans today—would that be accurate?"

"But that isn't what you said."

"Maybe you could offer a term in place of mine, sir. Put it in your own language so I'll understand."

"I don't think so."

"She was no traveler of any kind, I gather. I'll just need to make some indication here. Would you care to give me her name?"

"Fuck you."

"That's unnecessary, sir. What was she, sir, if not a traveler?"

I am the backwards traveller, ancient wool unraveller—this was a lyric Harris Murphy had regularly crooned at his adopted boy, when Murphy most wished to console Sergius or lull him, in his sobbing, to sleep. Sergius had never known the origin of the tune, though in Murphy's rendition it seemed to call to him from some distant Celtic isle. Sergius wondered now where Murphy was, whether he was still alive. Too late, it was all too late.

"No traveler at all," said Sergius. "She's an Occupier. Write that down. And so am I."

"So you are what, sir?"

Backwards traveler. Time Pilot. By birthright an American Communist, Sergius wished he could say. *You've apprehended an American Communist.* Yet he hadn't the first idea what these two words really meant even apart, let alone when you ran them together. *And we were sailing songs, wailing on the moon.* That was where the backwards traveler had ended up, in Murphy's lyric.

"I meant we were Occupying your fucking bathroom."

"Sir, I wish you to understand the seriousness of this situation and suggest you roll the untoward language back a few degrees so we can all get on the same page here."

"We did it, right in your pokey little Jetport. You got me, you caught one."

"One what?"

"*You tell me.*" This was not the rejoinder of Sergius's wild vicarious dreams. In fact it might be a kind of plea. You tell me, please. Tell me, if you can.

"Sir, this is the very facility Mohamed Atta used to begin his journey. I was there that day and I'm not proud to say we waved him through. On that day my personal American innocence died and I'm here to say right now *never again*, not on my watch. Will you please put both your hands on the table there now, thank you." In the manner of the baseball manager lifting in coldhearted reluctance the bullpen telephone, the supervisor nodded to the woman with the radio. "Go ahead," he told her. "You better tell 'em to pick up the girl."

Sergius lay his hands on the table. His plane by now gone. This, all this, as it was meant to be. Sergius, arrived here in this crucial indefinite place, this undisclosed location, severed from the life of the planet yet not aloft. Arrived at last at this nowhere in which he became visible before the law.

A cell of one, beating like a heart.

Thanks: Fred McKindra, Marjorie Kernan, Judith Levine, Phillip Lopate, Vivian Gornick, Matthew Specktor, John Hilgart, Sarah Crichton, Brian Berger, Peter Behrens, Jonn Herschend, Saïd Sayrafiezadeh, Ayelet Waldman, Joel Simon, Carlos Lauria, Taylor Kingsbury, Guy Martin, Michael Szalay, Lydia Millet, Karl Rusnak, Michael Chabon, Zoë Rosenfeld; Sean Howe and Rachel Cohen for walks in the Gardens; the readers in the Hole; Bill, Richard, Eric; my family.